PERILOUS TIMES

PERILOUS TIMES

THOMAS · D · LEE

orbitbooks.net

ORBIT

First published in Great Britain in 2023 by Orbit

Copyright © 2023 by Thomas D. Lee

The moral right of the author has been asserted.

A CIP catalogue record for this book
is available from the British Library.

Hardback 978-0-356-51852-7
C format 978-0-356-51853-4

Typeset in Caslon by M Rules
Printed and bound in Great Britain by
Clays Ltd, Elcograf, S.p.A.

Papers used by Orbit are from well-managed forests
and other responsible sources.

Orbit
An imprint of
Little, Brown Book Group
Carmelite House
50 Victoria Embankment
London EC4Y 0DZ

An Hachette UK Company
www.hachette.co.uk

www.orbitbooks.net

For my high school English teacher, Mrs Parker
Because I said I would

Part One

1

Kay crawls up from under his hill, up through the claggy earth.

For the last thousand years, the land around his hill has been dry. Drainage and farming and modern miracles kept the water away. He remembers. Now the ground is waterlogged, as it was when he was first buried. Before the fens were drained. He starts to wonder why, but then he gets a worm in his eye, which is the sort of foul development that drives the thoughts from your head. He makes a small, disgusted sound and wipes the worm away.

This part's always disagreeable, the brute scramble up towards daylight. He burrows through clay, grabs at roots, until the earth falls away and he's looking up at a vaguely yellow sky. He gets his head out first, and then an elbow, before taking a break to catch his breath. The air doesn't taste particularly good. The sun is baking down on his face. It must be midsummer.

He has another go at getting free. The earth's pulling down on his legs, but the slippery mud slickens his chainmail and provides lubrication. Finally there's an almighty squelch, and he feels the earth let go. His leg comes free. His hips get past the roots. When he's out to his knees he almost slips, falls back into the strange hollow that he's climbed out of, but he manages to stop himself. He gets his shins above ground, and then he's up, kneeling in the sun, panting in the heat. Wearing a coat of mail and a green wool cloak, both rimed with muddy afterbirth. His dreadlocks are matted with earth.

Sure enough, his little burial hill is surrounded by bog. The waters have risen. This is how it was when he was buried, before the tree grew from his stomach.

He gulps down air, trying to fill his lungs, but the air feels heavier than it ought to feel. It doesn't look like there's anyone here to wake him up this time. In the old days there were bands of horsemen, sometimes even a king, in person, when the need was dire. Then it became army lorries, or circles of druids in white shifts, slightly surprised that their dancing had actually achieved something. More recently, a man in a raincoat, checking his wristwatch, with a flying machine roaring on the grass behind him. Nothing today. It must be one of the more organic ones, where the earth itself decides to shake his shoulder. Something shifting in the spirit of the realm. Or maybe the birds in the sky have held a parliament and voted to dig him up. He looks around. No sign of any birds, either.

'Bad, then,' he mutters, to nobody.

Kay drags himself to his feet. First thing to do is to find his sword and shield. They usually get regurgitated somewhere nearby, though there's no exact science to it. He's not sure that the earth fully understands its obligations. The covenant with Merlin was fairly specific. *Make this warrior whole again and surrender him back to the realm of the living, whenever Britain is in peril. Return him with his sword and shield and other tools of war, untarnished.*

When peril is bested, let him return to your bosom and sleep, until peril calls him forth again.

It couldn't have been much clearer. But mud is mud. Mud struggles with written instructions. There were bound to be some misunderstandings.

There's something new across the bog. He squints at it, because the sun is bright and reflecting off the metal parts. An ugly cluster of low buildings, with pipes running everywhere like a mass of serpents. In the centre is a silver tower shaped like a bullet. A fortress? Bigger, though, than Arthur's fortress at Caer Moelydd ever was.

'Didn't used to be there,' he says to himself.

It seems like a good place to start, if he's going to figure out why he's back.

He heads downhill, the earth squishing underfoot. His sword might be in the bog somewhere, hilt protruding from the wet earth. Hopefully he'll just stumble onto it. That's usually how this works, the various ancient forces of the realm conspiring to make things easier for him. That was always one of the perks of being in Arthur's warband. You'd blunder into the forest and you'd happen upon a talking raven who could tell you where to find what you were questing for. How else would idiots like Bors and Gawain have achieved anything, if they hadn't had assistance from white hinds and river spirits, guiding them on their way? Not that they ever showed any gratitude.

Across the bog, the mess of buildings glistens. Strange that whoever built this thing built it so close to his old hill. But it's no stranger than white hinds or talking ravens. Riding through the old forests, you could never shake the feeling that there was a quest around the corner, put there by some greater power, whether that power was the Christ King or the Saxon gods or some older goddess of the trees. Arthur never seemed to notice.

It seemed natural to him that things of import should occur in his proximity. If anyone else noticed, they knew better than to mention it. Only Kay would bring it up occasionally and earn himself a scowl from Merlin or a jibe from Lancelot.

There's a thought to make him angry. Lancelot on his white horse, sneering. Whispering in Arthur's ear. *Look, sire, a brown Nubian covered in brown filth, and no browner for it.* It's a good thought for fuelling you through a bog. He imagines Lancelot in the distance, goading him. He imagines pulling Lancelot down from his horse and punching him in the jaw. Drowning him in the mud. That's a nice thought for getting you through a bog, too.

The mud isn't so bad, at first. He wades through it with barely a grimace. It's no worse than Agincourt, or the Somme. At least there's no bullets flying, no hot shell fragments raining down or French coursers charging at him. The only problem is the mail, which weighs him down. And Christ, it's a hot day. Summers never used to be this hot, he's sure of it. It's a day for resting in the shade, not wearing mail, or wading. If it gets any thicker he'll be right back underground again, slowly choking, lungs filling with mud. And what would happen then? He's died in forty different ways over the years, from Saxon spearheads and Byzantine fire and Japanese inhospitality, but he's never drowned in mud before. That would be a new one to add to the list.

He can't help but notice that there's something odd about this mud. It has a slickness to it, a purple sheen, that reflects the sunlight more than mud really ought to. He's up to his knees in it, now. No sword yet. He casts his eyes around, throws up his hands in hopelessness.

'Nimue?' he asks. It's worth a shot. 'Bit of help, maybe?'

No answer. No pale arm shoots skywards from the oily waters, holding aloft a gleaming sword. That only works for Arthur's

Caliburn, apparently. Not common swords like his that soil themselves with blood now and again.

It's made him careless, coming back from the dead. He'd never have walked blithely across a moor in the old days. Suicide. He's used to being pampered now, cars and helicopters and warm beds whenever he's above ground. He's forgotten the basics. If he does drown here then it will be his own fault and no-one else's. No wonder Nimue isn't helping. She's probably got more important things to do in another lake somewhere. More important than helping errant knights find their bloody swords.

He's thinking of wading back when a sound breaks out across the moor, a modern sound. There's still a part of his mind that thinks of old-fashioned explanations first. It's a beast that needs slaying, or else a signal horn. But no, it's a klaxon, a warning siren. Coming from the mass of buildings. That piques his interest. If it sounds like peril, it's probably peril. Onwards, then. Through the heat.

After five minutes of trudging, he reaches a wire fence. Cruel razors coiled on top of it to make the passage even more unpleasant, and thorny bushes planted thickly on the other side. Slim chance of cutting through it all, without his sword. But there are some signs on the fence which he reads out slowly, sounding out the words with dry lips. The first sign says, SECURE FRACKING FACILITY. Some kind of fortified brothel? They didn't have secure facilities for that sort of thing, the last time he was up and about. Times change. The second sign is more interesting. It says, THIS SITE IS PROTECTED BY SAXONS. There's red heraldry of a nasal helmet, which doesn't look like any helmet that he ever saw on a Saxon head. In the corner of the notice are the words SAXON PMC. *PROTECTION YOU CAN RELY ON.*

He is confused by this sign. How can there be Saxons guarding places again? Have they overthrown the Normans, finally?

Have more Saxons come from Saxony, as invaders? Perhaps that's it. Invaders have overrun Britain's shores, and it's his job to stop them. Classic peril. The sort of thing he used to be good at, a long time ago. Pushing Saxons back into the sea. If he finds Saxons in this place then he will kill them. Then maybe he can go back to sleep.

First, he must pass the fence. He has climbed the walls of Antioch and stormed the beaches of Normandy, so a wire fence shouldn't pose much difficulty. Except he is slick with mud, and there are no footholds, and the whole process takes much longer than it ought to. He falls into the mud more than once, caking himself further. The razor wire cuts his hands and face, and would tear the flesh of his body too, if not for his mail. He gets caught halfway over, his cloak snagged and his mail hooked; hanging at a strange and painful angle, over the fence but unable to get down, no matter how hard he strains.

This is a fine situation. He imagines Bors and Gawain standing at the foot of the fence, laughing up at him. The klaxon is still blaring out over the marsh. But now he hears raised voices as well, people shouting from the silver tower and the ugly buildings.

And then he hears gunshots. Stuttering fire, like the guns he learnt how to use in the last big war. They've probably built better and deadlier guns since then. He misses the days when Saxons only carried axes and round shields. Maybe a longbow, at worst. But he's not picky. He'll kill anything that needs killing if it means he can get back to his slumber afterwards, undisturbed.

They're not aiming at him, yet. Someone else here, then, some other reason for a gunfight. But it would still be prudent to get down off this fence. There's some distance to the towers, with wet ground in between. Makes him think of Flanders, back in the first big terrible war with the Germans, when he used to sneak across the blighted fields and drop down into the foe's trenches.

Do some old-fashioned slaughter with sword and club and bayonet in the black of night. One time he got tangled on the way over and couldn't get free. Was still there at dawn, exposed and helpless in the open. Had his throat blown open by a German sniper. He's not keen to let that happen again.

He reaches back with bloody hands to try and unsnag himself. His mail is caught in two or three places, the wire having hooked through the iron links, and it's the devil to get it unhooked again. This is where Bors or Gawain would have got hopelessly stuck, thrashing and roaring until they were tangled even worse. They'd have to wait for some passing fay to take pity on them and help them down, make some terrible pact in exchange for their freedom. But he's always had a bit more patience than them. He works with careful fingers.

The last link of mail can't hold his whole weight by itself. It breaks, with a tiny clink, and suddenly he's free. He drops five or six feet and lands in the bushes, banging his jaw on something hard and wooden.

There are faeries dancing in his eyes, for a moment. Angels singing in his ears. When he's done groaning he turns over, clutching his face. Then he starts laughing to himself. He landed on his shield. It's here waiting for him, lying face down in the mud. The earth knew to put it in his path. That must mean he's going in the right direction.

He picks it up and brushes the mud off it. The shield is solid oak and iron rimmed. It is painted with the face of Herne, the Horned God, a crude drawing that might be a tree or a stag's head, depending on how you look at it. White, on a green field. In the centre is an iron boss for breaking people's noses. He lashes it to his forearm and feels better for it. Then he stands and heads towards the peril.

The earth is drier on this side of the fence. Soon he can walk, rather than wade. Then he begins to run. Around the silver tower and the ugly buildings there's a great mass of pipes and tanks and walkways, none of which he understands the purpose of. The tower looms over everything, gleaming in the sun. He's struck by the size of it. He always is, with these new things that people build. The gunfire is coming from within, so he ventures into the maze. Ducking under scaffolds, stepping over cables, moving warily between rows of machinery. It all hums with the movement of something, some fluid or energy. The air feels prickly, charged with strange potential. He has no sense of what this place is. A mine? A power mill? He doesn't know why people would choose to come here and shoot at one another, but that's the kind of detail he can figure out later. Maybe once the Saxons are dead.

He's close to the fighting now. Beneath the wail of the siren and the patter of gunfire he can hear shouts, footfalls, the clatter of men running with war gear. But he can't see anything, yet. There is a metal staircase, the colour of lemons, leading up over a row of tanks. He's about to climb it when another three shots ring out. A bullet tears through the air above him, through the place where his breast would have been if he'd started climbing three seconds earlier. It leaves a dent in a tank behind him, and a question worms its way into his mind. Not a Bors or Gawain question, but a Merlin question. What is in these tanks? Does it marry well with bullets? He somehow doubts it.

This question is still in his mind when a small person dives down the staircase and lands in front of him. They land like somebody who throws themselves down staircases on a fairly regular basis and knows how to do it without breaking an ankle. Then they draw themselves up and stare at him, panting for breath.

They look like a woman, but that doesn't stop them from being a Saxon. They are wearing black and khaki: thick boots and a heavy backpack. Head covered by a knitted hat in rainbow colours, with only holes for their mouth and eyes. They are not the eyes of someone who was expecting to run into a man in chainmail. They aren't carrying a gun, as far as he can tell. More than anything, they look exhausted.

'All right,' he says. 'You in peril?'

'What?' asks the woman.

She's speaking English, the bastard horse-trading language that people have been speaking since the Normans arrived. It still sounds new and vulgar to him, ringing strangely in his ears, but Merlin's magic makes it so that they can understand each other. Part of the covenant. The gift of tongues. *Give him knowledge of the words which are spoken by the people in the realm, so that he will not be a stranger in his own land.* He wouldn't be much use otherwise, going around speaking old Brythonic, not knowing a bloody word that anyone was saying.

'Sort of seems like you're in peril,' he says.

There's another patter of gunshots, closer this time, up from where this woman came. More bullets slam against the tank behind them.

'Who the fuck are you?' asks the woman.

'Never mind that,' he says. 'Go on, I'll try and keep 'em busy.'

'I . . .' says the woman.

'Head for the tree on the hill, if you can,' says Kay.

She seems to think about this for a few moments, while she catches her breath. Then she nods and starts running, down the alleyway between the pipes. Towards the fence, he hopes.

Which leaves him at the bottom of the yellow staircase. He can hear boots on metal, from somewhere up above. If he doesn't move quickly, he'll have some Saxon shooting down at him from the top of the stairs. Mustn't stop and think too much about it.

He raises his shield, putting his shoulder into it, his head low, his body sideways. Then he creeps up the stairs. One step at a time.

There's not much he can do with just his shield. Even his sword wouldn't help enormously. Ancient warriors risen from the very ground with their arms untarnished are less useful than they used to be, when there are men doing wicked things with automatic rifles. If Merlin foresaw everything that would come to pass, why didn't he account for guns? It was only about a hundred years ago that Kay learnt how to use them, after five hundred of refusing to touch them. But he doesn't have one now. His right hand feels strange being empty of a weapon, just clenching and unclenching at his side.

Over the tanks are metal walkways, branching off in different directions. He's almost beneath the silver tower now. When he peers over the rim of his shield he can see movement at the other end of the walkway. Men carrying rifles, wearing strange war gear, sunglasses and camouflage vests that stand out against their surroundings. The wrong colour for fighting in a place like this. He decides that these must be the Saxons. There's a lot of them. Almost too many. Why is this place important enough to merit this many guards? More useless questions. If they get past him they'll be down the stairs, in the alleyway, with a straight shot at the fleeing woman. That's all that matters.

The Saxons must have seen him. A shield is not just for protection. It's also for drawing attention. The face of Herne is painted white, and the iron boss will gleam in this bright sun. It's not much of a plan, but it's better than doing nothing. He plants the shield at the top of the stairs, driving the rim down between two bands of the metal walkway. Then he kneels behind it, lowering his head. Bracing himself.

A few inches of oak can't stop a bullet. Not even a few inches of oak with the Horned God painted on the front. The greater part of its power in the old days was in scaring people, making them think twice about fighting someone who was under Herne's protection. These modern Saxons won't even know what the symbol means.

But it had other uses, as well. There were several warriors in Arthur's court who wanted to cover all their bases. They didn't want to put all their eggs in the heavenly basket of the Christ King. Merlin accommodated that. He led them into the woods at night. Passed around mushrooms for them to eat, powders for them to place under their tongues. He took them far from Caer Moelydd, to places that weren't on any of his maps. He introduced them to the fay folk, to the minor gods of the earth, to people with strange powers. And he did things to their arms and armour. Drew up magic from the ground and poured it into their shields, imbuing them with strange properties. Powered by the earth. There might be enough magic left in the ground for the old charms to still do their job.

But a lead bullet, chemically propelled, pays as much attention to old fay magic as it might pay to a veil of cobwebs. It punches through his shield and hits him in the right thigh, breaking straight through a ring of mail and carrying it into the wound.

He's been shot before, but it's never any less painful than it was the first time. He stumbles, he screams through his teeth, without opening his mouth. He almost falls backwards down the stairs but steadies himself upon the planted shield. Dear Christ, it hurts, though.

The woman is getting further away. That's what matters. He's keeping the Saxons distracted. All he needs to do is stay where he is.

He learnt a few hundred years ago that sometimes the most useful thing he can do is to just let himself get killed. Merlin's covenant with the earth didn't grant him the strength of an ox, it didn't make his flesh repellent to arrows or bullets. It just allows him to return from the dead. So death, for him, means less than it might do for others. And somebody has to be the first one over the walls, the first one through the breach, the first one out of the landing craft and up the beach. Should that be somebody who can only die once, whose family would miss them? Or should it be someone who can die a thousand times, whose wife and family died a long time ago? There's no question, when you think of it like that.

Bullets are landing all around him now. Perhaps the magic has kicked in, and the bullets are curving away, flying off sideways at strange trajectories. Or perhaps the Saxons are just terrible shots. He can't be certain, because he still can't see them from behind his shield. Until one of them has the sense to get some height, climbing the stairs up to the silver tower and standing on a balcony. Kay sees him over the rim. The Saxon lowers himself to a crouch, bringing his rifle up to his shoulder like a good cross-bowman, and taking careful aim down the length of the barrel. Kay feels as though they share a moment of understanding before the Saxon pulls the trigger.

Death feels like God snapping his fingers. It's always the same. The old sorcery flies out of him like a raven bursting free of a pie, and the spell is broken. His bones remember their age and turn accordingly to dust.

There is always the briefest of moments, while his skin is still curling into parchment, when he can feel the morbid wrong-ness of it. Like opening a musty tomb and seeing the shrivelled thing inside of it and knowing that he is trespassing somewhere haunted. Except that the shrivelled thing is him. He is a living fossil, and then he is nothing, grains of sand in the wind, a bad smell lost in the many bad smells of war.

Then it gets worse. This is his least favourite part of the whole process, where he isn't sure where he is or what is happening. Nothing but darkness, and the sense of being bodiless but still falling through a space between worlds, between death and rebirth. He's always worried that he'll get stuck here forever if he isn't careful. But he never lingers in the darkness for long. Half a moment, and he is mercifully drawn back into the world. In the earth again, in the mud beneath his tree. Not knowing quite how long it's been.

There's a period of uncertainty. Is he flesh again, or is he still putrid clay, a cludge of wet earth, recongealing? He opens his eyes, wriggles his fingers, feels his leg and shoulder remade, the bone and sinew knitted back together. Not painful, but peculiar. Then he climbs up out of the soil, scrambling, more quickly this time, elbowing his way towards the light. His mail is repaired. How can the earth remake a coat of mail? How can it remake him? Questions that don't bear thinking about.

He gets his head and shoulders above the ground, again. It's still a hot day. Whether it's the same hot day is a different question. Decades might have passed.

But he can hear the sirens. He can still hear gunshots in the distance. When he climbs up further from the mud he can see that the fleeing woman has followed his advice. She's wading towards him, across the bog.

'Oh, *now* you ...' Kay says, to the earth. His shield is now lying helpfully at the base of the tree. His sword is buried in the roots, waiting for him to draw it out. Sometimes the earth has a sense of humour.

Once he's out he straps his shield back onto his arm and wraps his hand around the hilt of his sword. It slides cleanly out from the tree, leaving a narrow slit behind. He uses his cloak to wipe the sap from the blade. It's not a great kingly sword like Caliburn, with garnets cloisonned into the pommel; the blade is not emblazoned with the word of God; the crossguard isn't inlaid with silver or fashioned like the True Cross. It's just a well-balanced sword in the Roman style, good for spilling guts; a bit weighty in the hilt because he likes to be able to turn it round and break people's collarbones with the blunt end of it. It's served him well, over the centuries. There are swords to be wielded by kings and then there are swords to be wielded for kings, with which to do their dirty work. His is the latter.

The woman is close now, wading as quickly as she can. The Saxons are following her, tiny figures in the distance, moving slowly and uncertainly through the bog. But their rifles are still sputtering, and the air is live with the crack and sting of bullets.

'Come on!' he shouts.

She finds firm footing and hurries up the hill, collapsing back against it near the top. One of her boots has gone missing. She pulls off her hat to catch her breath more easily. She is young, angry, mostly bone and hollow, with skin almost as brown as his. Black hair plastered to her forehead. She looks him up and down with narrowed eyes.

'Yeah, me again,' he says.

'How . . . ?' she asks, catching her breath.

'I get around,' he says. 'You need any help?'

She shakes her head. Pulling her backpack around to one side and reaching into it, to pull something out. Kay doesn't know what it is. A small device, a modern thing with buttons. Too big to be a cigarette lighter, too small to be a radio. Or is it? He doesn't know what radios look like these days. There's a kind of screen built into it, a little glowing box.

'I think I'm all right,' she says.

She presses a button on her little device, and something across the bog explodes.

Kay has seen castles crumble and warships explode on the ocean. He was riding with Fairfax when the church at Torrington was blown to ruins, and they were both carried clear from their saddles. He was at the Somme when the Lochnagar mine went up. None of it has quite prepared him for this explosion, which briefly rattles God's creation and sends a plume of fire half a mile into the sky.

A hot wind picks him up and slams him into his own tree. Across the bog, the ugly pipes burst open. The storage tanks explode one after the other like thundering dominos, with angry orange blooms. And then the silver tower itself pitches sideways and erupts in fire. But this is a strange explosion. A rainbow fireball of blue and green and orange, which sends lightning coursing through the black smoke. Kay doesn't have time to figure out what that might mean before the bog itself catches fire, a sheet of flame spreading outwards with terrifying speed. Squinting into the inferno, Kay can just about make out some Saxons burning, like ants caught in a hearth.

The fire creeps all the way to the foot of their hill, spreading across the slickened water. It continues out towards the sea behind them, but it does not climb the hill and bother them. Old magic. Deep roots. His tree has been around for too long to be concerned by this sort of thing. Or so he hopes, anyway. It's never had to fend off a fire like this before.

The woman's eyes are wide and panicked. She is swearing to herself. 'It wasn't supposed to do that,' she says.

'What was it supposed to do?' he asks her.

But either she doesn't hear him or she doesn't want to answer. She buries her head in her hands, then brings her scarf up over her nose to guard against the fumes. Kay brings his cloak around to do the same. He puts his shield beside her, face down, and perches on top of it. Keeping her company.

They sit together for a while, coughing and watching the bog burn, because there isn't much else to be done until the fire dies down. When the woman looks up again, her eyes are red from smoke or tears or both.

'So, again,' she says. 'Who are you?'

'My name's Kay,' he replies. 'What's yours?'

'Mariam,' she says. 'Why did you help me?'

'I help people who are in peril. You looked like you were in peril.'

She looks strangely at him. 'Wasn't anything I couldn't handle.'

Kay nods his head at the inferno. 'Clearly,' he says.

'Thanks anyway.'

The smoke is rising in a great black column from where the silver tower used to be. Lightning courses through it in sudden bursts, every now and again. Thunder echoes across the moor. The earth is still shaking. Kay gets the sense now that the tower was for digging or drilling. Burrowing deep into the bowels of Britain and bringing something up. His bowels would be quaking too, if something like this happened to them.

'Are you with the Army of Saint George, or something?' asks Mariam.

Kay shakes his head. 'I don't know what that is.'

'I was gonna say,' says Mariam. 'You don't look the type. Apart from the shield, and everything.'

'How do you mean?' he asks.

'Never seen a black knight before,' she replies.

'You'd be surprised how many people say that.'

Mariam is confused. 'So, what are you? Are you up from Manchester? The communists? Who are you with?'

He doesn't understand the question. 'I'm with you,' he says. 'On a hill.'

'... Okay,' she says.

'Are there lots of people in peril, nowadays?' he asks.

She looks incredulous. 'What, have you been living under a rock?'

'Under a hill,' he says, patting the earth.

Mariam is staring at him as if he is mad. He's grown used to that, over the years. He's had worse. He remembers how Queen Victoria looked at him the first time she saw him, saw his skin.

Lightning arcs through the smoke. Then there's a new sound from across the bog. It sounds like a writhing beast again, something ancient and terrible. It's probably another modern sound. Metal twisting, or gas burning. Something succumbing to the fire.

'Yeah,' says Mariam, eventually. 'Yeah, there's a lot of people in peril.'

'I see,' he says.

'Are you ... going to try and help them?' she asks.

'Well, I'll see what I can do,' he says. He smiles at her. Then he frowns.

There is something moving in the inferno. The smoke is twisting into something tangible. It's a shape, it's a thing, crawling. And Kay knows exactly what it is. He stands up and straps his shield back onto his forearm.

It's been more than a thousand years since he saw a dragon.

It's a big one too, an adult female, the kind that were always the hardest to kill; the kind that used to rule over bull dragons like queens surrounded by fools. It would take Arthur's whole household to slay a dragon like that, all forty of his best warriors, with a thousand-strong levy of common fighting men, spearmen and archers, and all the war machines and incantations that Merlin could devise.

Or it would take Caliburn, Arthur's sword, which could cut through anything. Caliburn which has slept beneath the water for all this time, so that fools can't get their hands upon its hilt. He hopes it can stay sleeping there for a little while longer.

The dragon doesn't see them across the flaming bog. It coils itself on the ground, wreathed harmlessly in fire. It sniffs the air. It knows that something isn't right in the realm. And before Kay can think about how he's going to kill it, the dragon leaps upwards, beating the smoke down with its wings. With a few good strokes it's high in the air, trailing its long body behind it, rising on the column of heat from the burning tower. And then it's gone, high above the smoke. Far too high for him to see where it is going.

'What the fuck was that?' asks Mariam, in a quiet voice.

'I think it's the reason I'm back,' says Kay.

2

Lancelot wanted to be buried next to Galehaut, on the Holy Island, off the coast of Brynaich. They talked about it more than once, in the old days. They liked the idea that their trees might grow together, bound into one great oak. Intertwined for all eternity.

That's not what happened, in the end. You can't always control where you get buried. He ended up in the tangled heart of Windsor forest, when it was bigger and wilder and less penetrable to interlopers. Now it's a deer park, bare and manicured. His ancient oak stands alone, set apart from younger trees, overlooked by statues of dead kings.

It's not ideal. But it's an easy commute into central London.

He climbs upward, reluctantly. Lethargically. Only motivated by the off chance of a cigarette and some decent Scotch. Maybe he'll have time to visit a day spa, this time. Get some sort of deep pore cleanse. Sleeping in the London soil does nothing for his complexion.

He wishes he could stay dead for longer stretches of time

without anybody bothering him. Just a few centuries of being mud and not having to worry about anything. Small chance of that. There's a filing cabinet somewhere in the city with dossiers on all of the secret places in the realm, all the buried dragons and sleeping knights. They know where to find him, when they want him to do something for them.

Marlowe's already here, standing on the grass. Wearing his hat and his long grey raincoat, even in this hot weather. He updates his wardrobe once every hundred years or so. It used to be doublets and pantaloons. Then it became tailcoats and powdered wigs. Since the First World War it's been brogues, briefcase, three-piece suit. Now he's smoking a cigarette and checking his wristwatch. There's some kind of new-fangled flying machine waiting on the grass behind him.

Lancelot wipes the muck from his face and sighs from deep in his throat.

'Dear Christ,' he says. 'What do you want now?'

'Woken up on the wrong side of the tree, have we?' asks Marlowe. '"What power art thou, who from below, hast made me rise unwillingly and slow . . ."'

'Don't start. What do you want?'

'England's in peril.'

Lancelot levels a muddy finger across the park. 'It's not the Falklands again, is it? I should have thought I was perfectly clear about that last time. The Falklands aren't part of England, and they never have been. They're well outside my purview.'

Marlowe smokes, patiently. 'It's not the Falklands.'

'What is it, then?'

'All in good time.'

'It had better be some serious bloody peril. That's all I'm saying.'

Marlowe smiles thinly and walks towards him, offering him a cigarette. 'Let's get you into some fresh clothes. Then I'll explain.'

Lancelot mumbles his thanks. He takes the cigarette and pinches it between his lips. Marlowe stands close and lights it for him, smelling of hair cream and something else as well. The faintest whiff of brimstone.

Marlowe enjoys a different kind of immortality, achieved by different means. No magic acorns or slumbering under trees. He sold his soul on the dotted line, joined an exclusive members' club. Eternal life. But not eternal youth. He used to be gorgeous, in the old days. Marlowe the playwright, man about London, spying for the Crown. Getting into barfights. Dabbling in the dark arts and rousing ancient warriors from their slumber. They used to have fun.

But now Marlowe is older and careworn, crushed under centuries of manilla envelopes. He has the permanent aura of cheap tobacco and lunchtime pints. There's still something haggardly endearing about him, though, like a hound that's getting too old to hunt. The tired old spook. Last of a dying breed.

'All right,' says Lancelot. 'Christ, I need a drink.'

'I thought you might.'

They walk towards the flying contraption, over the yellow grass. Lancelot can't help but notice that the park is somewhat less verdant than it used to be. The trees look mostly dead. No indication of any deer. And it's far too warm. Like Kenya or India, where he went in the time of Queen Victoria. Not like England at all.

Still, if England's less cold and dreary than it used to be, that's not necessarily a bad thing. He remembers in the old days when they planted apple trees on the Holy Island and the apples froze in the cold. Galehaut tried to eat them anyway. It might be warm enough to grow them now. Eat them by the handful, looking out to sea. Warm sun on his face.

The flying machine has something in common with the helicopters that he saw in the 1980s, the last time he was up. Except it's smaller, clearer, more fragile. He gets the sense that it's not meant for military use. Just a glass orb with two seats and four propeller arms.

'What precisely is this thing?' he asks.

'Oh,' says Marlowe, disparagingly. 'They call them "quad-pods". Latest thing from Dubai. Think of it like a flying taxi.'

'Not a patch on my old Spitfire.'

'Times change, old boy.'

Once they're sat down and strapped in, the canopy rolls shut and the rotors start spinning. Marlowe swipes a finger across the control pad until he finds the right destination, then taps on it twice. The quad-pod springs upwards, blowing dead leaves away in the downdraught from its propellers, spiriting them high above Windsor. Then it turns and bears them towards London.

'It flies itself?' asks Lancelot.

'It does.'

'Disconcerting.'

'It's perfectly safe.'

They suck on their cigarettes, filling the pod with smoke. Marlowe in his raincoat, Lancelot in his muddy chainmail. Neither willing to admit before the other that smoking in here might be a bad idea. Both trying not to cough. Until an alert pops up on the canopy: a female voice tells them, in Chinese and then in English, that no smoking is permitted. Marlowe loses the game of courage and stubs out his cigarette against the armrest of his chair. Lancelot takes a last drag on his before following suit.

'Ghastly machine,' says Lancelot.

'I know.'

They follow the old course of the Devil's Highway, across the Thames. Then the city stretches out below them, far bigger than it used to be. Lancelot's nose wrinkles. He has fond memories of Marlowe's London. Thatched roofs and cobbled streets, theatres and alehouses. Back-alley encounters. Amorous evenings boating on the Thames. And then there was London in the last big war, with Galehaut, when they both came up to fight the Germans. Pubs and music halls and red double-decker buses. Matching scarves, in the cold months. Kissing secretly in dark air-raid shelters. The thought of that makes him smile. But beneath those Londons is the old Londinium, which he always hated. Festering and joyless. Tribes and gangs and Jutes and Saxons fighting over Roman ruins. Kay and Arthur crawled up from its gutters, which is more than enough reason to hold it in contempt.

'A lot's changed since you were last up,' says Marlowe. 'I'm not sure where to start. You might find that it's a bit damper than it used to be.'

They start to lose altitude around Belgravia. The pod takes them lower, for its own inscrutable reasons. Giving them a better view of the streets below. Lancelot has to lean forward, frowning through the canopy, to try and make sense of it all.

It looks more like Venice than London. The river has swelled its banks enormously, flooding Chiswick and Shepherd's Bush. Half the city drowned with floodwater, glistening in the sun. The underground railways and the air-raid shelters must be lakes and rivers now, below the earth. The dark places where he kissed Galehaut in the last war. He can't imagine what could have caused this, except the wrath of some angry sea god. But it wouldn't surprise him in the slightest to learn that Britain had angered a sea god since the last time he was up and about. Nothing surprises him any more. Not wars or revolutions or plagues or famines. He just comes up and does what Marlowe tells him to do, in the hope of going back to sleep as soon as possible. He'll probably keep doing that until Judgement Day. If it hasn't come already.

Even the dry parts of the city look pretty miserable. Hyde Park has been turned into some sort of camp, with rows and rows of white tents. The streets around it are cordoned off with barriers and roadblocks. Barbed wire and men with guns. From their little pod they can see crowds of people being pushed back. Clouds of smoke drifting on the breeze like mustard gas at the Somme. Smaller flying machines are buzzing like hornets, firing things down at the crowd. Getting things thrown up at them in return. Their quad-pod drifts overhead, too high to worry about stray bricks.

'All getting a bit fruity, is it?' Lancelot asks.

'That's one way of putting it,' says Marlowe. 'Hard to find room for everybody when the water's this high. We've had to abandon Parliament, Whitehall. So government business is being done from the City, for the time being.'

'No change there, then.'

'We're moving it all offshore fairly soon, but I won't bore you with the details.'

Their pod gets away from the fighting, heading east, over the monstrous Thames again. Past Westminster Palace, which is drowned and crumbling in the floodwater. Lancelot frowns.

'We're not going to the Department?'

'Ah, no,' says Marlowe. He clears his throat. 'As I said, there have been one or two changes.'

'Such as?'

'Well, the whole sector's been privatised. Musty old intelligence agencies broken up and sold to US private equity firms. That sort of thing. The services previously provided by the Department are now rendered by a transatlantic corporation called GX5.'

'What does it stand for?'

Marlowe sniffs with a dark kind of mirth. 'Why should it stand for anything, Lance?'

They draw closer to the banking district, which looks like an upended drawer of glass knives. Skyscrapers rising from the floodwater and piercing heaven, far larger and more hideous than anything he saw the last time he was up and about. Jagged, ugly things. They have skybridges built between them and pods like theirs buzzing back and forth. It must make things easier, in this new London, if you don't have to go below sea level.

One of the larger buildings has a roof garden, green and artificial. Their pod touches down on the grass, just next to the tennis courts. Once the rotors have spun down, the canopy opens, and they climb out onto the roof.

'Hideous,' says Lancelot.

'Oh, it's not that bad,' says Marlowe. 'The bar's this way.'

They walk over the fake grass, past the fake shrubs, to a penthouse bar that rises from the roof. Televisions showing an indeterminable sport. Old racquets and boat oars mounted on the walls. Nobody here apart from the bartender, cleaning glasses. He doesn't seem fazed by the mud and chainmail. If there are government functions up here then the bartender has probably seen stranger things.

Marlowe puts down his briefcase and slides into one of the bar stools. 'There's a changing room, over there,' he says. 'Take your time.'

Lancelot always tears off the mail and tunic as soon as he can, whenever he comes up. Would be much more convenient if the magic worked differently and the earth revised his wardrobe every now and again, as the centuries wore on. But Merlin didn't think of that, did he? There was a man with no conception of fashion.

Now he dumps his old war gear in the corner of the shower room, a heavy heap of iron and linen that he won't be needing again. Marlowe has arranged for a washbag and change of clothes to be left here for him. Soft white towels folded neatly on one of the benches. When he's peeled the muddy hose and braies from his legs he strides into the shower and turns it on. Scouring the mud from his flesh. Washing it out of his hair. Scrubbing it from under his fingernails. Hot showers are one of the few pleasures in this endless nightmare.

Whisky, motorcycles, good bars with loud music. Italian coffee. Cashmere. Hotels with good soap. They make all the rest of it slightly more tolerable. All the endless war and death and horror. He'd much rather be dead and consigned to oblivion, but he exempted himself from death a long time ago. If he blows his brains out, or drowns himself, or leaps off a tall building, he just ends up under his tree again. He's tried it before, a few times.

If he does have to keep coming up, he'll keep enjoying life's little indulgences as often as he can.

When he feels passably human again, he strides out of the shower and stares at himself dripping in the washroom mirrors, admiring himself from different angles. That's another small mercy. If he has to keep coming back until the end of time, then at least he can do it in this body. Firm buttocks. Broad shoulders. Sharp cheekbones. Curls of blond hair. Still handsome enough that he could get RAF officers to sleep with him in the last big war.

He finds various lotions and rubs them into his skin, until he smells of grapefruit and mandarin. Then he goes through the clothes that Marlowe has picked out for him. Grey boxer shorts. White linen suit. Green pastel shirt. Brown leather loafers to wear on his feet. All very much to his taste.

He's grateful for Marlowe. Not just for the shirts and shoes. There was a long time before Marlowe where everything was gloom and horror. One war after another, charging around on horseback. Mud and murder and mad kings. Henries and Edwards and Richards, and all the others. It all felt pointless, endless, hopeless. Eternal warriors, questing about aimlessly, all longing for oblivion. Then Marlowe came along and brought some structure to their afterlives. No more of this fruitless questing about; he gave them useful things to do. Stealth work. Spy work. Gave them all a sense of purpose again. *The intelligent application of extraordinary assets.* Made them feel as if they were actually helping. Making the realm a better place.

When he's finished pampering himself, Lancelot joins Marlowe back at the bar. Marlowe has ordered three double whiskies and knocked one back already, nursing the other while he watches the news on the big television screens behind the bar.

'Feeling better?' asks Marlowe.

'Somewhat,' says Lancelot. 'Thank you.'

They clink their glasses together, and Lancelot takes his first grateful sip. But the whisky tastes cheap, unsophisticated, cloyingly sweet. He frowns. 'Is this American?'

'I'm afraid so,' says Marlowe. 'We're having some trouble getting the good stuff down from Scotland since they declared independence.'

'Things must be worse than I thought.'

'I've still got a bottle of the old Terrantez knocking around,' says Marlowe, smiling. 'The 1704. We can crack it open once you've finished this job.'

Lancelot sighs. The thought of good Madeira wine makes the world seem like a kinder, better place for half a moment. Then he starts listening to the news.

Efforts are continuing to refloat Hull and reclaim land in the Gulf of Peterborough. It's hoped that these areas will be suitable for resettlement within the next fifteen years, if sea levels don't rise further. The Chinese trade commissioner is demanding extra security for the Essex International Development Zone, or Beijing will have no choice but to land troops and protect their assets. Another arctic methane 'super pocket' has been detected, in Siberia. It will be released from the permafrost within two years if global emissions aren't significantly reduced. An explosion at a Lancashire fracking facility may be the work of FETA, the Feminist Environmentalist Transgressive Alliance, a dangerous group of extremist eco-terrorists. The government will be expanding their anti-terrorism contracts in the north of England with Saxon and other private military companies. Residents of Greater Manchester are reminded to make their way south of the Mersey, to avoid being caught up in efforts to retake the city from socialist insurgents. Finally, construction has been completed on the Avalon platform, in the Bristol Channel. A state-of-the-art offshore facility for oil extraction, civil defence and strategic coordination. The government will start relocating there within the week. It's expected to boost the economy by several billion pounds.

'Christ,' says Lancelot, knocking back his drink.
'Hm,' says Marlowe. 'Another?'
'Please.'
Marlowe nods at the bartender, then reaches down for his briefcase and lays it out on the bar. He pops it open, retrieving a manila folder sealed with red tape.
'Urgh,' says Lancelot, quietly. 'Can't it wait?'
It's a plea for something else. A different conversation, an evening off, before he has to pick up his sword. But Marlowe isn't sympathetic. He slides the folder across the bar.

'Afraid not, old thing,' says Marlowe. 'My people are keen that it gets done quickly.'

Lancelot doesn't open the folder just yet. He stares down at it, wishing that it would go away. It's never been quite clear to him who Marlowe's 'people' are. It's not just the people in government, the people in the halls of power. Marlowe has different masters, older masters, who expect their due. But it hardly matters, does it? They tell Marlowe what needs doing. Marlowe passes it down to him, and Kay, and the others. They get it done. They get to feel like they're doing something useful. That's how it's been for three hundred years or so. Funny time to start questioning things now.

It could be anything, inside the folder. Marlowe uses his Arthurian assets for ordinary cloak-and-dagger work, not just for the weird stuff. It could be a war in Asia that needs winning. Somebody in South America whose throat needs slitting. An ancient monster in Wales or Ireland, risen from its slumber, which needs quietly vanquishing. It could be a week before he's back under his tree, or it could be three years.

New drinks are put down in front of them. Lancelot takes a measured sip, scowling at the taste. The only way to take control of this situation would be to go back outside and throw himself over the edge of the roof. But then he'd wake up under his tree again. He'd only have to crawl back up. Take another shower. Marlowe would still be here, at the bar, with his folder.

'If I'd known it was going to be like this,' he says, eventually, 'I never would have agreed to it.'

'Well,' says Marlowe. He clears his throat and pats Lancelot lightly on the shoulder. 'Chin up, old boy.'

Lancelot waits until he's sure that no further counselling is forthcoming. Then he sighs. He picks up the folder and starts tearing the tape.

'What is it, wetwork?' he asks.

'More in your line than usual, actually,' says Marlowe. 'These were taken in Lancashire, yesterday.'

The envelope contains two black-and-white photographs and a dossier that he can't be bothered to read. The photographs show an industrial facility, which seems to have exploded. In the first photo there's an old queen dragon, huge and mighty, writhing up out of the ground with flames around her. The second photo is of a man with a shield. Lancelot barely glances at the dragon photo before casting it aside. He's much more interested in the photo of Kay.

Kay, Arthur's brother. Kay, who didn't give him refuge when he needed it. Kay, who rode north against him with wild fury in his eyes.

'Old friend of yours,' says Marlowe.

'Hardly,' says Lancelot. 'Did you reactivate him? Before me?'

Marlowe smiles. 'No, he appears to have sprung up of his own accord. And now he's making a nuisance of himself.'

Lancelot scoffs. 'Doesn't surprise me in the slightest.'

'We're rather more concerned with the dragon, of course. Last spotted over Burnley, heading east. But it's proving somewhat difficult to track. Not showing up on radar.'

'No, well, it won't,' says Lancelot, picking up the other photograph again. He knows all too well that dragons are not real creatures. They are manifestations of magic, entities from a different realm. Bursting through from the Otherworld in a monstrous form. They don't usually appear for no reason. Usually they need a bit of help, from this side of the veil.

'Dragons don't just pop up out of nowhere,' he says. 'It takes a lot of magic to bring them into the world. Blood magic, or earth magic. What was this place, before it exploded?'

'Just a fracking site,' says Marlowe. 'Taking oil out of the ground. But then there's these terrorists, FETA, who probably caused the explosion. A group of highly spirited young women with far too much time on their hands. They might be dabbling in some amateur hocus-pocus.'

'That's a bit of a stretch, isn't it?'

Marlowe scowls. 'Oh, you'd be amazed how many women are turning to paganism nowadays, Beltane and Samhain and all the rest of it. It's all got even worse since the flower-power years. Can't just burn them at the stake any more, of course. This is an age of tolerance and free speech. Look where it gets us.'

Lancelot raises an eyebrow but says nothing. It's at times like this that Marlowe really does look like an old man grumbling into his whisky. But he never did like women very much, especially women who used magic. That strange breed of Elizabethan gentleman who studied the dark arts but would burn anyone else for doing the same.

'I haven't seen a wyrm this big since that mess at Passchendaele,' he says. 'The blood sacrifice. It takes more than petty witchcraft to summon a big queen dragon like this.'

'Do you think you can do it?' asks Marlowe. 'Slay the beast?'

'There's only one sword that can kill a dragon like this one,' he says. 'I'll have to go and get it.'

'You know where it is?' asks Marlowe, smiling significantly.

'Yes. And I'm not telling you.'

Marlowe sighs. 'If only I knew where it *was*, I could look after it properly. Lock it away in the vaults, keep it from falling into the wrong hands. Only bring it out in situations like this.'

'It's very well protected already,' he says. 'Even with the sword I'll still need some assistance. RAF support, that sort of thing.'

Marlowe pinches the bridge of his nose. 'Well. As I said, there've been some changes on that front. The defence sector's been privatised.'

'Which means?'

'The armed forces of the United Kingdom have been broken up and sold to foreign multinationals, in the spirit of free enterprise.'

Lancelot blinks, parsing this news into terms he can better understand. 'You've replaced Britain's professional army with hired mercenaries.'

'They prefer to be known as private military companies, but that's the essence of it.'

'Marvellous,' says Lancelot. 'We tried the same thing in my day.'

'Oh yes?'

'Hired an awful lot of Angles and Saxons to guard our borders for us, after the legions packed up and left.'

'And how did that turn out?'

'Not particularly well, as it happens.'

'Indeed.' Marlowe clears his throat. 'There are some ongoing contractual disputes.'

'Any other changes I should know about?'

'Well, let's see. Wales and Cornwall have declared independence, along with Scotland, although we refuse to recognise them. Most of the north has organised itself into a kind of socialist bloc. And we've sold Essex to the Chinese.'

Lancelot finishes his drink with a shrug. 'I never much liked Essex, anyway.'

Marlowe smiles a thin smile. 'In any case, our forces will be at your disposal. Such as they are.'

'There might be a certain amount of collateral damage. Bridges, infrastructure.'

'As long as it's north of Stoke, you'd actually be accelerating several government initiatives.'

Lancelot nods, happy with the terms of engagement. 'What about Kay?' he asks.

'Talk to him, if you get the opportunity. Try to bring him back into the fold. Get him on side.'

'And if he refuses?'

'I thought I'd leave that up to you,' says Marlowe, smiling. 'Then . . . come back here for debriefing?'

Marlowe reaches over and places a hand on Lancelot's knee. Lancelot looks down at the hand, and then back up again. Marlowe might look old and gaunt nowadays, but there's still a gleam in his eyes. Some of that old mischief. It's easy to smile back at him.

'Filthy old man,' he says.

Marlowe chuckles. Squeezing his knee. 'You'd better be going. Time passeth swift away, and all that.'

'I'll get my things.'

He goes back outside to the roof garden. The plants are artificial, but the old magic can be surprisingly accommodating, when it wants to be. His sword and shield have materialised in a plastic topiary bush. If he doesn't pick them up here then they'll keep appearing in his path until he trips over them. He knows that from experience. So he takes up his sword from the soil, drawing it halfway from its scabbard and running an eye along the blade before sliding it back. A long and light and balanced blade, good for piercing chainmail and killing enemies who move slowly on their feet. It will be useless against a dragon, though. For the dragon he will need Caliburn, the Hard-Cleaver, which cuts through almost anything. But first he has to go and get it.

He girths the sword onto himself, sword belt fastened tightly under his suit jacket, slung down over one hip. Shield lashed to his arm, golden lion on a field of blue. Ready to slay dragons. He comes back inside, striking a pose at the threshold to the bar.

'How do I look?'

'Divine,' says Marlowe. 'Crusader chic.'

35

Lancelot smiles. 'Perfect.'

'Try to come back in one piece.'

'I always do.'

He walks towards the flying machine, leaving Marlowe at the bar. Thoughts of Caliburn and dragons fly quickly from his head, replaced by thoughts of Galehaut, and apples, and warm gardens.

3

There are flying machines in the night sky, of a kind that Kay hasn't seen before. Small and murderous things that scour the blackened moor with hungry searchlights, hanging in the firmament and buzzing like hornets. Surely too small for anybody to be piloting them.

He could never have imagined machines like these in the old days. But there was a time when he couldn't have imagined plate armour or gunpowder, either. He's been doing this for long enough now that he's grown to expect new marvels whenever he comes up. Horseless carriages, music boxes, telephones. Machine guns. He saw helicopters in Malaya, the last time he was up. Those were new and ungainly machines. These whirligigs must be their deadlier grandchildren. He's never surprised anymore by the new means that men dream up for killing one another. Or the new reasons.

Memories of Malaya threaten to surge up, and he forces them back down.

Beneath the whirligigs the Saxons are searching on foot, spread out in wide ranks through the darkness. All that Kay can see of them is the glare from their helmet lights.

Kay and Mariam have to move like ghosts. He's done plenty of this sort of thing over the years, stealth and shadow work, but it's been a good five centuries since he's had to do it on English soil. Mariam seems good at it, knowing when it's safe to run, when it's better to crawl, when it's best to settle in the reeds and wait. Good fieldcraft. He wonders where she learnt it, and why she had to. How old she is. When she chose this life.

It's a poor time to ask any of those questions. She might ask him his age in return, and he'd have to say, 'Well, I was born in the year when the harvests failed, and old King Vortigern was burnt in his keep'. He can never quite remember which year that was, in new money. Nor does he know which year this is. How long has he been under? Long enough for the realm to change beyond recognition. This used to be his land, his manor. His little scrap of Britain, handed to him by Arthur, to hold against the Angles. He used to know every hill and dale. Now he can barely tell north from south. The Rhypol was once a narrow river, but it's become some sort of monstrous tidal loch, with soaking wetlands all around it. So they must go east, inland across the flooded plain. Mariam leads the way, and he must follow.

You can get into trouble, following people. He followed Arthur for almost all his life, and look where that got him. He followed one king all the way to Palestine. Now here he is following Mariam, because it seemed like she was in peril. He'd like to ask more questions about who she is and who she fights for, but the questions can wait until they're somewhere safe. He'd rather not get overheard and killed again. Twice in one day would be a new record. He'd never live it down, if Gawain or Caradoc found out.

New sounds in the dark sky, heavy wingbeats and a huge

indignant roar. The kind of noise that echoes back from heaven, even as it shakes the marrow in your bones. Then there's the drone of the flying machines converging, red lights blinking overhead, spotlights arcing wildly. A brief snap of the dragon's tail lit up against the darkness. One of the whirligigs starts to spin, batted out of the sky. Kay hears the plaintive sound of an engine in distress, the shattering crunch of the machine crashing down to earth. It makes him wince.

The Saxons panic, breaking ranks, firing upwards with their machine rifles. Not scouring the reeds any more for errant knights.

'Now's our chance,' says Mariam. 'Let's go.'

She's right. But he lingers for a moment. Long enough to see the dragon swooping low to toast some distant Saxons, long body snaking through the air. Where did she come from? She's not some shrivelled little wyrmling, or a firedrake the size of a horse. She could have laid cities to ruin in the old days. Somebody somewhere must be messing with some serious magic to conjure up a beast of her size. He thinks of the place they have just left, the silver tower, the strange explosion.

He has questions for Mariam which he cannot ask her now. So he follows her into the night, away from the gunfire, away from the Saxons being roasted behind him. Arthur would call him cowardly, slinking away like this. Perhaps Arthur would be right. But there's no sense facing a big wyrm like that with just his sword and shield. Bors or Gawain would charge over there and get the fat cooked off their bones, putting valour before wisdom. See dragon, slay dragon. He's not foolish enough to do as they would do. He will choose his moment, muster allies. Wake up some of the other lads, if it comes to that. Get Caliburn, if he must. Face her again when he has a chance of triumph.

Eventually the ground stops squelching and becomes firmer. They go through hedges, across farmland that's been left fallow, through fields of rotting cabbages. After two or three fields there's a dense copse of trees with thick undergrowth. Beneath the bracken the ground is suddenly harder. Concrete, not soil. There was a fence here, with wire and mouldy posts, but it's fallen down to ankle height. He almost trips over it.

Squared off by the fallen fence is a structure, a metal box, hard to identify in the dark. Some machine for farming, left here abandoned in the trees? He's still wondering what it might be when Mariam climbs up onto it and opens a rusty hatch.

'You first,' she says.

He feels all the old fears. Maybe the box is something evil, a portal to the fay realm. Or maybe it's just empty, and Mariam is going to lock him in and leave him behind. He's starved to death before. It wasn't an experience he'd care to repeat.

He decides to trust her, for the time being. It's easier to be free with your trust when death isn't permanent. He gets his shield off his arm and hides it in the undergrowth. Then he climbs up after her, feeling for handholds in the dark. The hatch plunges downwards into deeper darkness, but his feet find the first rung of a ladder. So he follows it down, into a dark place which smells of rust and mould and neglect. Eventually there's a concrete floor, covered by an inch of water. He stands not knowing how big the space is, or whether there is anyone down here with him.

The hatch screams shut again. He can hear Mariam's footfalls, one boot and one damp sock, following him down the ladder. Then he can feel her beside him in the darkness. She moves further into the space, rummaging with something. There's a promising hum. A dim orange light flickers to life.

Kay squints at the place. A tiny rectangular room with white walls, ventilators in the ceiling, instrument cases on the wall. There is a bunkbed, a cluttered desk, a dartboard, a mouldy canvas chair. A notice nailed to one wall says ROYAL OBSERVER

CORPS and has a list of instructions beneath it: *REPORT EXPLO-SIONS AND MAINTAIN DIARY.*

'What is this place?' he asks.

'They . . . built them in the fifties,' she says. Looking through a rucksack. 'For the Cold War. People forgot about them. Should be safe to hide here for a while. PMCs don't know about them, as far as we can tell.'

'All right,' says Kay. 'Who's we?'

'You don't need to know that,' she says. She finds what she's looking for and pulls a pistol out of the bag, pointing it at his chest. She knows how to hold it, how to work the action. It's not too different from one of the guns he was issued in the last war. This is the first time he's seen her clearly, bathed in the amber light of the bunker. She looks like a roe deer that's been dragged through a hedge backwards, layers of rugged outdoor clothing padding out a narrow frame. Parka, dark green trousers, muddy boot on one foot, filthy sock on the other. When she pulls off her woolly hat she looks young and angry, her hair plastered against her forehead. Her mouth curled into a snarl.

'Seriously, though, who the fuck are you?' she asks.

'I thought I explained,' he says. He's not putting his hands up. He fell out of the habit centuries ago. 'I'm Kay. I help people who are in peril.'

'Bullshit,' she says. 'Who are you with?'

'Nobody.'

'So you just turned up out of nowhere at exactly the right moment and saved me from some Saxon mugs who couldn't shoot straight? Seems awfully fucking convenient.'

'Pretty much,' he says. 'A lot of convenient things happen to me. You get used to it.'

'That must be nice,' she says. 'Here's what I think this is. I think you're a plant.'

41

Kay screws up his face at her, genuinely baffled. 'What? No, I'm not ... I mean, I grow back under a tree, so I might be part plant. I'm not exactly sure how it works, to be honest. But the tree grew out of *me*, when I died. I'm more mud than plant, if anything.'

'Just, shut up!' says Mariam. She looks as confused as he feels. 'Now I'm supposed to take you back to my people so you can spy on us for Saxon. Is that about right?'

'I told you. I help people who are in peril. You looked like you were in peril.'

'How did you get here, then?'

'You wouldn't believe me.'

She moves nearer, holding the gun closer to his chest. 'Try me.'

'All right,' he says. It can't hurt at this point. He breathes out, thinking of where to begin. 'I'm an old warrior. From long ago. Arthur's time.'

She pulls a face at him. 'What, King Arthur?'

'Yeah,' he says. 'King Arthur. Didn't you see the dragon, back there?'

'I don't know what I saw,' she says. Eyes wild. 'It was just a hallucination, or the fumes, or something. Now tell me why you're here. Tell me the truth.'

'I don't know why, exactly,' he says. Trying to do just what she asked, and tell her the whole truth. 'I've been sleeping under a hill. Like in the legends. Back in the old days we all ate these things, these resurrection stones, that Merlin had done his magic on. And they took root, inside us, so that when we died they'd still be there, and they'd grow into trees. So the idea was, whenever Britain was in peril, we'd come back from the dead and sort things out. That was my tree, up on the hill. That's where I was buried. And now I climb up from under it whenever things go south. Whenever people need help. So maybe it was

42

the dragon, or maybe it was you, but ... that's why I'm here. I'm here to help.'

There's a long silence in the little bunker, apart from the buzz of the generator that's keeping the lightbulb on. Mariam's eyes are white and unblinking.

'You're right,' says Mariam. 'I don't believe you.'

'I told you that you wouldn't.'

'You're fucking mental.'

'Probably,' says Kay. 'But I swear, by the blood of Christ, I'm telling the truth.'

'All right, then,' she says. She's clearly reached a decision. 'Prove it.'

'How?'

'Come back from the dead,' she says.

She pulls the trigger.

Twice in one day. New record.

Falling through darkness for another brief infinity, confused and terrified. Time is meaningless. It could be years or hours or seconds.

His last body will be turning to dust in the bunker, but he never needs to worry about that. The old body dies, and a new one is made. The tree just remoulds him every time from the clay and earth. He saw a printing press once, in Queen Anne's war. Churning out paper from dead trees. It made him wonder about himself. Maybe that's how the tree works, and he's just a crude copy of the original. Something churned out of the ground. No soul in his breast. Some kind of tree ogre. Not a pleasant thing to think about.

He never asked for any of this. He wanted to be buried in Mamucium, next to his wife. Beside the ruins of their home. Lie beside her in the earth and sleep, or join her, up in heaven. That would still be his strong preference, if anyone offered him the choice. But he sold his soul to the wrong gods. Died in the wrong place. Ate Merlin's resurrection stone and sealed his fate. Now all he has to look forward to is more of this nonsense, until the end of days. Forever coming back, over and over and over again.

At least this time he has something to prove. He's ready to climb up from under his tree and find his way back to Mariam. See the look on her face. But he finds it tougher than usual to piece himself back together. His flesh and bones seem to pause for longer as soft mud. He feels the hardness of bark, the creaking of timber, before he feels the familiar litheness of flesh and sinew. He catches a glimpse of his hand in front of his face, in the light coming down through the soil. It doesn't look quite right.

There's something gone wrong with the printing press this time, he can tell. Something caught in the wheels. That's never happened before, not once in the last thousand years. But then he's never been remade from the earth twice in one day before. Maybe the tree needs time to recover. Needs time to draw magic up from the ground and gather the raw stuff to mould him back together. That might be it. Or it might be the fire and the oil and the devastation. Maybe the land is poisoned. Maybe a floating ember has set his tree on fire. He starts to panic, clawing his way up through the soil. Keener than usual to get free.

And then he's up there, kneeling at the foot of his tree, catching his breath. All in one piece, as far as he can tell. The bog is still burning in the darkness, a lake of fire with few safe paths across it. He can see the ruins of the fracking place, still belching out smoke against an orange night. He hears the roar of the dragon in the distance, further away than it was before.

His hand looks normal when he raises it in front of his face. A bit stiffer, maybe, when he flexes his grip.

It takes him a moment to notice the ache at the centre of his chest. He reaches up and presses his hand against his mail, probing through the links with his fingers. No wetness of blood or sharp stab of pain, just a dull twinge. But it's in the same place where Mariam just shot him.

He freezes. That's never happened before.

Normally he comes back brand new. He's been beheaded, burnt to a crisp, and he never came back with any scars. So why now?

Probably nothing. Just faerie pain. The bullet's ghost, still lingering. Sometimes wounds stick in the mind long after they've healed on the body. He learnt that a long time ago. Yes, that'll be it. All in his head. It'll wear off, in time.

He can't check now, anyway. Can't shrug off his mail here in the darkness and check his chest for gunshot wounds. He has to get back to Mariam. He has something to prove. His sword is gone from his hip, as usual, but he's sure it will turn up somewhere. Like it always does.

It's a struggle getting back to the bunker without Mariam's help, but eventually he finds the copse of trees again. He climbs up onto the metal box and knocks on the hatch.

His old body has turned to mulch by the time he climbs down, wasting away to nothing. Just a few leaves left floating in the floodwater and an earthy smell. Mariam is staring at him in wide-eyed terror, holding a string of beads tightly in her right hand.

'Have you got any food?' he asks. 'Haven't eaten since 1952.'

It gives her something to do. She starts nodding, slowly. Then she gets two cans of baked beans down from a store cupboard and opens one for him.

He says a short prayer and then gratefully devours his food. Mariam mumbles a prayer as well. He's heard that language before, beneath the walls of Antioch and a few times since. Safir and Palamedes used to speak it back in the old days. Strange that he can understand it better now, with Merlin's gift of tongues. Strange to hear a young woman like Mariam giving thanks to God, when most young people had stopped doing that the last time he was up and about. He doesn't try to understand it all. He just thanks God for his beans.

Mariam isn't eating. She just sits on the old desk and stares at him. The gun sits next to her, where she can reach it.

'Okay,' she says. 'What was that thing, back there?'

'That was a dragon,' he says, between beans.

'Are dragons real?'

'That one was. Looked pretty lairy, as well.'

Mariam stares at the floor, nodding. Lots of people get nauseous when you tell them that dragons exist. He sighs and tries to explain.

'They're not real in the same way that me and you are real. Or a horse, or a cow, or any other beast. But when you get some spare magic released into the world, then the magic doesn't like being idle, so it takes the form of something. If it's only a little bit of magic then it'll just be a gnome or gremlin or something. If it's a *lot* of magic, you get dragons popping up.'

'Okay,' says Mariam, scratching her arm. Eyes still downcast towards the floor. Talk of magic doesn't seem to be making her feel better. 'Why was there . . . why did magic get released?'

'That's a good question,' he says. 'What was that place back there? Before you blew it up?'

46

'The fracking site? It's . . . they use it to get gas out of the earth. They blow stuff up, deep underground, and the gas gets released. Then they pipe it up so they can burn it.'

'Like a mine?' he asks.

'Yeah.'

He squints at his beans. Strange things can happen, with mines and caves and tunnels. Especially if they're left abandoned. A crack can form between this world and the Otherworld. Smaller monstrosities can squeeze their way through. But he's never known a big queen dragon to slither through a faerie hole like that. They're proud creatures; it would be beneath their dignity.

'They weren't doing anything else down there?' he asks. 'Nothing . . . nefarious?'

She shrugs. 'Well, not unless you count drilling for gas, and using it to fuel bomber planes, and polluting the atmosphere, and destroying the ecosystem.'

He can't help frowning at her. 'What?'

'Climate breakdown? Global warming? Ever heard of it?'

''Fraid not.'

She stares at him for a long moment, weighing him up. Eyes moving over his muddy chainmail. Then she buries her head in her hands. 'You really have been under a hill, haven't you?'

''Fraid so,' he says.

'Did you actually just come back from the dead?'

'You saw the body.'

'Fuck.'

'Yeah, I know.'

'I'm having trouble processing this.'

'Sorry.'

'I've had a really long day. And I'm very freaked out right now.'

'I don't blame you.'

Mariam starts breathing deeply into her hands. He waits for her to calm down. There's a reason that he doesn't normally tell people who he is. Usually he has some alias or another. The last few times he was up and about, the Department gave him a cover story, made up all the paperwork for him. Sergeant Knight or Mr K. Spared him from having to explain himself to people. It might make things easier if he went down to London again and found Marlowe. Report in, like a good soldier. But he swore he wouldn't work for Marlowe again. Not after Malaya.

A few minutes pass before Mariam lifts her head, staring thoughtfully at the wet floor.

'So,' she says, 'your whole deal is that you sleep under a tree, and you come back from the dead to help people out whenever England's gone to shit?'

'That's about the size of it, yeah,' he says.

'Why?' asks Mariam.

It takes Kay a moment to understand what she's asking. He blinks at her. 'Why what?'

'Why do you bother coming back and saving people? What do you get out of it?'

He opens his mouth to say something about honour and duty and sacred oaths, but it dies in his throat. That hasn't rung true for a while, really. He's not sure he can say it with a straight face any more.

'Honestly, I just want to go back to sleep,' he says. 'Sooner I deal with the latest mess, sooner I can get back underground.'

Mariam starts nodding to herself. He's finally said something that makes sense. Now she picks up her can of beans and eats a forkful. He takes that as a good sign.

'Okay,' she says. 'Well England's definitely gone to shit. So, good thing you're here, I guess.'

'Would you mind bringing me up to speed?' he asks. 'There wasn't a war on, last time I was up and about. Well, there was, but it was far away. Not here in Britain.'

She breathes out, wondering where to start. Then she begins. It's the same old story, for the most part. Rich people trying to make themselves richer. Poor people getting sick of it. Rich people blaming it on foreigners. Britain cutting itself off from the world, turning on itself like the hungry serpent that eats its own tail. The people are starving. The people are angry. New enemies have to be found, to put in front of their anger. He nods as she goes along. None of it surprises him in the slightest.

She tells him other things as well. Corruption in the air, and the world getting warmer. The ice melting in the far north and the waters rising. People flooded out of their homes. It doesn't make much sense to him, but the strangest thing is that it rings a distant bell. Didn't Merlin used to talk about something like that, every now and again? One of his half-baked prognostications, casting chicken bones and licking moss and staring strangely at cave walls. Men of great wealth will burn oil and tarnish the sky, until the seas rise and drown us all. Everyone thought it was more of his usual bollocks. Look out, lads, Merl's been on the mushrooms again. But maybe it wasn't. He got other things right, after all. Steam trains. Egg whisks.

'Are there any more of these fracking places?' he asks. 'Anywhere else where they're doing the same thing?'

She is sitting on one of the bunks now, with her socks up on the stained old covers. Hugging her knees. Giving him a strange look. 'Yeah, loads. Why?'

'Whatever they were doing there, it had something to do with magic,' he says. 'And when people start messing around with magic, it's usually my job to try and stop them.'

'Okay,' she says. 'Well, they have fracking sites and oil rigs all over the place, but the biggest one's down south, in the Somerset flood zone. The Avalon platform.'

The name sends a chill through him. Ynys Afallon is the Isle of Apples, the land of strange plenty which sits in the Otherworld beyond the mists of time. Avalon is where his brother lies sleeping, waiting to return. Mariam can't be speaking of the same place. It must be some modern thing that has borrowed the name, some clanking place of steel and smoke and industry. But he can sense the shadow of something else, like a sea serpent lurking beneath the surface.

'Tell me about it,' he says.

She sits up straighter. Cautiously excited, now. 'Well it's the same kind of place, but worse. It's everything that's wrong with the world, all in one place. All the pollution, all the corruption . . . it's a hotel and an oil rig and twelve other things at once. All the CEOs and the media men, all of the rich tossers, they think they can just sit out the end of the world in their big, air-conditioned luxury fortress while everyone else overheats or starves to death.'

'Doesn't sound good,' he says.

'We – the group I work with –' she says, 'we want to blow it up. Or, not blow it up, but find a way of taking it out, without hurting the planet. Do you . . . maybe want to try and help?'

She's trusting him, now. He doesn't take that lightly. And helping her might be the thing he's here to do, the quickest way back to sleeping under his hill. If a big queen dragon came from this small fracking place, and the Avalon rig is bigger, worse, more powerful . . .

He destroyed places like that in the last big war, steelworks and iron foundries and secret bunkers where the enemy was brewing strange horrors. He sees no reason why he shouldn't do the same thing now. And he'd find it hard to say no, at this point. There's a delicate hope in Mariam's eyes.

'Why do you need my help?' he asks. 'You're pretty good at blowing things up, as far as I can tell.'

She winces, embarrassed. 'I didn't actually want to blow it up,' she says. 'I just wanted to put it out of action. I put the charges in the wrong place.'

'Seems like it went pretty well to me. Whole place was up in flames.'

'Exactly,' she says. 'That just releases more ... argh. You don't get it. I just made things worse.'

Kay looks at her, this tired young warrior being hard on herself, feeling the weight of the world on her shoulders. Now who does that remind him of? It makes him smile. Maybe that's why he's followed her this far.

He'd like to try and tell her some of what he's thinking, but he's never been very good at speaking his private thoughts. Dredging up his feelings and airing them like dead fish. He'd rather fight the Saxons again, at Badon Hill. But she looks like she needs consoling, so he clears his throat and tries his best.

'You said you're on the side that tries to make things better,' he says.

'Tries to.' It's muffled against her knees.

'Well,' he says, 'there've been plenty of times where I felt like I was just making things worse. But as long as I'm *trying* to make things better, I think that's what matters, in the end.'

She stays still for a long moment, head buried in her hands. Then she looks up at him, over her knees.

'The whole world's in a mess,' she says, 'and I don't know how to fix it. But that's what you do, you fix things? You help people?'

'I try to.'

She nods to herself for a while. Then she clears her throat. 'Will you help me?'

'I'll do my best.'

51

Mariam sighs and closes her eyes. The first time he's seen her relax, even for a moment, since they met. Like she's passed something on to him, a heavy pack that was weighing her down. And now that she's passed it on to him, she can rest. But there's still a wariness in her eyes. She stifles a yawn, tries to hide it, tries to show him that she's still in charge. The gun is still on the desk, beside her.

He's still wearing his swordbelt, and his coat of mail. So he does what he would have done in the old days, if he was a guest in someone's hall, to show that there aren't any warlike thoughts in his mind. He ungirths his sword belt and puts it on the counter. He unlaces the leather strips around his wrists. Then he bends over forwards and starts shrugging off his mail. It's not the most dignified display. You have to stick your arse in the air and roll your shoulders, grunting like a pig. But then, that's why he's doing it. Disarming himself, making a fool of himself. Getting it tangled around his head and his hair and bunched in his armpits, until he's firmly stuck. He hears her laughing, and grins against the mail.

'Could you tug on the sleeve?' he asks. 'Easier with two.'

There's a moment's pause. Then he feels her taking a strong grip on the loose sleeve. Nearly pulling him over onto the bed, until he braces himself. And then the mail unbunches and comes free, slinking down over his head with its own weight. It leaves him twenty pounds lighter, with chafed ears, standing in just his hose and his linen tunic, feeling like he's about to float away towards the ceiling without the iron weighing him down. There's still that strange pain in the centre of his chest, but he'll worry about that later.

Mariam has collapsed back against the bed, still clutching the sleeve of his mail. Looking up at him with a different expression. No longer wary. Almost curious. He feels her gaze pass over his ancient clothing, which must look strange to her. Thoughts moving through her head. Here they both are, covered in soot and grime from the burning marsh. But he can feel the eyes of God on the back of his neck, looking down at him from heaven. He imagines Hildwyn looking down at him as well, through the smoke and the earth and the ceiling of the bunker. And he clears his throat, pulling the sleeve of mail away from Mariam's grasp. Bending to gather up the rest.

'Thanks,' he says. 'That's what we used to have squires for.'

She frowns at him. 'What's a squire?'

'A servant,' he says. 'Not that you—'

'I'm not going to be your servant for you,' she says.

'Wouldn't dream of asking,' he says. 'I'll take the top bunk.'

He heaves his mail onto the countertop and spreads it out so that it won't get tangled overnight. Mariam stands up behind him and gets something out of one of the cupboards. When he turns around to face her, she's holding his sword. She offers it to him uncertainly, by the hilt.

'When you turned to dust, or whatever ... it just fell on the floor. Like it knew you were coming back.'

Well. That tells him everything he needs to know.

4

They agree to try and sleep. Kay clambers up into the top bunk, shaking the whole bedframe and feeling slightly ridiculous. Mariam stays on the bottom bunk with the gun under her pillow. She switches off the light, plunging them into abject darkness.

He waits long enough that he thinks she must be asleep. Then he gathers his tunic to his waist and reaches up inside it, to the place where his chest still aches. His fingers brush against something hard. The linen is crusted to his chest.

'What?' he mouths to himself.

When he peels it away there's a strange stickiness, not blood but something else. Like dry honey. He rubs it between his fingers. Feels around for a hole or wound, but doesn't find anything.

Easier to check it in the morning, when there's light. So he lies staring at the dark ceiling inches from his face. Not knowing what to think.

Hopefully he won't die overnight. Even if he did, he'd only

end up back under his hill. No harm would come to him. You have to have faith, in magic. It's strange and unknowable, but it's also strong. Everlasting. Drawn from the ground itself. It's survived for this long, through all the wars and changes in the realm. There's no reason it should stop working now. That's a nice enough thought to lull him off to sleep.

He's not actually sure if he needs sleep when he's up and about. It's always a strange experience. Never restful or restorative. He can never lie down for forty winks without it being bloody prophetic. This time he finds himself in a forest. Not a modern forest, trimmed back and ornamental. This is ancient woodland, the kind that can hardly be found any more in the waking world. Ghostly elms and foreboding oaks. Snaking branches drenched in moss. Thick green carpets of liverwort and saxifrage. The trees are close, and the light is strange. The air has a damp and fetid quality, a fungal must. Mushrooms climbing halfway up the tree trunks and thriving in the damp crannies between the roots. They seem to mark his path, leading him forward through a wide deer trail.

It seems churlish not to follow. Foolish to stray from the path. There might be other things in this forest, long gone from the waking world. Beasts and phantoms. Kay watches the shadows, wary of movement. This remade body is still human. Even in a dream, it has hackles that can rise. It tells him to fear things that lurk the darkness.

When he sees a figure looming through the trees, he feels a stab of fear. His pulse climbs to a thunder in his ears, then climbs back down again. He knows who this is. Not that it makes him feel much better.

The trail of mushrooms has led him to an open glade, where the trees thin and the moss thickens. In the centre of the clearing is a huge oak, furry with lichen, wider than any tree could be outside of a dream. When he looks up he cannot see the branches, because they rise clear above the mist. Any falling fruit would crush castles beneath its weight.

The roots of the tree reach out like grasping hands in every direction. Between two knuckles, at the very foot of the tree, there stands a great throne. And sitting cross-legged in the throne is Herne. He wears a long tunic of rotten pelts, home to whole dynasties of moth and maggot. In this aspect he has an empty deer skull for a head, but he can take any aspect that he wants: a huntsman with his bow, or a warrior with holly leaves for flesh. He is Cernunnos, the Horned God of beasts and trees and forests and the vale. Warden of Albion, older than Rome or Babylon. Never a pleasure to see.

Right now he's plucking at a bone harp with his oak fingers. As Kay draws closer, the old hunter clears some moths from his throat and begins to speak in lilting verse.

> *'When crown returns to Arthur's head*
> *And knights awaken from the dead*
> *The earth will stir, the trees will sing*
> *The realm will recognise its king!'*

Kay groans. 'Is that what you do all day? You sit here in the Otherworld coming up with shit poetry?'

'There's not much else on my calendar, these days,' says Herne, placing down his harp. 'No festivals, no hunts. No kings coming to visit me and ask me favours. And no offerings, either! Nobody has time to pour out libations for old Herne anymore. Lucky if I get a scented candle lit for me nowadays.'

'Yeah, my heart bleeds for you,' says Kay. 'Now what's this about? I'm trying to sleep.'

Herne leans forward, clutching the arms of his throne. 'You've slept for long enough! Realm's gone to the dogs. Or hadn't you noticed?'

'I noticed.'

'I made a deal. With your brother. I'd make him my champion and I'd look after his warriors, if he promised to protect the realm from peril.'

'I know.'

'Seemed fair enough to me. That'll save me some bother in the long run, I thought. But now here we are. Waters rising, forests cut down, and you're doing bugger all about it.'

'I'm going to kill this dragon, as soon as I figure out where it came from,' says Kay.

'Oh, you're going to kill a dragon, are you? That'll sort everything out, I'm sure. Dig deeper than the topsoil, Kay. There's a lot more going on than just one dragon flying around.'

'Like what?'

Herne starts counting off calamities on his strange, oaken fingers. 'Fields barren, rivers full of filth. The birds and the bees dying off in droves. There's nary a worm left in the ground! And now there's fools cracking the foundations of the earth, draining the soul of the realm. It's not just a question of killing the right dragon.'

'What do you expect me to do about it?' he asks.

'I think it's high time to wake up your brother,' says Herne. 'Wouldn't you say so?'

The dream forest seems to mirror how Kay feels. A baleful wind blows its way through, rustling leaves. It leaves him chilled to the bone.

'Arthur?' he asks. 'Why would you want to wake up Arthur?'

Herne seems to bristle in his chair. 'Weren't you listening to my poem? The earth will stir! The trees will sing! There's magic in the realm, while Arthur's king!'

Kay sighs. He'd trade good iron for a god who didn't speak in riddles. But he knows what Herne's trying to say. The veil between the Otherworld and the mortal realm became thinner while Arthur was king. Then it was drawn shut when he died, trapping sundry horrors behind it. Albion on one side, Anwyn on the other. That was the arrangement. Bringing Arthur back might make the veil thin again. Might let magic back into the mortal realm. Might let other things back through as well – dragons and giants and worse. Would that help anyone? Would it be worth it?'

'I can't see him making things much better,' he says.

'Well, he can hardly make them worse, can he?' asks Herne. 'And I'm not the only one who thinks so. Let's set things in motion, shall we? You'll be wanting this back.'

Herne flicks his hand upwards, and a huge black bear comes padding out of the forest, moving slowly across the moss. There haven't been bears like that in Britain since before the Normans came. It's carrying something heavy in its teeth, a gnarled piece of wood that makes Kay's heart skip a beat.

It's his old oak staff, from when he was Arthur's steward. Arthur never blooded him, never made him one of his brethren warband, his bodyguard of riders. He was always on the outside, Kay the Cupbearer, making sure the cellar was stocked with wine, making sure the hounds were fed and the horses watered. He was only a knight in the oldest sense of it. A fighting man who could ride a horse. Not in the newer sense of being halfway noble. And this staff was his reminder of that. Arthur's way of keeping him in his place. He didn't have an enchanted sword, or a golden helm, or a harp to make the angels weep. Just a wooden stick, a gnarly cudgel, weighty at one end. Good for nothing but breaking teeth. It was only after Camlann that it became something else. One of the components of the spell.

He didn't want anything to do with that. So he took his stick deep into the forest and buried it. And now it's here, in his dream, in the mouth of a bear.

'How did you find that?' he asks. His voice sounds quiet in his own ears.

'I know where every squirrel keeps every acorn!' says Herne. 'Did you think I wouldn't know where it was? I've been keeping it safe for you. But you'll be needing it back, if you're going to wake him up.'

The bear drops the staff, spits it out like a bad salmon, then lumbers away with barely a growl. The staff lies against a mossy stone. Kay stares down at it, not bending to pick it up. There are other weapons he can use before he resorts to using that staff. Weapons that he knows how to wield. Weapons that he can control. He remembers how Arthur was, in the last few years of his reign. He remembers how things ended.

'Even if I did want to bring him back,' he says. 'I'd need more than just the staff. There's the other talismans. I'd need the sword. I'd need Bedwyr's charm stone. Or Galehaut's ring.'

'You can find the sword by finding Nimue,' says Herne. 'And you know where to find her, don't you?'

This is his dream, and the memories bleed into it before he can stop them. He remembers Mamucium, going down from the fort to the riverside and sitting among the reeds, on the weir where the eel catchers stretched their nets. Waiting for a silvery movement in the water. Yellow eyes staring up at him. They'd speak about eels and harvests and other things. Then he'd pick up his wet feet and go back up to his wife, who'd scold him for walking muck into the hall. *Have you been talking to false gods, again? You know I don't like it when you do that. I'll pray for you again, later.*

He sees himself now, lying in bed with Hildwyn. Talking and laughing beneath the furs. He closes his eyes before he sees anything else. Thatch burning and rafters falling. He doesn't want to go back to Mamucium if he can help it. Walk that dead ground again.

'You'll need the sword to slay this dragon of yours, won't you?' says Herne, with an oaken chuckle, like branches creaking or a deep tree hollow collapsing upon itself. 'So once you've killed the beast, what's to stop you going south and waking him from his slumber?'

'People wanted him back when the Normans landed,' he says. 'And again, in Maud and Stephen's war. And in Cromwell's war, and every war since. We did all right without him. Managed to keep things ticking over. We'll manage this time as well.'

'Ah, but this time it's the realm that's suffering, not just the people,' says Herne. 'And I don't care about the people. I don't give a toss who's on the throne or how the country's run. But now the trees are dying. And if things carry on as they are, there won't be a realm left to govern. Arthur promised me once that he wouldn't let that happen. So now I'm holding him to that. You're his brother. Take the staff. Find the sword. Bring him back.'

'It's not come to that yet,' he says.

'And when will it come to that? Eh? When every tree in Britain's been cut down? When every lake and river has run dry? When every beast is lying dead, and there aren't even any flies left to pick their corpses clean?'

'There's people in the realm, Herne,' says Kay. 'People suffering. And I reckon they'd suffer even more if we brought Arthur back.'

'They've only brought it on themselves,' says Herne. 'As far as I see it, people could do with a bit of suffering. Remind them to respect the earth they live on. Remind them to fear it!'

'I'm leaving now,' says Kay. 'Nice catching up with you.'

He turns and heads out of the glade, leaving the staff where it lies. But behind him he can hear baleful sounds. Wood twisting, bones jangling. Moths fluttering. An angry wind blowing through the trees. Herne is drawing himself up into another more fearsome aspect. When he speaks again, his voice echoes from every tree trunk.

'It'll be the end of us both, Kay, if you don't bring him back! If you don't make things right in the realm!'

That's enough to make Kay stop and turn around. Herne is standing in front of his throne and has turned himself into some huge abomination, some horrible beast from before human memory, dark and terrible and muscular, with a cone of insects buzzing around him. New antlers sprouting from his skull and curling atop his head. Thirty foot high and growing. Kay's never seen any man or creature that he'd less like to trade blows with. He'd rather fight a whole battalion of Germans single-handed. But that's not what scares him. What scares him is the fear he can hear in Herne's voice. The fear he can sense when he looks into the dark holes of Herne's skull. Gods shouldn't be afraid of anything. But here's Herne, frightened of something and angry about it. What could frighten Cernunnos, the god of beasts, the oldest god?

He's still dreading the answer to that when Herne points down at him, levelling a finger at his chest. Kay looks down. With the logic of dreams, his mail and tunic have disappeared. He's standing stripped to the waist. And from his breast, where Mariam shot him, there is something growing. A twig that thickens and becomes a knotted branch, sprouting leaves. Before his eyes it turns into an oaken hand, with twisted bark instead of bones and sinew. It grabs suddenly at his face.

And then he is awake and panting in the dark bunker. Slick with sweat. He sits up and bangs his head on the ceiling. When his hand goes to his chest, it finds nothing, no growths or warts or wooden hands. Just the slight crustiness of whatever was there before.

5

Mariam wakes up feeling a familiar despair.

    She's resigned to it, at this point. It's like a stone sitting on the centre of her chest, sitting there for years and getting heavier with time. Knowing that the planet's getting warmer. Knowing that nobody with the power to stop it is actually trying to stop it. Knowing that half of England's underwater, and the other half is starving needlessly. Seeing it all get steadily worse, despite the best efforts of everyone trying to stop it. When she first felt that despair, it felt like grieving, like the death of a relative. But now it has become normal. Dull background heartache, muffled by confusion and frustration and exhaustion. She's gotten better at ignoring it, even as things in the world have become more hopeless. But it still crushes her against her bed from time to time.

    There's daylight finding its way down into the bunker through old shutters and ventilation grilles. Dust floating in the sunbeams. From her bunk she can see the barometer on the wall which measures air quality up above them. Designed for nuclear war, not for climate breakdown, but it still does the same job. Yesterday it said CONTAMINATED. Now it's moved up to SEVERELY CONTAMINATED. That's probably her fault.

She reaches up in bed and runs her hands down her face. Nothing at the fracking site went the way it was meant to go. She wasn't meant to get seen, or shot at. She wasn't meant to plant the charges near the fuel tanks. There wasn't meant to be fire, and death, and a burning oilfield. There wasn't meant to be a dragon, or a strange man with a sword.

Maybe he's gone. Maybe he was just a jinn, or a helpful ghost, who appeared in the hour of her greatest need, and all of that bollocks. But when she peers up through her fingers, the mattress is still bulging down towards her. There's still a pile of armour on the countertop. His sword, in its sheath.

Her nose wrinkles. It can't be true, what he's been saying. She didn't think King Arthur was real. But then she doesn't know much about that kind of history. The British history that she knows about is Partition and Amritsar and the Bengal Famine. She never cared much about knights and dragons. It's never felt like her history. It's old and vague and belongs to other people. White people. And she'd feel a lot happier if it stayed that way.

But maybe it is her history too, if there were black men in England back then. Black knights. Last night Kay made her feel like she could trust him. Like she could pass the heavy stone to him, instead of having to keep it on her chest all the time. Like she could ask him for help. It made a weird kind of sense while she still was shocked and sleep deprived. Now it seems mad.

But one of the nice things about the climate war is that you don't have much time to lie around in bed second-guessing your-self. Mariam hauls herself out of bed, aching in some places and itching in others. Her general despair at the state of the world feels less immediate when all of her muscles are sore. If you keep moving and doing useful things, the despair doesn't catch up with you.

Kay is still lying in the top bunk. Looking worried in his sleep. She takes a moment to watch him without being observed. Her white knight. Except he's not white, of course. Craggy brown face. Strong cheekbones. Salt-and-pepper beard. Mess of dreadlocks, black and grey. If she saw him back at camp, looking like this and saying the things he's been saying, she'd think he was off his face on mescalin. Her first thought wouldn't be that he was actually mates with King Arthur.

She takes the gun from under her pillow, then tries to get her stuff together as quietly as possible. Refilling her backpack from the supply cupboard. Protein bars. Toothbrush. Rehydration powder. Reusable pads. 9mm rounds. Semtex. Climbing gear. It might not do much against a dragon, but it's better than nothing.

It doesn't take her long to get ready, the drawstring pulled tight and her parka zipped back up. She laces her one boot back onto her foot, wishing she hadn't lost the other one. Then she's all ready to go.

She could leave without him, if she wanted to. Sneak up the ladder and go back to camp alone. Forget about everything that happened. The tree, and the dragon, and the way his body crumbled into nothing. The way he came back. It still gives her chills, thinking about it.

That must have been how he got to the tree so quickly. If he hadn't appeared from nowhere and distracted the Saxon pigs, she wouldn't have got away from the fracking site. She'd be dead, or worse – getting waterboarded at some Saxon black site. And he was willing to die to give her a chance of escape.

She buries her gun in the side pocket of her parka. There's a gas stove down here in the bunker, and a couple of old enamel mugs.

Teabags that she stole from ration packs. She boils the kettle. Starts being loud on purpose. Banging the cups down against the desk harder than she needs to.

It doesn't take long for Kay to wake up. He sits up as if there's an emergency, banging his head on the ceiling. Then he grunts and settles, rubbing at his forehead.

'Careful,' she says.

'Yeah,' he says.

'Sleep well?'

'Not really.'

'Doesn't look like it.'

'Cheers.'

He climbs down from his bunk, and she gives him tea. He mumbles gratefully, blows on it, slurps it. They drink tea together awkwardly, for a minute or so.

'Did they have tea, back when you're from?' she asks, to fill the silence.

'Sort of,' he says. 'Only really druids who drank it. Magic roots, and all of that.'

'Right,' she says. Nodding like she understands what he's saying.

'Didn't start drinking it myself until recently. Well, recently for me. In the last big war.'

'Which one?' she asks.

'The one with the Germans. The second one. Dunkirk, French Resistance, Normandy landings . . . '

She finds herself smiling slightly. 'You were in World War Two?'

Kay pulls a face. 'Daft name for it.'

There's sound from above, chattering down through the earth and metal. The sound of an engine. Kay throws down his tea and draws his sword, standing in a pose that starts to look ridiculous after he's held it for a few moments.

Mariam resists the urge to roll her eyes. Even from down here, she can tell that it isn't a diesel engine – it's not noisy enough. It's a jittery rattle, not a low grumble that you can feel in your bones. Which means it's not a big Saxon APC. It's something smaller. Probably running on potato alcohol to get around the fuel rationing, in which case she thinks she knows whose car it is. The weight of general despair in her stomach had settled slightly while she was talking to Kay. Now it ties itself into a familiar knot.

She puts her eye to a tube on the wall, where there's a periscope going upwards, above ground. The car is a Land Rover, towing a trailer behind it. Just like she thought it would be.

'Saxons?' asks Kay.

'No, just terrorists,' she says.

'Oh,' says Kay. 'That's all right, then.'

Mariam gets her backpack on, and Kay starts getting back into his chainmail. She doesn't stick around to help him this time. This is going to be difficult enough without her having to explain why he's here. Maybe he'll choose now to vanish. That would be helpful.

When she pushes the hatch open the air tastes of ash and fuel. The sky is a sickly shade of yellow. She coughs and climbs out into the open, squinting at the sunshine. Quickly checking the sky for dragons before she steps forward.

The passenger-side door of the Land Rover cracks open as she walks towards it. A black Labrador drops down and bounds across the grass. Dando. Two seconds later she kneels to give him some attention, and he slobbers all over her face. It's almost enough to make her feel better.

She hears both doors of the Land Rover slam shut. She hears boots in the mud. She knows who it will be before she looks up. Teoni is running towards her, with Willow following behind. Willow has her bright blue wig on today, which goes well with the scowl on her face. Teoni's wearing an orange tank top, camo trousers, and a brittle smile. They are both furious with her, though they have their different ways of showing it. Teoni's way is to kneel down and wrap her in a big bone-breaking hug.

'Oh my God,' says Teoni. 'I'm glad you're not dead. I'm gonna kill you, though. Soon as we get back to camp, I'm gonna kill you.'

'The fuck did you think you were playing at, Mar?' asks Willow. She sounds more disappointed than angry.

Mariam doesn't reply right away. She stays crouched, scratching Dando's belly. Letting herself be hugged. Not making eye contact with either of them. It would almost be easier if they were shouting at her, but they just stand over her and wait. The silence is worse. More oppressive, more heartbreaking. She has to swallow before she can speak.

'Look,' she says, eventually. 'I wasn't trying to start an oil fire. I was just trying to blow up the distribution valve. Knock it out of action.'

'Oh, well,' says Willow. 'That's fine then. If that's what you were *trying* to do. That makes all the bloody difference.'

'Don't be like that,' says Teoni.

'There were too many guards,' she says. 'I had to drop the charges in the wrong place.'

'Yeah,' says Teoni. Pulling back from the hug. 'And that's what happens when you run off and pull some crazy bullshit without anyone there to help you.'

'We voted it down, in a meeting!' says Willow. 'When a vote doesn't go the way you want it to go, you can't just ignore it. That's not how votes work.'

Mariam squeezes her eyes closed. 'Meetings aren't going to save the planet.'

Willow holds up her hand. 'Look at the bloody sky, Mariam. Is that going to save the planet?'

Mariam looks up at where Willow is pointing. The despair breaks through the last of her barriers, like water bursting through a dam.

A dirty plume of smoke is rising from the northwest, where the fracking site and the bog surrounding it must still be burning. Carbon entering the atmosphere, making things warmer, making things worse. She was trying to keep it in the ground. Stop people from burning it as fuel for tanks and warplanes and whatever else. All she's done is cut out the middleman. No planes needed. That fire alone has probably undone every good thing she's done for the climate, every damaged pipeline, every carefully planned piece of sabotage. Every risk she's taken, and the risks taken by her sisters too, all rendered worthless in the great balance of things.

The smoke begins to blur, because tears are forming in her eyes. 'It was an accident,' she says. Her voice is in danger of breaking.

Willow has to walk away and take a moment to compose herself. Mariam keeps playing with Dando, grateful that Teoni was thoughtful enough to bring him along. Dogs don't care whether or not you're a climate traitor. They're just happy to see you. She buries her face against his neck.

Teoni rubs Mariam's arm. 'Hey,' she says. 'So you blew up a fracking facility by mistake. So what? Easy mistake. It's not the end of the world.'

Mariam looks up long enough to narrow her eyes.

'Okay,' says Teoni. 'Maybe it is the end of the world. But it's not *entirely* your fault.'

She has to laugh at that, through the tears. They hug again, squashing Dando between them. He doesn't seem to mind.

'Try telling that to Roz,' says Willow, from a distance.

Mariam clears her throat, to get rid of the lump. 'Is she pissed?'

Teoni winces. 'That's putting it mildly.'

'And we're pissed as well,' says Willow. 'Us. Your friends.

'Cause you lied to us about why you were coming out here. And us being a pair of idiots who like you and think you're a nice person, we believed you. We drove you out here. You played us for fools. How do you think that makes us feel?'

Mariam rubs the toepads on Dando's paw between her thumb and forefinger. The guilt comes in solid waves.

'I'm sorry,' she says, weakly. 'But—'

'I don't want to hear "but" from you right now,' says Willow. 'Come on, get in the trailer. We're taking you home.'

Mariam is about to do as she's told when she hears the bunker's hatch opening behind her, the scream of rusted metal. That will be Kay, climbing up. Dando scrambles up and bounds away to say hello to him instead.

Willow's eyes go wide. 'Who the fuck is that?' she asks.

Mariam fights off the urge to crawl into a hole and die. Nobody should have to go through all of this in one morning. She has to swallow her guilt and dry her tears and clear her throat before she speaks.

'That's . . . Kay,' she says. 'He's safe. He helped, with the Saxons.'

Willow's mouth is hanging open. 'Did he sleep in there with you last night?'

Mariam finally looks over at Kay. He has climbed down from the top of the bunker, wearing his cloak and his chainmail. He seems more interested in Dando than he is in anything else. Saying hello and tousling his ears and making stupid dog noises. Dando bounces around his feet, like Kay is a long-lost friend.

'He did, yeah,' she says.

'He's a very handsome dog!' says Kay, calling over to them.

'Thank you!' Teoni shouts back, slightly bemused. 'He's not normally that friendly with strangers.'

'I think he sort of knows who I am!' In Kay's excitement, he doesn't seem to notice that he's interrupting an argument. He finds a stick in the grass and hurls it far into the woods, laughing a deep belly laugh. Something melts slightly in Mariam's stomach. It must be nice playing with a dog when you've been sleeping under a tree for hundreds of years.

'Well I'm glad the fucking dog likes him,' says Willow. 'But I don't. Did you plan this, with him? You met up with some random bloke to blow up a fracking site?'

'No.'

'. . . like a *date*?'

'No!'

'That's kind of cute,' says Teoni.

'Who's he working for?' asks Willow.

'Nobody,' says Mariam. 'He's just . . .'

She looks back over at Kay, who is searching for his shield in the grass. Dando bounds back from the bushes with a massive stick between his teeth, far bigger than the one Kay threw for him. He drops it at Kay's feet and sits panting, proud of himself. Kay stops searching. He kneels down and picks up the big stick, rubbing Dando's neck as if the fun's gone out of it.

Eventually, Mariam says, 'He wants to help.'

'I think he seems nice,' says Teoni.

'T, don't be daft,' says Willow. 'We've no bloody idea who he is.'

'I want to bring him back with us,' says Mariam. 'I think we can use him.'

Willow reaches up to pinch the bridge of her nose, doing some breathing exercises. Then she breathes out and sweeps the hand away.

'That's right,' says Teoni. 'Let it go.'

'Mariam,' says Willow. She speaks slowly, as if she's talking to a child. 'You're already in *more than enough shit*. Without turning up at camp. With some random bloke. Who we don't even know.'

Mariam runs a hand down her face. They do have a point.

Normally she'd be against one of the others bringing a strange man back to camp. It's supposed to be a sanctuary for women who need a place of refuge, and Kay might not understand that. He might not understand their rules. He might not understand Willow. They probably didn't have trans women in the Dark Ages, or whenever he's from.

But they're always trying to keep people out of their movement. Keeping the tent buttoned up against outsiders. Finding reasons not to trust people, and not to trust each other. Maybe they should try to let new people in every once in a while.

'He's an asset,' she says. 'If you drive us back to camp, I'll try to explain. Can you just ... trust me?'

'Big ask, right now, pet,' says Willow.

'I mean,' says Teoni, 'you did literally just go behind our backs and blow up a fracking facility. So yeah. Might not be the best time to be talking about trust.'

Right. This isn't even about Kay. It's about her. 'Look, I'm sorry,' she says. 'I did something stupid. And I put myself in danger, and I went behind everyone's backs, and I didn't tell you guys about it first. And I shouldn't have done any of that. I should have told you what I was doing.'

Willow shakes her head. 'Yeah, you should've,' she says. 'We'd have stopped you, you silly mare. We'd have talked you out of it.'

'Or maybe we'd have helped?' says Teoni. 'If you'd trusted us enough to tell us about it.'

'I know you would,' says Mariam. 'That's why I didn't tell you.'

Willow sighs enormously and runs her hands down her face. 'Go and play with Dando for a bit. We'll have a chat about what we're gonna do with you. Go on.'

She does as she's told. Getting up sheepishly. Scratching the back of her neck. Walking towards Kay, who is still kneeling in the long grass, turning the big stick over in his hands. It looks strange, not like a random branch or fence post. More like a walking stick.

'You all right?' she mumbles.

'Hm,' says Kay. 'Are you?'

'Erm,' she says. Looking back at her friends.

'I think I have to go down to Mamucium,' says Kay.

It takes her by surprise. 'Where?'

'Oh,' he says. 'Sorry, Manchester. Or whatever it's called now.'

Doubts fill her mind, again. She takes a step back from him, bare sock damp against the ground. 'Fuck off,' she says.

'Sorry?'

'That's where we're going. Me and my ... there's this conference. All the different rebel groups.'

Kay is nodding. 'That's good. I can go with you.'

'That's too much of a coincidence.'

He sighs. 'You get used to it, after a while. Things coming together.'

'Why do you need to go down there?'

'Had a dream, last night. Talked to Herne.'

'Who?'

'God of the forest? Antlers? He told me to go down there, see an old friend of mine.'

She stands, incredulous, blinking down at him. 'So we're going down to a super-secret rebel meeting in Manchester and you want to tag along because some guy with antlers told you to do it in a dream?'

'Pretty much.'

'And you expect me to believe that?'

He squints up at her. 'If I come down to Manchester with you then I might be able to kill that dragon. I might be able to go back to sleep.'

She hesitates. He could still be a plant. This could still be some

72

kind of Saxon trick. But she shot him. She saw him crumble into mulch. She saw him come back again.

If he looked like a knight out of her imagination, some white guy in gleaming armour, he'd be harder to trust. But he doesn't look like that. He represents something else, something ancient that she doesn't fully understand, something in the earth and the trees that can be woken up and put to good use. Used like a weapon against the dying of the world. And the thought of that does something to lighten the despair, for a moment. It's a feeling of relief. The slim hope of a bright future. Not something that she feels very often anymore. She'll take it wherever she can get it.

'Okay,' she says. 'Come with us.'

Kay nods and gets to his feet. He feeds the big stick through a loop of leather on his belt so that it hangs on his hip, which seems like a strange thing to do. It can't be comfortable. Dando paws at it, and Kay ruffles his ears, staring into the trees.

'All right,' he says. 'You lead the way.'

They walk together, with Dando trailing after them and sniffing at the grass. Mariam tries to overpower the feeling of awkwardness. Hard enough introducing new people to your friends, even when one of them doesn't live under a hill.

Willow and Teoni are still arguing, but the subject has changed. It's amazing how quickly they can turn an argument about one thing into an argument about something else. It happens in meetings. It happens on long car journeys. It happens in the shadow of burning oil fields.

'It's just common sense, love,' says Willow. 'Stop being impulsive for five seconds.'

'Stop telling me how to think!'

Mariam really doesn't have the patience for one of their tiffs today. She clears her throat. 'Kay,' she says. 'This is Willow and Teoni.'

'Nice to meet you both,' says Kay.

Willow and Teoni become a united front again. They look him up and down, taking in the sword and the shield and the chainmail. They look distinctly unimpressed.

'Why's he dressed like a Nazi?' asks Teoni, after a moment.

Mariam closes her eyes.

'This isn't ...' says Kay, confused. 'I'm not ... I used to kill Nazis.'

'Oh,' says Teoni. 'Well, I like him!'

'Urgh,' says Willow. 'Fine. Get in the fucking trailer.'

The trailer behind the Land Rover is full of two things: potato ethanol for the engine and menstrual hygiene kits for the relief camps. That's what their movement does, on the face of it. Their excuse for getting into the relief camps. Soap and clean underwear and reusable pads. It's supposed to stop mercenaries from prying. The depressing thing is that it works. Most Saxon goons are Americans and the kind of Americans who'd rather handle a live grenade than anything that says 'menstrual' on it.

Under the top layer of cargo pallets there's a hollow space in the bed of the trailer for more sensitive cargoes. There's barely room for two people, especially if one of them wants to bring a shield and a big stick with him. Mariam ends up closer to Kay than she would have liked, with her knees pulled up against her chest. Willow and Teoni don't give them time to get comfortable before they slide the pallets back into place on top of them. Then everything is dark.

They try to avoid eye contact. It's not a long drive to where they're going, but it is a bumpy one. Lying sideways over the trailer's axle makes it worse. She can barely see Kay, but she can hear him breathing. And she can smell him. In the confines of the trailer, they both smell worse than they already did. She knows what she smells like, armpits and caked mud and her manky old parka. Kay smells different. Like wet soil and old pound coins.

There's another smell before long. Sewage festering in the sun. It gets stronger as the Land Rover stops and starts, driving deeper into the relief camp. The camp stinks of hot rubbish, of unwashed bodies, of overflowing Portaloos. Like a music festival on its eightieth week.

The smell gets worse when the cargo pallets are removed. Mariam squints into the sunlight, filtered through the fake leaves of the army netting overhead. This part of the camp is all concrete hardstandings and offices made from shipping containers, with some covered loading bays as well. Willow and Teoni are frowning down at her. Dando tries to climb into the trailer with them until Mariam pushes him away.

'I don't have to hose this thing down, now, do I?' asks Willow.

Teoni scoffs and rolls her eyes. 'They were in a bunker together all night, why would they do it in a trailer?'

'I don't know,' says Willow. 'She's been making a lot of questionable decisions lately.'

Mariam wants to answer back, but Willow has already grabbed a box of hygiene kits and walked away into the camp.

Teoni keeps watch while they extricate themselves from the trailer. When Mariam climbs down, her foot disappears into the mud. It's almost as thick here as at the fracking site, and she's still only wearing one boot. Kay climbs out after her, dragging his shield with him. Mariam feels herself cringe, glancing over her shoulders.

She's not worried about guards, because there aren't any. The camp used to be run by the army, but then they pulled out, and nobody came to replace them. No Saxons, no peacekeepers. Just a sprawling mass of hungry people, fighting over scraps. So other groups started moving in. Gangs and militias and rebels and cults, and worse. Giving out food, but not quite doing it out of the goodness of their hearts. Some of them might not be too happy to see Kay, dressed as he is. Strapping his shield to his arm.

'You can leave that thing here for now,' she says.

'I'd sooner not,' says Kay.

'No, go on,' she insists. 'The car's not going anywhere. It'll save you lugging it about.'

Kay casts his eyes around the camp and then puts the shield back where it was. He must have picked up how she feels. It's not that they're in danger. Not yet. It's just that he sticks out like a sore thumb.

'I think we'll have a quick dive in the clothes bins,' she says to Teoni. 'Before we do anything else.'

'Yeah,' says Teoni slowly, looking Kay up and down again. 'Good call. But don't take too long, or Willow'll think you're up to something.'

Mariam sighs. 'I've really pissed her off, haven't I?'

Teoni wraps her in a hug. 'She'll get over it. Honestly, I think it was pretty badass, blowing up that place all by yourself. You're badass. Even if you did cause an oil fire.'

'Thanks,' she says, melting into the hug.

They leave Dando keening after them and Teoni sorting out the rest of the hygiene kits. Kay looks uncomfortable without his shield, but he's soon distracted by the state of things. This part of the camp is full of new arrivals waiting to be processed. People sitting on wet cardboard, with sallow faces and worn clothes, their lives gathered around them in shopping bags. None of them wearing chainmail or carrying shields. They have rags

76

tied over their mouths to guard against the latest strain of Arctic Microbe Disease.

The world warms up and ancient viruses get released from the permafrost. Spreading to humans. Tearing through places like this. Does Kay have to worry about that? Mariam looks back at him. Would the universe allow for someone like Kay to come back from the dead and then let him be killed by germs? That would be stupid. But then the universe is a stupid place, as far as she can tell.

'There's some clothes just over this way,' she tells him.

Kay nods, and follows her. 'This isn't Manchester.'

'No,' she says. 'We're stopping here first, for a day or two. This is Preston. Or it used to be. The camp's bigger than the town, now.'

'Where did all of these people come from?' he asks.

'Well, Blackpool's underwater,' she says. 'And Morecambe, and Southport. And most of Yorkshire. And it happened more quickly than anyone thought it would. So they had to set up this camp. It was run by the army, before the army got privatised. And the government said it would rehouse everyone, but it couldn't get any contractors to build affordable housing. So nobody got rehoused. That was years ago. Then the fighting got worse, so we ended up with even more people coming here from Manchester and Sheffield. It's all just a huge mess.'

'I can see that much,' says Kay. 'How many people are living here?'

'About ten thousand,' she says.

He doesn't answer, other than wrinkling his nose.

'Yeah, sorry about the smell,' she says.

'Oh, it's not so bad,' he says. 'London used to smell worse.'

The clothes bins are round the side of the triage tent. They're mostly empty now, or full of crusty rags. After digging for a while Mariam finds a khaki rain cape or poncho that looks to be in pretty good condition. It smells a bit funny, but it will be long enough to cover Kay's chainmail. She hands it to him.

'There.'

He takes it and looks confused. 'I've got a cloak already.'

'It'll help you to fit in,' she says.

He spends a moment rubbing the fabric between his thumb and forefinger, like he's trying to figure out what it's woven from. He does have that vibe about him, of someone who knows what things are made of, where stuff comes from. One of those authentic people who could actually live off the land, if he needed to. Build his own house. Hunt his own food. It weirdly makes him easier to trust.

'Fair enough,' he says, and whips off his own cloak. It's thick wool, dyed green, nicely embroidered around the edges and held in place by a fancy brooch. He folds it carefully and places it in the clothes bin for someone else to find. The brooch goes with it.

When he's put the rain cape on and figured out how to fasten the poppers, it only leaves a thin band of chainmail visible at the bottom. His legs still look weird, in tight brown stockings and weird leather shoes, but he's less conspicuous now. The cape hides his sword and his big stick. If you had to pick out a dead Arthurian knight from a line-up, you might not pick him straightaway. It will have to do.

'What now?' he asks.

'Well, I've got to go and see the others,' she says. 'Ask them if we can take you with us, down to Manchester.'

'All right,' he says.

Mariam finds herself a boot that fits and starts to rethread the laces. Kay is very obedient. She doesn't know how to feel about that.

'Do you normally just . . . wake up and . . . do whatever people tell you to do, or . . . ?'

He shrugs. 'Fastest way to find out what's going on, usually.'

'You just roll with it?'

He frowns at her. 'Roll with what?'

'Never mind.'

When she's ready, they move deeper into the camp. The shipping containers and the hardstandings become rarer. There are hovels built from cargo pallets and corrugated iron. Timber-framed constructions and huts made from recycled plastic. But the camp is mostly a city of tents. She's seen families of three living in the kind of tent that you might take for a day on the beach. People lying on mouldy mattresses, sharing them with the flies. Most of them know that they're not getting out of here out any time soon. But where else is there to go?

It's a strange mix of chaos and order. There's rubbish every-where, strewn around the tents in circles, floating in black pools of floodwater. They go past the library, which she helped to build. It has a turf roof and good foundations, with paint-ings of children playing on the front of it. She waves to Ruth, the librarian. Then they walk past a patch of blackened earth, where somebody has been starting fires. Kay stops, looking at the metal skeletons of tents that have been torched. The words *IMMIGRANTS GO HOME* have been sprayed on a nearby stretch of tarpaulin, flapping slowly in the hot breeze. Kay laughs quietly to himself when he sees it. Mariam finds that strange.

It is weirdly embarrassing to show him all of this. To let him see how bad things have got since whenever he was last awake. She feels the need to apologise. Sorry for the mess. Sorry for the racists. Sorry it happened on my watch.

She leads him the rest of the way, to the part of the camp that people call Parliament Square. It's just a patch of empty waste ground which has become a gathering place, a market among the rubbish. Somewhere to congregate, to settle disputes. Or start them.

Even in this heat there are punters huddled around the rubbish fires, ratcatchers cooking meat on spits and selling it to the crowd. Most of them are off their heads on muscimol, glassy-eyed and soaked in their own piss. There's an evangelist from the Church of Noah, the weird cult who are building an ark on the Isle of Lincoln. He stands on an empty water butt, wearing a scuba-diving mask, and preaches about the Second Flood while hymns blast from a boombox behind him. People are listening to him because they have nothing better to do. In another corner there's a group of commissars up from Manchester, wearing red armbands, shouting about self-actualisation. They have a smaller audience. Most of the people listening are Soldiers of Saint George trying to remember if they hate communists as much as they hate immigrants. The Saint George crowd are mostly shirtless, with scarves over their mouths. They carry cricket bats wrapped in barbed wire. Mariam steers Kay as far from them as possible.

She can feel Kay wanting to linger, wanting to take in more of what's happening. One of the muscimol addicts staggers past with his head at a strange angle, mumbling under his breath. Kay stops to watch him pass, looking around at the squalor, pursing one corner of his mouth.

'Lot of people in peril, looks like.'

'Yeah,' she says, weakly, feeling that embarrassment again.

On the other side of the square is the Moon Aid clinic. A camp within a camp. Five shipping containers bolted together, surrounded by a cluster of marquees and tents and awnings. Soggy cardboard signs hang from the canvas, written in English and Urdu. WOMEN'S HEALTH CLINIC. MENSTRUAL HYGIENE. SAFE TOILETS. GET AND WASH REUSABLE PADS HERE. There are timetables for sustainability workshops and yoga classes. Again, it's meant to keep men from prying; again, the depressing thing is that it works. The Saint George crowd don't come near, in case menstruation is somehow contagious.

Moon Aid isn't officially an eco-terrorist organisation. There's a lot of that kind of thing in the big displacement camps. The People's Food Kitchen isn't officially run by the communists, but it's still recruiting soldiers and sending them down to Manchester. The English Christian Refuge isn't officially run by the Army of Saint George, but it still does their dirty work. And Moon Aid volunteers aren't officially eco-terrorists, but they're all trained to blow up oil pipelines.

Willow is standing alone outside the clinic, arms crossed, waiting under one of the awnings.

'He'll have to wait out here,' she says.

Mariam sighs. 'Look, I know you're angry with me, but—'

'It's not even about that,' says Willow. 'The meeting's already started.'

Mariam pinches the bridge of her nose. They won't want Kay in there, where he might overhear their plans. She turns to look at him.

'You mind waiting out here for a bit?'

He shrugs. 'I do a lot of waiting.'

'All right,' she says. 'Try to stay out of trouble.'

'No promises,' he says.

That makes her pause. Should you leave an Arthurian knight unsupervised? If he survived World War Two, then he can probably survive on his own for ten minutes in a refugee camp. But she's less worried about him than she is about anyone he might encounter. She feels more and more like she's brought a fox into a henhouse.

She tries to think of something else to say to him, but Willow is holding the tent flap open for her to go through. So she ducks inside, feeling Kay's gaze on her back in a way that makes her shiver. Standing with her eyes closed while Willow steps through the canvas and zips it closed behind them.

6

Kay scratches the back of his neck. Long time since he had
to wait outside a tent. Probably the war against Napoleon,
down somewhere in Iberia. Generals in gold braid poring over
maps beneath the canvas. Now it's Mariam and her warrior
sisters, who don't look like any kind of army that he's ever seen.
What is it that they do, in these tents? When he reads the signs
on the canopy he has to look away and clear his throat. It's a
strange world he's woken up into.

There's something about the place that feels off-kilter,
stranger than just the words written on the canvas. Something
that makes him want to peek behind the curtains. But there's
something sacrosanct, as well, which makes him feel that he
shouldn't trespass. Almost like a convent. One of the really
old ones. A private world of women, guarding their sanctuary.
Nuns in sackcloth living in huts near a riverbank. That's what
it reminds him of. A convent of steel and waterproof canvas,
instead of stone and mud. Are these women some kind of

holy order? Warrior nuns? He's never known nuns to carry pistols before.

He looks out across the wider camp, feeling that he shouldn't tarry here for longer than he needs to. There's a dragon to slay, a dragon that could burn this camp in minutes if it swept down breathing fire and fury. And now Herne has set a path for him that he doesn't want to follow, a path leading down to Manchester. Find Nimue. Find Arthur's sword. But his own sword stayed with Mariam when he died, and that might be a sign to stick with her. He has promised to help her as best he can, and that's not the sort of promise that should be lightly cast aside.

It would have been nice, for once, to come up and find that he was free to choose his own path, with nobody telling him what to do. That's how it used to be. Climb up, get the lay of the land, pick a side. Find a banner to march beneath. Then it became Marlowe, sparing him the trouble of thinking for himself. Pushing dossiers towards him while he still had soil on his fingers. Monsters to slay, wars to win. Doing whatever he was told to do, however bleak and foul. However pointless it turned out to be.

Malaya was meant to be the end of that. He made a promise to himself. But when he's not getting orders from men in suits he's getting orders from old gods instead. Herne, silent for a thousand years, suddenly calling in his debts.

Hard to argue with a god like Herne, who lives in every bramble thicket, every maggot crawling in every carcass, anywhere in the realm. But he's not sure it would help these people, here in this camp, to have Arthur back as king. Arthur wasn't a great healer, a great mender of broken things. He was the one who did the breaking, more often than not. You can't give a man a magic sword and then expect him not to break things with it. That's what it means – Excalibur, Caliburn, Caledfwlch. HardCleaver. It doesn't mend divisions. It creates more of them.

It might kill the dragon, but it wouldn't help with Mariam's slew of problems. You can't wave Caliburn at the sun and expect the world to get cooler. You can't cleave corruption out of the air.

Standing and doing nothing makes Kay very aware of himself, the weight of chainmail and the itch of his wool hose. Flesh that ought to be long rotten. Bones that ought to be underground and turning brittle. There's still a dull ache in the centre of his chest that he doesn't want to think about. His wounds have never carried over before. Worrying that they should start to do so now. Unsettling. Like he might turn to mulch at any moment.

He's aware of feeling hungry as well. That's a more welcome feeling. His heart and mind both know that they should have perished centuries ago, but his stomach is less philosophical. There's a pleasure in eating that he wouldn't want to lose. It makes him feel like a man who ought to be alive and breathing. Not some foul ghoul that crawled up from a bog.

Mariam wouldn't mind, surely, if he went and found himself a bite to eat. Somewhere below the high tang of siege-camp dysentery there's the smell of meat sizzling, skin charring. He looks back at the tent for a moment and then trudges forward, following his nose.

Back into the common forum, the square full of people. People shouting about Jesus, people selling questionable food. Paupers and mendicants sitting hungry in the filth. There were places like this in all of the old Roman cities, mud underfoot and mosaics fading on the walls. Always used to be the best place to go, if you wanted to find out the mood of the people. Perhaps that's what he's doing.

The shirtless men with the clubs have gone elsewhere, and the square seems friendlier for their absence. Kay joins a queue for food, listening to some of the preachers promising redemption and revolution. He's heard it all a hundred times before. Reject your oppressors. Embrace Christ to survive the hardship.

It's nothing he wants to listen to for any longer than he has to. Especially not in this heat. He's already sweating under the weight of his mail. Has Britain ever been this warm before? The air itself is hot when you breathe it in. Damp, muggy, acrid, foul-smelling. Like Malaya. It begins to rain, as he stands in line. One drop falling on his cape, and then another. And suddenly the heavens open. Monsoon weather. Not British weather.

He doesn't have the money to pay for a roasted rat or a tin of beans. He never comes back with any money. His bondsmen were meant to bury him with all of his worldly treasure, but they must have kept it for themselves. A lifetime's worth of gold, silver, jet, rings, coins. Marlowe usually sorts him out with money, but there's no Marlowe this time. He's as penniless as any of the other people here, the paupers and mendicants.

One of them slams into him, shoulder against shoulder. There's barely anything of them, just skin and bone. They bounce back, frowning, swearing, stumbling. He grabs their arm to stop them from falling. They smell terrible, their specific ripe stink slightly worse than the general stench of the camp. When Kay looks into their eyes he can tell that they aren't really looking back at him. They can see something else, past him and around him.

'Sorry, brother,' they say, vacantly. It's like it takes effort, like they have to bring themselves back to this world long enough to speak.

'No harm done,' says Kay.

They stumble away, walking slowly and erratically, not quite in a straight line. Like they've got something tugging at them, at their brain. Kay stands in the rain and narrows his eyes. Where has he seen that before? Somewhere long ago. This is a day for half-remembered things.

The pauper shuffles over to a wide blue sheet that's lying on the ground with the corners weighed down by bricks. Water pools in the middle, rippling in the rain. Ten or twenty more of these glassy-eyed and faraway people are sprawled on the tarpaulin or stumbling around it. All skin and bone, all staring into their own dream worlds. Their clothes are soiled and torn, but none of them are flinching in the rain. Everyone else in the camp is avoiding them like a pack of lepers. Kay joins them on their sheet, cross-legged. He gathers his cape around him, crosses his arms, and squints against the downpour.

One of them turns their head towards him, with the painful slowness of a snail or turtle. 'Salaam, brother,' says the pauper. He isn't really looking at Kay but past him, over his shoulder. 'You want some musk?'

'Some what?' asks Kay.

The pauper reaches into a pouch on his tattered clothes and pulls out a little see-through bag. There's something in it, a mixture of flakes, brown and white together.

'Panther musk,' says the pauper. 'It'll change your world.'

'Think I'm all right for now, thanks,' says Kay.

'Well, that's your choice,' says the pauper, 'and I respect you for it. Because I love you, my friend. That's why this stuff's so great.'

The pauper leans over and wraps an arm around him, shaking his shoulders. Kay can't stop himself from grinning, despite the smell. 'Yeah?'

'Yeah, bro,' says the pauper. 'It makes you realise that really, everyone's choices make sense to *them*. Even those guys. And those guys. And that's beautiful, man. That's beautiful. You shouldn't judge people for what they think or what they do. You should just try to get along with them.'

The pauper opens the bag and takes a pinch of the powder from inside, rolling it between his finger and thumb. He holds it up to his nostrils and sniffs, snorting it up. There's a whistling sound that healthy nostrils shouldn't make.

'Not many people seem to be doing that,' says Kay.

'Doing what, fella?' asks the pauper.

'Getting along.'

'Oh, yeah, there's so much hate in the world,' says the pauper. 'So much hate. When we're all just part of nature, really. Part of the earth. Hating somebody is like hating your own hand, your own flesh. And if everybody just slowed down and opened their minds, they'd see that. You know?'

'Yeah,' says Kay. He feeds his arm around the pauper's back and pats him on the shoulder. The pauper's clothes feel slick. There's a sour smell, not just of urine or sweat but something fungal. Like the forest from his dream. Musk is the right word.

'Do you know where this stuff comes from?' asks Kay. 'The, uh, the panther musk?'

'It comes from Ambrose, man,' says the pauper. 'Ambrose provides. He's got his guys everywhere, taking it to the people. Spreading the love. Spreading the joy. He just wants to make the world a better place. You know?'

Kay has noticed something unsettling. The pauper is mostly barefoot, his shoes long disintegrated and his socks unravelling. Down between his toes there is a huge white growth, a clump of fungus. There's an actual mushroom rising out of it, thin and anaemic.

'And where would I find Ambrose?' says Kay.

'Aw, you don't find him,' says the pauper. 'He finds you. Or if you want to buy some musk, you can go and ask Mr Whippy over there.'

The pauper points at a motor van on one side of the square. Kay could have sworn it wasn't there the last time he looked. It's brightly painted and covered in strange drawings, with the words CAUTION: CHILDREN written on the back. Why should people be cautious of children? There's a window on the side, with somebody leaning out of it wearing sunglasses and a woollen hat. It's difficult to tell through the glasses, but they seem to be looking back at him. They regard each other across the square for a long moment and then Mr Whippy gives him a friendly wave.

Kay doesn't wave back. He's about to ask the pauper another question when he hears shouting and sees people running at the other side of the square. He can hear panicked voices, see panicked faces. If it looks like peril and sounds like peril, then it's probably peril. He pats the pauper on the shoulder.

'Sorry,' he says. 'Got to be on my way. Might want to get that foot seen to.'

'I'm already seen to, man,' says the pauper. 'Ambrose sees me. He sees everyone. He sees my foot. He sees you, brother!'

On the other side of the square there's a man who looks like he hasn't had a good meal in weeks, ranting in a language that isn't English. Most of the other people in the square can't understand him. Kay can understand him, if he chooses to. The gift of tongues.

'What's the trouble?' he asks. His words sound alien to him, but he somehow knows their meaning. He's never liked this kind of magic.

'Stop them!' says the thin man. He grabs Kay's arm. 'Help me stop them!'

'Hang on,' says Kay. 'Slow down. What's your name?'

'Yusuf, I'm Yusuf.'

'Okay, Yusuf. Stop who?'

'Those men,' says Yusuf. 'They're burning our tents. My family. Please.'

Well. That sounds like peril, as far as he's concerned.

'Show me,' he says.

Yusuf nods and starts running towards the sea of tents. Kay

glances back once before he leaves the square, but the window of the ice cream van is closed.

He hurries after Yusuf, down narrow pathways that are getting muddier underfoot as the rain drives down harder. Yusuf is sprinting barefoot, driven by desperation. Kay feels his mail weighing him down. He wants to go back and fetch his shield, but he doesn't have the time. And he probably wouldn't find Yusuf again, in this city of tents. They run past somebody who looks a lot like Mr Whippy, standing with a grin on his face. But he couldn't have gotten here any quicker than them, not without slipping through the Otherworld or flying here on winged sandals. Kay barges past him, struggling to keep sight of Yusuf.

The rain is pouring down by the time Yusuf stops. There's a crowd ahead of them. Kay sees what's happening pretty quickly. It's these zealots, the men with the clubs. The Soldiers of Saint George. They've decided to burn down a few more tents, and the rain won't stop them. They've brought jerrycans of petrol, which must be getting harder and harder to come by. They're willing to waste it on this, pouring it over the canvas while Yusuf's family kneel, shivering, in the muck.

Kay has stood by and watched a lot of foul deeds over the years, but he can't watch people getting burnt in their homes. He remembers riding back up from Caer Moelydd to his hearth and home and seeing the tower of smoke from miles away. He let it happen once. Can't let it happen to anyone else.

The zealots with the clubs aren't sure what to do with themselves while the petrol is poured. Like a dog that catches its tail. Do they want to kill Yusuf's family, or not? People like this often turn out to be cowards, Kay has found. They're content with shouting slurs for now. Some of them are making Nazi salutes.

Well, he knows what to do with Nazis. He had plenty of practice in the last big show.

One of the crowd steps forward and raises his arm for silence. Big ugly shirtless bastard, wearing a Saint George flag as a cape. He has skin like a parsnip, the same shade of yellow white, the same lumpy texture.

'These filth have come here wanting charity!' says Parsnip Features. 'They've never worked a day in their lives, but they're here trying to steal your jobs and steal the food from your families, without doing anything to earn it! Well we're not going to stand for that, are we?'

Up goes the cry of 'No!' Somebody shouts 'Kill 'em', a little squirrel-faced man, giggling with excitement.

Kay starts counting heads. There's about twenty of these clowns, all told. It'll be a bit awkward without his shield, but it's still doable. He's got his sword. He's got the staff hanging from his belt, if he needs to break any teeth with it. That's a far better use for it than raising dead kings.

'We're going to show them that Sharia law isn't welcome in this country!' says Parsnip Features. 'We're going to take England back to how it was in the old days. We're going to make Britain white again!'

'Nah, that's bollocks,' says Kay, stepping forward. He goes around the crowd, comes in from behind Yusuf's family, so he's standing next to Parsnip Features. He's still wearing his rain cape. It covers the fact that his hand is on his sword.

The racists notice him and stop cheering. Parsnip Features turns to sneer.

'Sorry, but that's just bollocks,' he repeats.

'You can fuck off and all, darky,' says Parsnip Features. 'Fuck off back to your own country!'

The crowd start making monkey noises. Kay can't help

laughing. He waits for the cheers to die down before he speaks.

'Funny thing, that,' he says. 'Fairly sure I've been here longer than you.'

Parsnip Features stares at him gormlessly for a second or two. Then he smiles, wheezes, begins to laugh. 'The fuck are you talking about?'

'Well my grandad was from Numidia,' says Kay. 'He came over when the Vandals sacked Hippo Regius. But my dad was born in London, and so was I. And that was a very long time ago. So I bet you anything that my lot have been here longer than yours. What's your name, if you don't mind me asking?'

Parsnip Features looks around at his companions, shaking his parsnip head. Asking them with his tiny eyes if they can believe this rubbish. Then he looks Kay in the face and grins. 'Humphreys is my name. What's yours?'

'See, now, that's a French name,' says Kay. 'That sounds French to me. So my idea is, whoever your family were, they came over with the Normans. Which was a good five hundred years after my lot arrived.'

Humphreys isn't happy with this. He walks closer, his face drawn into a scowl. 'So now you're trying to teach me about British history,' he says. 'Is that it? *You're* trying to teach *me* about where *my* family comes from?'

'Yeah, I am,' says Kay. 'You've got no right to tell me to fuck off back to my own country. 'Cause I'm standing in it. And if I wanted to, I'd tell you to fuck off back to France. But I'm not going to do that.'

'Oh, are you not?' asks Humphreys.

'No. 'Cause I believe in making people welcome, in my country, on my land, by my hearth. No matter where they came from. Especially if they've got nowhere else to go.'

'Well, I don't want filth like them living in my country,' says Humphreys. He's right up in Kay's face now, with wild eyes, grinning through his anger. 'Or filth like you. So what are you gonna do? Eh? What are you gonna do?'

Kay mulls it over. He scratches his beard. There's several things he could do. Mariam did tell him to stay out of trouble, but he's already in trouble up to the nethers. Might as well get in up to the neck.

'Well,' he says. 'If I'm being honest. I'll probably start by stabbing you in the face.'

'What?' asks Humphreys.

He's not being entirely honest. If he drew his sword and then brought the blade all the way around to stab Humphreys through the face, that would be two separate motions. Too slow. Enough time for the fact of the matter to sink through Humphreys' skull, enough time for Humphreys to move out of the way. That won't do.

So he settles for the next best thing. He draws his sword, then punches Humphreys in the mouth with his sword hand. That's only one-and-a-half motions, so it doesn't take as long. His cross-guard breaks Humphreys' cheekbone. Then, when Humphreys is dazed, staggering backwards, Kay has time to bring his sword-point to bear. He steps forward with all of his weight behind the pommel and drives the blade deep into Humphreys' chest. There's the slight resistance of fat, the scrape of rib, and then the soft plunge into heart and lung. He gives it a bit of a twist and then heaves it out again, the blade now wetted with blood.

Humphreys topples backwards to the ground, throwing up a tidal wave of mud.

Half the crowd run away, because that's what cowards tend to do when you stand up to them. The other half charge at him, with bars and bats and chains.

It's not the hardest fight he's ever been in by a long stretch. He fought Mordred's motley horde at Camlann, human soldiers standing as shield-brothers with snarling fiends from the Otherworld, with the rain driving down even harder than it is now. He's fought Saxons, the proper kind, with axes and round shields, who knew what they were doing. He was in the Wood of Sars at Malplaquet, strangling shoeless Frenchmen until they clubbed him to death with their empty muskets. These clowns are nothing. They don't know what they're doing. They charge in, swinging all over the place, paying no mind to their feet. Footwork's half the fight. Keep moving, that's the thing.

He lets them use up their energy, getting them riled up, figuring out their habits. It's not difficult to avoid them. They don't counter or follow through. They just swing and miss, then get angry about it and get even sloppier. If they were working together as a line he'd have a harder go of it, but they're not, they don't have the wherewithal. Each of them trying to be a hero, one at a time. None of them succeeding.

He'll get tired himself soon, though. Can't evade forever. The bloodletting has to start sooner or later. Might as well be sooner, while he's fresh.

So he gets to work. Little cuts at first, splitting biceps, lopping fingers. Or he can scythe across in neat little strokes, right across from one armpit to the other. Whenever he sees an opening he gets in nice and close and makes the odd thrust, the odd jab up under the ribs. There's a move he learnt from old Gawain, where you just wait for the other bugger to rush at you and then you hop back, but you stick out your sword arm at the same time. They run onto it, more often than not. Then you can pull your sword back out and start on the next man.

The mud's getting a bit redder than it was before. None of it's his blood, yet.

It's harder without a shield, of course. Harder when there's ten of them and only one of him. He's overconfident. One of them finally has the bright idea to get behind him and gives him a good smack on the back of the knee with a metal club, which sends him down. Another one follows through, makes contact for once. A cricket bat to the face. A flash of pain in his head. Not his finest moment. He kneels in the mud, blinking, angels singing in his ears. False angels. Don't listen to them.

Why does he never come back with his helm? It was a good helm, that. Stole it from an Irish war chief. Embossed iron, with leather banding and a boar crest on top. Cheek guards that tied under the chin. By rights it ought to be on his head whenever he climbs out of the earth. He told his bondsmen to bury him with it. Maybe they fancied it for themselves or sold it back to the Irish. That'd be just like them.

Anyway. Focus. These clowns have got him down in the mud, but down in the mud is where he's happiest. He can thrust up, into paunches, into groins. He can get his blade behind their ankles and cut their tendons. Gives him enough time to climb back to his feet.

Not having a shield does give him a free hand, as well. He can make use of that. One of them swings at him again, but he grabs them by the wrist. Holds it firm. Brings his sword down mightily above their elbow. Suddenly he's holding a severed arm, which he drops to the mud.

That seems to be the end of it. There were ten of them up and fighting, now there's six of them on the ground. Dead or groaning, crawling away through the filth. Two of the others have the good sense to run away. He's left standing in the rain with the last one of them, a man who's been hanging back from the fighting so far. He looks a bit cannier than his mates. A slightly brighter look in his eyes. Bald, broad-shouldered, grey cloth sweater with the hood pulled up. He's holding something out in front of him, but it isn't a weapon, as far as Kay can tell. Just a tiny metal box, the same kind that Mariam was holding earlier. Shining a pinprick of white light at him.

Kay squints into the light, panting slightly. Head still ringing. The pain in his chest is worse, now that he's been throwing his weight around. He tries to ignore it. He rolls his shoulders.

'Come on, then,' he says.

'You've got no idea what you just did,' says Bald and Broad.

Kay looks around himself. 'Maimed your little gang of toe-rags?'

Bald and Broad starts grinning. That's usually a bad sign. He presses a button on his tiny box. Then he puts it in the pocket of his sweater and walks away, into the rain.

Kay watches him go, confused. Then he looks down at the bodies around him. Corpses turning pale as the blood drains out of them. He feels the surge of disgust, anger with himself that usually comes after a bout of bloodletting. So he kneels in the red mud and plants his swordpoint in the ground, holding the hilt as a cross in front of him. Whispering a short prayer. Lord forgive me for adding these souls to a very long list.

Next thing he knows, Yusuf's wife is kicking him in the side.

'And what happens when they come back?' she asks him. 'Are you going to be here then? Are you? Are you always going to be here? To protect my children?'

'I was just trying to help,' he says. 'You looked like you were in peril.'

She keeps shouting at him. He stands up, trying to speak, trying to apologise, but there's no arguing with her. Her children are hiding behind her, looking up at him with fear in their eyes.

Eventually she tells him to clean up the mess he's made, and tells Yusuf to help him. Then she climbs back into their tent, bringing the children inside, and zipping it up behind her.

'Sorry,' says Yusuf, gesturing to the tent.

'That's all right,' says Kay.

'Thank you.'

'Least I could do.'

They get started, moving Humphreys first. Yusuf seems to know where he's going, shuffling backwards with Humphreys' legs. Kay follows, straining under the weight of Humphreys' shoulders. Heavy bastard.

Nobody they pass looks particularly surprised that they are carrying a corpse. There's a rough graveyard on a dry bit of high ground near the northern outskirts of the camp, just a rectangle of mud with rows of grave markers. Names painted crudely onto sheets of cardboard, or pebbles piled into tiny cairns. Two men with spades sheltering under a tarpaulin, scrawny Lancashire men with long ponytails and beards. Yusuf pays them with a box of cigarettes, and they start digging a new hole.

Kay and Yusuf go back for the next body. It's harder work than it should be, because of his wounds. But he feels he has to help with this part. Clean up his own mess.

Yusuf gets to talking. He came over from Syria with his family, three years ago, to escape the fighting there. They didn't believe the rumours about England. They didn't think that things could be as bad. They made it through the chaos in Germany, the riots in France. They crossed the channel on a rubber dinghy, with twelve other families. They were put in a camp down south and offered a choice between starving or going to Essex to work for the Chinese. So they came north instead, because Yusuf had heard that people didn't come back from the Chinese camps. He heard that refugees were treated better in the north.

'I guess I was wrong,' says Yusuf.

They drop the second body, then go and collect the third. The other three have crawled off to die somewhere else, or else get their wounds seen to. The severed arm is still on the ground. Yusuf picks it up and carries it by the wrist. Kay drags the body by himself.

'I thought people would be kinder to each other here,' says Yusuf. 'Maybe they used to be?'

'Not in my experience,' says Kay.

The sad thing is that none of this surprises him. Hate is the path of least resistance. He learnt that a long time ago. Far easier for people to hate each other than it is for them to love themselves, so that's what people do. That's what people did in the old days. People from Gwynedd found reasons to hate people from Powys, and the other way around. They steal our sheep. They don't worship the right gods. Only ever binding together in their common hatred of someone else – the Irish or the Saxons.

Doesn't seem like things have changed much in the time since. People finding new reasons to hate each other. Building themselves up by putting other people down. That's how it was, and it's how it is, and it's probably how it will be, forevermore.

Lots of people walk down that path. Making it into a well-trodden road, so it seems like the natural way to go. But you have to look out for the people who don't go down that road. They find their own path, through rugged ground. It's harder going underfoot, and you're more likely to get lost, and people will call you mad for it. But it's still the better and the kinder way to go.

It seems to him that Mariam might be one of those people. Taking the road less travelled. The path of kindness.

Yusuf has to haggle with the gravediggers to get all three men buried. Kay looks out over the little graveyard and leans on the old oak staff. People are going to the trouble to lay flowers, to tie ribbons around the markers, to surround the graves with little stone squares. It reminds him of another grave, down south, that he hasn't visited for a long time.

He kneels again, and crosses himself to pray.

7

FETA's Holistic Action Group for the northeast of England consists of six tired women and one black Labrador. Now they sit together in the meeting tent, cross-legged on the groundsheet, where the sun coming down through the canvas makes everything look greener than it actually is. The tension in the air is made slightly worse by the smoke from the incense burners, which Bronte has lit to promote serenity and mindfulness, and to cover up the smell from the compost toilets.

Mariam tries not to cough. Her sisters don't say anything at first, because there's nothing new to be said. They can almost read each other's minds after so many months of having the same argument over and over again. Mariam can feel Regan's weariness, Bronte's self-righteous superiority. Willow and Teoni are sitting in sad silence, with Dando sprawled between them hoping for belly rubs. She tries not to look at Roz, with her short hair and her lip piercings and her left sleeve knotted below the elbow. Roz, who lost her hand in their last big raid on the Sheffield oil terminal. Regan somehow managed to keep her alive and stable, preventing the wound from going septic or gangrenous during the long painful weeks that came afterwards. They voted after that to lay low for a while, focus on running the clinic, growing vegetables, helping refugees. Nothing dangerous.

Mariam ignored that vote. She breached their trust. Now she knows what she has to do. She clears her throat.

'I'm sorry,' she says.

'You should be,' says Bronte. 'Climate traitor.'

'Let's not call each other names,' says Regan. Old and wise and tired of infighting.

'It's not even about the oil fire,' says Roz. 'Obviously that's bad for the planet, but . . . you could have gotten yourself killed!'

'I know,' says Mariam. 'I know it was dangerous, and stupid. I just . . . I felt like we weren't accomplishing anything here.'

'We agreed, as a group,' Teoni says. 'We agreed not to do any more violent actions. We all voted to focus on the humanitarian stuff for a few months.'

'It's *been* a few months,' says Mariam. 'And I know that helping people here in the camp is important, but while we're handing out sanitary pads the Saxons and the oil barons are still out there destroying the planet, and . . .'

'Let's not go over all of this again,' says Roz, running her hand over her eyes. 'We voted against it, and you ignored the vote. It makes all of these meetings meaningless, if you're just going to ignore the outcome and do what you want anyway.'

Bronte straightens slightly. 'The FETA guidebook for regional Holistic Action Groups states that we act together as a sisterhood or we don't act at all.'

'Oh, get off your high horse, Bronte,' says Willow. 'You can take the FETA guidebook and shove it up your arse.'

Bronte feigns shock, the upward inflection in her voice

becoming more prominent. 'I think that's an extremely problematic and hurtful thing to say? This is supposed to be a space for practising radical empathy and compassion?'

'Radical empathy? Weren't you just shouting, "climate traitor" a minute ago?'

'I mean, she *did* just put herself in, like, fifty trillion tonnes of carbon debt,' puts in Teoni.

'Sisters,' says Regan, with infinite patience. 'I don't think there's anything to be gained now by dragging Mariam over the hot coals. Let's think about our immediate future, instead. It might be prudent for us to relocate again, given the circumstances – I'm sure Saxon will be sweeping the area before long.'

'They might even use this as a pretence to shut down the whole camp,' says Roz.

Mariam feels a stab of guilt. If they have to abandon the clinic then so many women in this camp will be left without shelter and food and medicine. Will that be her fault? All of the hunger, sickness, violence. Everything that comes afterwards.

'We were going to go down to Manchester anyway,' says Teoni. 'For the meeting.'

'We can't go down there now, can we?' asks Willow. 'Hi everyone, we're FETA, we just caused a massive fucking oil fire and made polar bears extinct, but we really care about the environment.'

'It does look really bad,' says Roz. 'From a PR standpoint.'

'Well, PR's an inherently bourgeois and capitalist concept?' says Bronte. 'But yeah, I do think we should disavow the action and tell the other rebel groups that we've punished the person responsible.'

'Punish her?' asks Teoni. 'What are you going to do, put her on toilet rota for a month?'

'Well, actually,' says Bronte. 'I think we should consider putting her on trial for ecocide.'

'Oh, now, really,' says Regan.

The tent falls silent, which is what tends to happen when Regan loses her composure. FETA groups aren't meant to have leaders, but Regan has been fighting climate breakdown since before the rest of them were born, which sometimes makes her seem like the sensible adult in the room. Mariam feels something like relief melting the tension in her shoulders.

'If we put anyone on trial for ecocide,' says Regan, 'it will be the oil barons and politicians and corporate warlords. Not our own sisters.'

'I'm sorry,' says Bronte. 'But like, I still think maybe there should be some consequences for Mariam, here? She can't just cause an ecological disaster and then rejoin the movement as if nothing happened.'

Mariam zones out, staring into space, listening to the rain pattering down on the canvas above their heads and ringing on the roof of the repurposed shipping containers. Usually that would make her feel safe and warm, being under canvas while the rain came down. Today it doesn't. The tension that Regan's words had briefly eased has knotted itself tighter than ever in her body. She wants to leave. Or be sick. Or sleep. Or possibly cry. That might help.

She hasn't even mentioned Kay yet. Would that come under Any Other Business? The fact that she brought him back with her at all seems suddenly ridiculous. Maybe he was just a jinn after all, or a hallucination, and he'll have vanished. That's easier to believe now that she's here. Back in this tent, listening to familiar arguments, while the world gets warmer and the waters rise.

There's a corkboard on one side of the tent with pictures tacked to it. Potential targets. Laminated photographs of oil rigs and pipelines and fracking facilities. The biggest, ugliest thing is the Avalon platform, looming over the reeds in the Somerset flood zone. Regan managed to get the pictures from a friend of hers, down south. Every moment they spend sitting here and arguing is another barrel of oil, another tonne of carbon pumped into the air, another glacier collapsing into the sea.

'I've met this guy,' she says.

The debate around her stops instantly. Willow squeezes her eyes shut and shakes her head. Roz and Bronte look incredulous.

'You've what?' asks Roz, voice breaking slightly.

'I've met somebody who wants to help us. I think he could help us to take out the Avalon rig.'

'Mar, you know we can't go after Avalon,' says Willow. 'Too fucking dangerous by half. We'd get massacred before we got anywhere near.'

Teoni runs a hand down her face. 'Mar, honey, I think you need to take a break between blowing up oil rigs. You shouldn't blow up one oil rig and then immediately go looking for the next one to blow up. It's not sustainable.'

'Yeah,' says Bronte. 'And like, sustainability should be our main focus anyway? We don't need to resort to violence and destruction when we can make the world better through non-violent activism. Maybe we should all go and plant some trees tomorrow, to try and make up for some of the damage that Mariam has done.'

Mariam sits where she is, feeling tired and staring at the groundsheet. The despair in her chest has leaked into her bones as well, so heavy that she wants the ground to open and swallow her up. Like Kay, under his hill. But she makes herself stand because she wants to leave this tent. Get out into the open and breathe some fresh air before the incense gives her a headache.

'I'm going outside,' she says. 'You can put me on trial for eco-cide while I'm not here, if you want. But this is exactly why I went and did what I did yesterday. Because we waste so much time in meetings like this.'

She leaves the meeting tent, stepping out into the rest of the clinic. The cluster of awnings and banners and shipping containers that is supposed to be a refuge, a place of safety. Hand-stitched bunting hanging limply in the warm air. Right now she wants to burn it all down.

She's zipping the tent closed again when Willow pops her head out of the door.

'You all right, pet?' she asks.

Mariam shrugs. 'Just need to go and find a hole to scream into.'

'Yeah, I know the feeling,' says Willow. 'Well, I'll go back in and vote for you. Find you afterwards?'

'Thanks,' she says.

Willow zips the canopy closed. And then she is alone, for the first time in a while. No sisters. No Saxons. No strange men from under trees.

Permaculture is one of the fifteen things that FETA cells are supposed to do to try and save the world. The clinic is meant to be self-sustaining, so they grow potatoes in old paint tins and plastic tubs and anything else that they can get their hands on. This is the right time of year for leaving some of last year's potatoes in warm, dark places, letting them grow a few sprouts before replanting them. She pulls back a tarpaulin and wrinkles her nose at the old tubers, now covered in gross little purple growths like little trees or hands reaching for sunlight. Definitely time to plant them.

The sun is baking down and her limbs want her to rest, but she has a lot of feelings to ignore, and planting potatoes seems like a good way to ignore them. So she grabs a spade from the tool store and cracks opens the compost barrel, spreading the contents evenly into empty planters. Then she drags the old potato tubers out into the sunlight and starts pushing them into the soil, one at a time. Turning them over in her hand, and knocking off some of the shoots with the pad of her thumb if there's too many of them on one potato or another. She spreads more compost on top, trying not to think about Roz or Kay, or the burning moorland twenty miles away.

She checks the flower beds for slugs, picking out five or six of them and flinging them out over the tents. There seem to be a lot more slugs in the world than there used to be. Maybe because there's fewer birds. Slugs might survive climate breakdown, even if humans don't. Is that a comforting thought? Not really. But it's nice to think about slugs in the ground, living their little slug lives without harming anyone. Slugs aren't trying to break the planet. They don't even know that the planet's broken. Nobody expects them to fix anything all by themselves. Maybe it would be nice, being a slug.

When everything's done she sits in a folding chair, worrying the string of prayer beads on her right wrist, staring at the sky to rest her brain. Somebody will find her, eventually. Willow, or Teoni, or Kay. She isn't expecting Regan, but Regan is the person who comes, stepping out into the garden with a wicker basket to take some clippings from her row of herbs. When she sees Mariam she looks relieved.

'There you are,' says Regan. 'We were worried that you might have run away.'

'No,' she says. 'I thought I'd plant some potatoes instead.'

'Very wise,' says Regan, tending her herbs with a pair of shears. Calmly, methodically. Humming to herself. Mariam watches her for a while, letting herself be soothed by it. It sometimes feels like Regan's the only one here who actually does any good in the world, making people feel better. She was an old-school peace warrior before the climate war, sneaking onto airfields and disarming fighter jets. Now she's here helping refugees. Treating gunshot wounds and providing herbal remedies for period cramps. Mariam is quietly her biggest fan.

'So, am I an eco-criminal?' she asks, after a while.

'Not yet,' says Regan. 'You'll be put on trial for ecocide just as soon as we've toppled the oligarchs, established a people's government, and set up a court for crimes against the planet.'

'Oh, so any day now,' says Mariam.

Regan's smile gains a mischievous quality. 'Yes, I wouldn't hold your breath. Until then, you remain at liberty to destroy as many fracking facilities as you wish.'

Mariam winces. 'Are you here to tell me how much of an idiot I am?'

'No,' says Regan. 'I'm here to get some basil.'

'Hmm.'

'But I'm also here to tell you that I'm proud of you.'

Mariam feels her face screw up. Praise from Regan normally makes her heart glow. Today she's too worn out to feel anything other than confusion. 'What?'

Regan looks over her shoulder, to check that they're alone. Then she puts down her shears. 'Mariam, listen to me. I've been around for a very long time. I've been in more protest movements than I care to remember. And if there's one thing I've learnt, it's that you never achieve anything in this world without making powerful men absolutely terrified for their lives. We're eco-terrorists. We should be sowing terror. And that's exactly what you just did. So yes, I'm proud of you.'

'I . . .' says Mariam. 'Thank you?'

'You're quite welcome.'

Mariam feels the urge to go over and hug Regan, letting all of her walls down, sobbing against her chest. But she doesn't do that. She sits in silence for a moment longer. Then she clears her throat.

'Do you believe in all of Bronte's pagan bullshit?'

'Not all of it. Some of it.'

'Pagan goddesses, and river spirits, and that kind of thing.'

'Yes. That kind of thing, I suppose.'

'Okay,' says Mariam. 'What about King Arthur? Knights who sleep under trees?'

Regan doesn't look up from her basil. 'Why do you ask?'

'I . . . think I've met one?' she says. Part of her knows she should stop talking. Keep this secret. She stares up at the yellow sky, not looking down at Regan while she speaks. It would be heartbreaking, now, to see bewilderment or scepticism on Regan's face.

'He helped me to escape. From the fracking site. He comes up from underground whenever England needs him. Or that's what he said. He might just be bullshitting me. But he wants to help us blow up the Avalon rig. So, there's that.'

'How extraordinary,' says Regan. 'What did he say his name was?'

'Kay,' says Mariam. 'His name's Kay.'

'Aha,' says Regan.

'You don't believe me,' says Mariam.

Regan does not mock her. She tilts her head and thinks the matter over, in her old and sensible way. 'Well,' she says, 'old legends often have a grain of truth in them. So it may be true. I suppose it would be easier to believe you if I could see him for myself.'

'He's waiting outside,' says Mariam. 'Or, he was.'

'Well, if he's waited all these years underground then he can wait a little longer,' says Regan. 'I was just about to grind these herbs. Perhaps you'd like to join me?'

Why not. That's what they do, in FETA. They grow potatoes

and grind basil and have endless meetings, while the world burns around them. She can't cause any more harm to the world in the next five minutes if she lets Regan tell her where to go and what to do. It's a relief. Handing over autonomy. Her tired feet will go wherever Regan leads them.

The heart of the clinic is a row of three shipping containers converted into a triage centre. Old mattresses in long metal boxes, with awnings hung between them and red crosses painted on their roofs. They are too hot in the summer and too cold in the winter but safe from intruders. Lockable from the inside. One or two of the beds have refugees sleeping on them. Women who need food and shelter and medicine and love. Bronte has hung charms everywhere to protect the patients from bad dreams.

Mariam follows Regan through to the little storeroom at the back, which becomes private when Regan draws a curtain across the width of the shipping container. This place feels more comforting and nurturing than anywhere else in the camp, despite the wind chimes and the dreamcatchers. Or perhaps because of them. It even smells nicer here. Old comforting smells. Regan gives her a mortar and pestle and a pile of delicate leaves. And they sit together at a collapsible table, grinding herbs in silence. Turning them into paste and powder that they can give to patients, to ease their pain. When she was still training as a nurse, she would have thought it was crazy. New-age holistic rubbish. But real medicine is hard to come by nowadays. The Red Cross parcels hardly ever get through to the displacement camps. When you don't have antibiotics you have to make do with oregano oil, or basil and tree bark and dandelion roots. Mariam doesn't know where Regan learnt all of this stuff, but she's grateful anyway. Grateful to have it passed down to her.

'Some of this is your fault, you know,' says Mariam. 'You told me to be more independent.'

'I do admit to *some* responsibility,' says Regan. 'Although if you could refrain from mentioning that to Bronte, I would be infinitely obliged to you. I don't want to end up being tried for ecocide as well.'

'I'm not a grass, don't worry,' says Mariam. 'And in fairness, you didn't know that I'd blow the place up.'

'Well, part of me suspected that you might,' says Regan. Her smile returns. The mischievous one.

Mariam marvels at her. 'Sometimes I feel like you should be running this place. We'd probably get a lot more done.'

Regan frowns and shakes her head. 'Oh, I'm far too old for all of that. I'd much rather step back and let younger people be in charge of things, nowadays. Like you, and Bronte, and the others. Helping where I can. Giving you a nudge in the right direction, when you need it.'

'Like you did with me.'

'Precisely.'

'But don't you get annoyed with the way we're doing things? Don't you want to take over and do it differently?'

Regan quirks an eyebrow at her. 'Do you?'

She wasn't expecting that. She looks away and shrugs. 'Um, sometimes, I guess.'

Regan nods. 'I wanted that once, to be in charge of things . . . or to work behind the scenes, at least, and have some kind of power. The power to do good. But it didn't turn out very well for me, in the end. You need to make a lot of sacrifices to be the one in charge. You end up with blood on your hands.'

Mariam feels herself grinning, delighted and intrigued by the idea of someone like Regan having a shady past. Her next question is halfway out of her mouth when she hears noises outside, in the clinic. Shouting and clattering.

When they pull back the curtains they see Kay limping into

the clinic, using his staff as a walking stick. As soon as he gets close enough he eases himself down onto one of the mattresses. But Roz is following him, shouting, telling him that he can't be here. Not in this space.

'I don't mean to trespass,' says Kay. Raising his hands. 'Was just looking for Mariam.'

Roz looks up at her, incredulous. 'Is this the guy you were talking about?'

'Um,' she says. Finding her voice. 'Yeah. It's . . . he's fine.'

Regan, takes over. 'Roz, I have patients here who are trying to sleep. Please try to keep your voice down.'

'Patients who probably don't want a man with a sword coming in here,' says Roz.

Kay looks up between the two of them. Then he slowly unbuckles his sword belt, grimacing with the effort. Handing up the belt and scabbarded sword as a single bundle so that Roz or Mariam can take it from him. 'If I'm causing strife by being here, then I can go.'

'No,' says Mariam. Surprising herself, as much as Roz. 'No, stay here. Long enough for us to take a look at you, at least.'

Roz looks hurt, confused, angry. 'Where did you even meet this guy?'

'I'll tell you later, okay?'

Roz stays for a moment without saying anything, before shaking her head and walking out of the clinic. Mariam takes half a step after her but stays because of Kay. He's proven that he can't be left unsupervised for longer than ten seconds. She feels absurdly responsible for him, like babysitting a toddler. So she takes the sword from his grasp, uncertain of how to hold it. Swords seem like such a toxic male idea of how to solve problems. More even than guns or warplanes. If you don't like something you can just stab a big hole in it with your big sharp stick. She sneers down at it in her hand.

Regan is trying to part Kay's nest of hair, to get a better look at his scalp. 'Goodness me,' she says, smiling fondly. 'You look like you've been in the wars.'

'Most of them, yeah,' says Kay.

'I'll get the oregano oil,' says Regan.

Mariam has ten or twelve questions and she doesn't know which one to ask first. Why did he wander off? What happened to his head? How did he find his way back here?

'What the fuck happened to you?' she asks, eventually. It has the advantage of being versatile.

'I got into trouble,' says Kay. 'Like you told me not to. Sorry.'

'I don't understand. Did you get into a fight?'

He nods. 'Killed some men. Nobody you'd have liked, I don't think.'

Her stomach clenches like a fist. 'You did *what*?'

'Some of those Soldiers of Saint George that you were talking about,' says Kay. 'They were going to hurt people. So I thought I'd stop them.'

'So you stopped them by . . . killing them,' says Mariam. 'With your sword? You stabbed them all?'

'Well, no,' he says. 'Not all of them. Some of them I more sort-of bludgeoned.'

'You can't just go around stabbing people!' she says.

'Why not?'

'Because . . .' she is lost for words. 'Oh my God.'

'That's what I do, mostly,' says Kay. 'Go around stabbing people. Killing bad men. Been doing it for a while now. It's worked out all right for me so far.'

'We try to avoid violence wherever possible.'

He gives her a look. 'You shot me readily enough, last night. You killed plenty of men when you caused that explosion, yesterday.'

'That's not the same,' she says, quickly. Not believing herself. Trying not to think about men burning in the oil fire. Bad men, Saxon men, but still men with hearts and minds, men with families they wanted to feed.

'No,' says Kay. 'No, it's easier. Killing men just by pushing a button. Takes you away from it. You don't have to look into their eyes while you do it.'

'I think he has a concussion,' says Regan, pursing her lips.

'Easier nowadays,' says Kay. 'Dropping bombs. Killing thousands of people just like that. At least in the old days you saw the look on their face, while your sword was in their guts. While the life slipped out of them. It kept you up at night. Made you think twice before doing it again. Not like that nowadays. Like in the last war. Kill a thousand people from half the world away and then sleep soundly at night. There's nothing better about that. Nothing more civilised. It's worse. Just makes you more likely to do it again.'

'He's delirious,' says Regan. 'I'll look after him.'

Mariam nods, walking away with the sword still in her hands. Glad to be spared from the terrible look in Kay's eyes. She wants to find a corner of the clinic where she can hide until her limbs have stopped shaking, but Roz is standing outside the infirmary, waiting for her.

'We'll have to leave soon,' says Roz. 'If the Army of Saint George find out that we've got him here, there'll be reprisals.'

'I know,' she says, with her eyes squeezed shut. 'I know. We'll take him with us.'

There's silence for a long moment, broken only by Roz's quiet breathing a few feet away. Then Mariam hears a sigh and feels a gentle hand on her shoulder.

'I hope you know what you're doing,' says Roz. She leaves Mariam standing alone hoping the same thing.

8

There's a cobwebbed old potting shed in Chingford where Lancelot keeps most of his things. He goes through it methodically, chainmail and quartered surcoats and sundry clutter from the last few wars. It doesn't seem as though anyone's broken in and taken anything while he was underground. The moths have got to his hussar jacket from the war against Napoleon, but he'll hardly be needing that again.

It starts to frustrate him, looking through this hoard of stuff. Centuries of useless clobber. Chests and suitcases that he'll never sort through. At least if you live a normal life and die eventually, there's only so much stuff you can accumulate. It doesn't just keep on building, the old buried under the new. Gathering dust.

He doesn't need much, this time around. There's a gadget on the side table that Marlowe gave him the last time he was up. He didn't end up going to the Falklands, but they went to a few gay clubs in Soho. Marlowe made him a cassette tape of all the best anthems. Now it's here, in this box. He plugs in the headphones and hangs them over his neck, slipping the cassette player into his jacket pocket.

Under a grimy sheet is his motorcycle, a Brough Superior. A personal bequest from an old friend. The bike's saddlebags are full of other little gifts. An Ordnance Survey map of England, circa 1934, with interesting churches marked in pencil. *Excellent brasses. Nice place for a picnic.* Poor dear Lawrence. There's a sand-worn copy of Malory's *Le Morte d'Arthur*, which Lawrence read over and over again while they were in the desert together. Lancelot can never get more than a few pages into it without scoffing and putting it down. Nonsense, for the most part. Spreading the great deception about him and Gwen, which everybody seems to take at face value.

He finds the white silk scarf from his RFC days and throws it over his shoulder. There's also the pistol that Lawrence used against the Turks, scratched by desert sands. Now he sits for a while and cleans it, oiling the mechanism, blowing dirt out of the barrel. It won't do much good against a dragon, but he finds it quite calming, stripping and oiling a revolver. One of the small pleasures he was thinking about earlier. He opens a box of cartridges and chambers six of them, slotting some spares into the gun belt in case he needs them. Then he snaps the barrel shut. Returns the revolver to its holster. Fastens the whole assemblage over his shirt, under his jacket, so that it hangs opposite his sword. Pulls the buckle tighter than it really needs to be. Lawrence would have approved.

One more thing that he can't possibly leave without. In an old whalebone box there's a serpentine ring with a dull red stone set into it. Much more precious to him than any of the bric-a-brac bequeathed to him by Lawrence. His only keepsake of a cherished time. He twists it onto his left ring finger and kisses the stone.

Ready to go, after that. He fuels up the bike from an old

jerrycan of petrol, hoping that it won't explode. Petrol can get volatile if you leave it for too long. But immortality would be terminally dull if you never took any risks.

It's harder than it used to be to get out of London. Somebody has built new walls around it – tall wire fences, iron henges, concrete walls. These mercenaries that Marlowe told him about are trying to keep people out. Between the checkpoints are pens full of poor folk in ragged clothes, sweltering in the heat. The sort of people who would just make the place look even filthier if you did let them in. He wrinkles his nose as he passes by them.

When he's left the city behind he rides north, up through the heart of England. Feeling like he can breathe again. Scarf fluttering behind him and Donna Summer blasting in his ears. Shield on his back and his sword at his hip. He doesn't bother with a helmet. If he flew over the handlebars and dashed out his brains he'd only wake up again in Windsor Park. Lawrence wasn't so lucky.

Modern travel has always suited him perfectly. Far better than in the old days, when you had to worry about trolls under bridges, or Saxon raiders, or suspicious old women in misty castles by the wayside. If you strayed too far from the path you could end up stumbling into the Otherworld, beyond the pale, kneeling before some shadow queen and fearing for your soul. All that's been done away with now. The worst he has to worry about are craters and the blackened remnants of abandoned vehicles.

There's a delicate feeling of excitement building in his breast. It's a long way up to Manchester. There are one or two stops he'd like to make first. If he's going to be slaying dragons, he could do with some reinforcements. Get the old warband back together.

He knows where most of them were buried. Caradoc's up in the Marches, under his hill. Bedwyr's in the old heartland, the hills of Powys. Bors somehow contrived to die in Ireland, which is just the sort of thing that Bors would do. Percival's off in the Holy Land, a parched old tree in an empty desert. Gawain's only down in Cornwall, but they didn't exactly part on the best of terms.

No, the closest is Galehaut. Galehaut whose ring he's wearing on his left hand. They were meant to be buried together, on the Holy Island, but they both went travelling through the realm in their old age, and that's how they ended up where they did. Galehaut didn't die in battle, or abroad on some damn fool quest. He entered holy orders. Joined a hermitage. Lived his last few years sleeping alone in a tiny cell, eating simple foods, spinning his own clothes. Denying himself the pleasures of the flesh. Lancelot suspects that Gally might have struggled with the last part. Cloistered together with lots of handsome novices? He wouldn't have been able to help himself.

It's not too much of a deviation from his journey north. He turns off the A5 just south of Luton, then coasts down some country roads, fuelled by warm memories. Whenever they could get away from Caer Moelydd and Arthur they would camp under the same furs. Lying under the stars together in some woodland glade, with the fire burning low beside them. Then came Gwenhwyfar and Arthur's mad jealousy, and the first of several pointless wars. But there were good times afterwards as well. Together on the Holy Island. Coming back up and stealing moments together in all the centuries since. Laughing in London pubs in the last big war. Poor Galehaut hasn't been up and about since then. He'll need to be brought up to speed on everything. Helicopters. Cassette tapes. Imagine Galehaut listening to ABBA. It makes Lancelot laugh. Worth waking him up just to see the look on his face.

He's knows that Gally's tree is around here somewhere, where the hermitage used to stand. But it takes him longer to find it than he'd like. Everything's changed. It's all been built up, new roads and new houses, rows of miserable little boxes in the middle of nowhere. An entire town that wasn't here ten years ago, let alone a hundred, or a thousand. Hideous. On the edge of the estate there's a huge precinct of shops and warehouses, with a sea of tarmac outside. He drives past it three times before he stops and reads the name.

It says HERMITAGE RETAIL PARK.

'Ah,' he says.

This is the place where Gally came to repent the sins of a warrior's life, casting off his worldly possessions. Now it's a place designed for shopping, where lazy people can buy things they don't need. He doesn't want to linger here any longer than he has to.

Gally's tree must be nearby somewhere. In the car park? They must have built around it, left it standing somewhere. There are laws about this sort of thing. Royal forests. Tree Preservation Orders. You can't just turf them up to make a retail park. Marlowe's people made sure of it. All of the ancient oaks are untouchable.

He does a few laps, looking for wizened oaks and revving the bike's engine thoughtfully – until he sees a building across the road from the car park, and his spine goes cold.

It's some sort of public house. A big new building made to look old, with fake beams and pointless chimneys. The sign outside bears the image of a tree in a green field.

The place is called the Royal Oak.

'No,' he says, incredulous.

Lancelot pulls up outside, staring at this place and already hating it. The doors and windows are boarded up. There's a laminated notice on the door announcing that it is closed and condemned. Somebody has scrawled the word AMBROSE on the window panels.

He could just ride away and leave this particular question unanswered.

But he doesn't. He cuts the engine of the Superior and kicks down the lever to keep it propped up. He gets the shield off his back, strapping it firmly to his left forearm. His sword is already girthed to his belt, and he draws it halfway before reconsidering. There could be all manner of reprobates taking refuge in a place like this. He draws Lawrence's revolver from its holster instead, feeling better for having it in hand. Like Lawrence is with him.

He tries to kick the door open and gives up after five or six attempts. There was a time when doors flew open magically for warriors of Caer Moelydd. He skulks around the building, muttering about the state of things to keep himself distracted, until he finds a metal trapdoor that somebody has left open. Stairs leading downwards.

The place has a cellar. There's a sharp feeling of wrongness expanding in his chest, which he tries to ignore. It makes him feel lightheaded. Slightly nauseous. He descends into the gloom, revolver levelled in front of him. It feels like entering a tomb.

The cellar is full of metal barrels. There are some sleeping bags down here, and empty plastic bottles. Whoever was using them seems to have gone. Strange mushrooms cover the sleeping bags, furry and numerous.

He stands silently for a few moments in the strand of sunlight coming down through the open trapdoor. He stares at the concrete floor. This cellar should be Galehaut's grave. There should be ancient roots coming down through the ceiling, and a warrior buried here with his sword and shield and all the treasure he accrued in life. But there is nothing. Just the cold concrete and the mouldy sleeping bags.

Perhaps he is in the wrong place. It's the only explanation that he can countenance. The tree must be somewhere else. But crossing the cellar still feels like walking over a grave.

There's a staircase going upwards, into the pub, with an unlocked door at the top. When he's through it he finds himself in some sort of eating space with lots of tables. The light is strange because the windows are pretending to be stained glass, and there are only slivers of rainbow sunlight making their way through the boards. It's all decorated like an old coaching inn, with pictures and paraphernalia from a few hundred years ago. None of it seems authentic. In one corner is a castle made from colourful plastic. Somewhere for children to play. A shallow pit full of hollow balls.

His feet move over the ugly carpet. There's a feeling like molten iron in his chest now. A cold, angry heat. They can't have done what he thinks they've done. They can't have built this place where he thinks they've built it. He moves through the half-darkness, not sure exactly what he's looking for, or whether he's looking for anything at all.

Then he finds it.

There's a figure standing in the gloom by the entrance. The same door that he tried to kick in from the outside. He levels his revolver at the figure's head in a moment's panic, but this person is too still, too flat. Insubstantial. Not a real person. Some sort of wooden likeness.

It's a knight. Fat and jovial and wearing plate armour, from at least the fifteenth century. They didn't have pauldrons like that any earlier. Certainly not while Arthur was king. But this cartoon knight is speaking. Words are printed next to him, in a wooden bubble. Lancelot walks up close to them and reads them carefully through the gloom.

Halt, children!, says the fat knight. *I am Sir Galehaut! You can't eat here unless you're worthy of dining with a Knight of Camelot!*

119

'No, no, no, no, no,' says Lancelot, backing away. His own voice sounds feeble in the darkness. He picks up a piece of paper from a stack near the door, as if it might help. Just a sheet of puzzles, for children. This fat knight is printed on every page, smiling from under his moustache. *Can you help me find my horse, Dobbin?*

He throws the paper down. Galehaut never had a horse called Dobbin. Is there anything here? A tree, somewhere? Did they build the walls around it? He looks for leaves, branches. Anything.

The only thing he does find is a stone circle inlaid in the floor, in the middle of the restaurant. It's decorated almost like his shield, like the Round Table, with a tree in the middle. Etched around it are words. He reads them slowly and begins to shake.

On this spot there once stood an ancient oak tree, which was said to be at least nine hundred years old when it was cut down. Legend has it that this was the burial place of Sir Galehaut, a Knight of the Round Table.

A ragged sound makes its way up through his throat. He isn't entirely conscious of what happens after that, other than that it's horrible. He used to have episodes like these in the First World War, when the bombardments were particularly fierce. His limbs shaking and his teeth clenched together. Breathing ragged. Something wrong with his throat. Unable to speak, other than in braying shouts. Very embarrassing for everyone concerned. In the trenches, it was Galehaut who calmed him down. Tried to drape something over him and make sure he didn't harm himself. But Galehaut isn't here now.

He glares at the wooden knight until his fury boils over and he levels his revolver at it, shouting so loud that it hurts his lungs. The dark room is lit up by six stabs of flame. Splinters fly. He keeps squeezing the trigger until the chambers are all empty and the cylinder is turning pointlessly. The knight has been disfigured, breaking into splinters. But he is still smiling, despite the hole where his cartoon eye used to be.

Lancelot sags to the floor, sobbing like a seething ox. His throat is still closed, still tight. His nostrils are burning with the smell of cordite. He sounds ridiculous. But he cries anyway, dropping the empty revolver and holding his head in his hands. Wondering how Marlowe could have let this happen. How anybody could have let this happen. There are meant to be rules to stop this sort of thing.

He holds his fist tight, feeling Galehaut's ring dig into his skin. He holds himself against his knees until the shaking stops. There is bile dribbling down from the corner of his mouth, onto the lapel of his jacket, the front of his shirt. He will clean it up later. For now he just lies where he is. Shivering. Pressing his hand against the cool stone in the place where Gally's tree used to be. Asking small questions into the darkness and receiving no answers.

Time passes. He's not sure how much time. Eventually he gathers himself up and drags himself to the bar. If Galehaut were here, he'd tell him not to drink. But Galehaut isn't here. So he searches for something to settle his nerves. Something to help him drown his grief.

The last person to loot the place was good enough to leave a bottle of terrible Scotch behind the bar, in case anybody like him came along who really needed it. Or perhaps they just missed it – would have taken it, if they'd known it was there. But he prefers to believe the former. You have to hold onto some notion of human decency, at times like these. Otherwise there'd be nothing left to hold onto.

Once he's found a glass to drink from he sits at a small round table with four empty chairs around it, opposite the splintered knight. He slides Galehaut's ring from his finger and leaves it on the table, staring down at it. Then he thumbs one of the spare bullets out of his gun belt and slots it into the cylinder of Lawrence's revolver. The revolver goes on the table, next to the ring. Just in case the mood strikes him to blow his brains out. He's done it before. It never seems to achieve a great deal.

He wishes that Lawrence was here to cheer him up. But Lawrence is dead as well. So few people left, in the world. One of the many shortcomings of living forever is that all of the beautiful young men in your life grow old and get fat and ugly and develop haemorrhoids and, eventually, die. He never expected Galehaut to be one of them. He thought that Galehaut would be around forever. Until the end of time. Like him.

Once he's had a few slugs of the bad Scotch he picks up the gun up again. Holding it awkwardly back on itself and pressing the cold hard muzzle against his right temple, straining to squeeze the heavy trigger. He can feel the slow tension of the hammer creeping back, then the shock of it snapping forward. An empty click. No world-ending bang and deadly blaze of cordite. He puts the revolver back down and pours himself another Scotch.

They played Russian roulette in the last big scrap – him and Kay and Galehaut and the other survivors. Lunatics for whom the consequences of losing were negligible, or much diminished. Now that was a good team. Z Section, SOE. 'The Unmentionables'. Churchill's circus sideshow. They used to have fun together. Sitting around in the pub between missions with little else to do. He remembers one game where Galehaut lost, picking up the pistol halfway through a story he was telling. It was Caradoc's story, the one about the snake. But Gally was halfway through telling it when he blew his brains out mid-sentence. The rest of them fell about laughing, banging the table. It still makes him chuckle, even now. It might have been the same revolver, actually. He can't remember.

Galehaut was back at the pub in time for supper the next day. He must have woken up here, where his tree used to be, where this pub is now. Strolled through the countryside to the nearest railway station. Caught the next train to London, wearing his mail on the train.

That's all that Lancelot would have to do, if he shot himself now. He'd only have to find his way back here. So he has another go at it. The hammer clicks disappointingly again.

He pours himself another Scotch, although Gally would tell him not to. But Gally isn't here. And he never will be, ever again.

9

Kay has begun to suspect that there might be magic in this place.

He is slumped back on a mattress in this infirmary, nursing his bandaged head, with his mail coat piled in a heap beside him. His leg hurts from being bludgeoned, and there's an aching tightness in his chest that he's trying his best not to think about. A strange hard scab where he was shot, which he pokes through his grubby tunic.

The place feels even more like a convent now that he's inside it. A cloistered space where women do good works, curing the sick and aiding the needy. But it can't be a convent, because Christ clearly isn't welcome here. He can see things hanging from the ceiling that look like old pagan charms, with beads and feathers dangling from them.

The other sign, of course, is that the oak staff is warm to the touch.

He remembers Camlann, standing on a blighted battlefield

over Arthur's corpse. Ravens already circling, diving, pecking. Dead Britons and dead Saxons and dead monsters strewn all around them, giants and dogheads and worse things that Mordred conjured from the Otherworld to bolster his forces. A handful of tired Britons still standing over their dead king. They all agreed that magic should be banned after that. Firm boundaries drawn between the Otherworld and the mortal realm. To stop something like Camlann from happening again.

He remembers Merlin doing his spell, closing the veil. Deciding how Arthur might be brought back, in case of emergencies. The objects needed to end his banishment. They just used whatever they had to hand at the time: ordinary bits and bobs, staffs and rings. Merlin took them and made them more than ordinary. Gave them special purpose.

So his staff has a weird polarity, resonating with any magic that's left in the realm. Channelling it like a lightning rod. If it's hot beneath his hand, that's because there's magical currents running through it. Someone or something around here is giving off waves.

It could be witches. Maybe this place is a coven, disguised as a nunnery. Arthur used to be terrified of any group of women sharing knowledge behind his back. He ordered the death of every fishwife in the realm, one morning in spring, because he dreamt that they were all selkies, turning into seals at night and placing curses on him. Draining his virility.

It isn't like that now, surely. There can't still be witches hiding in plain sight.

Maybe it's just latent magic in the earth. Most of the magic's bled from the realm now. But there's enough magic left in the rocks and trees to keep dead warriors like him ticking over. Old wards and weather spells, weak curses and protections, sunk deep into stone. A few stubborn spirits still haunting their cairns.

Maybe that's all this is, and these tents were pitched on a little magical wellspring. The bones of a giant, down there somewhere. An ancient casting circle. Nothing to worry about. But even that seems like too much of a coincidence for his liking.

He'll have to be careful with the staff. If it soaks up too much magic then things are wont to get queer, swiftly. Bump it against a table by mistake and he might turn the table into a manticore.

Right now he wishes that he knew some sort of calming spell. Mariam and her warrior sisters have been doing a lot of arguing since he arrived. He has caused some ructions by killing the men that he killed. Now he sits quietly and listens to the raised voices just outside the infirmary. He's sat through worse arguments. Battle of Tewkesbury – that ended with an axe in someone's skull.

The older woman, Regan, comes back over from her storeroom with something else for his head. She casts a searching look outside, then rolls her eyes at him.

'All this bickering,' she says. 'It can be quite tiresome.'

'I can imagine,' he says.

Regan squats beside the mattress and sets down the bowl she was carrying.

'Now,' she says. 'I'm a little worried about your head. Do you remember your name?'

'Kay.'

'Good,' she says. 'Do you know what year it is?'

'Haven't the foggiest idea,' he says.

'That's slightly worrying,' she replies. 'Unless Mariam was right, and you have been under a tree for a while.'

'Oh, she told you about that, did she?'

'She did, yes,' says Regan. 'Are you back from the dead, to save the planet for us?'

'I'll do my best,' he says. 'Probably start with just Britain.'

'That sounds very reasonable,' she says. 'One thing at a time.'

It's the sort of conversation that a healer might have with a child, to keep them distracted. It doesn't really matter whether or not she believes him. He plays along. Letting her do the sort of things that healers do, dabbing his brow with something that stings. It lulls him into a strange calm.

'Do you get a choice in when you come back?'

'Not really,' he says. 'Just sort of happens. Whenever there's a threat to the realm.'

'Aha,' she says. 'And what's the threat this time?'

He shrugs. 'I'm still trying to figure that out.'

'Well, it's all very exciting,' Regan says. 'Will King Arthur be coming back as well, or . . . ?'

He laughs a bitter kind of laugh. 'We'll have to see about that.'

'It might be rather a good idea if he did, I think,' she says. 'He could tell everyone to stop being so beastly to each other.'

'Yeah, well. You don't know him like I did.'

She smiles thinly at him, and for the shortest of moments she reminds him of someone else. Empress Maud? No. He's still trying to figure out who when the warrior women walk into the infirmary. There's only five of them including Mariam, still hold-ing his sword. Two that he hasn't met before. One has a missing arm and a shaved head and many rings of metal in her face. The other is pale and thin, with beads in her yellow hair. They stare at him for a long moment without saying anything, casting glances among themselves.

'Excuse me if I don't get up,' he says.

The woman with the shaved head narrows her eyes at him. 'We want to know who you are and where you came from. Who sent you?'

One glance at Mariam tells him that she doesn't want him talking about trees and resurrection. So he clears his throat and tries to lie.

'Oh, nowhere really,' he says. 'I just pop up and help, when I'm needed.'

'Really?' says the woman with the shaved head. 'You weren't helping us when you went and killed those men. We've already drawn enough attention to ourselves, with that oil fire. Now the Army of Saint George are going to come gunning for us as well. Did you think of that?'

Teoni puts her hand up. 'Am I the only one who thinks it's fucking badass that he just straight-up murdered a bunch of Saint George geezers?'

'It was pretty badass,' says Willow. 'Not gonna lie.'

The woman with the yellow hair looks troubled. 'Sisters,' she says, 'I feel like we shouldn't be celebrating violence? We should always try and avoid bloodshed, where possible. Like, even our enemies are worthy of radical compassion.'

'Bullshit,' says Teoni. 'You're trying to tell us we should show compassion to literal Nazis?'

Kay clears his throat. 'They seemed like bad men,' he says. 'I wanted to stop them from doing bad things. Killing them was the quickest way of doing that.'

'See, he gets it,' says Teoni. 'You don't have skin in the game, Bronte.'

'It doesn't matter whether or not he should have killed them,' says Mariam. Speaking up for the first time. 'What matters is that he did. And if they find out that he's here, they'll regroup and come after us.'

Mariam's friends fall silent, for the first time in a while.

Kay feels the serpent of guilt sinking its teeth into his stomach. If this place is destroyed by evil men, it will be his fault. He should know by now, after all he's seen and done, that man's cruelty is like the Hydra. Cut off one head in your brave zeal and two more heads sprout in its place, each with more teeth than the first. And they don't always come after you in their vengeance, those two new heads. They go after other people, too. You don't feel quite so brave or zealous after that.

'I never intended to put you in any danger,' he says. 'I'm happy to leave, if you want. Draw them away from you.'

'Good idea,' says Willow. 'Let's just let him go, before they trace him back to us.'

Roz is shaking her head. 'He knows too much. He could be a plant. If we let him go he could run back to Saxon and tell them everything.'

Willow sighs. 'If we keep him prisoner, then we need to feed him, and guard him . . .'

'I'm not saying we should keep him prisoner,' says Roz.

Teoni frowns at her. 'So what, are you gonna just shoot him?'

'You're not shooting anybody in my infirmary,' says Regan.

Mariam looks him in the eye, asking him a question with one eyebrow. It would be one way of convincing them. A demonstration of his usefulness. Nothing he hasn't done before, in different wars. Letting himself be pistolled dead in front of the Duke of Wellington, to prove a point. But he'd rather not go through all of that again if he can help it. And he still has the tight pain in his chest from the last bullet. He doesn't want to wake up with another strange wound that shouldn't be there.

He purses his lips at her, and she seems to understand.

'We should take him with us,' says Mariam. Quietening her friends. 'We should take him down to Manchester, for the rebel meeting. We can get away from here before the Army of Saint George comes looking for him.'

Roz runs a hand down her face. 'Am I the only one thinking about operational security anymore? We don't know who he is. We don't know where he came from. If we take him down to the

Manchester meeting he could spy on all the other rebels as well. And he's already proven that he's a liability.'

'How's he a liability?' says Teoni. 'If he's good at killing Nazis then we want him on our side, right?'

'I feel like killing Nazis isn't one of the FETA Core Objectives?' says Bronte. 'We're supposed to provide humanitarian aid and non-violently disrupt the oil industry. Not go around starting fights with fascists?'

'Don't start going on about Core Objectives,' says Teoni. 'We have to be flexible.'

The argument keeps going round in circles, and Kay resigns himself to sitting and waiting. It occurs to him again that he could leave, go down to Manchester by himself, spare these women from having to decide his fate. But after a moment he hears a new voice, from somewhere outside. It sounds like a man's voice. Eventually it gets loud enough that the warrior women fall silent.

'Where is he?' says the voice. 'I know you FemiNazis are looking after him. I'll fucking batter him!'

A man walks into the infirmary holding a cricket bat with barbed wire wrapped around it. It's one of the Soldiers of Saint George, from earlier. The short squirrelly one with the long teeth wearing the red sports clothes. He ran away from the fight as soon as it started, but now he seems to have found some courage. He might be on the panther musk, the way his eyes are casting about.

The sisters can probably fend for themselves, but he doesn't want to take any chances. Mariam has his sword. He picks up the staff instead.

As soon as he touches it, he knows he's made a mistake. There's a sharp crackle of pain in his hand, which makes his whole arm twinge. A loud whipcrack sound. He drops the staff and snatches his hand back, but it's too late. Suddenly there's a bright warmth in the room and a change in pressure. Something pings off the

130

metal around them. For half a second they can see the squirrelly man's skeleton glowing brilliantly through his skin. And then he disappears into his clothes, dropping the cricket bat, collapsing in upon himself. Leaving a pile of sportswear on the floor.

After a few moments, a grey squirrel wrestles its way out from the trousers. It stares at them all, small and terrified. Then it scampers away through the door of the clinic.

The staff lies on the ground, smoking gently. Seconds pass. The sisters stand silently, staring at the pile of clothes. Staring back at Kay.

'Am I going mad?' says Roz. 'Are we all on musk or something?'

'Look,' he says. 'Maybe I'd better explain.'

So he starts talking, and he keeps talking, until he's told them everything.

He wouldn't normally dream of doing anything half-magical in front of people. But it might have worked out in his favour, this time. Proving that his story has some truth to it. Stop these women from writing him off as a lunatic. It was always Marlowe who insisted on secrecy. Marlowe who told him to stay in the shadows and keep his mouth shut. He remembers a night outside a theatre in London, five hundred years ago or thereabouts. Him and Marlowe watching a bear being baited. Wearing silly ruffs and pantaloons. 'You must never tell men the truth,' Marlowe said, 'about your nature. 'To forfend turning their whole grand notion of the world upon its head.'

It looks to him as if the world's been turned over on its head already. Maybe if he turns it over once again, it'll be back upright. There's a thought.

The sisters leave the infirmary looking ashen-faced, like he's undermined the walls of the castle where they kept their sense of reason. Weakened their foundations. Then they start packing up their convent, moving and gathering in stunned silence. He offers to help and they turn him away, so he tries to stay out from under their feet. Sitting on a stack of wooden pallets on the outskirts of the convent, keeping an eye out for any other Soldiers of Saint George who might fancy being turned into squirrels. The staff is propped up next to him, in case he needs it, feeling slightly cooler than it did before.

This has been a strange day even by his standards. He watches the wider camp until the sun has reached its highest point and come halfway back down again. Dando comes out to keep him company, bounding up onto the pallets beside him. Lazing against his leg and panting. Tongue hanging out. He reaches down and scritches the back of Dando's neck.

When was the last time he had five minutes to sit and stroke a dog? Not for a couple of hundred years, at least. There's a dragon somewhere that he ought to be slaying, and a war against corruption in the sky that he doesn't fully understand. But right now he can pause the cavalcade of death to sit and watch the sunset, scratching a dog behind its ears. He wouldn't have had that luxury if he went down to London. They may not be very well organised, these rebels, but at least they're not sending him on suicide missions. There's nobody up here handing him envelopes, giving him bloody silly orders, telling him to jump out of aeroplanes.

Nobody except Herne, sending him south. Find Nimue. Find the sword. Bring Arthur back. He'd rather stay here and stroke this dog, for the time being.

When the warrior women have packed up most of their gear they sit and prepare their late-day meal. Going to a lot of trouble to burn a kind of fuel which doesn't give off much smoke. They cook their food in a huge plastic tub, making far more of it than they could ever need for just themselves. It doesn't make much sense to him until he sees people forming lines, coming forward from the rest of the camp. Hungry people with nowhere else to go.

He can't imagine Marlowe ever taking pains to feed the hungry, peeling the vegetables with his own hands. But here are these women, doing just that. Sharing whatever they have to share, instead of hoarding it for themselves. Doing it out of common kindness, not to appear kind. He'd rather fight for people like that, in any century, on any day of the week.

When the lines have died down, Mariam brings him a bowl of whatever it is they've made. A warm yellow slurry of spiced potatoes with a kind of flatbread to mop it up. He offers his thanks to God, then scoops up the first mouthful. Eyes widening. Spices dancing happily on his tongue.

'Mmm,' he says. 'What is this?'

'Did they not have saag aloo, in your day?'

He grunts and shakes his head. Too busy eating to answer.

She stands close beside him, stroking Dando's belly. He can tell that she wants to say something, but he's not about to try and force it out of her. Better to eat his food and wait.

'It must have been easier, when you came up before,' she says.

He frowns at her, flatbread halfway to his mouth. 'Easy's one word for it.'

'I don't mean the fighting, or whatever. I mean ... knowing what you're supposed to be doing. There's so much wrong with the world that it's hard to know where to start, and it's too hot to think half the time, and ... it's like walking through fog, sometimes. Usually I feel like I'm working backwards or going round in circles. Or not making any difference.'

'Most wars are like that.'

'I get why you killed those men,' she says. 'That's what I'm trying to say. When I get angry and confused with everything, I sometimes just ... lash out to try and change things. It's not always the smart thing to do, but at least I feel like I'm doing something to make the world better.'

He stares at the dry earth beneath Mariam's feet, until he swallows the stone in his throat. 'I lost someone in a fire, once,' he says. 'Don't like seeing it happen to other people.'

'Oh,' says Mariam. 'I'm sorry.'

'It's all right,' he mutters. 'Long time ago.'

He has surprised himself. When was the last time he told anyone about that? This is a day for telling people things that he'd normally keep close and secret. He'll have to be careful not to trust Mariam too much. Not to burden her with every detail from the old days, and everything since. He clears his throat and tries to change the subject.

'If you ask me, it's better to act without thinking than to think without acting. Easy to sit around worrying about this and that. Much better to get out there into the world and make some difference.'

Mariam stares away into the distance for a long moment, scratching Dando absent-mindedly. Then she hands him back his sword, in its belt and scabbard.

'Come with me,' she says.

She leads him back into the convent, through the tents that haven't been packed away yet. He follows, girthing his sword as he walks, through a labyrinth of canvas and hanging carpets to some kind of inner sanctum. He feels like he's trespassing, being inside. In this most private part of the convent he can see guns on the table and photographs on the wall, a board where these women have mapped out their plans and schemes. Scribbled notes and printed pages. Pictures of some massive thing, a great towering fortress, standing on four legs like a monster rising from the sea.

'Here,' says Mariam. 'This is the place I was telling you about last night.'

'Everything wrong with the world,' he says, remembering her words. 'All in one place.'

'Right. I want to knock it out of action, but I don't know how.'

'Why don't you just blow it up, like you did the other place?'

Mariam sighs. 'First off, it'll be really well guarded. But also 'cause I don't want to cause another oil fire. We'd just release shit-tons of carbon and probably kill everything in the flood zone, too.'

He looks at the pictures, at the flooded plain beneath the dark fortress. The reeds and the wet marshland. It's the sort of place where herons would have nested, in the old days. The sort of place where you might have found Nimue skulking in the shallows if you knew where to look for her. You'd have made a quick offering to her, for safe passage, before you tried to cross the water. That gives him an idea.

'Remember I said I had a friend, down in Manchester?'

'Yeah,' asks Mariam. 'Why?'

'Ever heard of Nimue? Lady of the Lake?'

Mariam blinks at him. 'Um ... yeah?'

'She might be able to help you,' he says. 'If we can find her. Is the River Medlwc still there?'

Mariam is looking at him strangely. 'What, the Medlock?'

He nods. 'That sounds about right. If we can get there, I'll try and speak to her.'

'How's she gonna help?'

'I think this Avalon place would be ... in her element, so to speak.'

She looks him up and down, for a moment. Still untrusting. But there's something in her eyes that might be hope.

'Okay,' she says. 'Cool. Wait here. I'll go and tell the others.'

She ducks back out of the tent, and he looks at the board of photos, for want of anything else to do. These women have mapped out their plans and schemes, leaving them here for anyone to see. He remembers rebels in the last big war, houses in France with secret cellars. They didn't tend to keep anything written down. But Mariam and her sisters have left it all here. Photos and maps with sites circled in colourful pen. There's a list of targets, with numbers written next to each. Guards? Casualties? A couple of them have TOO HIGH written beside them.

He's joined enough rebellions over the years, when the realm was being badly governed. Helped Maud against Stephen. Brought King John to the treaty table and King Charles to the chopping block. He could do that now, pledge his sword to these women and carry them to victory. But the problem with victory is that time keeps happening afterwards, and people keep being people, killing each other for daft reasons. Men like Cromwell rise up on the tide of change and cause even more misery, more bloodletting. Paradise stays distant, just over the horizon. Waiting to be chased by the next band of hopeful rebels.

Maybe he's too old for politics. Just ancient mud, soon to be mud again. Maybe he should stick to the weird stuff. Slay the dragon. Find his brother's sword. Destroy this new Avalon, this fortress of doom, before its masters can bleaken the world further. Stop any more dragons from slithering through the gyre. Then back to sleep again beneath his tree, and let the world keep turning. Let the future look after itself.

That would be too easy, wouldn't it?

He's not sure he entirely understands these women, the evils they're fighting against, the dreams they're fighting for. But he knows that they want to change things, and it's foolish to try and stop the world from changing. No good digging your heels in, fighting for the old world when the old world's already gone. All you can do is live in the new world, however strange it might be. Try to make it a better place for the people who live in it.

That's what Mariam wants to do. If he can help her, he'll do his best.

10

Marlowe is high above London, sharing a quad-pod with a man he doesn't like. They're always supposed to pod-share, as part of the government's new environmental initiative. A bit like closing the stable door after the horse has died and turned to dust. He's not overly fond of these little buzzing death traps, but they're the only way to keep your shoes dry nowadays. And they do have other advantages, as well. He looks down through the canopy at the speeding ground below.

The man in the seat beside him is called Godfrey Scrope. He has a nonspecific high-level post at the cabinet office. Right now he's showing Marlowe a video on his computer tablet, posted online by one of the accounts linked to the Army of Saint George. TERRORIST IMMIGRANT KILLS LOYAL ENGLISH PATRIOTS IN SHOCKING RACIST ATTACK. The video appears to show Kay, their errant knight, roundly butchering a dozen troglodytes.

'Pithy title,' says Marlowe.

'Should we have it blocked?' asks Scrope.

'No, no, let it through,' says Marlowe. 'They might do our job for us.'

'Right,' says Scrope dolefully. 'I suppose I'll tell the social media chaps.'

He sounds almost despondent. Marlowe does his best to assume a friendly, trusting countenance. 'Not having second thoughts, are you, Scrope?'

'No,' says Scrope quickly. 'No. Well, yes. Somewhat. I have some reservations. But I'll raise them at the meeting.'

'I look forward to hearing them,' says Marlowe. Inwardly noting that Scrope's reservations might need addressing sooner rather than later. He glances down at the ground as the pod swoops low over Marylebone, slowing as it nears its destination. They're far enough north of the river now that the flooding isn't as bad, but it's still a problem. Regent's Park is damp and stagnant. The boating lake is twice the size it used to be. There's a big grey Edwardian building overlooking the park, keystones and colonnades and grand voussoirs. Their pod settles down in the damp forecourt, behind the Saxon security barriers. When the blades have spun down, the canopy rolls open, and they step down into the puddles.

Marlowe stops to light a cigarette, while Scrope gathers his things together. The building stands in front of him, as it has always stood. The plaque on the door says WESSEX PLACE and divulges no further information. There's a concrete unicorn on one side of the entrance, and a concrete dragon on the other. The whole façade is old and austere and reassuring. But that's all it is – a façade.

He tries to square his conscience, while he smokes his cigarette. This used to be The Department, The Shadow Bureau, The Office of Things that Go Bump in the Night. Very old and very secret and known by many names. This particular incarnation of it was founded in 1912, but it's been around for a lot longer than that, in different semblances. It passed through the smoky cellars of obscure Victorian dining clubs and the country manors of peculiar viscounts. It was close to the throne in the time of Elizabeth, the first Elizabeth. Respectable Protestants communing with demons in their townhouses by the Thames. That was round about when he got involved, young and eager for illicit knowledge. Secret power. But the organisation was already old when he joined. A holy order with an ancient purpose.

Some of the older members of the order might accuse him now of forgetting that ancient purpose. Betraying their immemorial principles. But those old members are dead. And the sad truth of the matter is that he doesn't care, anymore. The government used to pay him to deal with threats that they didn't want to know about. Now they outsource it instead. The building has been sold to GX5, which has no immemorial principles to speak of. He's making a lot more money as a private consultant than he ever did as a government man.

He grinds out the cigarette beneath his brogues, then trudges up the stairs. The lobby is empty, with aspidistras wilting in the planters. Once upon a time the porter would have bumbled out from behind his desk and called the lift for them, asking him how they were keeping. Complaining about immigrants. He'd held that post since the Battle of Salamanca. But most of the staff in the building were made redundant when the place was bought out. Most of the offices upstairs are empty. The ceiling tiles stained with seventies cigarette smoke. The filing cabinets gathering dust, full of reports on faerie kingdoms and flying saucers.

The lift arrives, and they take it down. Going underground is a luxury in this new London, where the tube is flooded. There aren't many watertight places. But the vaults beneath Wessex Place were reinforced in the Cold War, tanked in steel and concrete. There's a tedious series of security precautions before the vaults will open. They turn keys and swipe cards and type codes into number pads. Then the light buzzes green. A reinforced steel door unseals itself and swings open, into a huge space that is cold and mostly empty.

Nessie scowls down at them from the ceiling. The last dragon to rear her ugly head, in '33 or '34, he can't remember. Killed in short order and shipped south for further study. Then her taxidermied corpse was strung from the ceiling arches. Scrope seems unnerved by it. Marlowe barely looks up. Walking beneath the monster's jaws, its serpentine body, its grasping claws.

It's like a museum, down here. The vaults at Wessex Place used to be a repository of sorts. Artefacts of Empire, ransacked from across the world, or from other worlds altogether. Most of the articles have been sold to private collectors. The spear of Longinus. The keys to Xanadu and Shambala. Old display cases stand empty and undusted. There are a handful of legendary swords left on the rack. Balmung and Skofnung and Zulfiqar. They must have sold the Emerald Shamshir since the last time he was down here. Excalibur is still conspicuous in its absence.

At the far end of the vault there's another security door with a sort of cloakroom in front of it. There are already several coats hanging up, and umbrellas in the hat stand. The meeting has begun without them.

Marlowe and Scrope take off their overcoats and change into hooded robes, black silk with red trimmings. Then they present their thumbs to a pinprick device which takes a sample of their blood. The old arrangement was much worse, slicing one's palms, letting the blood drip into a cup of fire. This is much more convenient. If a little less sanitary.

The light buzzes green. Their blood has been accepted. The door swings open.

The inner sanctum used to be lit by torches, blazing in sconces on the wall. Now there's a tasteful electric lighting fixture in the ceiling. The dominant feature is the Round Table which once filled the hall at Camelot. It's not a small circular affair but a great ring, twenty feet across, big enough for Arthur to banquet his whole warband. But the ring is not complete: there is a gap through which one can walk. Then one is standing in the centre floor, surrounded by councillors. Marlowe can vaguely imagine Roman emissaries standing in the centre while the knights of Camelot sat in judgement around them.

Sitting around the table now are ten other men in black robes. Good old Protestant men. They have nonspecific roles in various government departments, or on the boards of private companies. Newspapers, social media, finance, oil exploration, private defence. Marlowe isn't overly fond of the current line-up. This order used to be made up of the finest noblemen and scholars in England. John Dee and Francis Walsingham. Now there are Australians present. Men born in Moscow and Wisconsin. It raises the hackles, somewhat. But that's how things are done, nowadays. No sense railing against it.

The table falls silent as they enter. Scrope mumbles an apology and hurries to his seat. Marlowe walks through the opening and into the circle, standing before the altar.

Any suggestion that the Round Table has no head is hopelessly naïve. Opposite the opening a large segment of the table is painted with bands of gold and forest green. The chair behind it is grander than the others because it was once Arthur's chair. Sitting in it is Brother Warden, in his red robe. He is gaunt and liver spotted under his red hood. He leads their order because he has cheated death for longer than any of them.

'I'm glad you could finally join us, Brother Tamburlaine,' says Brother Warden. 'We have been eagerly awaiting your report.'

'Things have been set in motion,' says Marlowe. 'Kay and Lancelot have risen. They're both more or less on the right path. All we can do now is wait.'

'So we're just expecting them to bump into each other?' asks Brother Pursuivant, one of the old guard. 'The chances against it must be astronomical.'

'I can't guarantee anything,' Marlowe says, 'but magic doesn't obey the ordinary laws of probability. It's not a question of chance. Think of it like ... streams, going downhill. They're bound to meet up eventually.'

'Spare us the metaphysical horse-crap,' says Brother Pilgrim. One of the Americans. Grating, to hear his drawl inside the chamber. 'Is this gonna work, or not?'

Marlowe sighs. 'All of the right elements are in play. I think we can safely proceed to Phase 2 of the operation.'

'And your undercover asset,' asks Brother Pursuivant. 'You're sure she can be relied upon?'

'She wants the same thing that we do,' says Marlowe, 'for different reasons. She'll do her part.'

Warden seems satisfied. He looks around the table at the other members of the committee. 'Very well. Brother Tamburlaine has proposed that we proceed to Phase 2. Are there any objections?'

The sanctum falls silent, until Scrope clears his throat. 'I don't wish to reopen old discussions here, but ... are we absolutely sure that we want to go ahead with this? Are we certain that it's necessary?'

'Oh, for Pete's sake,' says Brother Pilgrim. 'We've been over this.'

'I think it's worth going over it again,' says Scrope. 'This order was founded to protect the realm from peril. What we're about to do ... would have been unimaginable, even a few decades ago.'

Marlowe is getting tired of having this argument. 'I understand your concerns,' he says. 'But we've all seen the numbers. There's no way to reverse the damage to the planet, at this point. Not without a considerable redistribution of labour and resources. The future looks increasingly bleak. If we want to keep living comfortably then we have to make alternative arrangements. Phase 2 is the only viable option remaining to us.'

'Damn straight,' says Brother Pilgrim. 'I ain't spending the rest of my immortality raking muck in some hippy commune. I wanna go out in style.'

Marlowe waits. The men around the table spend a few moments wrestling with any vestigial shame that they might be feeling. Except for Brother Pilgrim, for whom shame seems to be an entirely foreign concept. But none of them have souls left to save any more. They made their choices a long time ago, and now they're facing the consequences. He's offering them a way out.

'Your objection is noted, Brother Trevelyan,' says Brother Warden. 'If there are no other objections then we'll proceed with Phase 2. Return to your departments and begin the relocation to the Avalon platform.'

The committee file out of the sanctum and pick up their suitcases in the antechamber, becoming bankers and CEOs once again. Oil men and media men. Walking out through the vault, beneath the bones of Nessie. Marlowe pulls his raincoat back on and places his hat back atop his head. Then he catches up with Brother Trevelyan, who is just plain Godfrey Scrope again without his robes.

'Shall we double up again, Scrope?' he asks. 'I'm going your way.'

'Oh,' says Scrope. 'Yes, all right.'

There's more than one quad-pod waiting, when they make it back outside. Some of the other committee members are frowning at their phones, waiting for their own pods to arrive. Marlowe and Scrope climb back into theirs and take off again.

144

The first few minutes of their flight go by in silence. Scrope starts shuffling papers in his briefcase, to give himself something to do. Marlowe waits until they're high up over Covent Garden before he speaks.

'I know it's hard to stomach,' he says. 'But think of the alternative. We didn't know about the climate when we signed up for immortality. Neither of us wants to live on a barren, lifeless planet until the end of time. If we want to avoid that, then Phase 2 is the only option.'

'Do you not feel absolutely wretched about it?' asks Scrope. 'It's shameful, what we're doing. It's morally repugnant. I'm ... I'm not sure I can stand for it.'

Marlowe sighs. 'I was afraid you'd say something like that.'

He doesn't have to do this himself, but it'll be much neater if he does. Fewer loose ends to tie up. So he reaches for the control pad in front of him and types in his administrator access code. Opening all sorts of options that aren't available to ordinary passengers.

'What are you doing?' asks Scrope.

'Just getting some fresh air,' he says.

He taps the canopy release button, and the cold wind roars into the pod. Scrope's neatly ordered papers are scooped up by the breeze, scattered on the winds, raining down over London. Scrope is still trying to save some of them when Marlowe grabs him by the ankle and tips him over the side of the pod.

He cranes his neck long enough to watch Scrope fall, plunging towards the pavement with his limbs flailing uselessly, grabbing for safety that isn't there. Immortality doesn't mean invulnerability. A fall from a great height still kills one of them. And when they die, the devil takes his due. The trick is to avoid death for as long as possible. Which is exactly what Marlowe intends to do.

He taps the canopy controls again and straightens his tie.

11

By the time they make it out of the relief camp there are streaks of pink in the sky.

There's seven of them altogether. Not the smallest force he's ever marched with, nor even the strangest. He knows the courage of women, from the last war, and from wars before that. Roz and Willow don't surprise him. He has fought with one-handed warriors before, like Bedwyr. He has fought with men who were born as girls, like Silentius, and known women who were born as boys, like the old maids of Cybele in Caer Catraeth. It might be the first time he's marched with only women. Just himself, six women, and one dog, walking down to Manchester overnight. They've left Teoni's motor car somewhere in camp, covered by a sheet. But Dando is with them, running ahead and darting under hedges.

They go east before they go south, putting the sunset behind them. Kay has the sense that the coast is perilous. These new Saxons can swoop in off the sea like their forebears, from ships and sea forts, raiding as they please. It makes sense to get inland – a bit further from Neptune's grasp. But it does mean they're heading further into Herne's domain. He eyes every blighted bush more warily than he might do otherwise. It feels as though the bushes are staring back. He finds his hand resting on the end of his staff. It's still got that warmth to it.

Once he would have led the column, knowing the land hereabouts better than anyone else. This was his land, for a brief time in the far olden days. Everything north of the Mersey, south of the Lun. He knew every stream, every deer track. Now it's all foreign to him. There are big new towns in the Blakewater valley, lights blazing, lending an orange underbelly to the dark clouds. The sisters give them a wide berth. Soon enough they make the turn south, down into open farmland. Winding their way down narrow country lanes.

His knowledge is ancient, useless. The country is changed. He wouldn't have any idea where he was going, if he didn't have these warrior women to lead him along. Hard not to feel unmanned by that. But they know better than him, and he knows better than to pretend otherwise. No good leading them in circles, looking for tracks that time has washed away, just to slake some fool's notion of how men ought to act. So he follows, with his shield strapped to his arm. Forming the rear guard. Letting himself be led.

The women seem happy enough with that arrangement. They don't have to remember that he's with them, or that he's real, if he walks behind them. They can stay ahead and talk among themselves. Mariam is in the middle of the group, talking to Willow and Regan. Glancing back over her shoulder every now and again.

Teoni's giving him odd looks, as well. She starts to slow down. Letting him catch up. When the others are far enough ahead, she starts plaguing him with questions.

147

'So you're, like ... from the past?'

'Yeah.'

'I bet you met all sorts of famous people.'

'One or two.'

'Did you know ... Henry the Eighth?'

'No.'

'Did you know ... Shakespeare?'

'Nah, never bumped into him. Had a friend in common, though.'

'Did you know ... Winston Churchill?'

'Hmmph. Unfortunately.'

Teoni gasps. 'Oh my shit, really? You were mates with Churchill?'

He makes a face. 'We weren't exactly mates, but yeah.'

'What was he like?'

He gives it some thought. 'Didn't like the way I looked. Didn't much care for anyone but himself, as far as I could tell. But he liked that I was from the past. Asked a lot of questions.'

'Sorry, I'm totally doing that right now.'

'Nah, I don't mind.'

'Okay. Were you, like, at the Battle of Hastings, or whatever?'

He swallows. 'Yeah. Yeah, I was.'

'What was *that* like?'

He remembers. In with the common fyrd, as usual. Holding the shield-wall together. He thought they'd won, marching down into the valley after the fleeing Normans. But then the Normans came back. Thundering downhill on horseback, calling the names of their saints, with their mail ringing and their swords held high and their banner flying behind them. Breaking men underhoof. Filling the valley with death. First time he ever died of being trampled. He'll never forget that, no matter how many times he dies or comes back.

'It's the shouting, that you remember,' he says, after a while.

'More than anything else. All the confusion. Nobody's got a clue what they're doing. You just keep fighting as best you can, and you keep standing, until you realise that it's all over. One way or the other.'

Teoni seems to have realised that it wasn't a great question. 'Sorry,' she says.

He tries his best to laugh. 'No, it's all right. You're bound to be curious.'

'I guess ...' she says. 'I just didn't know there were people back then, who were knights and shit, who looked like you and me. You know?'

He nods. It makes sense suddenly, why she's taken such a liking to him.

Funny, how much the world changes. He's sure that in the old days people didn't trouble themselves overmuch with how other people looked. There were black soldiers in Britain, black missionaries, black merchants. People moved around all over the world, before Rome fell. Nobody seemed to mind. Whether you were pagan or Christian was the more important thing. That's what people got up in arms about.

It was only after he came back from the dead that people started noticing his skin. Only in the gunpowder wars, with the muskets and the powdered wigs, that he started to feel judged. Loathed, because of how he looked. People inventing new reasons to hate each other.

It's never something he claimed to understand. He'd like to try and explain it all to this young woman, but he can't find the words. So she puts on a burst of speed and gets ahead of him, to join the others.

He sighs, and keeps moving. Trudging after them. The walk down to Manchester will be thirty miles or so, but none of these women are complaining. Not even Regan, who must be

149

seventy or so. They carry an arsenal of gear on their backs, and he only recognises half of it. He knows guns, ammunition, rope, carabiners, tents, medical supplies, shovels, canteens, blankets, bad rations. Had them in the last few wars. He doesn't know about the rest. Machines and devices that might as well come from Mars.

They leave the fields behind them and walk uphill into a dead woodland, covered in tree stumps, in fallen trunks and black undergrowth. The sky grows darker. Purple clouds and patches of pink through the empty treetops. Kay stops to pass his eyes over everything, looking for anything green. Anything growing. He can't see anything. Dando decides to help, charging into the bracken with wild confidence.

You can see what these women are fighting for. Stopping this, whatever it is. This war on nature. Maybe Herne is right. Nary a worm left in the ground, he said. What happens when it's too hot for plants to grow? When all the animals start dying? How can you stop that? They never used to think about that, in the old days. The idea of men killing God's creation, being more powerful than the beasts and the trees. That would have been heresy. Madness. Only Merlin would have thought like that. Arthur wouldn't believe it for a moment, unless you showed him. Really made it plain to him. Even then it would take a lot of convincing, surely. To make him want to do anything about it.

He gets dragged from his thoughts by a nearby commotion in the bracken. Dando has found something, something else alive in there. He is chasing after it, bounding through the leaves. After a moment a squirrel comes bolting out of the undergrowth, chittering in squirrel language. None of the sisters will be able to tell what he's saying, but Kay can hear him. The gift of tongues.

'Help me!' the squirrel is screaming. 'Fucking help me!'

The squirrel runs over to him and scales his leg, scrambling up his leg bindings, clawing its way desperately up his mail. When it gets high enough up his body, Kay grabs it by the bushy tail and holds it aloft, letting it dangle and squirm. It's hard to tell one squirrel from another, but he's fairly sure that he recognises this one.

'Oi!' says the squirrel. 'Get your filthy hands off me! I'll fucking have you!'

The squirrel starts clawing at his arm, but his arm is covered in mail, so that doesn't achieve much. Dando runs up to Kay and sits waiting, panting. He thinks this is a game. Kay holds the squirrel a bit higher.

'That dog's fucking dangerous!' says the squirrel. 'It should be put down. Nearly fucking killed me!'

'I wouldn't mind if it did,' says Kay.

'Bastard!' says the squirrel. 'You turn me back into a person, and I'll wipe that grin off your face. Go on! Turn me back, and we'll see if you're still smiling.'

'You're not making a very good argument for it, honestly.'

'Fuck you!'

Dando leaps up and snaps his teeth beneath the squirrel's dangling head.

'Shit!' says the squirrel.

Kay looks up the path at the warrior sisters, who are slowly getting away from him. Mariam is standing and waiting, with a question written on her face. But she can't hear the tongues of animals. To her, the squirrel is just chittering.

'Turn me back again, you bastard!' the squirrel is saying. 'Fucking voodoo magic. Turn me back again or I'll bite your fingers off!'

'No,' says Kay. ''Cause you're a nasty little bugger and this'll teach you a lesson or two. I hope you get eaten by a buzzard.'

'You can't do that!' says the squirrel. 'It's not fair! What about my rights? This is discrimination!'

Kay gets into a good javelin-throwing pose, one foot in front of the other, shield arm out in front of him. Then he flings the squirrel into the treetops with all his strength. The squirrel goes flying, shrieking and spinning over itself until it disappears into the brown pine needles. Dando bolts after it as if it was a stick or a ball.

Kay brushes the dirt off his hands and catches up with Mariam. She doesn't look impressed.

'Bit harsh?' she says.

'Yeah, well,' says Kay. 'He wasn't a very nice squirrel.'

Dando catches up with them, and they walk for an hour or two into the failing light. Their way takes them up into the hills. Between Preston and Manchester there is brown moorland with scraggy brush growing on it. They go through cloughs and fells, gills and brooks, flat heaths and steep valleys. This has always been wild country. It used to be wilder, of course. Wild woodland, like the forest in his dream. But there are still bowl barrows and stone circles from long before Arthur, long before the coming of the Romans. Time was, he'd have been wary, walking over an old heath like this. Wary of things that might crawl up out of their barrows and come lurking in the night, hungry for his soul. But nowadays it's him who does most of the crawling up from under hills. Seems daft to be frightened now.

Dusk gathers itself around them, and the sun falls below the distant hills. Mariam's still next to him, keeping pace.

'We walking through the night?' he asks.

'Yeah,' she says. 'Best time to do it.'

He frowns. 'Night marches are dangerous. Do you have good scouts at the front? I could go up and guide the way.'

'Nah, we just thought we'd wing it,' says Mariam. 'Worst that can happen is that we all fall off a cliff or something.'

He blinks at her. 'That's a joke, is it?'

He can see her smile, even in the twilight. 'We've done this before. You don't need to mansplain hiking to us. We've got GPS.'

The gift of tongues, again. *Give him knowledge of the words which are spoken by the people in the realm, so that he will not be a stranger in his own land.* It's mad, how it happens. Does the earth soak up words from people's lips, and then the knowledge soaks through to his brain while he's under his tree? He's suddenly aware of things in the heavens, blinking and beeping. Spinning at impossible speeds. After a moment he realises that he's stopped in his tracks, staring upwards. Staring up at the purple sky and trying to fathom everything.

Mariam is waiting again, staring back at him.

'Sorry,' he says. 'We didn't have GPS, in the old days.'

They keep walking, over the quiet moor. Soft footfalls in the deepening twilight.

'It must be a lot to get used to,' says Mariam. 'All of this.'

'Nah,' he says. 'Not really. I've got used to change, now. World's always changing. No good trying to make sense of it. Just have to keep putting one foot in front of the other. Come up and do what needs doing. Then go back down again. Try not to be too baffled by it all.'

'Why don't you just ... stay up?' she asks. 'Wouldn't that be better than being under a tree all the time?'

'Doesn't work like that,' he says. He tries to think now of the longest he's ever been up without getting killed. It might have been in the last big war, at some point. But then there was the whole crusade as well, traipsing all the way to Antioch before getting Greek fire dumped on top of him. That's probably it.

'I don't usually live to see the victory parade,' he says.

Mariam shakes her head. 'How long have you been doing that? Just ... coming back and ... doing what you do.'

'Oh,' he says, 'a long time. Just try and tell myself that it's all for

153

a reason, I suppose. It was all Merlin's idea, having warriors in the ground. Keeping us in reserve. Must have known we'd come in handy for something. Some great battle, sometime in the future.'

'But he didn't tell you what it was?' she asks.

He feels his hackles rise at that. Like he ought to stop talking. Pull up the drawbridge. Not let her into the keep. But he tries to relax. He can tell that the question wasn't meant unkindly. He shouldn't be unkind in answering.

'Well,' he says. 'No, he didn't. But that's just how he was. Never explained anything he didn't need to. But he never did anything without a good reason, either.'

'So you just volunteered for it?' she asks.

'Sort of,' he says. Smiling to himself. Arthur wouldn't have countenanced it, if any of his warriors had refused. He can't explain how it was at Caer Moelydd. The tension between them all. Vying for Arthur's favour in a smoky mead hall, like a pack of dogs. None of them wanting to seem the weakest.

'I'm not sure I would have done,' says Mariam. 'Seems like such a big sacrifice.'

He looks up at the sky again. Not for stars and satellites this time, but towards heaven. Hoping for a glimpse of Wyn looking down at him.

'Somebody has to do it,' he says. 'You're making a sacrifice as well, fighting this war. Living like this. You must have a home and a family you could go back to.'

'Not really,' she shrugs. 'I was . . . a foster kid. Didn't really have a family until I joined FETA. These are my sisters.'

That makes him smile, in the dark. Foster kid. Now who does that remind him of? Red-haired boy raised under a strange roof. Never feeling quite at home there. Knowing he was destined for something greater.

'I guess it is reassuring,' says Mariam. 'To know that there's people like you, keeping everyone safe from dragons and whatever. It does make me feel a bit safer.'

'Seems like you and your friends know how to handle yourselves,' he says. Only half lying. 'Don't need me to keep you safe.'

'Yeah, but we're not . . . heroes, or knights, or whatever. Not the same way you are. We can't do magic. We're just ordinary people.'

'Well, if there's anything I've learnt in all my time coming back it's that ordinary people can do amazing things if they put their mind to it. They can do miracles, if they choose to believe in themselves. And that's as good as magic. Or almost as good, anyway.'

She snorts at that. Not entirely convinced, but smiling in the darkness.

When the night turns entirely black the sisters stop their progress long enough to unpack something from their bags. Tubes of light which glow a soft green colour when you crack them slightly. Too dim to be seen from very far away, but bright enough to guide the path in front of them. You can see the person ahead of you and follow their light. Would have been useful in the old days, and a few times since. The women hang the tubes from their backpacks and walk forward in the strange green radiance. And then they begin to sing. It starts somewhere further up the line. First one voice, then several. It makes its way back. Mariam clears her throat and joins in, singing quietly next to him, perhaps a little embarrassed.

He doesn't quite catch the words, but he likes the tune. It's something about struggle, about how struggle will bring about something new. Giving birth to a new world. He's heard songs like that before. Seen the new world come and go often enough that songs like this should make him scoff. But there's still something beautiful about it. Sung by women, in the night, to guide their way. It's a nice thing to hear. He starts to hum along.

They've finished one song and got most of the way through another one when Kay hears one of the women walking back down the line. One of the glowing sticks bobs towards them until they can see Willow's face lit up dimly by the green light. She looks worried.

'We can't find Dando. Either of you seen him?'

'Oh, fuck,' says Mariam. 'No, not for a while.'

Kay feels a pang of concern. He can't think of the last time he saw the dog. On the trail somewhere, before the light went entirely.

'Shit,' says Willow. She looks around at the moor, but everything is dark. 'It's not like him to wander off.'

'I'm sure he'll turn up,' says Mariam.

The rest of the women have stopped and huddled around. Teoni isn't far behind Willow. She cups her hand to her mouth and shouts 'Dando!' into the darkness, at the top of her lungs. The rest of the women shush her.

'Fuck are you playing at?' Roz whispers.

'What?' asks Willow.

'There might be patrols. Somebody might hear us.'

'We were just singing!'

'*Quietly*. We were singing quietly.'

'What else are we supposed to do?'

Bronte's face appears in the green glow, stepping between Roz and Teoni. She clears her throat. 'Sisters, obviously there's some disagreement here. So why don't we vote on whether or not to stay and look for Dando? We can . . .'

'Oh for fuck's sake,' says Mariam. 'Let's just spread out and look for him. We can spare five minutes. If we stay in groups, we should be fine. Make sure you can all still see each other's glowsticks.'

And with that, Mariam turns and leaves. Willow and Teoni follow her example. Kay doesn't linger to see what the other women do. He catches up with Mariam, not wanting her to go off by herself.

They walk out over vaguely level moorland, fighting their way through knee-deep gorse and quietly calling Dando's name. When he looks over his shoulder he can see glowsticks bobbing away in different directions. He can't help shaking his head. It's madness. Stopping to look for a black dog in the middle of the night. Somebody might snap their ankle or fall down a sudden crag and end up dead. There are bogs and lakes and worse that people could sink into. He thinks again of the cairns and barrows and the spirits that come wandering above the earth while the sun is down. It seems more of a concern now than it did earlier, when it was still light.

'Let's go back,' he says, after a while.

'Why?' asks Mariam.

'Look,' he says. 'He's a lovely dog, but this isn't the smart thing for us to be doing right now.'

Mariam replies without even thinking about it. 'It might not be the smart thing to do,' she says, 'but it's the right thing to do, so we're doing it.'

Kay stops again in his tracks, like he did when he looked up at the stars. Except now he's looking at Mariam, fighting her way through the gorse. Maybe that's the mark of a good leader. Someone who understands the difference between those two things and does the right thing every time, without even thinking about it. Can it be as simple as that?

He's still trying to answer that question when somebody screams across the moor. One of Mariam's sisters shouting at the top of her lungs. He's heard a lot of screams over the years, whole corpse-fields of men lying half-dead and bellowing with pain, but this one puts a chill in his bones. It doesn't sound like fear or pain. It sounds like horror.

He draws his sword. Mariam is already running, so he runs with her. The scream came from somewhere further up the moor, the same way they were going in the first place, but they can't see much with just their glowsticks. He can see faint spheres of green light in the distance – the other women moving towards the same sound. He can hear their voices, calling to each other.

There's another sound as well, a shifting sound of something large being dragged through the gorse. Larger than a person. Kay can't think what it might be until the light from Mariam's glowstick reflects back from something in front of him, barely five feet away. A huge tail sliding through the undergrowth.

Dando barks three times from somewhere ahead of them. And then the dragon responds, lighting up the night with a bloom of fire. In the sudden blaze he can see the creature in her entirety, sitting on the moor with her long white body coiled beneath her and her tail snaking towards him. He can see a much smaller body on the ground burning, but he can't tell from this distance whether it's Dando or one of the warrior women. And he can see the dragon's face, the thick mane of hair around her neck. The liquid flame spilling from her jaws. The terrible fury in her eyes.

The gout of flame comes to an end, and the dragon's head disappears into darkness again. But the moor has already caught ablaze and started to burn around them. It will only spread, until the whole hill is burning. They have to get down off it and find safety somewhere before anyone else gets roasted alive.

But somebody has to distract this dragon, and it probably has to be him.

'Kay!' says Mariam. It's not quite a question, but he knows what she's asking.

His opening move certainly isn't the smart thing to do, and it might not be the right thing either. He charges towards the drag-on's tail and jumps astride it, like a horse. It's not a comfortable seat. The trick with dragons is to get your sword edge under one of their scales and work away at it until it breaks off. Then there's soft skin beneath that you can plunge your blade into. But big queen dragons like this one are covered in a hard scutum from head to tail. Like trying to cut through rock. Only Caliburn would cut through it.

Kay works away with his teeth clenched, looking for chinks in the armour, trying against hope to get a scale loose, but this dragon isn't going to give him the chance. He can hear her shifting her head, growling deep in her throat. He can feel, even through the darkness, something large looming over him. He risks a glance upwards, meeting her indignant gaze.

She doesn't waste her breath on grilling the skin from his bones. She just snaps her tail and sends him flying through the darkness. In the warm air, with his arms wheeling, for a good long moment. Landing face down in a gorse bush, in the darkness, feeling bruised. Listening to the sisters shouting at each other. He hears the dragon breathing fire again, casting an orange glow over everything. He pulls himself up, scrambling uphill.

There's a wall of burning gorse between him and the dragon now. Green lights dancing wildly on the other side of the blaze. He can hear gunshots, Teoni or somebody else wasting their ammunition. He learnt up in Scotland in '34 that bullets don't do anything against dragon scales. Teoni hasn't learnt that lesson yet.

He charges through the fire, leading with his shield, moving as quickly as he can. The shield doesn't catch fire, but his rain cape goes up like it's soaked in pitch. What do they make clothes out of, nowadays? He shrugs it off as quickly as he can, leaving it to burn on the ground. Left standing in his gleaming mail, which catches the light from the fire. Hopefully that'll draw the dragon's gaze.

There's a thick heat coming off the blazing gorse, but there's something even hotter pressing against his right hip. He looks down, expecting his tunic to have caught fire, but the only thing there is the oak staff. When he reaches for it, his first instinct is to snatch his fingers away. It's painfully hot.

But then, of course it is. Dragons are magical beasts. This one is huge and old and powerful. She must have a huge magical field surrounding her, and his staff is drawing from that. Filling itself with potential, once again.

Well, that might be of some advantage, if he can figure out what to do about it. He sheathes his sword. Draws the staff from its belt loop, instead. Presses forwards, towards the dragon.

There's a ring of fire spreading slowly across the moor, within which all the gorse is dead and burnt already. Mariam and her sisters are trapped inside it – all of them except for the older woman, Regan. He doesn't have time to wonder about what happened to her. The moor is burning so brightly now that he can see the dragon's head even when she isn't breathing fire. And she is staring directly at him. Her whole length begins to writhe and constrict around the crest of the hill, and suddenly he understands her strategy. She has surrounded them with herself. Now she tightens the noose, slowly herding them together, pressing them against each other, forcing them into a tight huddle with walls of impenetrable dragonhide on every side. Mariam is suddenly behind him, taking hold of his arm, above his shield. At least she's still alive.

When there is barely room for them to breathe, the dragon stops. Not crushing them but inspecting them. Looking down angrily with wide eyes.

And then the dragon roars at him. Not at the others, but at him in particular. It might be the loudest thing he's ever heard, resonating through his bones. And because he has the gift of tongues, he can hear what she is saying.

WHY HAVE YOU SUMMONED ME?

Kay is confused. He stammers for words. 'I ... didn't?'

The dragon doesn't like that. She moves her head closer to him, lower to the ground. Baring her teeth. Each one of them is big enough to bite him in half.

WHAT HAVE YOU DONE TO THE WORLD?

'Oh,' says Kay. 'Right. Well, I wasn't really around for most of it, so in my defence—'

'Kay, what the fuck?' asks Mariam, with a shaking voice.

'Hang on,' he says. 'We're having a chat.'

The dragon roars again. WHAT HAS YOUR KIND DONE TO THE WORLD? YOU HAVE BEFOULED THE AIR. IT TASTES OF YOUR CORRUPTION.

'We've ... been burning fuel,' he says. 'And it's been making the sky wrong, as far as I understand it. And things are getting warmer. So the oceans are rising? I might not be the best person to explain it to you, in fairness.'

ARTHUR PROMISED US THAT THE REALM WOULD BE PROTECTED.

'That was a long time ago, and—'

HUMANS CANNOT BE TRUSTED TO KEEP THEIR PROMISES. THEY CANNOT BE TRUSTED WITH CUSTODY OF THE WORLD. YOUR KIND MUST BE PURGED WITH FIRE.

'Hang on. These women here, they're on your side. They want the same thing as you.'

But the dragon is rearing her head back, drawing in breath. Her mane flares around her neck, and her wings unfurl to either side of her. He can see a bright glow forming at the back of her throat.

It must be a powerful kind of magic that lets dragons conjure up flame in their lungs. He thrusts the staff upwards with all his might, not knowing what he's hoping to achieve. He thinks about saving Mariam, and her sisters. He thinks about Merlin and Caer Moelydd. The things that Merlin used to say, when they ate mushrooms in Merlin's cave and travelled with him across the realm. Not by horseback or on foot, but within their minds. Waking up in different places with no memory of how they got there.

He realises that he's shouting, without meaning to. And then he can't see the dragon any more, and he can't feel the heat from the burning gorse. Because they have moved. They are no longer standing on the moor, where they were. The staff has taken them elsewhere.

12

Mariam doesn't know much about what just happened, but she knows that it was strange and horrible, and it made her feel sick. She knows that Kay has somehow saved them, by moving them to somewhere else. Now they're in a dark place, indoors somewhere. The green light of the glowsticks is enough to reveal low ceilings and each other's panicked faces. Rubble strewn on the floor. Wherever they are, it's far away from the dragon and the burning moor. They stand there swearing and shivering, not from cold but from the terror burnt into them. Bronte is throwing up in the corner of the room.

'Oh my God. Oh my God. Oh my God.'

'What even was that thing? It can't have been real.'

'It was, though. We all saw it.'

'Is everyone all right?'

'It got Dando,' says Teoni. 'It killed my dog.'

'Oh, pet,' says Willow. 'Come here.'

'It killed my fucking dog!'

'I know it did. I'm sorry.'

Mariam swallows down the lump in her throat. 'Is everyone else okay?'

'Think I'm all right,' says Willow.

'Where the fuck are we?' asks Roz. 'What even happened, just then?'

'I don't want to leave Dando out there,' says Teoni. Tears in her voice. 'I don't want to leave him out there all alone.'

'Don't be daft,' says Willow, gently. 'We can't do anything for him now, can we? No point charging out looking for him and getting yourself killed by a dragon as well. We don't even know where we are right now.'

'We're somewhere safe,' says Mariam. 'That's what matters. Why don't we just camp here and get some sleep? That was fucking horrifying for everyone, and we all need some rest. We can figure out everything else in the morning.'

There's a long, silent moment, and then everyone does what she told them to do. Pulling out their sleeping bags and laying them down on the hard ground. She's not sure why anyone is listening to her. Maybe people will listen to anyone when they're tired and scared.

She sinks to the ground and shrugs off her backpack, barely finding the energy in her shocked limbs. In the last two days she has blown up a fracking facility and met a magic knight and fallen out with most of her friends and seen someone get turned into a squirrel. And now she's almost been cooked and eaten by a dragon. She doesn't have the energy left to do anything but sleep.

Somebody looms over her in the emerald gloom. Kay, staring down at her.

'I'll go and scout about outside,' he says. 'Figure out where we are.'

'Right,' she says. 'Okay.'

He's gone before she can tell him to be careful. It does make her feel slightly safer, knowing that he'll be out there. Watching over them. But then he came up with the dragon, didn't he? They come from the same time, the same old weird place. They might not have met the dragon, if he hadn't been with them. Dando might still be alive.

Sleep comes quickly, despite the hardness of the floor. She can hear crying and whispering in the darkness. Part of her keeps expecting Dando to pad over and join her, like he sometimes did back at camp. She dreams once or twice that he's there beside her, snuggling down next to her, trapping some of the sleeping bag with his weight and warmth. But when she reaches out to stroke him, she finds that he isn't there.

Mariam finally wakes to the smell of weed and the sight of daylight streaming in through the broken windows. She doesn't feel any less tired.

It's hard to tell what kind of building they're in. The windows look old, with tree branches growing in through the shattered panes. The walls are cinderblocks, covered in peeling paint. There's some kind of plastic castle sitting in one corner of the room, like a children's play area. But the floor is hard concrete, and the ceiling is a mess of metal poles and corrugated steel. People have sprayed their tags everywhere. Twenty different names and nicknames and signatures. One of them is AMBROSE, like in the bunker.

The smell of weed is coming from Willow and Teoni. This is normally the time when they'd get up and feed Dando, squeezing ration bars into his little bowl and mushing them up for him.

But they're not doing that today. They're just sitting in their big double sleeping bag and smoking a joint together. Willow waves glumly at her. Teoni's just hugging herself and staring at the floor. Kay doesn't seem to be back yet, from wherever he went. Roz and Bronte are still asleep on the other side of the room. And there's no sign of Regan anywhere. Not even her gear or sleeping bag.

'Has anyone seen Regan?' Mariam asks.

Willow shrugs. 'Not since I woke up.'

Mariam feels a pit open in her stomach. 'Did she come here with us? Did we leave her out there?'

'I don't know,' says Willow. 'It was dark. Fuck knows what happened.'

'I . . .' says Mariam. 'I'll go and look for her, outside.'

'Hey, don't panic, pet. She might have just got up early and gone looking for mushrooms or something. You know what she's like.'

Mariam sits feeling unconvinced for a few moments, then starts pulling her boots back on. There are too many sharp emotions in this room for so early in the morning. Grief and panic and confusion. She needs space, and air, and somewhere to scream without waking anyone up.

When she heads out through the open doorway she has to raise her hand to her eyes, briefly blinded by the sun. Everything outside is overgrown, like an abandoned airfield, a flat sheet of concrete with plants poking through the cracks. But on the other side of the concrete are three white spires, with the sun behind them. The towers and pointy turrets of a fairy-tale castle. Somebody built it here, long ago, in the middle of nowhere.

It doesn't make any sense. But then, nothing has made much sense recently. She walks a few paces out into the middle of the concrete and stands there listening. It's the kind of time in the early morning when the world ought to be silent except for birdsong. But there aren't many birds left to sing. She feels like she has to move quietly, in the heavy silence, in case she disturbs the world. Like she could summon the dragon down from nowhere with a loud footstep.

Eventually Willow comes outside and puts an arm around her. They stand together, staring together at the white castle. Feeling a sense of mutual devastation.

Willow smokes thoughtfully on her joint. 'You know,' she says, 'I might be wrong but I think I came here when I was a kid. Way back when.'

'What is it?'

'Just a naff Camelot theme park. There used to be a dragon ride.'

'Weird.'

'It's not far from where we were before. Just off the M6, I think. Still in Lancashire.'

Willow offers the spliff to Mariam, but she shakes her head. She wants to stay focused, for the time being. It feels like the wrong time to relax.

'I'm sorry about Dando,' she says.

Willow sighs raggedly at the ground. 'Thanks. It is what it is.'

'Is Teoni going to be okay?'

'Not any time soon. I'm giving her a bit of time to herself.'

'Right.'

'She really loved that dog.'

'I know.'

'Bastard dragon.'

'Yeah.'

'I mean, fuck,' says Willow. 'How are you feeling about the fact that dragons exist? I'm not feeling great about it, to be honest.'

Mariam looks down at her feet. Then she looks away across

the tarmac, into the trees. She tries to form words but feels a lump rising in her throat. Pinching her eyes closed against the tears. It's only when Willow rubs her back that she starts full-on sobbing.

'It's my fault,' she says.

'How on earth's it your fault?'

'I knew,' she says, her voice strange and deep from crying. 'About the dragon. I let it out, when I blew up the fracking site. I saw it fly away. If I hadn't been an idiot then, it would still be underground or wherever it was, and Dando would still be here . . .'

'Come here,' says Willow. Pulling her into a hug. 'Don't be daft. You weren't going to think, "Oh, I'd best not blow it up, just in case a dragon pops up out of the ground", were you? You'd have needed to be bloody psychic to know that that was going to happen.'

Mariam sniffs against Willow's shoulder. 'Suppose you're right.'

'You could maybe have told us about the dragon a bit earlier, though.'

'You wouldn't have believed me.'

'Maybe not. But look. You need to stop blaming yourself for stuff that isn't your fault. D'you know that?'

'Yeah.'

'World's gone mad, and you're doing your best. That's all that matters.'

She dries her eyes and nods. Grateful to have someone who still wants to hug her and make her feel better, despite everything.

'Thanks,' she says.

'Course,' says Willow. 'Do you fancy a walk? Have a scout around for Regan, maybe. Feel like stretching my legs.'

Mariam doesn't complain. They wander out slowly across the tarmac. It feels like the set of a cowboy film, an empty courtyard with low white buildings all around it. Behind the cracked façade of Camelot there is just a giant metal box with nothing inside, like a barn or warehouse rusting in the sun. Whatever it contained is gone now. The two of them go elsewhere. Further into the greenery. Picking their way over rubble and broken fences. The whole place is long abandoned, with bracken growing on the old rides. Fake turrets and low walls that can't hold back the bushes.

'You were right about this Kay fella,' says Willow, as they walk along. 'I'll give you that.'

Mariam tucks a strand of hair behind her ear. 'How'd you mean?'

'He's a useful bloke to have around in a tight spot. I didn't know what to think of him at first, but ... if it's the fucking end of the world and there's dragons popping up out of nowhere then I suppose we want someone like him on our side, don't we?'

'I suppose,' she says.

'And he's not bad looking, either.'

Mariam wrinkles her nose. 'He's like ... at least a thousand years old. And I don't even have the space in my brain to think about that kind of thing at the moment. I don't know how you and Teoni manage.'

'We manage just fine, thank you. And it helps that— Oh shit, look!'

Mariam feels a stab of panic, expecting the dragon again. But it's just a deer. It steps out of the undergrowth in front of them, about twenty feet away, from under the old roller-coaster. It isn't scared or furtive. Probably because it isn't expecting to find any humans in this place. They stand as still as they can, watching it graze in the spots where plants are poking up through the tarmac. Then it sees them and raises its head. Panicked.

'Aw, we're not going to hurt you, lovely,' says Willow.

But the deer isn't taking any chances. It bolts away, back into the bushes.

'Okay, bye, then,' says Willow. 'Hope the dragon doesn't eat it.'

Mariam sighs. 'Does kind of makes you wonder. If we all just died, everyone on the planet, maybe everywhere would look like this. Green and overgrown. Animals everywhere. And the world would get better again. We could stop blowing up oil rigs.'

'Yeah,' says Willow. 'But then we'd be dead.'

'Hm,' she says. 'That appeals, sometimes.'

'Maybe we should just let that dragon fly around murdering everyone, for a while.'

'I can think of worse ideas.'

They find a wild trail where moss has grown to cover the concrete path, walking beneath part of the dragon ride, which has become a kind of trellis for hanging vines. Among the ruins they keep seeing plastic legs and torsos, brittle and broken and turned grey by the sun. Willow is high enough that she wants to explore, taking Mariam's hand and leading her down strange pathways. There's a long metal tunnel that used to be part of the dragon ride, strewn with faded rubbish. One of the little carriages sits abandoned, looking like a plastic cartoon dragon. On the walls are signs, telling the story of King Arthur in flowery writing. *The sorcerer Morgan le Fay bewitched Arthur and his knights in the guise of a fair maiden. Lancelot and Guinevere's secret love was discovered and this wrought the downfall of Camelot.* Somebody has sprayed the word LIES over the top.

The end of the ride is overgrown, and they have to push aside brambles to get through. Mariam stops suddenly because she can see the deer again, standing in a nearby patch of trees. And somebody is kneeling down to speak with it, feeding it or stroking its nose. It's like something from a tapestry, framed by tree trunks, with dappled sunlight streaming through the leaves. The kneeling woman looks like a stranger, for a moment. But then the light shifts, and her face becomes familiar. Mariam can't believe her eyes.

'Is that Regan?' asks Willow, softly.

'I think so,' says Mariam. Not wanting to disturb the moment. Feeling the need to stay silent, observing Regan without being observed themselves.

'Well there you are,' says Willow. 'She's fine. No need to worry.'

'Yeah . . .' she says. She knows that she should feel relieved. But there's something strange about this scene. The deer was so skittish with them earlier. Now it's eating berries from Regan's hand.

They slip away eventually, leaving Regan and the deer behind them. Heading back towards the others, in the vague direction of the white towers.

'I wonder how she keeps going, sometimes,' says Willow.

'How d'you mean?'

'Well, fuck knows how long she's been doing this. Decades. Trying to save the world and make things better, when everything's just getting worse. But she keeps going somehow. Finding the strength from somewhere.'

'Hm,' says Mariam.

'What does "hm" mean?'

'I don't know,' says Mariam. 'Do you ever get . . . weird vibes, from her?'

'Like what?' asks Willow. 'I know she's a bit old-school, but I think she's pretty on the level. Never given me any trouble about you-know-what.'

'Nah, it's not that. It . . . it might be nothing. Forget it.'

They find their way back to the empty courtyard by the white castle. The building where they spent the night looks bigger from the outside. Crumbling white paint on the walls, and wooden shields hung everywhere. They venture back inside.

There's still no sign of Kay, but the others are awake, sitting in a circle and breaking open the ration bars. Bronte looks a thousand miles away. Roz is looking over the maps and the GPS. Teoni is still smoking, with a blanket over her legs.

'There you fuckers are,' says Teoni in a low grumble. 'Was worried about you.'

'We was just having a nosey around,' says Willow, getting down under the blanket with her.

They sit for a while and chew on soy protein bars in miserable silence. Dando's absence still feels new and strange. Mariam keeps expecting to see him padding into the room. Her hands still want to stroke his back and feel the softness of his fur. She wants to say his name quietly while scratching him behind his ears and see him smile.

Regan returns after some time with nuts and berries and mushrooms, which make their breakfast seem slightly less depressing. Mariam isn't very hungry, but she takes the berries anyway, forcing herself to smile. If Regan saw them earlier, spying on her from the bushes, then she doesn't acknowledge it now.

Roz puts the maps away and runs a hand down her face. 'Okay,' she says. 'I think I know where we are. Question is whether we still want to go down to Manchester.'

Willow frowns at her. 'Why wouldn't we?'

'Because there's a lot of open ground between here and Manchester,' says Roz, 'where we could get attacked by a dragon. I thought we might want to avoid that.'

'Fair,' says Willow.

'Who even cares about the other rebels at this point?' says Teoni. 'There's dragons, there's magic, it's the end of the fucking world. Nothing that we can do is going to change that.'

'No, babe, come on,' says Willow. 'Don't talk like that.'

Teoni shakes her head. 'It's all gone to shit already. Let's just stay here. Or go back to camp. Or whatever.'

Mariam rubs her eyes. 'Kay has a plan,' she says. 'We need to go down to Manchester to find his friend. She can help us.'

Roz shakes her head. 'I'm not being funny, but we still don't know who he is, or who he works for. Just because he can do magic it doesn't mean we can trust him.'

'He did just save us from a dragon,' says Willow. 'I think he's chill.'

'He's not one of us,' says Roz. 'I don't trust him to look out for us.'

'Well, I trust him,' says Mariam. 'I know that's weird. But I do.'

'It is weird,' says Roz. 'He's not going to magically save the world all by himself.'

'I know that, but—'

'No, listen,' says Roz. 'People don't need knights in shining armour to come along and save them. People need to start saving themselves. That's how we get out of this mess. That's how we fix the planet. By all banding together and saving ourselves. But people don't *want* to do that: they want somebody else to do it for them. If you've got a hero around, you don't need to do anything. You can sit back and relax and let them do all the hard work. It absolves you from having to take action yourself. That's why people like the idea of heroes. Maybe that's why you like having Kay around.'

Something crumbles in Mariam's chest, like a sandcastle hit by the tide. She tries to build it back up again.

'That's not true,' she says.

'Isn't it?'

'He wants to help. He's trying to save the planet, just like the rest of us.'

Kay chooses that moment to come back through the door with a dead deer over his shoulder, throwing it down in the middle of the room. It lands against the concrete with a wet slap. He's holding a metal pole, which must have been part of the park at one point or another. Now the end is sharpened and stained with blood.

Bronte screams and stands up, scrambling back towards the edge of the room. Everyone else stays where they are, too horrified to move.

'Thought some meat might cheer everyone up,' says Kay, panting from his exertions.

'Kay,' says Mariam. 'I really hate to tell you this, but we're all vegetarians.'

Kay frowns. 'What?'

'We don't eat meat. It's bad for the planet.'

He looks from her to the deer in confusion. 'How?'

'He *killed* a *deer*!' Bronte is wailing. There are tears on her face. Willow goes over to give her a hug and calm her down a bit. Teoni is staring at the deer silently. The last thing she needs to see right now is an animal carcass. Kay doesn't seem to have thought of that.

'But,' says Kay. Clearly struggling with this. 'It's an animal. It's not burning fuel.'

'No,' Mariam says. 'But ... God. Okay. People cut down trees so that they can farm cows. And they use fertilisers. And the cows give off methane, which is just as bad as carbon dioxide. So, we don't eat meat, as a protest.'

'But this isn't a cow.'

She has to close her eyes. 'No, I know it isn't.'

'He does have a point,' says Regan. 'One dead animal doesn't do the ecosystem any harm. He didn't cut down any trees or use any fertiliser. It hasn't been processed or packaged. He carried it here on his back. I imagine the carbon impact of eating it would be very small.'

174

'That doesn't matter,' says Roz. 'We all took an oath not to eat meat when we joined FETA.'

'Oh,' says Kay. Up until now he looked indignant, angry, confused. Now the tension leaves his limbs. 'So it's ... like a holy vow?'

'Kind of,' says Mariam. 'If you want to think of it that way.'

He nods, looking down at the deer. 'Well. Wouldn't want you to break your oaths on my account. Not sure I can eat the whole thing by myself, though.'

'I'll help,' says Teoni.

That's the last thing anyone was expecting. They stare at her, and she shrugs.

'My dog just died,' she says. 'I can try some deer meat, if I want to.'

'Right,' says Kay. 'If anyone wants to see how to skin a deer, you're welcome to come and watch.'

He grabs the deer carcass by the forelegs and drags it back out through the door.

Two hours later the hall of Camelot is filled with woodsmoke and the smell of chargrilled venison. Kay has salted some meat for the road and is eating the rest of it now, chewing on a massive greasy deer leg. Regan has cooked her foraged mushrooms for the rest of them, bringing out a few spices that she had hidden away in her herb collection. They might not be eating the same dish, but there's something about the feast that seems to soothe their spirits, bringing them close together around the fire.

When Mariam has eaten more mushrooms than she can

stomach, she wipes her mouth on the back of her sleeve. Then she addresses the rest of the group.

'Okay,' she says. 'So this dragon killed Dando. And it's probably going to kill everyone else on the planet as well. And right now we might be the only people who know about it. So as well as saving the ecosystem and destroying oil rigs and everything else, I think we should make it one of our Core Objectives to try and kill this dragon.'

'We can't *kill* it!' says Bronte.

The other sisters look to Bronte for an explanation. She looks back at them in horror. 'I mean, it's probably an endangered species?'

'Oh my God,' says Willow. 'Bronte, *we're* gonna be the endangered species if we don't find a way of killing that thing.'

'And how are we planning on killing it, exactly?' asks Roz.

'Well, I'm hoping Kay will help us with that part,' says Mariam. 'But I think we should go down to Manchester and tell the other rebels about the dragon as well.'

'Fucking hell,' says Willow. 'Yeah, I'm sure they'll take that well. "Hi guys, we're the eco-terrorists who just blew up the fracking site in Preston. By the way, there's a dragon on the loose! And this is Kay – he used to be mates with King Arthur, now he goes around stabbing people!" That will put us in a great fucking negotiating position.'

Roz makes a noise in agreement. 'The communists will think we're insane.'

'The Welsh and the Cornish might like it,' says Regan. 'There are lots of old legends about dragons and Saxons.'

'It might be tough to convince them,' says Mariam, 'but we need to try. I don't see how we're going to kill it by ourselves.'

She looks to Kay, chewing thoughtfully on his deer leg. He shakes his head. 'She's not going to go down without a fight.'

'Wait,' asks Bronte. 'The dragon's a she?'

'Yeah,' says Kay. 'The females are bigger.'

'Well . . . maybe we can try and convince her to help us?' says Bronte. 'Like, don't you guys think that there's something really empowering about that? She could join our collective.'

'Bronte, I swear to Christ,' says Teoni.

'I think we're past the point where she wants to negotiate, pet,' says Willow.

'It killed my dog,' says Teoni. 'I want to get even.'

Mariam looks over to Kay. 'Would you know how to kill it? If you saw it again?'

'Well,' says Kay. 'My sword won't do much good against it, but there is one thing that might work.'

'Fab,' says Willow. 'Are you gonna tell us what it is, or . . . ?'

Kay sighs. 'There's another sword, down in Manchester. If I can find it, then I might be able to kill a dragon with it.'

Mariam blinks at him, feeling weirdly hurt. 'Why are you only telling us this now?'

'Because it's Excalibur,' he says. 'It's the sword that brings King Arthur back. And I'm supposed to wake him up.'

There's a long silence around the fire. Kay throws a deer bone over his shoulder, where it clatters against the wall. Dando would have gone after it, if Dando wasn't dead.

'Am I the only one wondering why Excalibur's in fucking Manchester?' asks Willow, eventually.

'I wasn't gonna say anything,' says Teoni.

'It's not,' says Kay. 'It's . . . well, Nimue's looking after it. Lady of the Lake. And I know a place down there where I might be able to talk to her. But I don't want to use the sword unless I absolutely have to.'

Mariam feels her trust turning brittle around the edges. 'Why not?'

'Mate,' says Willow. 'Are you waiting for things to get worse?'

'Yeah, bring King Arthur back,' says Teoni. 'Why not? He can't be any more shit than the people running things at the moment.'

'You'd be surprised,' says Kay.

Mariam narrows her eyes at him. 'So you just wave the sword and say abracadabra and King Arthur pops up out of the ground?'

'No,' he says. 'Not quite. There's other components that you need as well.'

'Ah,' says Regan, smiling. 'Eye of newt? Toe of frog?'

Kay doesn't seem to find that amusing. 'No, just whatever we had to hand when he died. Staffs and rings. You only need two of them to make it work. But then you need Excalibur, as well. And the blood of a dead king.'

'Oh,' says Willow. 'Is that all?'

'Was Merlin's idea,' says Kay. 'It was supposed to be difficult. Didn't want just anybody being able to bring him back.'

There's a strange wind outside that whistles through the broken windows. Trees scraping at the other side of the stained glass. Kay looks tense. Vulnerable. Like he regrets steering the conversation in this direction. Mariam clears her throat and tries to come to his rescue.

'So that's our new plan, then,' she says. 'We go down to the conference in Manchester. And while we're talking to the rebels, we see if we can find Kay's friend and get this sword.'

'Sounds good to me,' says Willow. 'Who votes for making "Slay the Fucking Dragon" one of our Core Objectives?'

Every hand goes up, except for those of Roz and Bronte. After a moment, Roz sighs and raises her hand as well.

Mariam finds herself smiling. 'What's our new Core Objective?'

'Slay the dragon.'

'Slay the fucking dragon!'

'And if that doesn't work, we've got King Arthur as plan B,' says Teoni.

Mariam smiles at Kay, but he's not smiling back at her. He's staring gravely into the fire.

13

Lancelot wakes up under the table, not under his hill. He is lying with his cheek in a thin, cold pool of his own vomit. His joints ache where they've been lying against the floorboards of the pub. He hasn't died again. It just feels like he has.

It takes him a little while to remember where he is, and why he's there. Then the grief hits him again, merciless and blunt like a charging ogre.

He moans. He moves gingerly, head like a drum, mouth like a badger's arse. Stomach yawning for food or coffee. He manages to haul his carcass up into a weary kneeling position, accidentally penitent. The stained-glass windows of the awful pub are blazing with morning light. Perhaps prayer would be a good idea. Cleansing. Detoxifying. But he already knows that he's going to hell.

When he's remembered how to stand, he goes to the pub toilets to try and clean himself up, but there's no running water. He finds some leftover paper towels and uses them to wipe the worst of the vomit from his face and clothes. Staring at his sorry reflection until he can't bear the sight of it any longer.

There's no sense staying here, in this awful place. He needs to find the sword and kill the dragon. Then perhaps he can go back to being dead for a while. He checks the revolver, straps his shield to his back, and girths his sword to his waist. Then he twists Galehaut's ring onto his finger, kissing the stone with his eyes squeezed shut. Heading back out through the cold basement and walking up into the light.

The bike is still there. Nobody has stolen it or slit its tyres. Is there nobody left in this part of Britain? Is everyone in a camp somewhere? Is everyone dead? Lancelot doesn't know the answers to these questions. He just mounts the bike and kicks it awake. Leaving the awful pub behind him, without looking back.

He listens to the Weather Girls until he has to tear the head-phones off. Pushing the bike's engine to its limit. Flying past flooded fields and dead woodland, through the blighted realm. As if he can somehow outpace the sorrow and the heartbreak, if he travels fast enough.

It helps to focus on the route ahead. He'll follow the old Roman roads as best he can, up to High Cross, where the fortress of Venonis used to stand and is now gone. Then west towards Uriconium, the old seat of Powys. North from there to the City of the Legions, and further north to Mamucium. Kay's old holdfast, in the dingy north.

Hard to flee from sorrow in a country that's haunted by the past. Ground waterlogged with memories at every step. Riding towards Manchester is riding towards guilt, the kind of guilt that he doesn't have space for, alongside his grief.

Well, there's nothing for him to feel guilty about. War is what it is. Chaos is unleashed, and people face the consequences of their decisions. Kay chose the wrong side. He always seems to choose the wrong side. Maud and Stephen. Charles and Cromwell. Arthur and Gwenhwyfar. He's on the wrong side now, as well. And he'll have to face the consequences for that.

He rides west towards Powys until he can see the Uricon in the distance, standing lone and tall over the new towns and the old fields. The hill where King Charles marshalled his cavaliers for the war against parliament. The hill where druids used to worship, in the old days. Now the way is blocked by boxy war machines, grumbling down the road towards him. Blurring the air with their exhaust fumes. He stops to let them pass, but the whole convoy grinds to a halt. A single mercenary pops his head out of a hatch to speak with him.

'Nice bike, mate!' says the soldier.

'Thank you,' he mumbles.

'I'd turn back if I were you. Any further and you'll be in Wales.'

'And?' says Lancelot. Indignant. 'I've been in Wales before.'

'It's these New Gwynedd nutters,' says the soldier. 'They've taken Shrewsbury now, and Chester. They're just down the road, shooting at anyone who looks a bit English. We're pulling back!'

Lancelot looks at the war machines, scored with bullet holes. It would be a shame to damage the bike. And the fuel gauge on the bike is already beginning to droop. He doesn't fancy refuelling in enemy territory.

'Thanks for the warning,' he says.

He turns the bike around and rides north for a while, down narrow country lanes. Until he's hopelessly lost and has to pull over on a grass verge. Checking Lawrence's old map, to figure out where he's going. Planning his new route with a stubby pencil.

Stopping was a mistake. The grief catches up with him as soon as he cuts the engine. He thinks about trying the revolver again. But no. He might as well get this bloody mission done. Kill this dragon. Batter Kay to death, if he can spare the time. That would be therapeutic. Then he can sleep again. Sleep for a hundred years. Forget about all of this.

Lawrence's map says that there's a petrol station just outside of Nantwich. It also says that there's a church with *Wonderful Acoustics*, but the petrol station is more immediately useful.

Nantwich used to be Nametwych, the sacred wellspring of the druids. Lancelot fought a battle there in the war with Charles and Cromwell. It was just a paltry village then. Now it's a ghost town. The petrol station is a blackened ruin, burnt and twisted. Somebody has sprayed something on the tarmac, the words FETA and CLIMATE JUSTICE.

He sighs. What kind of war is this? At least in the war with Charles and Cromwell he understood the terms of engagement, the *raisons de guerre*. People fighting for their king, or grubby men like Cromwell fighting for themselves. But people are always finding new causes, new reasons to kill each other and cause chaos. Now he has no petrol, and it's all because some idiot tried to make the world a better place. He drives away again, running on fumes, to see how far he can get. North and further north. Past low hills and brown hedgerows. Past a giant metal dish pointed at the sky. He can't think what purpose it might have served. It looks old now, rusty and neglected. It's always hard to reconcile how quickly things change. Here is this great iron wonder which he never could have imagined in the old days, now abandoned and left to ruin.

Not far south of Manchester Lancelot finds himself in a nicer part of the realm which doesn't seem as badly blighted as the rest. There are still verdant trees on either side of the road, their leaves touching above his head. It gives him meagre solace for about five seconds, before the bike begins to sputter. He stops and kills the engine before the fuel is gone entirely, kicking down the stand.

Then he sits on the bike, in the middle of the road. Trees rustling quietly above his head.

'Bugger,' he says to himself.

Walking to Manchester feels beneath his dignity. But he doesn't see many other options. He doesn't want to leave the bike for somebody to find and break up for scrap, so he pushes it along by the handlebars. Walking north, beneath the trees. He is still thirsty and hungover, but it isn't entirely unpleasant. The trees give him some shade from the sun. There's a sweet and earthy smell in the air, not of manure or burnt diesel but of untrammelled nature. All of this chaos must be letting the realm go wild again, in some places. That can't be a bad thing.

It doesn't take long before he begins to resent the motorcycle. Lawrence wouldn't want him to abandon it, but it is becoming a nuisance. At least horses never required you to wheel them along when they got tired. You could stop and let them forage, to get their strength up. One would have less success trying that with a bike.

The grief rises up in him again, walking like this. Grief behind him and guilt in front of him. People dead who oughtn't be dead. People still alive who oughtn't be alive anymore. Like him. This endless farce. How does it end? Somebody might come and cut down his tree as well, if he's lucky. Build a pub on top of it. But what happens to him then? Would he be trapped beneath the earth forever? Would the spell finally be broken, and he'd float off up to heaven? More likely down the other way, in his case.

Lancelot would like to know what happened to Galehaut. He'd like to know if there's someone he could ask. But there isn't, of course. There's just the road ahead of him, and the sun blazing down, and the wind whispering in the trees.

He stops by a sign with an oak leaf on it that says ALDERLEY EDGE. Then he takes the shield from his back, strapping it over the bike instead. The jacket comes off as well. His shirt is sticking to his back with sweat, getting damp at the collar. He rolls up his sleeves and mops his brow with a handkerchief. The thought occurs to him that he would sell his soul for a cup of ale.

When he looks up again he sees a pub by the side of the road. He could have sworn that it wasn't there a moment ago. It's not a foul new pub like the one in Hertfordshire. More like pubs from the war against Napoleon. Old and overgrown and painted white, with big square windows. Even more notably, there's a white horse tethered outside in the car park. The horse is staring at him.

'Oh now, really,' he scoffs.

He's not falling for it. This is the sort of thing that used to happen in the old days. Faerie taverns springing up out of the forest just when you started getting thirsty. Your horse would go lame, and you'd walk for a while through the wilderness, think- ing to yourself that you'd renounce Christ if only some old god would send a horse for you to ride. And then one would appear, as if it had trotted up from a hole in the ground. Christ testing your resolve. Or the old gods tempting you over to their side. Or some other power preying on you in your moment of weakness.

This horse is probably a demon that will gallop to the near- est lake and drown him if he climbs up onto its back. The ale in the pub will poison him. He should just ignore it and keep going. There might be a better pub further down the road. His reward from Christ for ignoring temptation. That used to happen sometimes.

Or maybe it's just a pub with a horse tied up outside, and the sun's getting to his head.

Wheeling the bike closer, he can see that the pub is called THE WIZARD. There's a painting over the door of a figure who looks a lot like Merlin. And somebody has left a sign outside. NO COMMUNISTS OR TREE-HUGGERS, written in chalk.

It sounds like his sort of place. And he does need a horse. Perhaps it's worth the risk.

He wheels the bike into the car park, and the horse steps closer to him, to the end of her tether. You might have called her a palfrey back in the day, with the kind of build she has. A good messenger's horse, or an even better hunting mount. She has a beautiful coat with only a few blemishes on her flanks. He spends a bit of time fussing over her when he's done with his bike. Why might she be here, of all places? Taverns used to have horses hitched outside of them, but he thought that sort of thing had stopped, with there being motor cars everywhere. Maybe it makes sense, having a horse, when the realm's in chaos and there's barely any petrol to be found. It wouldn't be a bad thing, to his mind, if people started riding horses again to get from place to place.

He goes back around the front of the pub and falters by the door with the painted wizard staring down at him. This might be a bad idea. But he has his sword at his hip and Lawrence's revolver at his side. He's not sure what .455 rounds will do against the fay, but its weight makes him feel better.

There aren't any fay inside when he pushes the door open – or, there don't appear to be. But then that's the problem with the fay. Never what they appear to be. What he sees is locals in flat caps, frowning at him over their beers. If they're fay, then they're good impressionists.

The place is comfortingly old-fashioned. Beams and panelling and tasteful furnishings. Brass plates on the walls. Far better appointed than the other place, down south. It doesn't make sense that this pub should be here and open and serving beer at a time when all the realm's in chaos, but if it's some sort of faerie pub he's too grateful to care. Maybe it's just what it appears to be. Even when there's war and doom and peril in the realm, there are still men in flat caps who want to sit in pubs and frown at newcomers. That's an oddly heartening thought.

The landlord could win county squinting competitions. Lancelot approaches him with a manufactured smile.

'Good morning!' he says to him.

'Don't think I've seen you in here before,' says the landlord.

'No, you won't have done,' says Lancelot. 'My bike ran out of petrol. I don't suppose you have any, do you?'

'No,' says the landlord. 'We're a pub, not a garridge.'

'Well, never mind, then. Do you serve food?'

'Sometimes.'

Lancelot suspects that now isn't one of those times. He tries to ignore his hunger and maintain his smile. 'Perhaps I'll just have a drink, then. What have you got on?'

'We've only got Lionheart,' says the landlord. 'Can't get owt else nowadays. New licensing laws.'

There's a tap on the counter ornamented with the white-and-red cross of Saint George. The standard of the Genoese, picked up by crusading kings when they went to Jerusalem. Lancelot will never understand how it became the flag of England. It says LIONHEART across the red band, and ENGLISH ALE underneath. In small letters at the very bottom are the words, *Brewed in Massachusetts*.

'Lovely,' he says. 'I'll have a pint of that, then.'

'That'll be twenty-four pound ninety.'

Lancelot balks. '*How* much?'

The barman shrugs. 'Inflation.'

He swallows his outrage and fishes out a leather wallet from his inside pocket. Marlowe usually sorts him out with a bit of ready cash whenever he's up and about. He slaps a few bank notes down on the counter.

'Contactless only,' says the barman.

'What does that mean?' asks Lancelot.

'It means we don't take cash. And if you take that tone with me again you'll be out on your arse.'

He stares into his wallet, as if it might provide answers. There's a piece of plastic and a few hundred pounds of paper money. He gets about fifty quid out and slides it over. 'How's that? Keep the change.'

The landlord grumbles but pockets the money. He pulls a pint of the Lionheart stuff into a tall glass with no handle, not like the dappled tankards that Lancelot remembers from the last big war. But they could serve it in a shoe, for all he cares. He nods his thanks and raises the glass to his dry lips. Slaking his thirst.

Then he grimaces. Something must have gone wrong with the brewing process, somewhere. Maybe it went sour on the way here from America. He's tasted better ale in old hostelries with straw on the floor, where you ate from the common pot over the fire.

'What do you call this?' he asks.

The landlord shrugs. 'Progress.'

'I'm not sure I like it.'

'Neither does anyone else.'

Lancelot scowls at his beer. He can't bring himself to pour it out on the floor when he just paid a king's ransom for it. So he sits at the bar and drinks his awful beer, regretting it more with every mouthful. The landlord watches him.

'Are you a wizard?' he asks eventually.

'No,' says the landlord. 'I'm a landlord.'

'So why's the pub called The Wizard?'

'Old mines round here,' says the landlord. 'Up on the Edge. Supposed to be a wizard living in them somewhere. Whole host of knights sleeping in the ground. And the time'll come that they'll ride out and save England from peril. That's what the legend says.'

'Well,' says Lancelot. Smiling, now. 'If that's true, then perhaps you can help me. I saw you had a horse outside.'

'That's right,' says the landlord.

'I was wondering if you'd consider selling it to me.'

The landlord's eyes widen. 'Now look,' he says. 'Who d'you think you are, coming in here, flashing your cash around, asking if you can buy my horse off me? That horse belonged to my wife, before she died. And I'd sell my own arm before I dreamt of selling her to anybody. Specially not some flash git from down south somewhere. So if I were you, I'd finish your pint and clear off back to London, or wherever it is you're from. And another thing—'

'My name's Lancelot,' he says.

The landlord stops speaking, long enough for his brain to catch up with his ears. He opens his mouth to say something, then closes it again. 'What did you say?'

'Lancelot.'

'What – *the* Lancelot?'

Lancelot smiles like he's been asked for an autograph. 'Of the Round Table, yes.'

The landlord looks him over. He knows he's not exactly dressed how one might expect. So he draws his sword and lays it on the bar. Lending some weight to his claim.

The landlord stares at the sword for a long moment. He begins to nod.

'Up from under the hill, are you?' asks the landlord.

'That's right,' says Lancelot.

'Well,' says the landlord. 'Suppose I'd better find you something to eat, then.'

A short time later, they're sitting at a table in the back, with the window open to admit the breeze. There's a brass plate on the wall of a knight with his sword planted in the ground, staring nobly into the distance. The landlord has served up a board of bread and cheese, and found a jug of home-brew cider behind the bar.

Lancelot happily eats his fill. This is the kind of hospitality that peasant landlords ought to show to weary warriors on the road. It's how things used to be in the old days. If you stopped at any house in the realm, even the lowest hovel, you could expect those dwelling within it to offer up the finest food in their larder. They did it out of pride. There were laws of hospitality and kindness, in those days. Most people are too selfish nowadays. But not this chap.

'Back to sort out all this mess, then, are you?' asks the landlord. He's filling a pipe to smoke, tamping down the tobacco with one thumb.

'That's the general idea,' says Lancelot.

'Not before time,' says the landlord. 'World's gone mad, I tell you.'

'Mmm,' says Lancelot. 'This is very good cheese.'

'Could do with King Arthur back, to be rid of all that pack of vultures down in London. I'd trust him a far sight more than I trust them.'

'Well,' says Lancelot. He chews his bread and tries to think of something charitable to say. 'He certainly wouldn't be best pleased with the state of things.'

'And all this madness up round here,' says the landlord. 'People with their daft notions. I tell you, those Free Stoke Army communists, or whatever they call themselves, came here the other day wanting to take my horse off me and grind her down into meat! To be "distributed equally", that's what they said.'

'Barbarians,' says Lancelot.

'I sent 'em packing,' says the landlord. 'They'll be back, o' course. Can't fend them off forever. But I'll make a fair go of it.'

Lancelot feels a pang of sympathy for this man. There are armed Welshmen in the hills to the west, and dragons climbing up from the earth, and Christ knows what sort of pandemonium happening up north. But here's this man, keeping his horse fed, making his own cider, tending his bar. Minding his own business. He could have been here for a thousand years, undisturbed, letting the realm change around him. That brings something unfamiliar up from Lancelot's heart, something that he buried down there a long time ago.

'All the more reason to let me take that horse of yours, then,' he says. 'She won't get turned into meat as long as I'm riding her.'

The landlord thinks about it, pursing his lips. 'You'll look after her?'

'Of course,' says Lancelot. 'You can look after the bike for me, as collateral.'

The landlord nods. 'I'll put it under a tarp, round back. Then you'll know where it is, if you come back for it. How's that?'

'That sounds ideal,' says Lancelot.

The landlord reaches across the table, and they shake hands.

'Anything I can do, to help a knight of Camelot,' says the landlord. And he actually smiles, for the first time. His red face cracking into a grin.

Lancelot smiles back at him, politely. It's not quite a genuine smile, but he wishes it was. When was the last time that he actually felt happy enough to smile? Christ, he can't remember. He only ever seems to smirk, or sneer, or suffer fools. But that's what immortality does to you, as far as he can tell. Hollows you out. Saps the joy out of you.

When they've eaten their fill, the landlord leads their way outside. Brushing down the horse's coat, ready to be ridden. Getting the stones out of her shoes with a mattock. Lancelot wheels the Superior around the back of the pub, taking what he needs from the saddle bags. Map, revolver. Cassette player. He leaves the copy of Malory. But he keeps Galehaut's ring on his finger. He's not leaving that anywhere unguarded.

He'd like to take a moment to bid the bike goodbye, but he doesn't get the chance. The landlord covers it over, weighing down the tarp with four loose bricks. Then he clears his throat. Scratching the back of his neck. Sentimental, suddenly, about his horse.

'She's called Rhiannon,' says the landlord. 'My late wife named her that. Welsh, she was. Very fond of all the old stories.'

'Ah,' says Lancelot. He tries not to sigh too loudly. It would have been too much to ask that the horse would be called Beryl, or Snowdrop. He can't meet a horse without it being the queen of horses. He can't drink from a stream without it being the home of a water nymph. It's always been that way. His penalty for being one of Arthur's warriors. It's more exhausting than convenient.

He straps his shield back to his arm. The landlord gets Rhiannon's tack ready, saddles her up, telling him what she likes and doesn't like, how many times a day he ought to feed her, how fast she can go on roads or over open country. He remembers that he has some treats in the pub, so he hurries to fetch them. Putting a few of them into her saddlebags. Lancelot can tell that he wants to delay this. He doesn't truly want to part with this creature. He's having second thoughts. But Lancelot's patience is finite. He climbs up into the saddle with his shield on his arm.

'Well, er, mind how you go,' says the landlord. 'Give those Free Stoke Army fellers a good seeing too, if you come across any of 'em. And I hope you sort all of this out, you know. All this mess. You're always welcome at my table. Might not be round, but it's well-stocked. And that goes for Arthur too, if he's up and about!'

Lancelot knows just what to say, to someone like this. He smiles the noblest smile that he can muster, and nods in a princely fashion. He hopes the sun is shining from behind him, through his hair.

'Camelot owes you a debt of thanks,' he says.

Then he gallops out of the car park and down the road.

He breathes the air more deeply on his ride north. This is half of what it means to be English, as far as he's concerned. Horse trading, handshakes, hearthside hospitality. People like that landlord shouldn't see their taverns plundered and their horses ground down into meat.

The realm needs fixing. That much is clear to him. Will it help, killing Kay? Slaying this dragon? It might stop the land from sliding deeper into ruin. It might not achieve much else, though, for ordinary people. He wonders for a moment if there's anything else that he could do to help. That's probably what Galehaut would want him to do.

There's still some nice country between here and Manchester. He dons his headphones again and rewinds the tape, spurring Rhiannon to an easy gallop. She seems to know which way to go.

14

This false theme park Camelot is by far the strangest thing Kay has seen since he came up again. Stranger than the rising of the oceans or the buzzing whirligigs in the sky.

He's never understood why people think such grand things about Arthur and Caer Moelydd. The perfect kingdom, ruled by the perfect king. Where did that idea come from? Welsh bards, and later people writing stories. When he went crusading with the French kings of England, the Henries and the Richards, they all wanted to be Arthur. Moulding themselves after their notion of him. Churchill talked about Arthur with wide eyes, like a schoolboy who'd heard too many tales. Kay never had the heart to tell them the truth. They wouldn't have wanted to hear it.

Once, in the very old days, he rode back down to Caer Moelydd and found the whole place silent and morbid. It was Gawain who finally told him of what had happened. Arthur went to see a soothsayer, some crone throwing chicken bones in her hut. She said that a child had been born in the realm who would one day kill him, and the child had been baptised with a name that began with M. Arthur didn't like that, and Kay hadn't been there to talk sense into him. So Arthur sent riders out into his lands, looking for Christian children whose names began with M. They were dragged from their mothers' arms and piled up in wagons and carried all the way to Mona, the Isle of Druids, on the sea. Arthur rode up there himself to make sure that everything was done to his liking. All of the children were loaded onto a sleek ship, one of the dragon ships from Arthur's warfleet. And the ship was covered in oil and pushed out to sea and fired with burning arrows, so that the whole thing went up like dry tinder and burnt on the water in a great blaze. And any of the children who didn't want to burn had to jump into the water and drown instead.

Gawain managed to tell that whole story without weeping. He only wept right at the end. Because the worst thing about it all hadn't been the burning ship or the screaming children. It was Arthur's face. When Arthur rode home to Caer Moelydd and sat down at the round table he bit into his venison quite as calmly and cheerfully as if he'd just been riding with the hounds, for sport.

Kay can't imagine Churchill would have liked that story. But then, perhaps he would have done. Perhaps it would have made him feel more justified in doing foul deeds himself. Bombing cities and starving people in far distant India. If Arthur killed children in the name of righteousness, then why can't I?

He thinks all of this in a tired haze on the road down to Manchester. Mariam and her sisters have decided to risk daylight, following a wide road. Sun baking down on them. They'd rather get spotted by Saxons than run into any more dragons in the dark. He's inclined to agree. Even if he wasn't, he'd have a hard time convincing them. They've grown a harder band of women to disagree with. That battle with the dragon, and the feast afterwards, have brought them together, strengthened their resolve.

Mariam leads the column, with Roz close beside her, planning what they'll do and say when they get to Manchester. He guards the rear again, hanging back to keep an eye on everyone. But he is getting tired. He spent the whole night ranging, keeping watch, tracking deer. He hasn't slept since the dragon fight or the angry men the day before. The last time he slept was in the bunker, with Mariam, when he dreamt of Herne and Arthur and the hand bursting from his chest. He doesn't want another audience with Herne. No more midnight visits to the gloaming forest of the Otherworld, if he can help it.

Perhaps it's foolish to avoid dreaming altogether when he has to protect Mariam and her sisters. Now he's sluggish, fug-headed. Sour feeling in his eyes and limbs. Chest hurting in the place where Mariam shot him. Head hurting in the place where he was clubbed. He'd quite like to roll up in his cloak and go to sleep, but he doesn't have his cloak anymore.

There might be sleep in Manchester. Strange to be returning, after all this time. Will they be welcomed? Given food and somewhere to sleep? There used to be rules about it in the old days, when you spent the night beneath the thatch of someone else's hall. They gave you a cup of wine and a seat at the feasting table, and a place to sleep on the straw. That's the greeting he gave to strangers when he was lord of Mamucium, all that time ago. But this isn't Mamucium anymore.

They go south until they see a barricade across the road in front of them, with soldiers guarding it. Not Saxons, as far as he can tell. Motley partisans with armbands and wild-coloured hair. The sisters keep walking towards them, not bothering to conceal themselves. Kay tenses. Wishing he was better rested. Resting his hand on the hilt of his sword, for all the good that'll do him. These communists have automatic rifles held across their chests.

'We're from FETA,' says Roz to the sentry.

'Like the cheese?' says the sentry, after a long pause.

'We've been invited,' says Mariam. 'To the conference.'

'Oh,' says the sentry. 'Let me call this in.'

They're taken south eventually, marched through the empty towns on Manchester's outskirts. Each town far larger than Mamucium ever used to be. Now mostly deserted, as far as he can tell. They're kept under guard for hours in a vacant building while they wait for a new escort. Kay feels more like a prisoner than a guest. Mariam and Roz are still planning things, but Willow looks tense as well. Former soldier. He can tell that from a mile away. Good to know that there's another person here who could handle themselves if things went south.

Finally some transport arrives for them, a double-decker thing like the grandchild of the big buses he saw in London in the last few wars. The communists have turned it into a rolling fortress, bristling with guns and covered in corrugated sheets. Bronte wants to know if it's harming the planet before she'll get onboard, but her sisters are tired enough to overrule her. They settle in the back and let themselves be driven south. Kay tries to look out the window. His stomach always gets unsettled in motor vehicles. Never used to happen on horseback.

It's not long before they're surrounded by towers of brick and glass. Huge great buildings that reach up to pierce the belly of heaven. Even London didn't have buildings like this during the last war. He can't see the tops of them, even when he presses his head against the window of the bus. This can't be Mamucium, the old forgotten Roman holdfast with a few pigpens propped up against the old walls. It was a ruin even in the old days, but he rebuilt the walls a little, made a rampart around it. Put new thatch on the hall. Turned it into a home. Then when Wyn came to live with him she made it like a garden inside the walls. Planted mulberry trees and yellow celandine. It's probably under a car park now.

The Romans built Mamucium at the place where the two rivers met, the Medlwc and the Arwl. There used to be a shrine to Nimue in the confluence, a tall stone pillar rising from the water, with her Roman name carved into it.

He wouldn't know where to look, in this vast city, for the river, or the shrine, or the ruins of his home. Somewhere under these glass towers, these grey streets. Even the red bricks are old now, when they once seemed strange and new. It's this sort of thing that makes his bones remember their age. Easier to fool them when he's walking over moorland or through a forest. You can make them forget that they ought to be dust in the cold ground. But when he arrives somewhere like this, it feels even more profane than usual, his walking and breathing and thinking. Like his bones are questioning the magic. He has to hold them together by force of will.

There's distant gunfire, as they drive further. Mariam spends the bus ride explaining the differences between the factions to Kay. The people here were hungry, so they rioted. They were angry with the people down in London, so they had a revolution. And then the revolutionaries started fighting among themselves, which is what revolutionaries always do, as far as he can tell. Now there are roadblocks and barricades held by people from different groups with different armbands and different principles. There are too many acronyms and initials for him to fathom any of it. They are all communist, but some of them are more communist than others. Fighting over streets and buildings that didn't used to exist.

The more things change. Hate is the path of least resistance.

He remembers Britons fighting each other in the hills, over sheep and boundary stones, when they ought to have been fighting the Saxons. Finding reasons to despise the people that they had the most in common with, instead of banding together against the common foe.

The bus stops beneath one of the great glass towers. There's a statue outside of a man with a beard, and a great red banner hanging over the door. Words stitched into it in English. WELCOME TO THE PEOPLE'S REPUBLIC OF ENGELSGRAD.

Strange how the world turns. Kay remembers the winter of 1918, when they shipped him north to some frozen country. It was Churchill who sent him, rumbling balefully about the Red Peril. *'You must strangle Bolshevism in its cradle, Sir Kay! Before it spreads to our cities and infects our uninformed masses!'* He can remember the fear in Churchill's eyes. He can remember the men he served with, and the men he killed. They had fear in their eyes as well. Blood on the ice. Most of them barely old enough to shave.

Now there are young people here in Britain wearing red armbands, calling themselves communists. In his city, his Mamucium. So why did he have to go and kill those boys in the frozen north, however many years ago? Why did he have to fight them in Malaya? Stalking them through the jungle. Fire and death and more things he'd like to forget. Trees burning. People fleeing. What earthly purpose did it serve?

He's too tired and baffled to be outraged. It's always a mistake to try and make sense of things. Better to let it wash over you without fighting against it.

The communists show them up several long flights of stairs to a room which will be theirs for the next few days. Beds to sleep in and a table with food to eat. Mugs and kettles for making cups of tea. But the walls are made of glass. This is higher than he's ever been without flying in an aeroplane. The view's like nothing he's ever seen, looking out over the rooftops of a whole city in the evening light. It's dizzying. He's grateful for a place to rest his head. But how's he supposed to find Nimue in a place like this?

Morning comes suddenly. His wounds feel worse. Head pounding, where the Saint George men hit him with a pipe. When he reaches up to touch his scalp, he finds a hardness there that feels like wood.

The view outside seems friendlier in the morning light. When he stands by the window he can see for miles, to the outskirts of the city. The hills in the distance, low and grey, with white windmills turning on them.

This is still Mamucium. His old manor. Even if it looks different. Even if these communists have renamed it. It's still the same land, beneath it all. The same hills surrounding it. Worth remembering that.

They're all invited for breakfast in another room of the tower. It's not just them and the ten or twelve communist factions scowling at each other. There are rebels from other parts of the country, up from Cornwall and over from Wales and down from Cumbria. Delegations and envoys. People in modern war gear or strange clothing. Wild-looking men with long hair and their faces painted blue. The Welsh are here in huge numbers, wearing dragon armbands, with leeks and daffodils pinned to their uniforms. They look like a proper army. One that he might not mind fighting for, if they have their wits about them.

It's funny how it still lines up, how the mardier parts of Britain are still the same as they were two thousand years ago. Wild and unruly. The parts that won't suffer some honey-scented tyrant from Londinium telling them what to do. This is what they used to have to do when Saxons came knocking. Have a great meeting of the clans. Muster the war chiefs from Gwynedd and Powys, coax down the old northern kings from Rheged and Dun Eidyn. Get the Duke of Dumnonia on side. Hammer out an alliance. They didn't meet in glass towers in the old days, though. They met at Caer Moelydd, or other little timber forts. Hosting each other in their halls. Trying to put aside their grievances and work together for the common good. The good of the realm. Not a perfect kingdom, but a better one.

That's what these people are trying to do, as well, and they might be able to come to some kind of agreement. Save the realm from peril by themselves.

Then he might not have to wake up Arthur after all.

15

Mariam has never been keen on heights.

They're up on the forty billionth floor of this sky-scraper. She ends up standing by the window, frozen in horror. Staring down at Manchester, or Engelsgrad, or whatever it's called now. Somewhere in the grid of streets must be Stretford, where she used to live with her foster parents. Years ago. The house might still be standing, quiet and empty, or it might have been blown up by the Marxists or the People's Front or by some-body else who thinks they're right. She doesn't particularly want to go looking for it, either way. Not many happy memories buried in the rubble.

Her foster parents went south, when things got bad. Went to live with relatives in London. She stayed in Manchester through the food riots and the founding of the commune. She was there when the infighting started, the petty bickering. Different fac-tions disagreeing on how the city should be run. It started with meetings, then it became turf wars. Fighting street-to-street.

That's part of why she left Manchester, went up to Preston. Sick of the hospital changing hands every couple of days. Neither side giving them enough beds, enough bandages. Just more patients. She's not surprised now to come back and find them all still shooting at each other. The Marxists and the People's Front, who can't even agree on whether the city's called Engelsgrad or if it's still called Manchester. The Manchester People's Front aren't here, as far as she can tell. At least there's the Rainbow Liberation Army, with pride flags on their shoulders. Willow and Teoni are already getting friendly with them.

The other delegates are weirder than she expected. The Welsh have daffodils pinned to their combat fatigues. The Cumbrians have painted their faces blue. The Cornish have sent a pagan priestess, guarded by Morris dancers with submachine guns. There's a whole gaggle of priests from the Church of Noah, wearing their usual mix of dog collars and scuba-diving gear. And standing by himself is an ambassador from the Republic of Scotland, wearing an ordinary suit and tie, looking at the other rebels as if they're animals in Chester Zoo. Mariam can't help but feel for him.

Bronte knows the Cornish lady, somehow. They're talking about ley lines and healing crystals, so Mariam excuses herself and slips away. Standing at the edge of the room, with her back to the window, she offers a quick prayer and then tries one of the weird vegetable fritters that the Marxists have served up for breakfast.

There are probably people that she should be talking to. Mingling with. Making connections. But she was never very good at that kind of thing. She finds herself watching Kay instead. He's talking to the Welsh, asking questions about their army. It's comforting to have him here, making allies, asking the right questions. But she remembers what Roz said yesterday. It's always a relief to have a hero around. Somebody else to save the world, so that you don't have to do it.

One of the Welsh people comes up beside her, a red-haired young man with a leek pinned to his chest. He has a big jaw and rugby-player's shoulders, and he stares out the windows with a soft smile.

'Look at that view,' he says. 'I've heard you can see Snowdon from here, on a good day. But that's probably bollocks, eh?'

She nods and smiles. What do you say to a man wearing a leek on his chest?

'Have you ever been to Wales?' he asks.

'Uh, no,' she says.

'Oh, you should go,' he says. 'It's lovely. Especially this time of year.'

'I'll ... have to book a caravan holiday, sometime soon,' she says.

He laughs at that. 'I'm Gethin, by the way.'

'Mariam.'

'Who are you here with, then?'

'FETA.'

'What, like the cheese?'

She sighs. 'The Feminist Environmentalist Transgressive Alliance.'

'Oh, I know! You're the ones blew up that fracking place? Very nice work. That'll have pissed off a few people down in London, I should imagine!'

'Well it was ... me who set the charges, actually,' she says, unconsciously tucking a strand of hair behind her ear.

'Really?' he asks. 'Well, if you're in the business of blowing up oil rigs then there's another one you could do, for us. Just down off the coast of Cardiff. Hideous great thing.'

'The Avalon?' she asks.

'That's the one.'

Mariam feels a surge of hope, excitement, optimism. It's an unfamiliar sensation. Different from the despair and the creeping horror that she's become accustomed to. 'We want to blow it up as well,' she says. 'Or . . . well, we don't really want to blow it up. That would be bad. But we have another plan. A different plan.'

Gethin looks confused. 'Oh really? What is it?'

'Well . . .' she begins. She looks over at Kay. Finds her words failing her, and her mouth going dry. She can't tell this nice Welsh man about the Lady of the Lake.

Gethin looks like he's going to say something else when another Welshman lumbers over, draped in some sort of bearskin that doesn't look vegan. He glares down at Mariam without smiling.

'Ah, Dai, this is Mariam,' says Gethin. 'Mariam, this is Dai ap Llywelyn. The, uh, the King of Wales.'

She didn't even know that there was a King of Wales. 'Oh!' she says. 'Hi. Your . . . Majesty?'

'Mariam's with these eco-warriors, Dai,' says Gethin. 'FETA, they're called.'

'Fel y caws?' asks the King of Wales.

'Ie,' says Gethin.

The King of Wales looks her up and down and grunts. Then he says something to Gethin in Welsh and claps him on the shoulder before walking away.

Gethin grins sheepishly at her. 'Sounds like I'm needed,' he says. 'Nice to meet you, though! I'll talk to you later, if we get the chance.'

The communists are trying to get everyone together so that the talks can begin. Mariam stands by the window for a moment longer and takes out her brick phone. The device is so old that it can't run apps, which makes it harder for Saxon to track. She finds the number of her foster parents and types out a quick text message.

Still alive. Hope you're okay xxx

The communists herd them through to a conference room, where a narrow table stretches along the width of the building. The communists sit at one end, under a portrait of Friedrich Engels, with his massive beard. Everyone else hurries to sit as close to them as possible, fighting over seats.

Kay sighs, looking up and down at the long table. On the verge of saying something.

'What?' Mariam asks.

'This is why . . .' says Kay, making a circle with his hands. 'Ah, never mind.'

They sit down beside each other, somewhere in the middle of the table. It's only the King of Wales who stands back and lets the others jostle for seats. When they're all finished, he sits down by himself at the far end of the table. The other Welshmen stand behind him with their arms folded. A few of the delegates look as if they'd like to change seats.

The priests from the Church of Noah want to bless the meeting room before the conference starts. They stand and offer up a prayer, asking God to witness their efforts here today. Forgive their sins and make the Second Flood recede. That makes everyone else feel vaguely uncomfortable right out of the gate. Marxists and Cumbrians and everyone else briefly united in their embarrassment.

There are two communist leaders at the head of the table. The Rainbow Liberation Army commander is called Leo; they wear a pink beret on their head and a nonbinary pride flag on their combat gear. The leader of the Marxists is called Tarquin. He is bald and bespectacled and wearing a blazer with a red armband. He clears his throat.

'Comrades,' he says, in a Yorkshire accent. 'On behalf of the Central Executive Committee of the People's Republic of Engelsgrad, I'm thrilled to welcome you all here to Engelsgrad for these historic talks. I'd like to start by apologising for the absence of the Manchester People's Front, who have chosen to boycott these talks because they don't want to be seen as associating with Welsh nationalists or violent eco-terrorists.'

'Fucking centrists,' says Leo, quietly. There are a few jeers of agreement.

'However,' says Tarquin, 'the Rainbow Liberation Army and the Engelsgrad Revolutionary Guard are both keen to forge an alliance with eco-warriors. And we'd be very interested in any training workshops you'd be willing to run on how to destroy the machinery of the capitalist oligarchy.'

'Um,' says Mariam, swallowing.

Tarquin keeps talking. 'We're also particularly glad to welcome representatives from the Cornish Independence League, who've had a very long journey to get here—'

The King of Wales stands up, at the far end of the table. Grumbling deep in his throat. Tarquin falls silent. Once the king has drawn himself up, he takes a deep breath like he's about to blow their house down. Then he launches into a speech, in florid Welsh, in a booming voice so deep and resonant that it makes the windows rattle. Mariam finds herself weirdly hypnotised. It sounds beautiful, even though she has no idea what it means. He's obviously good at public speaking: stopping in all the right places, stressing all the right syllables, making all of the right hand gestures. He holds the attention of the room for two or three minutes. Then he sits down again. The whole Welsh delegation bursts into thunderous applause. Kay is chuckling to himself, beside her.

'Okay,' says Leo. 'If all delegates could agree to speak in English, for the duration of the conference . . . ?'

Gethin shakes his head. 'The King of Wales, Dai ap Llywelyn, refuses to speak the language of those who colonised our great nation. It will not sully his tongue.'

'Right,' says Tarquin. 'Are you happy to translate for him?'

'I do not speak for the King of Wales,' says Gethin. 'He speaks for himself.'

'Terrific,' says Tarquin. 'Can anyone else here speak Welsh?'

'I can,' says Kay. 'King Dai's saying that we don't have time for all this talking, and we ought to be forging an alliance as quickly as possible. And I think I agree with him.'

'And who, er, who are you?' asks Tarquin.

'I'm Kay.'

'And who do you represent?'

'The people of Britain?'

Tarquin looks dubious. 'As do we all,' he says. 'I'm sure we're all keen to proceed. So perhaps we could skip the rest of the opening remarks. But—'

'Aye, let's get on with it,' says one of the Cumbrians. 'First off, we're not keen on all of this communist bollocks. And we're not taking in any refugees, or any of that.'

'Aye,' says someone else. 'Cumbria for the Cumbrians!'

'Well . . .' says Tarquin. He swallows. 'The People's Republic of Engelsgrad expects that all parties represented here today will accept a *small* number of refugees from Engelsgrad and the flooded regions of Yorkshire . . .'

The delegates start shouting, and they don't stop. Whenever Tarquin calls for order, the Cumbrians shout him down. Dai ap Llywelyn stands up and starts orating again, pounding his fist against the table. Mariam tries to make her voice heard, but she is never quite quick enough. When she opens her mouth to speak, there are already three people talking. Eventually Willow speaks up, standing and shouting over all of these loud men.

'Before FETA gets into any kind of alliance with anyone,' she says, 'we need a commitment from all of you to go completely carbon neutral and embrace alternative fuel sources!'

'That would have to exclude Welsh coal,' says Gethin. 'We've been opening new pits. Coal power's the lifeblood of New Gwynedd.'

That's enough to stun Bronte out of her silence. 'Oh my God. That's, like, a crime against the planet? We're not working with *you*.'

'Comrades,' says Tarquin. He isn't smiling anymore. 'Comrades. We can focus on saving the planet once we've established a free and fair society that's equitable for everyone. We'll implement green energy solutions once the whole island of Britain is integrated into our communist system.'

'The whole island?' asks Gethin. 'The Kingdom of New Gwynedd is a sovereign nation, ruled by King Dai. It's not going to join your little student union any time soon.'

Leo wrinkles their nose. 'Well, monarchy's an inherently anti-communist and counter-revolutionary form of government. So I don't think we recognise the legitimacy of King Dai, or any other monarch.'

'There goes Plan B,' says Kay, quietly.

The Welsh start roaring for recognition, and the communists start shouting back at them, and the priests from the Church of Noah start praying for calm. The despair wells up in Mariam's chest and keeps rising until it's pressing down on her shoulders, compressing her heart. They lost Dando, coming down here. They left a lot of women in the Preston camp without protection. Because they thought that this conference would get them closer to saving the planet. Not because they wanted to come down here and have more pointless arguments.

She stands up and starts speaking, mouth moving faster than her brain. 'Listen!' she says. 'We all want different things, but we're all fighting the same people. We're all trying to get rid of the government and the oil barons and the private military companies. So let's help each other to do that. Then we can worry about making everything else better. And there's something else that we need to—'

There's the sound of something tearing through the air, and then the building shudders. A bang echoes from several floors below, followed by the sound of glass shattering. Kay is on his feet in an instant, reaching for his sword. Pressing Mariam's shoulder down with his free hand. She lets him push her down under the table, and then she wonders why. She should have pushed back. Stood her ground. She won't let him do it again.

There are other people taking cover. She finds herself face-to-face with Tarquin, under the table.

'Is it Saxons?' she asks.

'No,' says Tarquin. 'It's the Manchester People's Front. They've broken the ceasefire.'

'Fucking centrists!' says Leo.

'Comrades,' says Tarquin, 'don't be alarmed! This is just a brief mortar attack. Nothing to be concerned about. Happens every day. Let's all head down to the secure basement until it's over.'

So that's what they do, winding their way down ten or twenty staircases. Communist fighters charge up in the other direction, while the building shakes around them.

They sit in the basement for a long couple of hours, arguing pointlessly, while the shells fall above them.

As soon as the mortars stop firing, Tarquin calls a break for lunch. Mariam leaves the conference, storming out past the sentries, past the statue of Friedrich Engels. The glass tower stands next to the canal, or the river, or whatever it is. She can sit on the edge of a walkway and dangle her legs over the side, staring down into the water, which is just a stream really, trickling between two brick walls. There are bottles and shopping trollies lying along the banks. It's as good a place as any to despair about the state of the world.

She realises after a while that Kay is standing next to her. Looming over her. She feels her shoulders tense.

'Just . . . fuck off, for a minute,' she says. 'Give me some space.'

'You should be careful,' he says. 'Might be snipers about.'

She scoffs at him. 'And what are you going to do if there *are* snipers? Are you gonna throw your sword at them?'

He looks out across the river, like he's considering the physics of it. She stares back down at the water below her feet, listening to it trickling for a while.

'I don't need protecting,' she says. 'And I want some space. So go back inside and leave me alone.'

He doesn't. He stays where he is, turning over loose stones with one toe of his leather boots. Eventually he clears his throat.

'Do you want to tell me why you're so angry?' he asks.

It explodes out of her. 'Because of everything! Because of all that bullshit in there. The world's getting warmer every second and everyone's too busy arguing to do anything about it. We're not going to get anything done if we keep demanding too much from each other. We're focusing on all of these tiny differences when we should be organising and working together and looking at the big picture. So this whole thing is a pointless waste of time.'

'Why don't you go in there and tell them all of that?'

'Because they won't listen. Nobody's going to take any refugees, and the Welsh are never gonna go green, and we're never gonna swear allegiance to a guy calling himself the king of Wales.'

'Smart move sometimes, to have a rebel king,' says Kay. 'Or queen. Someone that the people can rally behind. You know, when Maud was fighting her cousin Stephen, she ... '

'And then there's you!' says Mariam. She turns around and glares at him. 'With your fucking *sword*, and your fucking *dragon*. You shouldn't even exist.'

'I know I shouldn't,' he says, quietly. He reaches up to scratch his scalp, squinting up at the tall buildings around him. Then he leans on the barrier next to her. She can smell him, that smell of soil and metal and old forgotten things. She looks sideways at the thin leather bindings around his feet, then up into his face. Realising for the first time how tired he looks.

'It's hard, this kind of thing,' says Kay. 'It never comes easy.'

'What kind of thing?'

'Leading people,' says Kay.

'I don't want to lead people.'

'Well, banding people together. Making them set down their little grievances and fight alongside each other. Kill the real enemy, instead of killing each other.'

'Ugh,' says Mariam. 'Killing people doesn't help anyone. I don't understand why people think that trying to kill each other is going to make any kind of difference.'

Kay sighs a long and weary sigh, through his nostrils. 'People die, in war. Sometimes killing people is the only thing that can make a difference.'

'Does it, though?' she asks. 'You keep coming back and fighting in wars and killing people and feeling like you've saved the world ... but it doesn't actually make things better, does it? It doesn't stop the wars from happening. Have you ever actually made the world better by killing someone?'

He looks hurt, confused. Maybe even angry. But he doesn't have an answer to that question. He stares into the river, saying nothing.

She sits with him for a little while longer, in case he has anything else to say. But she feels the growing urge to leave this place, to go and do something useful. So she stands up and brushes off her hands. Walking away up the path, towards the city.

'Where are you going?' he calls after her.

'I'm done arguing,' she says. 'I'm going somewhere I can make a difference.'

She can leave the knights and dragons and communists behind her for a little while, at least. The hospital's only a ten-minute walk.

16

Kay stands alone on the path above the river, watching Mariam walk away into the city. Nothing to be gained by chasing after her now. Better to let her come back in her own time. He remembers learning that, in the very old days. When he did one thing or another to aggrieve Hildwyn she'd saddle her horse and go off riding in the greenwood by herself. And he'd fret for her safety, thinking she might fall from the saddle or be set upon by bandits along the road. But she always came back, in time.

At least he's found the river. There's a metal sign which says that this is the River Medlock, and he can hardly believe it. The Medlwc was a proud, surging thing. Now it's reduced to a stream trapped between buildings, following an artificial course, rendered old and strange by the city looming over it. The water is shallow and murky, full of rubbish. A strangled trickle over a bed of rocks.

Kay checks to see that no-one's watching, then he ducks down under the barriers, making his way carefully down the steep bank. He lets his feet carry him down until he's standing in the shallows. Old river mud is better than steel and glass and carpet. He stands there soaking his foot bindings for a few minutes. Closing his eyes. Trying to let his aches and his worries bleed from him. Trying to feel calm and clear-headed. Focusing on the sound of the water babbling around him.

Then he hears a sickly cough from further downriver. When he looks up, there's somebody sitting there who wasn't there before. She's perched on a stone ledge, under a red-brick arch, wearing a hooded jacket that looks like it's seen better days.

He wades over, with worry growing in his stomach. She doesn't look at all well. He can see the yellow eyes peering out from under her hood, but they look sadder than they used to. Her silver skin has lost its former lustre. Some of the scales on her face are missing, showing patches of sickly yellow underneath. The lower half of her body is covered by a sleeping bag, with her feet or fins soaking in the river. There's a plastic bottle of cheap cider or some other swill on the ledge beside her.

'All right, Kay,' says Nimue. Even in the old days her voice was faint and reedy, but now it has a croaking rasp to it that doesn't sound healthy. 'Looking well.'

'Christ,' he says. 'You look like shit.'

She tuts. 'Always were a charmer.'

'How did you end up down here?'

'Wish I knew,' she says. She looks up and down the river with a puzzled expression. 'Just where I ended up, I suppose. Can't do much about it. I go with the flow.'

'Right,' he says. He's sceptical, but he doesn't say as much.

He wades over and sits down next to her. There's a rancid smell. She shuffles away from him as if she's suddenly bashful. The sleeping bag flops once against the ledge.

'Been a rough few centuries for you, has it?' he asks.

She laughs. It's a heartbreaking sound, coarse and gurgling. 'You could say that.'

Nimue picks up the bottle and offers it to Kay with a webbed hand. It's not best practice to refuse gifts from river goddesses, so he takes it and swigs from the neck. It tastes like sour apples, picked up off the ground and bitten into after they've turned bad. He almost chokes on it, and she cackles at him.

'Why are you poisoning yourself with this stuff?' he asks.

'Weren't *my* idea,' she says. 'Somebody threw it off the bridge.'

He shakes his head. 'I don't know,' he says. 'The shit people throw away. Not worrying about where it ends up.'

She grins at him, with sharp black teeth. 'That's what rivers are for. Washing away shit.'

'Not this much shit, surely.'

'Hm,' she says. 'What brings you here, anyway? As if I don't already know.'

'I'm with these idiots,' he says, jerking his thumb towards the glass tower. 'Trying to sort out the realm.'

She makes a knowing kind of sound. 'Oh, aye. And how's that going?'

'About as well as you'd expect.'

She offers him the bottle and he takes another swig, regretting it immediately.

Nimue shakes her head. 'I can't see the point in trying, meself. Sorting all this out. Where would you start? It'd be like . . . standing against the current. Trying to stop the river from flowing. With a rusty sieve.'

'Well, we've got to try, at least,' he says. 'I know we can't fix everything overnight, but we can make a bit of a difference. That's all anyone can ever hope to do. Whether they're mortal or immortal or anything else.'

'Hmmph.'

He smiles at her. 'Be a lot easier if we had a river goddess on our side.'

She pulls a face. 'Oh, you know me. I try not to get involved. Affairs of mortal men are nowt to do with me.'

'Bollocks.'

'Bah.'

'What was that business at Nantwich, then? In Cromwell's war?'

Nimue tries to look innocent. 'Don't know what you mean.'

'Yes you do.'

'Sometimes rivers just thaw out on their own, all right? Sometimes bridges get swept away. It's not always me behind it.'

'Right. And if there's some cavalier geezer trying to bring his cavalry across the bridge when it washes away then that's just a coincidence, is it?'

Nimue takes another slug of cider before she speaks. 'All right, that one *was* me. But he was a right tosser, and he had it coming.'

'See, you pretend you're above it all, but you're not. You've got involved before.'

'Yeah, and look where it got me!' she says.

She puts down the bottle long enough to peel the sleeve away from her arm. The foul smell gets fouler. Whatever's under the fabric is hard to look at. It doesn't look like skin or scales. He doesn't want to know what it is, and he's grateful when she pulls the sleeve back down again.

'Never makes any bloody difference. Same fucking story either way,' she says. 'All these different people are as bad as each other. None of them give a shit about me. Don't see why I should give a shit about them.'

Hard to argue with her, after everything he's seen in the glass tower. He sits and scratches the back of his head. Thinking about the realm.

'Herne told me to find you,' he says.

'Well, Herne can sod off. Mouldy old badger-fucker.'

Kay laughs and shakes his head. 'I'll tell him you said that, next time I see him.'

'I'll tell him myself.'

He scratches the back of his neck. 'He's worried. About the birds and the beasts.'

'Worried about himself, more like,' says Nimue. 'Mind you, he's right to be. I don't even want to tell you how many fish have been dying recently. Too bloody depressing.'

Neither of them says anything for a while. Kay stares at a tin-foil packet that's trapped against a brick on the other side of the river, bobbing in the current.

'He reckons it's time.'

Nimue spits a globule of something foul into the water, then wipes her hand on her sleeve. 'Bollocks to him. Do you think it would do anyone any good, bringing your brother back?'

'I'm not sure,' he says. 'I thought these rebels might be able to sort things out, but they don't seem like they can find their arses with both hands. It might be that he's the only one who can fix things. I don't know.'

'You of all people ought to know better. When did he ever fix anything? Just broke things, mostly. With that bloody sword.'

'Have you still got it?' he asks.

Nimue snorts at him. 'What sort of question's that? Course I've still got it. Been looking after it for this long. I'm not just going to lose it, am I? Or give it to the likes of you on a whim.'

'Why not?'

'Fuck off, you don't really want it. Do you want to be King of the Britons?'

Kay thinks about it honestly, for a moment. Wielding that kind of power. He never wanted it, in the old days. Only held the sword aloft for the briefest of moments, when everyone thought it was him who'd pulled it free. People kneeling in front of him. And he was so young then that it scared him to his marrow, the idea of ruling the realm. So he told the truth, in that moment of terror. He said it was Arthur who'd pulled it out. He couldn't give it back fast enough. Throwing Arthur to the lions. His little brother.

Would it be any different, now? Having the power to help people, to really change things? It might be worth it. All the weight of responsibility. Maybe he could bear it. Maybe he couldn't.

'No,' says Nimue, after a while. 'That's what I thought.'

His eyes trail downwards. The sword isn't anywhere on her person, that he can see. But then this sickly form beside him is just one aspect of what Nimue actually is. She's every river in the realm, every stream or limpid pool. The sword could be anywhere or everywhere. Hidden in an underwater cave. Spread finely in the morning mist. Raining down on the mountains in the old north. She could fetch it at a moment's notice, if she wanted to.

'There's a dragon, Nim,' he says. 'I need the sword to slay it. Soon as I'm done I'll throw it in the nearest pond.'

'Oh, aye? Pull the other one. You'd be amazed how many times I've heard that. "I just need it for five minutes, honest, I'll give it back after." And do they? Do they fuck. It's always too tempting to just keep it. Once you've run out of dragons to slay you start looking for other things you can kill instead. That's what happened to Arthur.'

'You don't have to tell me that,' he says. 'I was there.'

'Aye, which is why you should know better. It's nothing but trouble, that sword. So I think I'll hold onto it, if it's all the same to you.'

He stares down at the river, dribbling along its course. Mariam won't be happy if he goes back to her without the sword. Herne

219

won't be happy either, if he doesn't do as he was bidden. But he tries to think about what would make him happy. What would make Wyn happy, up in heaven? Somebody has to set the realm to rights. If not him or Arthur then somebody else. Somebody who can be trusted. Somebody who desperately wants to do the right thing.

'Look,' he says. 'There's this young woman I know.'

Nimue makes an incredulous sound. 'Yeah, I heard her up there. Trying to take the world on her shoulders.'

'If you don't trust me with Caliburn, you could give it to her. Her heart's in the right place. Head screwed on straight.'

'Oh, well,' Nimue scoffs. 'Head screwed on straight. Is that all it takes these days? I don't give it to just any fucker, you know. They have to pass muster. Have to be pure of heart, and all that bollocks.'

Kay squints. 'Why did you give it to Arthur, then?'

'Why d'you think? 'Cause Merlin told me to. He says, "Here's this scrawny ginger lad, it's his destiny to fix everything, give him the sword", and I do. Because I was young enough to believe it, back then. Not because I thought he was pure of heart.'

'Right,' says Kay. 'Makes a lot of sense.'

'Not likely to do it again in a hurry,' she says. 'So I suppose I'll be looking after the bloody thing forever, until all the fish have died and all the rivers have dried up. Then any fucker can have it, if they can find it. I won't be around to worry about it, then.'

'Hm.'

'What's so special about this lass, anyway?'

'I'm not sure,' says Kay. 'Maybe nothing. Maybe everything.'

She grins at him, suddenly. 'You soft on her?'

'No,' he says. 'It's not like that.'

'Christ, when was the last time you got your leg over? Eh?' She elbows him in the ribs. 'You have shagged *someone* in the last thousand years, haven't you?'

'Don't see how it's any of your business.'

'So that's a no, then. That's tragic, that is.'

'Well, if you're going to be unpleasant, I'll be off. Got to make sure these rebels don't kill each other.'

'Better you than me.'

'Look,' he says, standing up. 'If you won't give me the sword . . . there's something they want to destroy, down south. This iron fortress, in the sea. And they can't do it with fire, as far as I can tell. So thought maybe you could do it with water, somehow.'

She frowns at him. 'I've told you, love, I'm not lifting a finger. Mortals can kill each other well enough without me getting involved.'

He tries to think of something to say, some trade or bargain that might win her over. You used to be able to bargain with the old gods, sometimes. But here she is, down in this dank place, turning sickly. There's not much he can offer her. He can't clean the rivers and make the realm right again.

'Well,' he says. 'Keep an eye on her, at least.'

She nods. 'I'll do that much.'

'Take care of yourself.'

'And you, pet. Nice to catch up. See you again in another thousand years or so.'

She shuffles slightly on the ledge where she's sitting, then leaps forward like a fish jumping upstream, further than a mortal person could leap. The river's not shallow enough for a person to disappear into it, but that doesn't stop Nimue. It's not even deep enough to cover Kay's feet. But she plunges into it as if it were a cavernous lagoon.

He shakes his head and wades back towards the tower, picking up an errant piece of rubbish on his way.

17

Mariam feels childish, storming away from her problems. And she feels bad taking them out on Kay. It's not his fault that the other rebels are useless.

Her feet take her through Deansgate and down Oxford Road, which the communists have renamed to something else. They're building something here, in this city, but they're destroying it at the same time. There are ruined buildings and piles of rubble, but there are soup kitchens as well. The posh hotels have become shelters for people who have nowhere else to go. They've turned the old law firms and office buildings into vertical farms, with different vegetables growing on each floor. It's almost nice, if you ignore the spent bullet casings rolling on the ground.

She walks all the way down, under the Mancunian Way, where homeless people used to sit beneath the overpass. Now there are anti-aircraft guns on top of it. One of the factions has parked a bus across the road, under the bridge, to use as a kind of barricade. Engine idling. Fumes blurring the air. The communists stand around it with their rifles, trying to stay cool in the midday heat. They don't do anything to hinder her as she walks past.

Mariam goes through the university, where she only spent a year and a half. Came with her mum for the open day. Had her first-year lectures in the big building that looks like a tin can. Went to Climate Action Now meetings in the Students' Union. It feels longer ago than it actually was. It still seemed possible back then that none of this would happen. That the world might continue normally, and she might be a normal person, with a normal life. Even then, though, she remembers feeling torn. Like there was a fork in the road ahead of her, or two branches stretching off from each other. Hard to know which future to expect – the one her foster parents imagined for her, or the one she felt was coming.

Eventually she reaches the hospital, which used to be the Royal Infirmary. Now they're calling it the Thora Silverthorne People's Hospital. She has no idea who Thora Silverthorne is or was, but as long as it's still a hospital it doesn't matter what it's called.

The communists must have run out of space in the hospital itself, so they've created a makeshift triage ward in the multi-storey car park. No cars to park there anymore, so that makes a certain kind of sense. There's a man outside smoking a roll-up, leaning back against the wall. He has a red cross armband sewn onto the sleeve of his jumpsuit.

'Hey,' she says to him. 'Do you know if I can just . . . do a shift? I was training as a nurse before all of this.'

'Be my fucking guest, love,' he says in a Burnley accent. His eyes are bloodshot behind his glasses, with grey bags under them.

So she pulls her scarf up over her mouth and goes inside, passing somebody lying in the stairwell. She stands to one side so that two people can awkwardly wrestle a stretcher down the stairs. The woman in the stretcher looks so pale that she must be dead.

The first floor is chaos. It's like the Preston camp, except worse.

There are more people and fewer beds. No precautions made for Arctic Microbe Disease. Patients sprawled on folding cots or lying in between them. Left on old mattresses if they're lucky. There are medics doing surgery right here in the triage ward, under lights powered by a car battery. This must be where the wounded fighters are brought in. Getting bullets dug out of their stomachs without anaesthetic.

She walks through in a daze, trying not to get in anybody's way. And eventually she finds a nurse's station and gets to work.

Two hours later Mariam is sore and sweaty and filthy and ready to collapse. But she doesn't feel done yet. When she thinks about the tower of smoke over Preston she feels like she still has debts to pay. Maybe she can pay them here.

She goes down another row of beds to see if anyone has wounds that need dressing. There's a woman sleeping with her leg amputated above the knee. Two or three more with only minor wounds. Then she stops at a bed and shrieks. Lying on the cot is Hassan Aboukir, who she went to school with. She hasn't seen him for years.

'Oh my God,' she says, automatically. 'Hassan?'

Hassan raises his head and his whole face lights up. He doesn't look a healthy colour, even from here. But his smile is so warm and surprised that she has to smile back at him.

'Yooo!' says Hassan. 'Mariam? What the hell, fam? Long time no see!'

'What are you doing in here?' she asks him.

'Well, I got blown up, didn't I?' he says. 'But that don't matter. It's good to see you, fam! How you been?'

'Yeah ... I've, I've been good,' she lies. She can hear her accent changing. Trying to talk like a roadman. She tries to resist it, but it feels so natural to slip back into it. Talking like she did when she was at school.

'So you're with these communists now?' she asks. 'Didn't think you were into politics.'

'Nah, not really,' he says. 'They give you more food if you do shit for them, though, innit?'

'Right,' she says.

'It's dead, though,' he says. 'That's what I was doing when I got blown up. Was down in Didsbury or some place, I don't know. With my crew. 'Cause they put me in this labour detail, yeah? Cleaning shit up. And then the progs blew up the house we was in, and all this happened.'

He gestures to the dressing on his side. He's got some kind of burn across his whole chest, but there's a big wound down by his right abdomen that Mariam doesn't want to think about until she has to. She's just grateful that he didn't get hit in the mortar attack. That would have been one more thing to feel guilty about.

'So is you a nurse, now?' asks Hassan. 'Gonna be looking after me?'

He grins at her, and she has to laugh, because that's exactly the same grin he used to flash at all the girls at school, in the canteen or on the corridor. And the fact that she's laughing just makes him grin ever wider. But he still looks ill.

'No,' she says. 'Well, maybe. I'm just ... I was over in Deansgate, where they're having the big meeting. And it was ... it was pretty dead. So I came down here instead.'

'No shit?' asks Hassan. 'You got friends in high places?'

'I'm not sure I'd call them friends.'

She's distracted because she has seen the yellow colour of the dressing on his side. He scratches at it absent-mindedly while they talk.

'When was the last time someone changed that?' she asks.

'Hm?' he says. 'Oh, I don't know. Bare time ago. It's starting to smell nasty now.'

She tries to keep smiling. 'Okay,' she says. 'Well I'll change it for you, but I've got to get some stuff. I'll be back in five minutes. Stay there.'

'Yeah, yeah,' he says. 'I ain't going anywhere.'

Mariam scours three whole floors of the car park, ignoring other patients and medics, looking for clean gauze and tape and gloves and everything else that she needs. Then she finds her way back down to Hassan and sits by the side of his cot. There is a faint smell as soon as she gets near him. When she peels off the old dressing, it gets even worse. Probably infected. She feels something like an axe cutting down through her chest.

She'll have to find him some antibiotics. But where is she going to get those from? The wound needs dressing before she does anything else. She knows how to do that, even if she doesn't know how to save the planet or kill a dragon. She can change some-body's bandages. That makes her feel a bit better. Remembering her old training. She started skipping tutorials pretty quickly, as soon as her second year started and she went to her first few protests. Half of the lectures were only ever online anyway. But she knows how to do this.

'So you've been up there, yeah?' asks Hassan. 'Talking to the people in charge?'

'Yeah,' Mariam says. 'Although they're not really listen-ing to me.'

'Wha-at? They is dumb, then. You's like, the smartest person I know.'

'Aw,' she says. 'Thanks.'

'You've always been smart,' says Hassan. 'You've got them brains. You're educated, innit. So if they ain't listening to you, then . . . I don't know, fam. I hope they know what they're doing up there.'

'Well. All evidence to the contrary.'

'Wha?'

She smiles. 'They don't know shit, from what I've seen.'

He shakes his head. 'You know, that don't even surprise me? They just keep saying, "Aw, everything's gonna get better, if we all just keep fighting for a bit longer." But I think they're too busy fighting each other to actually make anything better. You get me?'

'Well, that's why I'm down here. I got sick of it all. I didn't feel like we were getting anything done. So I thought I'd come and . . . I don't know. Do something helpful.'

Hassan stares at her, with his head down against the pillow. There are beads of sweat on his forehead, from the effort of talking. 'Listen to me, yeah,' he says. 'I'm gonna lay down some wise Hassan advice for you. So listen up.'

'Okay.' Mariam laughs.

'If you've got that influence, yeah?' he says. 'If you've got a voice up there, and them people listen to you? Then don't you dare give that up, fam. 'Cause I've got no voice down here. And if I could go up there and tell them what I think, then I would. I'd tell them to stop messing about and sort this shit out. But I can't do that. So you've got to do it for me, yeah?'

'I will,' she hears herself saying. Before she can even think about it. Because what else can she say? 'I'll talk to them.'

She tries to find some antibiotics for him, but there aren't any in the whole hospital, as far as she can tell. By the time she leaves there are tears on her cheeks. She walks back up Oxford Road in a daze, not really noticing anything on the way back. Shaking with anger and purpose.

18

Lancelot stops south of the Mersey, staring at the long and empty road ahead of him, the blasted tarmac and the ruined overpass. Remembering another journey, long ago. When he rode up here with Galehaut, and Gwenhwyfar, fleeing from Arthur's rage. Looking for sanctuary. Sanctuary that Kay wasn't willing to give them.

He's never forgiven Kay for that. If Kay had just opened his hall to them, it could have prevented everything that came afterwards. But Kay had lain down his sword. He didn't want to pick it up again and wield it against his brother. And that was the cause of everything that happened after. The whole realm, crashing down around their ears. Every innocent slain, every hall burnt. It was all Kay's fault. Not his.

He crosses the Mersey with the Bee Gees blasting in his ears.. Trotting north through the outskirts of Manchester, past rows of ugly houses. Wondering how any of the miserable people in this miserable century find their way back to their miserable homes at the end of the miserable day. He's just starting to enjoy the music when the road is blocked by men with guns, fanning out from behind a row of wheely bins. They're wearing too much tactical gear, pointing their rifles at him. Screaming for him to get off the horse.

They sound American. Lancelot's hand goes to his sword. It would be therapeutic to spill a bit of blood. But they might shoot Rhiannon, and he's not sure he could cope with the death of his horse, after everything else recently. Not when he promised the poor barman that he'd look after her.

So he puts up his hands, pursing his lips, and climbs down from the saddle.

They grab him by the collar of his new jacket and drag him down the road, through a gate, into a sort of park. Not the kind of park where you could hunt deer. The kind of park where miserable modern people go kick footballs around. Now it's been turned into a sort of army camp. Huts and tents and giant sandbag walls, topped with barbed wire. Grass churned to mud by tyres and treads. There's a legion of tanks with their engines grumbling, idling in the mud and going nowhere. Flying machines sit with their rotors still. Air wavering with the heat of exhaust fumes. Soldiers sit on their machines or stand around looking bored. Almost as bored as he feels.

It's strange, this camp. There's a flag hanging limply from a pole, but it's not the flag of any nation. Just some letters on a blue field. Most of the soldiers have the same sigil somewhere on their body armour. He can't help but notice that there's something slightly off about their war gear. None of it matches. Piecemeal, different colours, different sizes. They're wearing caps and sunglasses. Baggy trousers. He's been present in enough wars to know that good soldiers pack light. These men are wearing far too much, especially for the weather. Laid down with useless clobber. Strange scarves and gorgets around their necks. Not soldiers. Men dressing up as soldiers. That doesn't bode enormously well.

He's dragged over to some portable cabins and shoved into an office that smells vaguely of sour meat. The plaque on the desk says COLONEL NASHORN. Some sort of American flag hangs from the wall, although it looks like there's something wrong with it. There are framed pictures of Colonel Nashorn standing over dead animals, grinning and wearing sunglasses. Colonel Nashorn with a rifle and a dead elephant. Colonel Nashorn with a longbow and a dead zebra. Colonel Nashorn with a fishing rod and a dead trout. The real Colonel Nashorn is reclining on a sofa, red-faced and pig-eyed, wearing a padded vest and an oversized set of combat fatigues. He is not grinning. He is chewing something and playing a video game on a widescreen television, murdering aliens with a Gatling gun. When Lancelot and the soldiers enter the cabin he looks over at them, but his thumbs keep moving on the controller.

'Who's this queer?' asks Nashorn.

'Not a god-damned clue, sir,' says the mercenary on Lancelot's left. 'Caught him on the perimeter, riding a fucking horse. Says he wants to talk to you.'

'Well, shit, Tyler, you should have just put a cap in him,' says Nashorn.

'Want me to do that now?' asks Tyler. He pulls a pistol out from his cargo pants.

'Ah, I wouldn't do that, if I were you,' says Lancelot, on his knees. 'My supervisors in London would be very upset if they found out that you killed one of their agents.'

'Agents?' asks Nashorn. He scrunches up his face, which makes him look even more like a walrus than he did already. 'What kind of agents?'

Lancelot reaches very slowly into his breast pocket, retrieves a piece of plastic, and throws it across the floor. The card is mostly meaningless, but it looks official.

Nashorn pauses his game and stands up, cursing under his breath. He seems to have trouble bending down to pick the card up, but he makes it into a performance of manliness, like a hunter kneeling down to look at bear shit. Grunting slightly too loudly. Squinting at the card like it's written in a foreign language. Lancelot isn't particularly impressed.

'My name's Mister Lake,' he says. 'I'm here representing the interests of His Majesty's government.'

'Well, shit,' says Nashorn. Grinning, suddenly, like in the pictures. 'How about that. It's a pleasure to meet you, Mister Lake, just a real huge pleasure. I'm sorry for any trouble our boys have given you, but they get a bit too excited sometimes. They're good boys, really. They're just protecting your investment! Keeping your country safe. Go on, boys, let him up.'

'Thank you,' says Lancelot, rising to his feet. 'Yes, they made me feel very safe.'

Nashorn claps a hand on his shoulder, shaking him firmly. 'So you rode in here on a horse? Never done much riding myself, but we could get a round of golf going, if you're up here long enough. Golf courses are just about the only good thing in this shithole country. If you'll pardon my saying so. We oughta just turn the whole place into a golf course.'

Lancelot forces himself to smile. 'Another time, perhaps.'

'My name's Augustus Nashorn. You can call me Gus. I'm Vice President of Urban Conflict Management with Saxon's Defence Solutions Team here in north England.'

'A pleasure to meet you, Colonel,' he lies.

'Well, I'm not strictly speaking a colonel anymore,' says Nashorn. 'Not officially, anyway. I tell you, one or two friendly-fire incidents is enough to end your whole career, nowadays. But the private sector's got more sense, of course.'

'Clearly,' says Lancelot.

'Now I assure you, Mister Lake, your government's investment is going to some real good use. Come outside, let me show you some of the hardware that you're paying for. We've got a shit-ton of tanks out here, and all sortsa other shit.'

They head outside the cabin. An entourage of other Americans appear, seemingly out of nowhere; some of them are in combat gear, others in suits and bulletproof vests. Nashorn leads them down a row of grumbling vehicles, talking endlessly but saying nothing.

'We've got a hell of an operation going here,' Nashorn is saying. 'I mean, some of this stuff's crazy, like science fiction. Look at this SOB! I love this thing. Wyatt, you tell him what it does.'

The soldier called Wyatt stands to attention. 'Uh, the primary armament fires bursts of microplastic fragmentation that don't appear on x-rays, which reduces the chances of surgical extraction and increases infection-related mortalities among enemy combatants.'

Nashorn slaps the side of the vehicle. 'Isn't that the coolest thing? They banned it in Europe, but we aren't in Europe anymore, are we? I always tell people, the Brits are our favourite clients. You never let regulations get in the way of a bit of fun.'

Lancelot tries to swallow but finds that his mouth is dry. 'I'm sure it's all very impressive, Colonel,' he says. 'But why is none of it moving?'

Nashorn was stroking the mudguard of his monstrosity, but now he stops, breathing loudly through his mouth for a few moments. 'Uh, moving?' he says. 'Oh, it all moves. It moves just fine! It's great at moving.'

'Why isn't it moving now?' he asks. 'You're supposed to be fighting these rebels, aren't you?'

Nashorn licks his lips, then moves a half-step closer. Bringing Lancelot into his confidence. 'Well, between you and me, Mister Lake ... all these woke snowflake types seem to wanna kill each other just as much as they wanna kill us. Hell if I know why. If they all stopped shooting each other and started shooting at us, we'd be in a whole heap of trouble! But as it is, we like to sit back and let 'em waste their ammo on each other. It'll make it easier for us when we do roll in.'

Lancelot can't argue with that. *Divide et impera*. But he's not going to sit and wait in this siege camp with these awful Americans for one second longer than he needs to. 'Colonel,' he says, 'there's something in that city that I need. It would be in the interests of national security if you could provide me with an escort.'

Nashorn looks gormless. 'Uh, you don't want to be going in there right now, Mister Lake. We're keeping tabs on a meeting of rebel leaders. Delicate situation. But we've got the situation monitored. Ain't that right, Troy? We've got situation monitored, don't we?'

'Yes, sir,' says a soldier in sunglasses. 'We have the building under observation.'

Lancelot is confused. 'You know which building they're in?'

Nashorn grins. 'Yes sir, Mister Lake. That's exactly the kind of premium intelligence that your government's paying for. Come on up this way and we'll show you.'

Beyond the ranks of armoured vehicles there's a kind of observation platform. Once he's standing on it, he can see glass towers in the distance. Four of them, glinting in the sunlight, past the treeline and the nearby houses. Far taller than any church spire. This can't be Mamucium, Kay's soggy little northern holdfast. Why would you build skyscrapers here?

The soldier named Troy hands him a pair of boxy binoculars,

which he raises to his eyes. The towers are even more ugly up close. One of them has a red banner hanging from it.

'The rebels are in that building?' he asks.

'That's right,' says Nashorn.

Lancelot feels something tighten in his stomach. Kay might be in that building.

'Can't you just fire a missile at it?' he asks.

'I love your thinking there, Mister Lake,' says Nashorn. 'You're a real connoisseur at this kind of thing, I can tell. But the thing is, Mister Lake, you see, most of those big skyscrapers over there were paid for by big ol' Chinese corporations.'

'Right.'

'They've got a lot of capital tied up in those buildings. And personally, I'd love to blow 'em up, just to piss off the goddamn Chinese. But the thing is, Mister Lake, you see, a lot of our shareholders are operating out of China as well. There's a lot of money coming out of China. And we don't want to piss off our shareholders. Even if they are Chinese. So I hear what you're saying there, and we do really value the interests of the British government – like I said, you're our favourite clients! But my hands are tied. We have zero clearance to, uh, engage any hostiles in the vicinity of those buildings.'

Lancelot is listening with one ear, but he is also looking through the viewfinder. He has seen something that makes him smile. Something large and serpentine in the distant air, winding its way towards the glass tower.

'And what about dragons, Colonel?' he asks.

'What's that now?'

'See for yourself.'

Nashorn snatches the viewfinder like a child snatching a toy. He peers through it, craning his neck and hunching his shoulders, until suddenly he freezes.

'Holy shit,' asks Nashorn. 'That's real? That ain't CGI?'

'Dragons have been native to England for over a thousand years,' says Lancelot. 'You could be the first man in centuries to kill one.'

Nashorn is still staring through the viewfinder, so Lancelot can't see his eyes. But other parts of him are betraying his thoughts. He is breathing very deeply.

'Well, holy shit,' he says. 'We got clearance to kill that thing? Where's that damn lawyer?'

The lawyer appears, thin and sallow, with a bulletproof vest over his suit and tie. He rearranges his glasses before he speaks.

'Uh, unfortunately, Mister Lake, any ... dragons, cryptids, or other large exotic animals wouldn't be covered by your government's current contract with Saxon PMC. If your government wants us to devote our resources towards dragons, that would require a contract renegotiation and a corresponding increase in the cost of our services.'

Colonel Nashorn makes a pained grumbling sound. Lancelot smiles. The trick with killing dragons is to find a chink in the armour. A loose scale to work your sword under. Get some leverage and prize it up. Colonel Nashorn has plenty of loose scales.

'Colonel,' he says. 'You're not the kind of fellow who lets regulations get in the way of a bit of fun, are you?'

Nashorn looks around at his lieutenants and then steps closer, so that Lancelot can smell his breath. 'Don't get me wrong, Mister Lake,' he says, in hushed tones. 'I'd sure as shit love to shoot this dragon down for you. Love to. It'd be my pleasure. But if I get on the wrong side of the legal department I'll be in a whole heap of trouble. They've got my balls in a vice.'

'Uh, sir,' says Troy. 'It appears that the flying creature is approaching the target building at this time.'

'See?' says Lancelot. 'If you shoot that dragon down, you'll just be protecting the investment of your shareholders! You'll be a hero.'

'Well, I . . . ' says Nashorn.

'You could pose with it, when it's dead,' he says. 'I'll even take your picture. They'll call you Colonel Dragonsbane, after that.'

'Sir,' says the lawyer, 'I really don't advise—'

'Ah, to hell with your advice,' says Nashorn. 'Saddle up, boys. We's goan' dragon hunting! Get these wagons rolling. Mister Lake, sir, do you wanna ride shotgun with me?'

'Thank you *very* kindly for the offer,' says Lancelot. 'But I brought a horse with me, and it would be a shame not to use it.'

'Get a load of this guy,' says Nashorn, grinning. 'I like your style, Mister Lake. All right, now, let's move on out!'

The camp descends into chaos. Men running in every direction, drones buzzing like hornets, war machines trying to roll out of the camp all at once. Lancelot finds his way through the traffic jam to the edge of the camp, into the narrow band of green that still exists around the edge of the park. Rhiannon is waiting for him, so he vaults onto her back.

19

Kay waits for Mariam outside the conference room, wondering what he will say to her. He'd like to try and mend the bonds between them, but that sort of mending has never been foremost among his talents. He'd rather mend a shield, or a straw roof. Apologising might be a good start in this situation. It might make her less angry when he moves on to the bad news.

The lift doors open and Mariam walks out of them looking like she's ready to win a battle against the Scots. He falters for words.

'Did you talk to Nimue?' she asks.

'Um . . .' he says. 'Well, yeah, I did, but—'

'Good,' she says. 'Come with me.'

He doesn't have much choice but to follow, trailing her into the conference room.

It doesn't seem as if they've missed much. Now the Cumbrians are threatening to block the aqueducts and let Manchester go thirsty unless the communists do what they want them to do. The communists are talking about the importance of the dialectical method. But they all look up when Mariam storms into the room.

'Your hospitals are a fucking disgrace,' she says.

The communist called Tarquin looks stunned. 'Erm,' he says. 'We'll be having a sub-committee meeting to discuss healthcare provisions on Thursday, but right now we're—'

'What is the point of all this if you're not even providing healthcare for people?' Mariam asks. 'Why are you bothering? Is it just so you can dress up like Lenin and feel good about yourself?'

'Mar,' says Willow, quietly. 'Why don't you sit down?'

'No, I'm not going to sit down,' she says. 'There's people suffering, all over the country. In the hospitals, and the refugee camps, and in their own homes, and everywhere else. If they could see how much time we're wasting in here, they'd be angry with us. Because we're their only chance of something better. Nobody else is going to come along and make the world a better place. That's down to us. So let's *stop arguing* with each other and start thinking together about how to beat the Saxons and the oil men and all the other bad people in the world. We don't have to be best friends. We don't even have to like each other. We just have to work together, and help each other, and figure out what to do next.'

Kay feels his heart glowing. Wishing that he had Caliburn right now, so that he could hand it to her on the spot.

'Felly beth ddylen ni ei wneud gyntaf?' asks the King of Wales, after a long moment.

Kay clears his throat. 'He's asking, what do you think we should do first?'

'I think we should destroy the Avalon rig,' she says. 'It's everything we're fighting against, all mixed up together. So let's make a plan and blow it up. To send a message to people. To show people that we mean business.'

'Yes,' says Tarquin. Warming to the idea. 'Yes! It's a physical

238

manifestation of the corporatocracy! Destroying it would send a powerful message.'

'We could wait until they've moved the government there,' suggests Gethin. 'Take them out all at once.'

The Scottish ambassador straightens his tie. 'The Republic of Scotland wouldn't necessarily oppose such a course of action.'

'How are you gonna do it, though?' asks Leo, from the RLF. 'I mean, yeah, great, smash capitalism, bash the fash. Well up for that. But won't it just cause another oil fire? Like the one in Preston?'

'Well,' says Mariam, 'my friend Kay here is going to explain.'

Kay wasn't expecting that. His stomach turns to ice, and he searches for words. Where to start? Does he start with himself? With King Arthur? With all the long history? Or does he just stick with the basics. Nimue. Water. Even then, he'd be lying. Nimue said that she wasn't going to help. There is no plan, no hope of destroying this sea-fort thing without blowing it up. He can't tell them that. But he has to tell them something.

'Well . . .' he begins, 'you might not believe this, but—'

He's rescued from saying any more when the Preston dragon sweeps past the windows, showing her armoured underbelly, close enough to rattle the glass with her wingbeats. Her long tail trails after her, spiked and knobbled like a club. The rebels are already standing up out of their chairs, turning around and hardly believing their eyes, when the dragon's tail flicks absent-mindedly and shatters the windows, sending shards of glass streaming inwards and exposing them all to the cold wind.

Kay's eyes meet Mariam's across the room.

'Stay here!' he shouts over the wind.

Then he runs, out of the room, into the corridor. He finds a grey-walled stairwell at the end of the corridor and charges up it, feeling his heart soaring in his chest. You shouldn't feel relieved or delighted when a dragon attacks, but that's what he feels. This is the kind of problem that he can solve with just his sword.

On each floor he stops long enough to peer through the door, checking to see if he's high enough yet. After four floors he can see sky, so he shoulders the door open. And he is standing on concrete, with the wind blowing fiercely, and only pillars above him. This tower is still unfinished. An orange fence is blowing in the wind around the sides of the building. Nothing else between him and the sky.

He can see over the whole city, past the maze of glass and stone and metal to the distant hills, with the white windmills. He can see beyond them, away to the west, over the plain and towards the sea. The lion's share of northwest Britain laid out before him. Most of it was his manor, once. Between the Mersey and the Vale of Lune. People used to mock him for it. Call it a backwater. The arse-end of Britain. He disagrees. It looks lovely, as far as he can see. Even now he can spare half a second to admire it.

But only half a second. The dragon writhes past, circling the whole building once before she pulls in her wings and drops out of view.

It's not just the dragon, either. The sky is full of Saxons and their machines. These buzzing whirligigs look even deadlier in the daylight than they did in darkness. Muscular things with four or five rotas, bristling with weapons. They are strafing the building, their guns sputtering downwards. He can't quite tell from here whether they're firing on the dragon or on the communists. The bigger machines have men hanging off them, dangling on ropes, trying to land on the building. He preferred it when Saxons came in boats.

After the view and the dragon and the whirligigs, the fourth thing Kay notices is that he's not the only person up here.

Standing near the netting is Regan, her hands outstretched and the wind blowing through her hair.

It dawns on him, then. He wonders why he didn't see it earlier. She isn't holding a magic wand or chanting ancient words, but he can tell from the way she's standing, from the fact that she's not frightened. She knew that the dragon was coming because she has summoned it here, to this place. She has been calling it up.

When she sees him, she makes no effort to hide it. She smiles at him, instead. Then she begins to change herself. Her clothes sprout spines and plumes. Her feet become talons. Her eyes widen. Her face becomes a beak. And then she leaps over the side of the building, plunging downwards.

Kay draws his sword. He runs to the barrier, looks down after her. Sees a feathered form take wing and glide towards the ground.

Sometimes if you kill the summoner, the beast disappears. Maybe the dragon will return to its slumber if he takes Regan down. He'd rather fight a witch than a dragon any day of the week. But how to get down? He can't turn into a bird, but there's some sort of chute leading downwards, at an angle. He doesn't know what it's made out of or whether it can hold his weight. But it leads all the way down.

He must be twenty floors up, at least. He could just turn around and hurry down the stairs. But then he'd lose her.

He sheathes his sword again, long enough to untie his shield from his arm. After a moment of fretting, he drops the shield down the chute. He doesn't like the speed with which it disappears. The sounds it makes as it goes down. But he's thrown it down, now. He has to go after it.

Kay pulls his staff free from its leather frog and throws that down as well. He drops his sword, blade-first, hoping that he doesn't land on it and do himself an injury. Then he whispers a prayer for Christ's protection and jumps down the chute himself.

He's done madder things over the years, but he can't think of any off the top of his head. He realises, very quickly, that this was not a good idea. The chute leads almost straight downwards. It's not a solid tube but a soft-sided thing that shifts around him, not slowing him down in the slightest. He is plunging through it like a stone. He will probably hit the ground and shatter his legs, then die slowly and wake up under his tree. It would serve him right for being an idiot. He realises that he's screaming, bellowing at the top of his lungs.

But the tube suddenly becomes more substantial. It's ribbed and hard around him, and segmented. Like being moved through the bowels of a plastic giant. It hurts more. He strikes his ribs on each of the narrow openings, then crashes through to the next one. But at least it's slowing him down slightly.

And then the chute curves gently, and he finds himself on his back. Still moving quickly. Too quickly. When the tube ends it shoots him out into daylight, into a pile of painful things. It knocks the wind out of his lungs.

He lies there, staring up into the sun, long enough to get his breath back and to realise that he's not dead. He is in a midden of some sort, a metal box for broken glass and bags of waste and other things that have been thrown down the chute. Nobody was thoughtful enough to throw down any pillows or mattresses.

Regan is down here somewhere. He has to find her. That's the only thing that makes him move his limbs, makes him pick himself up. Heaving himself upright isn't particularly fun – he may have cracked a rib or three – but that's fine. He's been through worse. No limbs broken, as far as he can tell.

He finds his shield, his sword. Buried up to the hilt in some brownish mess that he doesn't want to know the nature of. He wipes it on his cape. It takes longer than he might have liked to climb out of the rubbish, getting himself down to ground level. He's in a construction yard. There are machines around that must have once been used for building the glass tower. None of them will help him.

The staff is lying on the ground. When he picks it up it's hot to the touch. Crackling with potential.

The yard has a thin blue wall around it, with a gate leading out. It hurts to put weight on his right leg, but he hobbles over and peers into the street.

Outside there is war. Saxons are moving up the road towards the tower, armed with rifles and a kind of metal shield that he hasn't seen before. He'd never have foreseen shields making a comeback, but here they are. They don't seem to be doing much good, though. The communists are holding the entrance to the tower and firing down from the upper floors. Kay wouldn't want to storm a building like this, with the foe raining down bullets from five and ten floors above. But there are armoured vehicles coming up the road. Their cannons speak. Suddenly it's glass raining down instead of bullets. And then the Saxons make a run for it, charging the doors with battering rams.

If they've noticed him, they aren't doing anything about it. Enough to worry about without stray knights. He could go over and murder a few of them, but there's half a battalion here. They'd probably murder him back.

Another moment of confused loyalties. These men with the battering ram are just soldiers doing a job. He's been in their place more times than he wants to remember. Beneath the walls of a rebel town, hammering on the gates, with arrows and stones and hot oil and buckets of shit raining down on him. If things had been different he might be standing there with them. Marlowe could have woken him up, sent him to Manchester to deal with some rebels. Would he have done it? Maybe. Then he'd have been sheltering with the Saxon men, waiting to burst through the doors and slaughter some rebels. It might have been Mariam and the others whom he killed without a second thought.

All these years and he still thinks too much during battle. That's what gets him killed, more often than not. While he's busy thinking the Saxons break down the door and charge inside. Moving huge numbers into the lobby. Well, that's that. They've taken the ground floor. Now they'll have a hard fight to get upstairs. Getting Mariam out safely has just become a lot harder. And he still has a dragon to kill, and a witch to—

A white horse appears from between two armoured cars, and all other thoughts vanish from Kay's head. The horse is spooked by the noise and the chaos, but the rider knows how to handle his mount in a way that few people do nowadays. He calms the animal down, brings it around. Lets it gallop down the road to use up some nervous energy. There can't actually be a horse here, so it must be a vision, something from the Otherworld, a horse sent to him by the old gods. Except it isn't. The man on the horse raises his round shield above his head to protect himself from falling debris, and the shield is a golden lion on a blue field.

Something odd happens in your bones and stomach when you see someone you've hated for fourteen hundred years. It's been half a century, at least, since they last saw each other. It doesn't feel like long enough.

Lancelot comes closer, reining in his horse and staring up at the tower. Dressed in a suit. There can only be one reason why he's here.

Kay waits and spies on him. He could come around the corner with his staff brandished and turn Lancelot into a salamander, if he really wanted to. But it's hard to know whether the staff will heed his wishes at the best of times. It might turn him into a lion, or a dragon. That would be worse than having to deal with Lancelot in human form. But only slightly worse.

Instead of using the staff, Kay steps out from cover. The first wave of Saxons is already through the door now. It's just the two of them left in the street, with ten or twenty paces between them.

'Lance,' he says.

Lancelot recoils slightly in the saddle. His face shows something like relief, for the briefest of moments. Then it gets papered over by something closer to contempt.

'Kay,' says Lancelot. His eyes flicker downwards. 'Is that your old staff, or are you just pleased to see me?'

'I'm never pleased to see you.'

'No, well, the feeling's mutual,' says Lancelot. 'What, precisely, do you think you're doing up here? I'd love to know.'

He shrugs. 'Serving the realm.'

'You're on the wrong side, again. Why are you always on the wrong side? Do you just get a perverse pleasure out of it?'

'Looks like the right side to me,' says Kay. 'I'd rather try and make the realm a better place. Not just do whatever the men in London tell me to do.'

Lancelot pinches the bridge of his nose. 'Do you think bringing Arthur back is going to make the realm better?'

Kay doesn't have the patience for this. He squints and shakes his head. 'I don't want to bring him back!'

'So why are you here? Why do you have the staff?'

'I'm not planning to use it,' he says. 'Just looking after it. Make sure nobody else gets their hands on it.'

'Do you expect me to believe that?'

The dragon roars somewhere above them, loud enough to shake the ground and rattle their bones. They can't see it, but they can hear it. Lancelot looks up at the tower and his confidence falters.

Kay tries to swallow his pride. He tries to think of Mariam and the others, trapped in the tower.

'Look,' he says. 'We can fight that thing together, if you want. Just call off your men first. I've got friends in there. Don't want them getting shot.'

Lancelot seems to consider it for a moment. But then a goading smile appears on his face. 'I don't think I could call them off now, even if I wanted to,' he says. 'You know how it is. The dogs of war.'

Kay feels anger swelling in his chest. He remembers riding home to Mamucium and finding his home burnt to the ground. Wyn lying dead under the fallen rafters. It was some Saxon brigands who carried out the deed. Not these modern imitators but real Saxons from over near Brynaich, sacking any keep that flew Arthur's dragon banner. Lancelot's silver clinking in their purses. It wasn't Lancelot himself who barred the doors or threw the burning brands onto the thatch, but it might as well have been. It was never a distinction that mattered much to him.

'Call them off,' he says, through his teeth.

'Give me your staff and I'll consider it,' says Lancelot.

'I won't give you the staff,' says Kay. 'And if you're here for Caliburn, I won't let you have that either.'

Lancelot's smile broadens. 'I was hoping you'd say that,' he says.

They draw their swords. They each have advantages and disadvantages in this situation. Lancelot's mounted; he's got speed, downward thrust, the raw weight of horseflesh. Gravity and momentum on his side. He's not armoured, though, and neither is the horse. Plenty of soft places, plenty of vitals to pierce and arteries to nick. It's not pretty, seeing the blood gush out of a horse. But it gets the job done.

Kay stands in a fighting posture behind his shield. This fight won't be the best use of his time, but it won't take long. He wants to wipe the smirk off Lancelot's face.

Lancelot's already spurred his horse. He's coming at the gallop, charging down the street. There's a raw battle cry in his throat – not the name of Arthur or Britain or any of the saints, just his contempt, his indignation at being inconvenienced, all tearing up from his lungs. He stands in the stirrups and raises his sword high above his head, the better to bring it crashing down.

The other advantage Kay has is that Lancelot thinks he's an idiot. It's always worked in his favour, over the years. He brings his shield up over his head, as if he plans to shelter beneath it. Holding it up against Lancelot's downward blow. Which means Lancelot's going to change his sword stroke. Not from above but from below. Bringing the blade down beneath the shield to slice through Kay's chest.

Here he comes. Still shouting. Sure enough, Lancelot leans sideways in the saddle, until he's almost falling out of it. His weight isn't astride his horse anymore; it's off to the right. Only his knee on the saddle to keep him there, and his shield hand clutching the bridle. He is level with Kay. Eyes locked under the shield. His sword's about to fall, about to scythe through flesh.

Kay brings his shield back down in front of him, putting his whole weight behind it and bracing his feet. He wishes he could see the look on Lancelot's face, but he can't see through solid oak.

An almighty slam. Lancelot stops and the horse keeps going. Kay collapses backwards. The crash of Lancelot-against-shield knocks all the breath out of him, knocks him reeling, onto his arse. The horse gallops straight past him, catching his sword arm and nearly breaking his shoulder. Lancelot falls the other way, landing hard on his shoulder.

They are both sprawled on the floor, now. They allow each other a few moments of pain and groaning. Recovering their breath. Then they start to gather themselves up. Whoever does it the fastest will probably kill the other.

They're still scrambling to their feet when the Saxon cannons start to thunder once again. The armoured cars, firing into the air. Not at the glass tower, but at the dragon, which is now plunging from the sky, huge and terrible. Boring into Kay's soul with her massive eyes. Fire spills from her jaws.

This isn't a street that Kay wants to be on anymore. The tarmac is melting. The armoured cars are burning. Their ammunition goes off all at once, cooking and bursting. Lancelot's horse bolts to safety, screaming in the way that horses do. Kay helps Lancelot to his feet before Lance can protest. Leads him out of the inferno and away from the tower, towards the safety of the Medlwc. They agree without words that this is a short truce, just while they save their bones from being turned to ash. Then they can get on with the business of trying to kill each other. Kay risks a glance back over his shoulder and sees the dragon's head appear behind them. She breathes in deeply, and breathes another jet of fire after them.

They run with the fire at their backs. Kay reaches the railing and dives straight over it, landing on the bank of the Medlwc ten feet below. Rolling down into the river muck. Lancelot crashes down beside him. The fire shoots overhead.

And then they have to pick themselves up all over again. Grunting at new pains and indignities. They are in the river now, with the ancient dribble of its waters beneath their feet. Crisp packets still bobbing against the current. Nimue nowhere to be seen. The dragon doesn't seem to have followed them. It has turned its attention back to the tower, fire melting through glass and steel.

Mariam. Still in there, caught between the dragon and the Saxons. He shouldn't have let himself be drawn into this. But Lancelot is upright, rolling his shoulders. Getting into a war footing with one knee behind his shield.

'Wait,' he says. 'We need to—'

But Lancelot's not stopping for that. He charges forward and they meet swords again.

It's a harder fight by a country mile than the Nazis in the Preston camp. Centuries have flown by since the last time he had to spar like this, and it takes him a while to remember how. Lancelot makes the most of that. He was always among the best of them as a swordsman. He comes on strong with clever little feints and jabs. Beautiful wristwork. And always good at irritating people, getting under their skin. He checks his watch between sword strokes. Face so smug that it makes you furious. But if you act on that anger, if you lash out at him, then he strikes you like a serpent from the grass.

So you have to stay calm. Fight from behind your shield. Kay gives ground, wading carefully backwards, uncertain underfoot. And Lance comes on with all the old panache, all the flair and dash that used to impress the ladies. Ladies who didn't realise that Lancelot didn't return their interest.

Well, this isn't a show fight. Might be time to remind Lancelot of that. Kay ducks a lazy sword swipe, then comes up with his shield facing the sun. One quick jab with his shield arm, smashing Lancelot's top lip with the iron rim. Lancelot reels back, crying out, bringing his own shield up quickly to cover his vitals while he recovers from the blow.

That's bought Kay a moment's advantage. He could follow through right now, go in for the kill, get his swordpoint around Lancelot's shield and stick him in the bowels. Or else a nice bear hug, blade round the back, severing the spine. But he finds that he's quite enjoying this. He hasn't had the chance to give Lance a bloody nose for a good couple of centuries. Not since Naseby. So he takes the moment to recover his breath. Grinning and flexing his sword arm.

Lancelot sees the mirth in his eyes and growls at him. His

perfect teeth are red with blood. He comes forward with a cold new fury that Kay doesn't recognise, raining down blows from all quarters. Trying everything. Cutting below the rim of his shield, going round the side to pierce him through the ribs, swinging down from above to cleave through his neck or shoulders. Lunging at openings with his blade forward, straight for the heart. Kay blocks, moving his shield one way and then the other. Turning with it. Trying to spin on his heel and bring his own sword down as Lancelot goes past him, but Lancelot doesn't give him the opportunity. He has to give more ground, let himself be pushed downriver. He's never seen Lancelot fight like this before.

Eventually he runs out of ground to give. Brick walls close in on either side of him. The Medlwc disappears into a low culvert, or tunnel, with buildings over it. Quick glance over his shoulder and he can see the reflection of daylight, somewhere at the other end of the tunnel. So he ducks back into it, into this strange passageway with slimy walls. There are plants growing from the water, and empty bottles floating on the black surface. Kay wades back through them, into the darkness, trying to lure Lancelot after him. But Lancelot stops at the threshold to get his breath back. Wiping the blood from his mouth. Still seething from that blow to the face. There's something else there as well. Plenty of fuel on that fire. All Kay did was throw sparks on it. He tries to keep his own anger burning, but his curiosity builds until it gets the better of him.

'What's got you in such a foul mood, then?' he shouts, from the gloom.

'Fuck off,' says Lancelot.

'Nah, really,' says Kay. 'You . . . all right? Want to talk about it?'

'I want to kill you, slay the dragon, and go back to London,' says Lancelot. 'Unless you want to yield?'

'Not particularly.'

Lancelot sighs. 'Well, then.'

He wades forward. Kay raises his shield. They trade a few blows in the tunnel, but it's dark enough that neither of them can see a bloody thing. Bad place to make a stand. Worse place to die. The noise from the larger battle echoes strangely off the brickwork, the patter of automatic rifles and the rending dragon sounds. But their own fight is louder, more immediate. Their laboured breath and their feet moving through the water and their swords biting into each other's shields. Hard to focus on anything else.

Kay backs away further, and they're out the other side of the culvert, into daylight again. He was hoping it would lead somewhere half-defensible, but no such luck. They're in a small artificial lake, shallow and black-surfaced and full of rubbish. Brick towpaths on either side, and a metal footbridge over it. What has happened to the Medlwc? Does it just empty into this basin now, becoming a canal, losing all sense of itself as a wild thing that flows down from the hills? Kay hates it, the way people treat the world. People used to worship rivers. Now they brick them in, they make the water bend to their own will. They play at being gods themselves.

It's a mistake to start lamenting the state of the realm when you're halfway through a swordfight, especially if it's a swordfight against Lancelot. Kay gets caught out, has to block at an awkward angle, has to expose himself. Suddenly Lancelot is darting past him, ending up behind him. Whisking his sword across to catch him neatly on the hand. There's a crunch of steel passing through bone, and then he feels a mighty shock of pain. His sword drops from his hand and disappears beneath the water.

So there he is, swordless, bleeding. Clutching his injured wrist with his shield hand. It'll heal once he comes up from under his tree again, but that doesn't help him much in the present moment. Lancelot's sword tip appears at his throat, hovering close enough to kill him in half an instant. He can hear Lancelot panting. He must think that he's won.

'Right,' says Lancelot, once he's caught his breath. 'That's that over with. Now give me the staff. Can't have you running around with it.'

'No,' says Kay.

Lancelot groans. 'If you drag this out for much longer I'll be too tired to kill that dragon.'

Kay raises what's left of his hand. 'We could have killed it together,' he says. 'But it's a bit late for that now.'

No answer to that. Lancelot's swordpoint moves close to his gullet, but it doesn't plunge any deeper yet. It's difficult to know how Lancelot is feeling, from the look on his face.

'I don't have to kill you,' says Lancelot. 'Just give me the staff and you can go back to ... knitting your own yoghurt, or whatever it was you were doing with these tree-worshippers.'

'What, so you can bring Arthur back? Don't think so.'

'Why would *I* want to bring him back? He thinks I slept with his wife.'

'He's not overly fond of me, either.'

Lancelot growls at him. 'You stood with him, in the old days. In the last battle.'

'Because of what *you* did.'

'Just give me the staff!'

Behind Lancelot, a Saxon whirligig appears in the sky. Weaving out from behind a building on a frantic course. The reason for its arrival becomes plain when the dragon's head snakes out after it, trailing smoke from its nostrils. It breathes a gout of flame so bright and warm that Kay can feel the heat from where he's standing. The machine is consumed by fire. It falls from the sky, burning and misshapen, and crashes down somewhere on

252

the far side of the canal, where the roofs have caught fire and the plants are burning.

Lancelot turns to look at the dragon, so Kay grabs the head of his staff. He casts it up out of its belt loop and catches it further down the haft. Taking a firm grip with his injured hand, fist slickened by blood. When Lancelot turns back he's greeted by the staff's head, swinging sideways like a club. It meets him in the mouth and knocks his head sideways.

There's a tremendous crunch. Kay sees teeth flying. Lancelot staggers backwards, nearly falling back into the water. Wide-eyed. His bloody mouth pressed against his sword arm and screaming into it. The look in his eyes changes from shock and pain into something else. Unbridled rage.

'Well, you did ask for it,' says Kay.

Lancelot roars, showing his bloodied gums. He comes forward with his sword held high. Kay raises his shield against the blow. And they keep fighting, while the city burns around them.

20

Mariam wishes that she had a sword. Then she could run away from her responsibilities and charge upstairs to try and slay a dragon. It must be nice to be able to do that, whenever a dragon rears its ugly head.

'We need to get down to the bunker again,' she says. Following Tarquin and the other communists down the corridor.

But Leo is shaking their head. 'Nah, the fash have already taken the lower levels,' they say. 'We'll have to stay up here until we've fought them off.'

The dragon roars loud enough to shake the building. There are communist fighters charging up and down the corridor, carrying machine guns and rocket launchers and boxes of ammunition, most of which are stamped with Chinese characters. Tarquin leads the other rebel delegates back to the reception room, where the food is still laid out from breakfast. The windows here are bigger and south-facing. They are vibrating. The sky is full of Saxon drones and gunships, buzzing towards the tower.

The dragon snakes past them, shaking the windows with each wingbeat. Flying away from the tower towards the swarm of drones. It can't have any idea of what drones are, in its ancient dragon brain. And the drones can't be programmed to recognise what a dragon is. But that doesn't stop them from deciding to destroy each other. The sky fills with rocket trails and muzzle flashes, followed by a plume of dragon fire. The dragon uses its whole body as a weapon, biting and clawing, shattering drones with the end of its tail.

Mariam stands watching the violence, and so do all of the other rebels, until one of the windows is shattered by a stray bullet and brings them out of their trance. Rainbow soldiers are turning tables over and building barricades. Mariam ducks behind one of them, with the communist leaders.

'Look, comrades,' says Tarquin. 'It's mostly targeting the forces of capitalist oppression. Perhaps the dragon is an ally of the revolution?'

Leo shakes their head. 'Dragons are inherently bourgeois. The whole concept of dragons was invented to justify the existence of the land-owning warrior elite.'

'Ah,' says Tarquin. 'Yes, comrade. It must be destroyed by the people, to reaffirm the obsolescence of the feudal system.'

'Dragons are the national animal of Wales!' says Gethin from behind a different table. 'Killing it would be an act of aggression against New Gwynedd!'

'No,' says Dai ap Llywelyn.

It takes Mariam a moment to realise that Dai has spoken in English. She turns to look at him, but he is staring out the window with a hardness in his eyes.

'Welsh dragons are red,' says Dai. 'This one's white. Which means it's an English dragon. Not a Welsh one.'

'Oh,' says Gethin. 'So we *can* kill it, then?'

'Comrades!' says Tarquin. 'Comrades, we can discuss the dragon, or what to do about it, at a later time. Right now I suggest we continue with our negotiations. Our soldiers will keep us safe. We can deal with the dragon once we've secured an agreement that brings us closer to the international liberation of the workers.'

'Nah,' says Teoni. 'It killed my dog.'

Teoni has found a rocket launcher. One of the rainbow soldiers must have left it unattended. Now Teoni is resting it over her shoulder, kneeling next to Mariam and aiming through the window. Mariam can't say or do anything before Teoni pulls the trigger.

The blast feels like a nail being driven into each eardrum. Mariam covers her ears too late. She sees the rocket as a black shape flying away, punching through the air, leaving a trail of vapour behind it. It doesn't seem as though it will actually hit the dragon, but then the dragon twists into its path. She sees a bloom of flame somewhere near the dragon's head, the side of its neck. It writhes and recoils.

Teoni is punching the air in triumph, and Willow is trying to wrestle the rocket launcher away from her, but Mariam can't tell what either of them are saying. Her ears are still ringing. It sounds like she's underwater. But she can see what the dragon's doing. It has lost interest in the drone that it was chasing. Now it looks around at them. It stops where it is, dangling its long tail, beating its wings quickly to remain in the same place. Following the rocket's trail of smoke. Back to the source.

'Oh, fuck,' says Mariam. But her ears are still ringing, and she can't hear herself speak.

The dragon lunges forwards. Wings beating. Head getting bigger and bigger. Fire spills from its jaws. The communists break cover and run for safety, and she follows their example, fleeing with everyone else towards the corridor. Her hearing comes back in time for her to hear the windows shatter inwards. And then there is a sudden blaze of heat against her back. There's a corridor in front of her and death behind her, so she keeps running, until somebody grabs her arm and pulls her into a conference room.

Then someone is batting at her jacket because the sleeve is on fire. It's Teoni, swearing at a rate of four shits per second. The rest of FETA are in the same room. All except for one.

'Where's Regan?' Mariam asks.

'Bigger problems right now,' says Willow. 'Like how do we get out of here?'

'I thought we said we were going to kill the dragon,' says Roz. 'Remember? Core Objective? Slay the fucking dragon?'

'Don't look at me,' says Teoni. 'If a rocket launcher doesn't do anything then I'm out of ideas.'

Mariam shakes her head. 'I don't know. Let's ... let's just get out of the building. We can't slay the dragon if we're all dead.'

The corridor is burning. They pull their scarves up around their noses and venture out into the smoke, moving together. Mariam ends up leading them, without any idea of where she is going. But they're following her anyway, so she has to lead them somewhere.

They stumble into the Welsh delegation, moving quickly to keep their king safe. Gethin jerks his head for them to follow him. 'We've got boats down on the canal. We're going to make a break for it. You're welcome to come with us.'

It makes about as much sense as anything else that's happening. They find their way to a back staircase, down twenty flights of breeze-block walls and cold metal railings. Then they are outside, in a builder's yard, with gunfire close around them.

The street isn't any safer than the tower. Communist fighters are holding out against a Saxon army, who are coming down the road with drones and APCs and all sorts of other things that Mariam doesn't want to get killed by. But the Welsh are still moving forwards, down through a passageway to a quay at the side of the canal. And down in the water, against all logic, she can see Kay. Fighting with somebody. A man with golden hair, hammering Kay's shield with a sword.

'Kay!' she shouts to him.

But Kay doesn't answer her. The man with the golden hair must be some other knight, she realises. Somebody who Kay knows from the old days. But they're not fighting like knights. Not how she would imagine knights fighting. There's nothing brave or noble about it. It looks like two idiots wrestling in a canal, which is exactly what it is.

'Come on,' says Gethin. 'The boats aren't much further now.'

There's a red-brick bridge across the canal. They can run under one of its arches, towards safety. But the sky fills with death, as they draw close. The dragon crashes down in front of them, landing hard enough to shake the ground and knock them from their feet. It moves too quickly for something so large, draping itself across the canal bridge. Blocking their path with part of its coiled length. Not trying to kill them, yet, but looking upwards at a passing drone. Breathing a jet of fire across the sky.

They are trapped on this old stretch of dockside, waiting for the dragon to kill them on a whim, if the Saxons don't break through and kill them first. The communists and rainbow soldiers have formed a rear guard behind them, fighting and retreating. Saxons fill the square of daylight at the end of the passageway. Tarquin appears at her shoulder suddenly, a wild look in his eyes. His blazer is burnt and bedraggled. There are too many people on this towpath, too many guns firing, too many bullets taking chunks out of the brickwork. The King of Wales goes down suddenly with a stray shot to the stomach. Blood splattering the stones beneath his feet.

This isn't how Mariam wants to die. Somebody has to do something. But Kay and his friend are still wrestling in the basin. Both of them wet through and covered in mud, trying to drown each other, down there with the traffic cones and the floating rubbish.

'Kay, there's a fucking dragon!' she shouts, letting all of her anger rip out of her throat. 'Do something!'

'Bit busy right now!' Kay shouts back at her. He looks like he might be winning, but then the other knight pins him down, holding him under the water. Punching him in the face, again and again.

Neither of them look like they're going to do anything useful. She looks down into the basin to see if she could climb down there. Maybe, if the basin's shallow enough, she can lead the rebels under the bridge and away to safety. Or just wade over to Kay and slap some sense into him.

She can't see the bottom of the canal. What she can see is much stranger.

There's a woman's face beneath the water, pale and wide-eyed. Grinning up at her, with a mouth full of sharp teeth.

Mariam stares down at her. And everything else seems to stop.

She feels briefly as if she's somewhere else. Standing on the banks of a gentle river, in the middle of the forest. Leaves on the ground. Mist floating through the trees. She sees this woman rising from the water in a sodden white dress, looking less fishlike. Holding the sword aloft, by its hilt. There are voices singing quietly from somewhere behind her, angels or sirens or something else.

But then she is back on the towpath, and the woman in the

water bursts up from the canal, streaming water. Covered in scales. She doesn't bother to introduce herself or push the damp hair back from out of her eyes. She just thrusts out her hand, holding the blade of a sword. The handle is pointing upwards for her to grab.

'Here, love,' says the fish-woman. 'Have this!'

Mariam doesn't want to take it, but she doesn't see what else she can do. She leans down and grabs the handle. The woman in the water lets go and sinks back beneath the surface, still grinning her wide and toothy grin.

The sword doesn't feel special or powerful in her grasp. She doesn't even know if she's holding it right. But now she has a sharp piece of metal, which is more than she had three seconds ago.

Tarquin chooses that instant to try and make a run for it, leaving the rainbow soldiers to die behind him in service of the proletariat. He sprints down the canal towpath, trying to get past the dragon, but the dragon's head turns with him. Following him with its gaze. Snaking down low to the towpath and breathing an angry stream of fire.

While the dragon's head is turned, its neck is exposed. And Mariam can see a patch of pinkish flesh that isn't covered in scales. The place where Teoni hit the dragon with her rocket launcher.

Even if she had a clue what she was doing there wouldn't be any time to think about it, so she just runs up to the fucking dragon with the sword held awkwardly in both hands and plunges it up through the soft white patch of flesh, just behind the dragon's cheekbone. She only realises she's screaming once the blade is in up to the hilt.

It's like a damn bursting. Blood surges from the ruptured flesh and meets her face with a horrible warmth and pressure. It comes in spurts, in time with the dragon's heartbeat. It is in her eyes, in her nose, in her mouth. Soaking her hair and clothes and shoulders. She chokes, horrified, pulling the sword back out again and trying to cover her face with her arms. Trying not to slip on the bloodied ground.

The dragon is writhing and squirming, lashing its head from side to side. Convulsing along its entire length. It demolishes a building further down the canal with an accidental twitch of its tail. It breathes a final arc of fire into the sky, raging against death. Then it falls into the canal, crashing down massively under the bridge, with one dead eye staring upwards. Leaving the way clear.

Mariam wipes the dragon blood out of her eyes and turns to the other rebels, pointing her sword down the towpath. 'Come on!'

They don't argue with her. Hard to argue with someone holding a sword and covered in dragon blood. She stands and waits for them to hurry past, the Welsh and the Cornish and the last surviving communists. Her sisters try to hug her and congratulate her, but she herds them onwards. King Dai limps past her with Gethin holding him up, stopping long enough to clap his hand on her shoulder. He says something in slurred Welsh. Then he stumbles onwards, with dragon blood on his hand.

She stays behind, for a moment. Holding the sword and looking down at Kay. Wondering what knights are even for.

21

Kay is half-drowning, mouth full of foul water. The staff is lost somewhere in the canal, with both their swords. But they are still fighting. Lancelot has him pinned down under his knee. Strangling him with one hand and punching him with the other. Not a particularly pleasant way to go, but he's had worse.

He reaches out for something to hit Lancelot around the head with, a pipe or brick or anything that might be lying on the bed of the canal. His hand passes through weeds and other gubbins until it finds the hilt of a sword. It could be his sword, or Lance's sword, or Nimue giving him Caliburn. Doesn't matter. He grasps the handle and brings it round. Drives the blade up through Lancelot's side.

Blood clouds the water. Lancelot convulses on top of him. The hand around Kay's neck loosens. So he pushes upwards, rolling Lancelot over. Sitting up through the water and tasting air again, gasping to get his breath back. Lungs burning.

It's Lancelot's own sword, in Kay's hand. He draws it back

out of Lancelot's side and throws it across the water, out of its master's reach. Lancelot might have the strength left to do some mischief with it, otherwise. He's not quite dead yet, but he will be soon. Dragging himself away through the water, staggering low, holding his side.

Kay gathers himself up, shakily. Looking around for Mariam.

What he sees is a dead dragon, bleeding into the canal, turning the water a murky shade of red. He sees Mariam standing over it, on the bridge. Covered in dragon blood. Holding Caliburn in her hand. She looks down at him as he stands up, and he feels something fall into place.

'Mar—' he says.

Then he hears a familiar bang. Something rips through him from behind, and the smell of cordite reaches his nostrils. He misses the days when damp powder would stop a gun from firing.

When he turns around he sees Lancelot collapsed against the side of the canal, holding a smoking revolver in both hands. He must have had it stowed away somewhere the whole time. Very chivalrous of him not to use it earlier. But now he has used it. Chainmail doesn't do much good against a .455 round. It's gone in through his back and out through his stomach, making a hole the size of his fist.

He's been shot forty or fifty times over the years, but that doesn't make it any less painful. His legs fail under him, and he falls to his knees. Water up to his midriff, above the wound. He looks up at Mariam, standing above him on the quayside. She doesn't need to say anything. He can see it written on her face.

'Mariam,' he says, again.

'I just killed a dragon, *by myself*,' she says. 'Because you were too busy . . . I don't even know what you were doing. Play-fighting with Prince Charming, over there.'

'Listen,' he says.

But she doesn't want to listen. 'That was fucking pathetic. Both of you. If you're not gonna kill dragons, then what's the point of you? What's the point of either of you? Why do you even bother coming back?'

'Listen,' he says. 'You need—'

'I don't think I need anything from you,' she says.

She stares at him for a moment longer, as if to convince herself. Then she follows the others under the bridge, taking Caliburn with her.

He watches her go. Then he sags where he is and lets his hands fall against his thighs, under the water. The whole basin is turning red, from the dragon blood, and his, and Lance's. Mingling together.

He looks back at Lancelot, who's still leaning against the wall, breathing heavily. And for lack of anything else to do, he goes and joins him. Better to die with some company than to die alone. Dragging himself slowly and painfully through the water until he falls against the wall as well, barely four feet away from Lancelot.

'What a nice young woman,' says Lancelot.

'Shut up,' says Kay.

They lie at the edge of the basin, dying miserably together. Once the rebels are completely gone, the Saxon troops creep onto the quayside, slowly and carefully. Shouting commands at each other. Too loud and too cautious. Rifles raised. Checking every corner. Like they're afraid of their own shadows.

'Rubbish, these lot, aren't they?' says Kay.

'Yes, I thought so,' says Lancelot. 'Dreadful soldiering.'

The word 'clear' is shouted, more times than it really needs to be. Then a Saxon leader steps out from cover and saunters down the towpath to where the dragon lies dead. He is laughing and joking with his men, slapping them on the back, leering at the dragon's body. If he sees the two old warriors bleeding to death twenty feet away from him, he chooses to ignore them.

'Urgh,' says Lancelot.

'D'you know him?' he asks.

'American,' says Lancelot. 'I met him earlier.'

The American tries to climb across from the quayside onto the dragon's head, but he can't quite manage it without a handhold. Two other men have to push and shove at him, shouldering his buttocks as if they're raising a flag, until their leader is standing heroically on the dragon's head. Then the Saxons take devices out of their pouches and pockets and start taking photographs. Their commander stands on the dragon's head, grinning and making V-signs with his hands.

Kay tries to put pressure on his wound, but there's not much point. Not much strength left in his arms. He's already lost the feeling in his legs. The pain in his gut is a constant, throbbing thing. You start to feel sleepy when you're dying of blood loss. Won't be long, now. Lancelot looks very pale.

When the Saxons have taken their pictures and filmed their videos, they start to move out. The drones and the war machines and the mercenaries move away into different parts of the city. Leaving them alone. One perished dragon and two perishing knights.

'Least the dragon's dead,' Kay says, after a while.

Lancelot grunts. 'No thanks to us,' he says. 'Your friend wasn't wrong. We weren't much use, really. Could have stayed in the ground.'

'Well,' he says. 'Be back there soon.'

'Hm.'

They're not alone for long. When the Saxons are long gone, and the coast is clear, the witch from earlier drops down into the basin. She is still more aquiline than person, still covered in

265

feathers, still moving with birdlike grace. But once she's standing in the water she begins to transform again.

'Urgh,' says Kay.

'D'you know her?' asks Lancelot.

'Witch,' says Kay. 'I met her earlier.'

Instead of turning back into Regan, the witch adopts a new appearance. The aspect of a younger woman, with curls of raven hair. Kay isn't sure whether this is her true form or just the form that she chooses to appear in, but it's one that he and Lancelot both recognise from the old days. She manifests with the same green dress that she always used to wear. The same golden circlet on her head. Just to make sure they know who she is.

'Fuck,' says Lancelot, quietly.

Kay manages to smile, gritting his teeth against the pain. 'Hi, Morgan,' he says.

Morgan the Fay smiles back down at them. 'Hello, boys,' she says. 'I knew I could rely on the two of you to murder each other.'

'Should have known it was you.'

'Yes,' she says. 'Even for you, that was particularly stupid.'

'Thanks.'

'I'll let you both get on with the business of dying in just a moment,' says Morgan. 'But I need to borrow a few things from you, first.'

She walks closer, trailing her wet dress through the water. Kneeling to retrieve something from the canal bed. It's his staff, Kay realises. Panic floods through him. He tries to move, tries to get over to her and snatch it back from her, but there's no strength left in his limbs. Nothing he can do but watch.

'Morgan,' he says. Hearing the weakness in his voice. 'Come on. You can't have that. There are rules. About bringing him back.'

'There was a time when I might have agreed with you,' she says. 'But I think we're rather past the point where the old laws mean anything anymore. Wouldn't you agree? I've taken it, and you're in no position to stop me. So, there we are. And Lancelot, if you wouldn't mind . . .'

She holds out her other hand, and Lancelot's limp hand rises from the water of its own accord. There's a ring on his finger which twists itself free.

'No,' says Lancelot. 'No, not that. Please.'

It's hard seeing Lancelot reduced to begging. Too weak to fight. The ring crosses the distance through the air to where Morgan is standing, settling itself in the palm of her hand.

'I know what it means to you,' she says. 'And I am sorry. But I need it to bring Arthur back. That was the point of all of this, if you haven't figured it out yet.'

Kay shakes his head. 'You can't think that bringing him back is going to solve anything.'

Morgan sighs. 'Well, there's a lot going on, Kay, and it's all very complicated, and I don't expect the two of you to understand it. But I'm tired of all of this. I've been working for a very long time to try and save men from their own stupidity. To try and stop them from poisoning their own planet. And it hasn't worked. So my intention is to bring back the one man who might actually listen.'

'He won't,' says Kay. 'He won't listen to you. Or anyone. He won't be any different to how he was towards the end.'

'He may have stopped listening to you. But he never stopped listening to me. I know how to put him in a . . . receptive frame of mind.'

'Urgh,' says Lancelot.

Kay shakes his head. 'If you bring him back, things aren't going to get any better. They're only going to get worse.'

'Well then I suppose you'll have to try and stop me, won't you?' says Morgan. 'I look forward to seeing you try. Lovely catching up with you both.'

267

She beats the staff once against the bottom of the basin and disappears upwards in a twisting spume of water, turning herself to vapour. Scattering herself on the winds so that she can rain down somewhere else. She takes half of the canal with her, leaving the surface choppy and restless until it settles down again.

'Fuck,' says Lancelot, again.

Kay waits for a moment before saying anything else. He almost falls asleep, yielding to the cold water of the canal. But sleep would mean death, and resurrection. There are things he needs to say first. Matters at hand. He rouses himself again.

'Was that Galehaut's old ring?' he asks.

'Yes.'

'Hm. Didn't know he, er . . . didn't know he gave it to you.'

'Well he did,' says Lancelot, quickly. 'And now Morgan has it. No thanks to you.'

'Don't see how it's my fault.'

'If you'd just given me the staff then we wouldn't have ended up like this.'

'Well maybe if you'd listened then we could have killed the dragon, together, without killing each other first.'

'Urgh,' says Lancelot. 'Hardly matters now, does it?'

'There's a lesson, in this,' says Kay.

'Spare me.'

'No, really. When we come back, after this, we need to work together. If we want to stop her. Stop Arthur from coming back.'

Lancelot sighs. 'What else does she need? If she wants to bring him back.'

'Well,' Kay says, 'she's got your staff. And Gale's ring. She just needs Caliburn. And the blood of a dead king.'

'Your friend has Caliburn,' says Lancelot. 'Where's she going to get the blood of a dead king from?'

'The Welsh have a king,' says Kay. 'He didn't look well.'

'Arse,' says Lancelot.

Lancelot starts coughing, and it doesn't sound good. When Kay looks over to him, he can see a line of blood trickling down from the side of Lancelot's mouth.

'Kay,' he says. It rattles, through the blood. 'I should tell you. Galehaut. I tried to wake him up, on my way here. But . . . somebody's cut down his tree. It's gone. They built a pub over it.'

Kay feels anger rising in his belly, even through the numbness of his wounds. 'They can't have done,' he says. 'I thought we were protected. Ancient oaks.'

'Apparently not.'

'Christ. I'm sorry. I know . . . I know that you and him were . . . well, that you . . . What I mean is . . . I know you felt very . . .'

'Hmm. Thank you. But there might be people out there coming after *our* trees, as well. So just . . . mind how you go.'

Kay doesn't know what to say. He's oddly touched. Lancelot has never said anything that kind to him before.

'Same to you,' he says. 'I know you and I have always— Lance?'

He shifts himself painfully and cranes his neck. But Lancelot is already decomposing, turning rapidly to compost. Kay watches his flesh rot and his mail rust and his bones turn to fine sand. It all diffuses nastily, staying as a brown scuzz on the surface of the water.

And then there's not much point in him sticking around himself. He takes his hands away from his wound, letting the blood out into the water. Waiting to black out. But then minutes later he's still there, cold and miserable. Wanting to be remade, without going through all the horror of being remade. Eventually he puts his head back, and kicks his feet up, and lets himself sink beneath the shallow water. Held down by the weight of his mail.

Part Two

22

Lancelot crawls up from the earth with more urgency than usual, knowing that he has a purpose to fulfil, although he can't quite remember yet what the purpose is. His brain is still mostly mud. It's like waking up from a dream in which he had something important to do. When he's finally kneeling in the open, breathing raggedly, mired in filth, the purpose is still unclear. It takes a few moments for it all to come back to him.

'Shit,' he says, to himself.

Windsor Park is warm and empty. The air is dry, and the grass is brownish yellow. He drags himself to his feet, weighed down by his mail. He always gets reborn from the earth with his mail, even if he wasn't wearing it when he died. But he never comes back with anything that he was carrying. His cassette player. Or his revolver. Lawrence's revolver, from the war. Now it's lying at the bottom of a canal in Manchester. He can't imagine the next time he'll be up there. Will he travel up and trawl through the whole canal looking for it, just for the sake of sentiment? Probably not. Well, there's something else he's lost.

He can't call Marlowe. But Marlowe usually seems to know when he's up and about. Marlowe seems to know everything. It's one of his more infuriating qualities. He'll probably be along in a little while, whenever it suits him.

So, instead of doing anything else useful, he sits down under his tree to wait, trying to get some of the mud out of his hair.

It takes him a few minutes to realise that there isn't any birdsong. Because there aren't any birds. Just bronze kings on their horses and yellow grass dying on the ground beneath their plinths. The park is silent. It is empty. Nothing moves or makes a sound.

Lancelot rests the back of his head against the bark of his tree and stares up into the cloudless sky, wishing that he had something to drink. But he doesn't. And when he gets sober for long enough he always starts thinking dangerous thoughts. He balls his fist against the dry soil and pulls out a handful of dead grass.

He has always felt his heart swell when he thinks of Britain. Even in the old days, when it was a backwater, forgotten by Rome, carved up between warlords and Saxon chiefs. He had a strange pride in it, even then. When he rode up to the brow of a hill and watched the sun setting over a gorgeous green corner of the realm, he felt something powerful. A pride, completely unjustified, completely solid in his breast, in some notion of what the realm was and what it stood for. It might be the only notion that he's ever felt any loyalty to, other than the notion of love.

He felt it in him whenever they defeated the Saxons, in the old days. Even if nobody else around him seemed to feel it. He felt it smothered and contorted during the last few years of Arthur's reign. He felt it begin to creep back when he returned from the dead. Felt it return with more strength each time he came up. A guilty pride. An aching feeling. Longing for something that was or wasn't there. Loving the land under his feet and the trees over his head, even if he didn't love the people that he had to share them with. Loving the hills and the fields. Fighting for them, in ten or twenty wars. Fighting with people who felt the same way. Mouldering in the trenches of Flanders and doing it for the thought of Britain. Letting false memories of the old Britain keep him warm when Galehaut wasn't there. It was always faintly embarrassing. Childish. But why be embarrassed? It kept him warm. It kept him going.

For so long now he has been serving the realm, or his idea of it. The two have become indistinguishable. Protect the realm by destroying its enemies. Fighting in its best interests. Following orders from Marlowe's people. Knowing that most politicians are idiots, but broadly trusting in the old establishments to keep things ticking over. To stop things from getting too bad.

He wonders for the first time whether that trust might be somewhat misplaced.

He doesn't give a toss about Manchester communists. But when Windsor Park looks as brown and dead as this, when he can't hear a single bird singing in the trees. Is there something wrong with the realm? Something that can't be fixed by the people in charge?

Something he ought to try and fix himself?

He's still sitting and thinking, sweating in his chainmail, when he hears buzzing in the sky. It's not a little glass pod coming for him but a bigger helicopter thing, the kind of thunderous machine that the Saxons were using in Manchester. It flattens the brown grass with the force of its propellers as it settles down. Shortly afterwards the door slides open, and there's Marlowe sitting in the back compartment, waving his umbrella jauntily.

He feels the absence of Galehaut's ring on his finger.

Perhaps he shouldn't ask about Galehaut's tree right away. Perhaps it should wait until later. Catch Marlowe at a better time, in an unguarded moment. Not that Marlowe ever seems to have unguarded moments.

He trudges over to the flying machine and climbs inside, sitting across the aisle from Marlowe. Facing backwards. Marlowe is still wearing his ridiculous coat, even in this heat. It doesn't look as if the warmth is bothering him. Perhaps he can afford some sort of miracle coat that keeps him cool. He has one knee crossed over the other, with one of his brogues dangling, showing an inch of foot. The bulge of his ankle. The slightly racy pattern of his socks.

'Went well, then, did it?' asks Marlowe.

'Not particularly.'

Marlowe makes a sympathetic cooing sound and fetches a hipflask from his coat, handing it across the aisle. Lancelot takes it greedily and unscrews the top, but he stops with the neck halfway to his mouth. He has the unusual urge to stay sober.

'Actually it went very badly indeed,' he says. 'We need to find Morgan. She's going to bring Arthur back.'

'Ah,' says Marlowe. 'And where is she now?'

'She was with the rebels.'

'Oh, that makes things easier. But don't worry about any of that, for the time being. You kept to your brief – the dragon is dead.'

'It wasn't me that killed it. Or Kay, for that matter. It was this girl. One of the rebels. She has Caliburn. We should try to track her down, as well.'

'It's all well in hand,' says Marlowe. He is entering commands into a little touchscreen in the armrest beside him. The doors slide shut around them, and the propellers outside the cabin begin to whine more purposefully. Lancelot turns his head and realises that even this contraption doesn't have a pilot. He's not sure whether he likes the idea of being flown around by a computer, but it doesn't seem as though he has much choice in the matter.

'Why are we in this infernal machine?'

'Oh, really, Lancelot, you know what it's called. It's a helicopter. Don't be so affectatious.'

'Then don't be evasive.'

Marlowe scoffs. 'Well. We're not going into London this time. Actually the whole government's bugging out.'

Lancelot scowls. 'What?'

'All getting a bit fruity,' says Marlowe. 'Like you said. So we're letting the protestors have the run of the mill, for a while. Give them a few days of painting murals and playing ukuleles, or whatever it is they do. Just to get it out of their system. Then the Chinese will roll in to protect their assets and clean things up a bit. The new government will be based offshore. Much safer that way.'

Is this really how the country is governed? Lancelot can never quite tell how serious Marlowe is being at times like these. He chooses to believe that he's at least partway joking, because it's easier than believing the alternative.

'So where are we going?'

'Avalon,' says Marlowe. Then he laughs, when he sees Lancelot's expression. 'No, not that Avalon. It's a sort of fortress oil rig thingy. You'll hate it.'

'Surely if the plebs take London then … they've won?' asks Lancelot. 'They can form a government. Or however it works.'

Marlowe sniffs with laughter. 'Well, they can form a citizen's assembly and feel very self-righteous for a few days. But they can't afford to pay the mercenaries. Or pay off the Chinese. Whereas we can. So we can govern from wherever we wish. The world doesn't work the way it used to, old boy.'

'I hadn't noticed,' says Lancelot.

Marlowe's eyes narrow by a fraction. It's not a good feeling, when Marlowe chooses to scrutinise you. Like he's weighing your soul with an old brass set of scales.

'Not like you to take an interest in politics,' says Marlowe.

'Idle curiosity,' says Lancelot. He shrugs and takes a nip of Scotch from the hipflask, which seems to satisfy Marlowe for the time being.

'As I said,' says Marlowe, 'it's all well in hand.'

The flight is short and fairly smooth. Lancelot tells Marlowe something of what happened in Manchester. He mentions the idiocy of Colonel Nashorn. He mentions the fight with Kay, without really telling him how it ended. He doesn't mention The Wizard Inn. And he doesn't mention Galehaut's tree. Now doesn't feel like the right time.

After an hour or so there's an annoying sound from Marlowe's touchpad, and he smiles. He taps the screen with a flourish and a pair of shutters open in the nose of the craft, where the pilot ought to be. Lancelot turns in his seat to look through the window.

There is something monstrous glittering in the Bristol Channel, something that Lancelot instinctively detests before he can even make sense of what it is. When you strayed into the realm of the fay in the old days you used to see things like this sometimes, shimmering cities and faerie palaces. But this wasn't built by the fay – he can tell that. It was built by the hands of men.

'You're right,' he says. 'I do hate it.'

The drone lands on a windy outdoor platform guarded by Saxon men. When the doors slide open Lancelot's nose wrinkles, greeted by the mingled smells of salt spray and crude oil. Marlowe leads him inside, out of the wind, and suddenly it's as if they're somewhere else. Not an oil rig but an expensive hotel. A luxury shopping mall. A day spa. Something like that. The corridors are softly furnished, fitted out in soothing colours, shades of beige and orange. There is art on the walls. There are potted plants. Lancelot can feel the cold breeze of air being mechanically circulated.

'What is this place?'

'I told you, it's Avalon,' says Marlowe. 'Our new government headquarters. Everything important has moved here, to get away from all the fighting. Defence, broadcasting, finance. Everyone vital to the economy.'

'Why is it . . . beige?'

'We're all doing very important work here. You can't deny us a few creature comforts, surely.'

Marlowe leads him through it all, past massage parlours and indoor water features, to an apartment suite. There's a mini-bar and a private sauna. Clean towels and a box of chocolates on the bed.

'This is us,' says Marlowe. 'Make yourself at home.'

So Lancelot goes into the en suite and closes the door behind him. Shrugging off his mail and tunic. Scouring away the grime and earth again, like he did in London. He doesn't particularly feel like admiring his reflection this time. When he's oiled and perfumed and reasonably clean he walks back out into the room, where Marlowe is waiting for him in the bed. The lights are dimmed. There are two martinis on the sideboard.

He's tired enough of everything that he surrenders himself to the luxury, lets himself be carried along by the good vermouth and the soft bedsheets. Marlowe makes it easy. His smooth confidence. His arched eyebrow. It's difficult to resist. Twenty or thirty or forty minutes where he doesn't have to think about saving the realm. He doesn't have to think about Kay and dragons and Morgan and Galehaut.

Afterwards they lie together in matching bathrobes, eating the chocolates. Watching the news together on the widescreen television. Violent terrorist insurgency, the newscaster says. State of Emergency extended. Government moved to the new highly secure Avalon defence platform. Chinese government have graciously offered to lend troops to the effort to restore law and order in the capital.

'I'll have to shower again, now,' says Lancelot.

'Hmm,' says Marlowe. 'We could shower together. Save water. I hear it's good for the planet.'

'Perhaps,' says Lancelot. And then he finds that he can't keep quiet anymore, so he clears his throat. 'I went to wake up Galehaut.'

'Oh yes?' asks Marlowe, vaguely. 'How was he?'

Lancelot stares at the screen, feeling a kind of numbness in his jaw. The crowd is running wild, on the television. People pulling down statues with a chain.

'He's gone,' says Lancelot. 'Somebody cut his tree down. Totally obliterated. Built a dirty great pub on top of it.'

'Ohh,' says Marlowe. More interested in the news. 'Oh, I'm sorry, Lance. That's such a shame. I know you were fond of him.'

They've both seen a lot of people die, in their lifetimes. When you've been around for a thousand years, it seems natural that your old friends should die around you. Death itself becomes an old friend. But Galehaut wasn't meant to be one of those friends. Galehaut was meant to last forever.

'I don't understand how it could have happened,' says Lancelot. 'I thought you said there were laws, to stop it from happening. Protected trees. That sort of thing.'

'There's been so much deregulation . . .' says Marlowe. 'People can build anything they want, if they have the money. Sometimes palms are greased, deals are made. Laws are circumvented. All the old protections worn away.'

The television shows people climbing the railings outside the

Tower of London. Then it cuts to a row of Chinese tanks forming up in Essex somewhere. Lancelot lies next to Marlowe for a while, suddenly feeling foolish. Snug in his bathrobe, with his martini, while all of this is happening in the realm. There's a knot of anger burning in his chest.

'Isn't it your job to stop that sort of thing?' he asks. 'Protecting the country? Saving the realm from peril? Pardon me for saying so, but you don't seem to be doing a terribly good job.'

Marlowe lets out a long and ragged sigh. 'There's been . . . a significant shift in power, since the last time you were up and about. Or maybe it had already started then. I'm not quite sure. But what you have to understand is that Britain isn't a country, anymore. Not really. It's an American meat export market. It's a private laundry service for Russian mafia money. It's a giant multistorey car park where Saudi oil princes can keep their Lamborghinis. But it isn't a country. It's the hollowed-out husk of a country. We help other countries with their dirty laundry, and then we send them the bill. Everything else is just here to prop that up. The people who I work for don't care about protecting the realm. And neither do I, really. Not any more. Because there's nothing left that's worth protecting.'

'That can't be true,' Lancelot hears himself saying.

'Come on, Lance,' says Marlowe. 'How long have you been fighting, without really knowing what you were fighting for? The only thing left that's worth saving is our own skins. Yours and mine.'

Lancelot stares at the mattress. He has killed a great many people, over the years, to keep this country safe – or, that's what he told himself he was doing. Sometimes he rather enjoyed it. Often he didn't. Was there any grand, noble reason for it? Did it make it easier to tell himself that there was?

'And how do we do that?' he asks, slowly. 'Save our skins?'

'By letting Morgan get up to her mischief. That's step one.'

'But she wants to bring Arthur back.'

'Precisely,' says Marlowe. 'That's step two.'

The ice in Lancelot's martini seems to spread through his whole body. The things happening on the television don't feel particularly important anymore. Like they're happening somewhere else, on a different continent.

'What?' he asks.

'I've been meaning to tell you.'

'You can't seriously think that bringing Arthur back will do anything to make the realm a better place.'

'My dear boy, I've just told you,' says Marlowe. 'I'm not particularly interested in making the realm a better place. And neither are the people I work for, anymore. It's all a bit late in the game for that sort of thing.'

'I . . .' says Lancelot. He swore an oath. A very long time ago. To defend the realm from peril. It would feel silly, saying that now.

Marlowe rests a hand on his leg. 'Why don't you make another martini and I'll explain everything?'

'In a moment,' he says. 'I'll shower first.'

Lancelot finds himself standing up and going into the bathroom. Closing the door between himself and Marlowe. Ignoring his reflection, in his soft white bathrobe. Sparing a glance towards the pile of muddy chainmail in the corner.

23

When Kay opens his eyes again, he isn't falling through the darkness between worlds. He is still floating on his back. Which is strange. That's never happened before.

The gloaming sky overhead tells him that he's not in Manchester anymore. He has slipped into the Otherworld. Back in the dream forest, near the throne of Herne.

He feels a fleeting sense of hope. He won't turn his back on Herne this time. He'll stay and ask about the realm. Find out how to fix everything. Restore the balance of nature.

But when he begins to sit up, he sees that the forest is changed. This isn't some lipid faerie pool but a huge sea of floodwater, swallowing the forest. The surface of the water is carpeted with dead leaves. The mist has thickened, and the strange light of the dreamworld barely pierces it. Where it does shine through the light doesn't find strong oaks or thick moss. It finds dead trees. Bare trunks, blackened and twisted.

Kay stands fully to his feet. Moving through the floodwater

as quickly as he can. Tripping on submerged roots. The last time he was here there were glowing mushrooms to guide his path. Now they are rotting in damp places, giving off a putrid smell. He must find his own way, wading half-blind through the mist.

He's not sure how long it takes to find the clearing. Weeks or months or hours. It doesn't seem to matter, in dreamtime. When he finally climbs out from between two blighted elms he sees that Herne's great world tree has been cut down by some force too powerful to comprehend. Only a hollow stump remains, giant and rotten. The fallen tree is nowhere to be seen. The only other thing in the clearing is the bear from last time, lying dead in the water. It has been dead on earth for a thousand years. Now it is dead here too. Not enough magic left to keep its spirit walking in the dreamworld.

Herne is gone as well. The throne is empty and bare, between the knees of the giant stump. Kay walks up to it without haste or purpose. Not much point hurrying when everything is already gone, when hope is lost and the gods have vanished. His leg catches on something hard-edged under the water, and he bends down to pick it up. It's an empty deer skull, which he holds up in his oak hand, letting the water drip from it. There is nothing in the eyes or nose, no black depth of power or knowledge. Just bone and the absence of bone.

Now he knows how to kill a god. You don't kill them with a magic spear or a legendary sword. You just wait. You chop down trees. You burn wood, and let the fumes into the sky. You poison the oceans. You have to be patient. But eventually you do away with them.

When he's finished turning the skull over in his hands, he sets it down carefully on the empty throne. It seems like the respectful thing to do.

But the moment his fingers leave the skull, the rotting trunk in front of him collapses entirely. The land beneath it starts to give way, opening into a yawning chasm at his feet. Shards of rotten wood swirl into abyssal darkness. The throne and the skull crumble into it. Kay backs away. He turns and tries to run. But the floodwater has started rushing into the hole, flowing against him. Pushing against his thighs. The whole forest is rumbling, falling in upon itself. He hears the howling lament of ancient beasts. Sees creatures taking flight in the distance. The water carries him backwards, and the ground beneath him gives way.

And then he is falling again, as usual. Through the darkness between worlds.

Normally his time here is short. This time it lasts longer. He seems to be falling faster, into deeper darkness. Maybe time is finally getting even with him, punishing him for his hubris, for cheating fate. He can understand why time might have grievances to take up with him.

Perhaps this is the end of everything. Maybe Herne's death has brought an end to the long battle, the endless coming back. Maybe Morgan or Marlowe or somebody else has sent men to cut down his tree. Maybe the magic has just stopped working by itself. And now there's only cold oblivion and hopelessness. He will fall until the end of time, or until he reaches whatever's at the bottom. He doesn't relish that thought.

Is this what's been waiting for him, at the end of days? A thousand years of saving the realm, and this is his reward. Not heaven with Wyn or a peaceful slumber under his tree. Just an endless plunge into the abyss. Merlin never mentioned that when he talked them into swallowing the stones, long ago. He never told them what would become of them in the end days. Maybe he didn't know. Maybe he didn't care. Kay can't decide which is worse.

When he's been falling for five centuries, or perhaps five minutes, he feels a cold hand close its grip around his chest. Slowing his fall. Not pulling him downwards, but lifting him back up again. Some unfathomable force has reached down into the darkness and scooped up his soul, bearing it back up towards a distant light.

Maybe he has friends in high places. Wyn's been up there long enough to have endeared herself to the right people. She's probably been baking treats for Saint Peter, who has provenance over this sort of thing. Walking down to the gates of heaven once a week with a wicker basket full of warm honey cakes. Talking idly about her heathen husband and how nice it would be to see him again. Kay never knew anybody who wouldn't do Wyn a favour once they'd tried her honey cakes.

When he rises high enough the darkness is replaced by light, and he feels a radiance that blazes through his soul, reaching the furthest depths of it. Maybe this is the moment of his salvation. Saint Peter has relented, wiping the crumbs from his beard and scribbling Kay's name into the other column of his ledger. God won't notice one heretic. Maybe he's finally being borne up to heaven to see his wife again. He allows himself to hope, for a few short moments. But then the radiance fades and he finds himself in the cold earth again, back under his hill. Saint Peter can only do so much. He can't open the gates for a heathen, especially not a heathen whose soul is still promised to the old gods. But perhaps he can save a heathen from oblivion. Set him back on his quest. Put him back in the ground and give him another chance at redeeming himself. Wyn's efforts haven't been for nothing.

The earth doesn't seem pleased, having him back in its bosom. It seems to be asking, 'You again?' It felt wrong, last time. Now it feels worse. Painful. Roots twisting and grasping around his bones, and the soil churning while his flesh is rendered new. It's like the tree has forgotten how to do it and is bungling through the process, resentful of its obligations. His soul felt bright and hopeful a moment ago. Now it feels as though it's been dragged by its ankles through a bramble bush. Saved from the darkness and thrust into radiant light, too briefly, and now here in the muck being wrought back into a human by a tree that can't remember its instructions properly. He's had better days, to be sure.

Normally this process is damp and alluvial, slurry turning slowly into supple flesh. Now he feels stiff and taut and inflexible. Parts of him are creaking and groaning as they reform. When he gains control of himself and starts to climb upwards, his limbs don't feel as lithe or limber as they should. Like he's been refashioned from tenser stuff than usual. Several parts of him feel wrong, even as he nears the surface. He wonders if he should have lain beneath the ground for longer, given the earth more time to get everything right. But it's too late for that now. His hands are grasping at daylight. Up through the hollow of his tree.

Morning, in this part of the realm. Still uncomfortably warm. The sky is a grainy yellow, and the oil fire has burnt itself out. When he's standing in front of his tree he looks at his sword hand and freezes. The wound has healed, but not as flesh and bone. Skin has been replaced with wood. Not solid timber but lissom bark, like a young sapling. He can still bend the wrist, which he does, curling and uncurling experimentally once or twice. He can hear it creak. Stiffer than flesh and bone, but tougher too. No bigger or smaller than before.

He keeps his right hand warily at arm's length, running his left hand over himself for anything else that isn't right. Sword's missing, but he expected that. He can feel something through his mail, in the place where Mariam shot him. Some growth or hard swelling that shouldn't be there. He shrugs off his mail shirt, breathing quickly, doing it too fast and getting it bunched up under his shoulders. Once it's in a pile on the floor he tears his tunic over his head, standing stripped to his waist in the morning heat.

There's a knot of wood in the centre of his breast, just like a knot that you'd see on a trunk of oak. Leaking sap and protruding from the flesh around it. Christ knows how deep it goes into his person. Does he have an oak breastbone, now? Are his ribs like the ribs of a longship, beneath his flesh? Does he have a core of heartwood, instead of a beating heart? Sap running through his veins, instead of blood?

He pulls his tunic back on over his knotted breast and fights his way back into his mail. Then he walks downhill, suspecting himself to be on borrowed time.

Can he walk back to Manchester, like this? Can he find Mariam, stop Morgan? There's no horse or motor car or flying machine to get him there more quickly, so he trudges forward on his own two feet. The bog is black and empty and firmer underfoot than it used to be, now that the oil fire has raged through it. There's no sign of any Saxons or their whirligigs. The fracking facility lies ruined and abandoned in the harsh yellow light of day.

He goes through it, rather than around. Only because it's the direct route. But as he gets nearer, he gets more curious. He starts to see the bodies of Saxon men who died in the explosion. They are half-cremated, and their masters have left them here to moulder in the bog. But there's something strange about their corpses. Like his new tree-hand. He turns one of them over with his foot and grimaces. This one is badly burnt, but above his bulletproof vest he has a goat's head and horns. White fur crisped and blackened by the fire. Cloven hooves emerging from his sleeves. He's fairly sure that the poor sod didn't look like that when he was alive. What kind of explosion could do that?

The fence was blown down by the blast and poses no barrier this time. He walks over it, into the ruin of the place itself. Buckled metal lying everywhere, fused together or torn apart. Pipes sticking up at strange angles, like stakes waiting for victims to be speared upon them. The Saxons here are even more disfigured, by fire and magic and sheer velocity. Broken carcasses. If some of them have pigs' ears or lizard scales then it hardly makes a difference. One of them has charred leather wings bursting through its clothes, and a broken tail of thorns lying in the mud behind it. Like it had half-changed into a manticore when the fire tore through it.

The place is utterly destroyed, and the machinery is stopped, but there is still a strange energy in the air. An electric tension. A humming sound. How can that be? Nothing here can still be operational, making power or drawing up anything from the ground.

He combs through the ruins, picking up odd scraps of metal, turning them over, casting them aside. Not sure exactly what he's looking for until he finds it. In the very heart of this place, where the silver tower once stood, he comes upon a deep hole. Wide and dark and foreboding. That makes sense. If this place was a mine, for drawing up oil, then there had to be a hole down into the earth. But this doesn't seem to him like any ordinary hole.

He begins to get the sense of what might have happened, here. When a lot of magic gets released at once it tends to manifest strangely. It doesn't want to just be magic floating on the air, it wants to take the form of something. That's what Merlin told him, once. So that's why the queen dragon appeared, from nowhere. Conjured suddenly from the Otherworld, because there was enough magic in the air for her to travel through the veil. Smaller fay spirits slipping through with it and trying to possess these poor Saxon men, in the half-second before the fire killed them. Good thing that it did. He remembers Mordred's army at Camlann, men turned into all manner of creatures. Hard to behold without going mad.

He starts seeing lights dancing in his vision. Faeries. Fay spirits in their purest form, frolicking in the air around this source of magic. If he still had his staff at his side then it would probably be red hot, standing here. He keeps moving, leaving the place behind him, before he gets turned into something foul and strange as well. But then, it's a bit late for that, isn't it?

When he's finally out of the bog he follows the burst banks of the Ribble, walking across country without really caring who sees him. There don't seem to be any Saxons around, anymore. Nothing worldly or otherworldly to delay his progress. No mercenaries or communists or dragons or wights or giants. The whole realm seems bleak and empty.

It only takes a few hours of solemn trudging to get near Preston. He knows that he's nearby because he can smell something in the air. Except it doesn't smell like siege camp dysentery, anymore. It smells like the siege is over, and the city has been burnt to the ground.

He quickens his pace.

Sure enough, when he gets there the whole camp is in ruins. The fences are torn down or sagging from the blaze, which has now ended. The ground is a carpet of ash and cinder. Burnt scraps of tent are blowing idly in the faint breeze. He wanders through the wasteland, not knowing when the dragon had time to come back and do this. But then he starts to think that it might not have been the dragon after all. There are tyre tracks through the ash. There are bullet holes in the sides of abandoned shipping containers. And the bodies that he can see are too neatly organised, like they were lined up and shot. He stands on something, then looks down to see what it is. A plastic dustbin lid, painted with a crude tree. Somebody must have seen his shield and liked it. Copied it. Now it has been warped and melted by fire.

Eventually he finds himself in the place that was once the central square, where he sat and talked with the paupers. In the middle of it there's still a groundsheet fluttering, blackened around the edges but weighed down by bricks. There are shapes underneath it, and he's seized by curiosity. He throws one of the bricks aside and lifts the corner of the sheet.

Then he wishes he hadn't. He covers his mouth and speaks the name of Christ.

He has witnessed many horrors over the years. He's seen and done a thousand dreadful things. This might be the most disgusting thing he's ever seen. Not the most morally foul or pointlessly cruel. But the most sickening, the most viscerally nauseating.

They are not quite corpses, and not quite mushrooms, but some ungodly union of the two. It's the glassy-eyed paupers, lying where they died. Killed by the fire or the smoke or by something else. Maybe they just starved. He can't tell because their bodies are so badly altered now. These mushrooms have used their flesh as mulch. They are furred over, with gossamer stalks sprouting from them like fingers reaching for the sun. Toadstools bloom from their groins and armpits. Their cheeks and thighs and stomachs are overgrown with wide discs of fungal matter.

He can't even bring himself to put the groundsheet back over them. He just turns around and vomits. What comes up from his stomach is mostly soil and black sludge. Stuff from underground. He's not much different from these mushroom men, really. No less strange or ungodly.

When he's done retching, he wipes his mouth on his cloak and staggers away from the bodies, shaking his head. Not lingering to cover them back up.

The coven where the sisters used to live has been destroyed as well, burnt to the ground and torn apart with particular venom. There are foul words sprayed on the walls of the shipping containers. Things blowing in the breeze, white pads that were neatly stacked in packages but have now been torn open.

He picks around the ruins for anything useful and eventually finds the wreck of Teoni's car. It's a blackened shell of what it was, with the windows staved in and the wheels removed. It looks as though it was battered with sticks before being burnt. But on top of the car there is a squirrel drinking from a can of beer. By sloping the can down the bonnet he can stick his nose inside the hole and lap it up, lying on his back, holding the can in place with both paws. He pulls his head out long enough to belch, but then he sees Kay, and the belch turns into a shriek. The can rolls down off the bonnet and spills its contents on the ground. The squirrel looks ready to bolt and disappear, but then a flicker of recognition crosses his small face.

'Oh, it's you!' says the squirrel. He sounds relieved.

'Yeah,' says Kay. 'It's me.'

There's a moment of awkwardness. The squirrel looks around at the ashes and shakes his head. 'Fuck,' he says. 'Can you believe all of this? It was my lot who did it. It was mad. Just … killing people for no reason. Setting the whole place on fire. All because they had beef with you. But you weren't even here.'

Kay closes his eyes and breathes a long sigh through his nose. So this is his fault, as well. All of the death and ruin. The Army of Saint George came here and did this because of what he did to them. Retribution. If he hadn't killed those men, if he hadn't rescued Yusuf's family, then this might not have happened.

'Do you, er . . . want a lager?' asks the squirrel. 'Found a whole pack of them.'

Kay opens his eyes and stares at the sky. Then he nods. 'Yeah, all right.'

He's tired. He sits down on the blackened bonnet of the Land Rover. The squirrel goes and retrieves a can of beer, then drags it over to him. He picks it up and nods his thanks. Struggles with getting it open, until the squirrel shows him how to do it. Then he slurps from the opening and swallows it down. It doesn't make him feel much better. His mouth still tastes of corpse rot.

They sit together in silence for a while. Kay takes the odd swig from his beer. The squirrel just stares into the distance.

'Suppose you could have stopped it,' says the squirrel, 'if you'd been here.'

'Maybe.'

'I kept trying to tell them to stop,' says the squirrel. 'But they just kept kicking at me. One of them set my fucking tail on fire. That put a lot of things in perspective, let me tell you.'

'I can imagine.'

'I mean, I never signed up for all of that. I know it's immigrants stealing all the food and everything, and they're the reason the country's gone to shit, and if it weren't for them then Britain would be the best country in the world. No offence.'

'Well—'

'But that's no reason to *set them on fire*, is it? I mean, Christ. That's taking it all a bit too far.'

'Hmm.'

The squirrel drags another beer across the bonnet, for himself. The beer's getting to him, clearly. He moves erratically, as close as a squirrel can get to a drunken stagger. When he's opened the next can and taken a generous slurp from it he looks up and shakes his head. 'World's gone mad. Fucking mad. I mean, what do you even do?'

'That's a very good question,' says Kay. 'Not sure I know the answer.'

'Can't just go around murdering everyone who disagrees with you, can you?' asks the squirrel. 'That's not going to make a blind bit of difference. Except everyone ending up dead. But what do you do instead? I don't fucking know.'

'Hmm,' says Kay again. He stares out over the wasteland and tries to think of a decent answer. 'You know, back in the old days, used to be that everyone hated the Saxons. They were the ones coming over here, taking our land and our women. My brother, Arthur . . . he took that hate and he made it worse. Like pouring petrol on it. I saw what happened to people, when they heard Arthur talking. All their little fears and struggles, none of that mattered anymore. They didn't have to face who they were. Didn't have to hate themselves for this or that, anymore. They could just hate the Saxons instead. Much easier. And I just wonder what might have happened if they all asked themselves why. Maybe if they'd . . . found a way of sitting more easily with themselves. Slaying the monsters inside. Staring down whatever it was that was really making them afraid. Maybe then they wouldn't have listened, when Arthur came round looking for soldiers. Maybe then they'd have stayed home on their farms, and they wouldn't have gone killing anyone.'

The squirrel stares at the floor for a long time, with wide squirrel eyes. Then he starts nodding. 'You're all right, you know. I had you down wrong.'

Kay finds the energy to smile. 'What's your name?' he asks.

'Barry,' says the squirrel. 'My name's Barry.'

'Well,' says Kay, 'my name's Kay. Nice to meet you properly, Barry.'

'Nice to meet you too, mate.'

They shake hands, Barry's tiny paw pinched between two of Kay's fingers.

'Look,' says Barry, 'I don't suppose there's any chance of you making me human again, is there?'

'I'll be honest with you, Barry,' says Kay. 'I'd love to turn you back. But I've lost my staff. And even if I still had my staff, I'm not sure I'd know how to do it.'

The squirrel sighs and deflates. 'I was worried you'd say something like that.'

'But I'm going to try to get my staff back,' he says. 'So if you come with me, we'll see if we can sort you out.'

'Sounds good to me, bruv.'

He drains the rest of his beer, then throws the empty can into the ashes. Offering an arm to Barry, who clambers up his sleeve of mail and perches on his shoulder. Then he sets out into the ruined camp again, looking for a path through the ruination.

As soon as he stands up he sees the ice cream van where the paupers used to buy their musk. Standing exactly where it was the last time he saw it, as if it had been there all along. It has somehow survived the flames entirely unblemished, without any burns or warps in its plastic hull. Kay sighs and walks towards it, puzzle pieces falling into place. The panther musk, the mushrooms, the strange happenings. And the man in the back of the van – who is not quite a man after all.

The van's engine is running. There are wind chimes jangling in the window, despite the lack of breeze. As Kay approaches, he grows sure of it: this is one of the fay. They look bored, sallow and

295

slender, all elbows and cheekbones. Leaning out of their window and sneering at what they survey, as if they've seen better waste-lands. Still wearing sunglasses and a beanie hat. When Kay gets close enough he can see the points of their ears, disappearing up under the brim.

'You are Kay, the Cupbearer?' asks the fay.

'Yeah,' says Kay. 'Who's asking?'

'We expected you sooner.'

Kay shrugs. 'I was busy.'

The fay lets out an almighty sigh. They're already bored of this conversation.

'Did you see what happened here?' Kay asks.

The fay shrugs. 'We saw. There was fire.'

'And you didn't think about stopping it?'

The fay smiles. Their teeth are too sharp to be human. 'Why would we do that?'

Kay isn't in the mood for this. He reaches up and grabs the fay by their hoodie, pulling them halfway out of the window. Their sunglasses shake loose from their face and fall to the ground, revealing their purple eyes. They shriek, but the shriek turns into shrill laughter.

'Does Kay the Cupbearer blame himself?' asks the fay. 'Could have stopped it, if he was here.'

Kay's fists tighten around the bunched fabric of the fay's hoodie. No sword to stab them with. He considers pulling them bodily from the van, throwing them down in the ash, kicking them in the ribs. But he has Barry chittering in his ear.

'Easy, big man,' Barry is saying. 'We were just saying, weren't we? No good going around battering people.'

Kay doesn't let go right away. He stares into the fay's eyes instead. But the fay wants him to do it. Wants him to lose his temper. Kicking them in the ribs wouldn't make him feel any less guilty, and the fay would probably enjoy it. He releases them instead and takes a few steps away to calm himself down. He runs his hands down his face.

'That's right,' says Barry, 'walk it off. Who's this geezer, anyway?'

'One of the fay,' says Kay. 'You'd probably call them a faerie or something.'

'Well, I wasn't going to say it, but yeah, I could tell that much.'

'They're not really human,' says Kay. 'They're just a kind of spirit from the faerie world that's taken a human form for a while. If you know what you're doing then you can bring them into the world and bind them. Like servants.'

'Right, right,' says Barry, as if he understands. 'So what do we want with him?'

'Them,' says Kay.

'Oh, er, sorry,' says Barry. 'Right. Them.'

'They can lead us to their master,' says Kay. 'And I think their master might be able to help us both out. Might be able to turn you back.'

'Right! Lead on, then, big fella.'

Kay braces himself and walks back over to the ice cream van, where the fay is still grinning.

'Would Kay the Cupbearer like a Calippo?' asks the fay.

'Not particularly, ta.'

'As you wish.'

'So you work for this Ambrose fella,' he says. 'Is that who I think it is?'

The fay nods. 'Emrys has bound us to do his bidding.'

'So what is his bidding?' asks Kay. 'Why are you here?'

'Emrys will tell you,' says the fay. 'We have something for you.'

They reach up to rummage on a shelf, behind a box of wafer cones. Then they extend their hand to Kay and unfold their fist. There is a small plastic bag in their outstretched palm.

Kay grabs it, dangles it from his thumb and forefinger to get a good look at it. It contains a single red mushroom with white spots. The label has something scrawled on it.

Kay.
Eat this.
Merlin.

What else can he do? Stand in the wilderness with this fay? Walk all the way to Manchester, looking for Mariam? Stumble through the realm looking for Morgan? Have an ice cream? No good options. None of them seem any more or less mad than eating a mushroom that some grinning fay has palmed off on him.

There is something comforting about the thought of eating it. Surrendering to fate, to oblivion, to the currents of the Otherworld. He hasn't done much good since he came up, questing around, trying to save people. He just gets people killed when he tries to puzzle things out for himself. He only needs to look up at the ashes to remind himself of that. Might be worth letting somebody else do the brainwork. That's what Merlin was always good for.

'What do you reckon?' he asks Barry.

'I trust you, mate,' says Barry. 'Do what you think needs doing.'

He nods. Then he tears the bag open and empties the mushroom into his palm. He can feel the purple eyes of the fay staring into his soul.

'What will this do?' he asks.

'It will remind you of the important things,' says the fay.

'Right,' says Kay. He takes a deep breath. He rolls his shoulders. He looks over at Barry.

'Here goes nothing.'

Then he palms the mushroom into his mouth and begins to chew.

It tastes foul. Nothing happens, for a minute or so. Then he's vaguely aware of his brain leaking down into his legs. He can hear Barry talking to him, but there seems to be hours between each word. The fay's grin widens, and their eyes seem to deepen, containing multiverses. It's not a pleasant sight. He's almost glad when the ground rushes up to meet him. It swallows him whole.

24

The boats take them out to sea and down the north coast of Wales, strangely untroubled by Saxons or anyone else. Mariam sits with the sword awkwardly across her knees. She wishes that she had somewhere sensible to put it, someone else to give it to. It doesn't feel right to just put it down in the bottom of the boat, between her feet, where it will get jostled about. It's still stained with dragon blood. So is she – her hair and her clothes and her skin. It stinks of iron and meat, and something else. She'd like to shower. Plunge into the sea and scrub it off. Anything to get clean. Not much chance of that any time soon, though.

They come ashore somewhere Mariam doesn't recognise, a seaside town that's now covered in sandbags and barbed wire. When Dai ap Llywelyn steps out of the boat he falls down on the beach, bleeding on the sand.

Mariam's nursing instincts take over. She tries to get through to help him, but the throng of Welshmen is too thick. They pick him up between them and carry him up the beach to the seafront, where there are lorries waiting with their engines running. Gethin makes sure that there's room for everyone, not just for the Welsh but for all of the other rebels as well.

'Mariam, you go in with your lot, now,' he says.

'Let me help,' she says. 'I trained as a nurse.'

Gethin looks her up and down. He looks at the sword. Then he nods and gets out of the way. 'Aye,' he says. 'Come on.'

They climb up together, just before the lorry starts moving. Dai ap Llywelyn is lying on the bed of the lorry, bleeding freely onto a canvas stretcher, with Welshmen arguing over him. Mariam kneels beside him and puts the sword down, using both hands to put pressure on the wound. She shouts around for a first aid kit, but nobody seems to have one. Her hands are still stained with dragon blood and now they're in contact with an open wound, trembling and red and slick. It can't be sanitary. Dragon blood and the king's blood mingling together.

The wound looks deep. Dai is already pale and slick with sweat. When she looks up into his eyes she finds that he's staring back at her.

'Blood of the dragon,' he rasps at her, in English. 'You killed it.'

'Yes,' she says quietly.

'The . . . lady in the water,' says Dai. 'She gave you the sword.'

He holds out a shaking hand and finds the strength to grab her by the wrist. She tells him to lie down, pushing his shoulder back against the bed of the lorry. It's easier to focus on keeping him alive than it is to think about what he's saying. Somebody does find a med kit and she gets busy with it, autoinjecting morphine into Dai's arm. That will shut him up. There's nothing she can do about any deep tissue damage or a perforated bowel. She's not a trauma surgeon. All she can do for now is clean and dress the wound. It's harder, in a moving lorry, over bumpy roads. But she manages, just about. Dai is barely conscious by the time she's finished. He grabs her wrist again, but his grip is weaker than it was before. His eyes are searching for her in a haze of morphine.

'Queen of Wales,' he says. 'Queen of Wales.'

Her spine freezes. Gethin says something in Welsh, and Dai rasps back at him. Even if they were speaking English she wouldn't be paying attention. Her heart is suddenly pounding.

'No,' she says. Her voice sounds small to her. 'No, no, no. I'm just. I'm not ...'

'You've got the sword,' says Dai, switching back to English again. 'Killed a dragon. That's all you need.'

'Dai,' says Gethin, 'look, she's a lovely lass, but you're not thinking right. You've lost a lot of blood. Just rest yourself, now.'

'It's up to me,' says Dai. 'Blood of the dragon.'

He slips into unconsciousness, eyes rolling upwards. Mariam sits back away from him because she feels like she has to. She steps on the sword by accident, which nearly sends her down onto her back. The Welsh are all staring at her.

'She can't be queen,' says one of them immediately. 'She's not even Welsh!'

'I don't want to be queen of anywhere,' she says, quickly. 'That's insane. I can't be queen.'

But the Welsh are arguing now, in English.

'Dai just named her as his successor. If he dies then we have to respect his wishes.'

'Bollocks. We never got around to writing the bloody rules of succession, did we? Didn't think we'd need to.'

'She just said herself that she doesn't want it! If it's anybody then it ought to be you, Gethin.'

'All right, that's enough of that,' says Gethin, louder than any of them. 'He's not dead yet. Let's worry about that when it happens.'

The Welsh fall silent. Mariam sits in silence, staring at Dai, until Gethin moves up and offers her a seat on the bench. She climbs over and sits next to him, eyes boring a hole in the canvas on the other side of the lorry. After a few minutes her hand starts to hurt, and she realises that she has the sword across her lap. She doesn't remember picking it up. She is gripping the handle so tightly that her knuckles have turned white.

They can't have driven for more than an hour. The lorries move quickly over smooth roads, then slowly over rougher ground. They seem to be climbing. Going up. Towards the end of the journey they have to hold onto the benches to stop themselves from falling. When they stop, they are herded out into a cold wilderness that Mariam wants to leave as quickly as she can. It's empty moorland, somehow even emptier and bleaker than the moorland in the Pennines. A wet desert, with craggy hills all around them, draped in thick sheets of mist. There are mountains lurking in the clouds like sleeping giants. The Welsh have a camp up here, tents and canopies and hardware that looks Chinese as far as she can tell. Missile launchers for shooting down drones. Everything damp and wet.

The ground feels hard and cold and unwelcoming beneath her feet. It doesn't feel like land that she has any right to rule over.

The Welsh carry their king into one of the tents, where it looks like there are proper medics waiting for him. She tries to go after them, but Gethin stops her.

'They've got it handled from here, I think,' he says. 'You just . . . look after that sword.'

'Where are we?' she asks, quickly.

'Deep in Snowdonia,' says Gethin. 'Nowhere safer. Now, if you don't mind.'

He jerks his head into the tent and disappears after his king. She is left standing in the mist, holding the sword and not knowing what to do with it.

There's a confusion of rebels standing around the lorries. Survivors from Manchester. The Cornish and the Cumbrians and one or two of the strange Lincolnshire priests. The Scottish ambassador made it all the way out here, in his dishevelled suit and tie, and he looks more confused than ever. Mariam's sisters are there, climbing down from the lorries and regrouping. All of them except for Regan. They must have left her behind. Somewhere in the crossfire, or the burning tower. Shot or burnt or captured by Saxons. None of those are fun to imagine. None of those are the kind of fate that Regan deserved.

They find a place to sit, among the lorries and the ammunition crates, and they stay there for a long time without speaking or moving. Mariam stares down at the sword in her hands.

'We slayed the fucking dragon,' says Teoni, when the worst of the shock has faded.

'Yeah,' says Mariam. 'Yeah, we did.'

She can't find the energy to smile, and nor can any of the others. That's the way things are now. Even victories are overshadowed by everything else that's happening in the world. They sit silently, squinting against the wind, until Willow pulls out a bag of weed and starts rolling a joint.

'Well,' says Willow, 'I think we should be bloody proud of ourselves. Because we just achieved one of our Core Objectives.'

'Hm,' says Roz. 'First time we've ever done that.'

'Yeah, we can cross that one off the list,' says Willow. 'Now we just have to stop climate breakdown, destroy capitalism, and dismantle the fossil fuel industry. Can't be that hard.'

'Right?' says Teoni. 'If we can slay a dragon, we can do anything.'

'Can we, though?' asks Roz. 'I don't see how we can do anything from here. Where the fuck are we, anyway?'

'Snowdonia,' says Mariam.

Roz shakes her head. 'Great.'

Willow takes a drag on her joint and then starts gesturing with it. 'It's not the end of the world,' she says. 'I mean, it is. But we might be able to work with the Welsh. Stop them from hurting the sky. That sort of thing.'

Teoni looks sceptical. 'Why would they listen to us?'

'Well,' says Mariam. She swallows. 'They were talking about making me the new Queen of Wales, just now. So that might help.'

'Fuck,' says Willow.

'What does that even mean?' asks Roz.

'I thought we were, like, in favour of abolishing the monarchy?' asks Bronte.

'Can I be your Prime Minister?' asks Teoni.

Mariam closes her eyes. 'Look, it's just ... It's just something that King Dai said while he was delirious. It was probably just the morphine talking. When he's lucid again he'll take it all back.'

'I think you'd make a great queen,' says Willow. She offers Mariam a drag on her joint and Mariam takes it, hoping that it might help. Steadying the sword with one hand and smoking with the other. Coughing and wincing as she hands it back.

'Thank you,' she wheezes.

They pass the joint around until Mariam starts to feel restless. The blood is itching on her face and hands. She scratches at it, gets it under her fingernails, but that doesn't seem to do much good. So she stands up, taking the sword with her, and goes looking for somewhere to clean it off.

Away from the Welsh camp and down across the bleak mountaintop there's a pool of stagnant water like a small lake. She walks over and kneels by the edge of it, in the red bracken. Laying the sword across her lap. Twisting the prayer beads around her wrist. She feels the urge to throw the sword away, down into the water, make it somebody else's problem. The strange fish-woman might rise from the lake and take it back.

She examines the sword properly for the first time, holding it by the handle and looking up and down the blade. It's not very big, or very grand. She has a mental image of the swords used by knights, and this sword seems smaller. Barely three feet long. Shouldn't it have some kind of handguard? It doesn't, really. Just an oval where the blade ends and the handle begins. The grip is made from something smooth and black that feels cool in her hand. And above the grip there's a wedge of gold or bronze or something else lustrous, with snakes and dragons carved into it. Then finally a beautiful thing, a little house of jewels at the very top of the sword. Like the windows of a cathedral, strands of gold criss-crossing over red and green panels which must be gems or glass.

She still wishes that she had somewhere to put it. Kay had a sheath of leather at his side that he could slide his sword into. That would be good. Since she has no sheath, she drives it into the ground beside her, pushing it down far enough that it stands with its handle sticking into the air.

Is that bad? Stabbing the ground with it? The first thing she stabbed was a dragon. The second thing she stabbed was the earth itself. She wonders what she'll stab with it next.

When she's finished scraping the blood from her skin Mariam draws the sword back out of the earth and goes to help the others pitch their tents. The Welsh are sitting in circles, talking nervously and quietly, eating oatcakes and Chinese ration packs. She's hammering one of the tent pegs into the ground with a spare rock when she hears her name and looks up to see Gethin standing over her.

'I think you'd better come with me,' he says.

She looks back down at the tent peg and ties the guy rope around it, making sure that it's good and taut. Finishing this one normal job. Only when she's happy with it does she pick up the sword and get to her feet, looking Gethin in the eyes. She's surprised by the expression on his face. It looks almost like fear.

He leads her through the camp to a big tent full of metal boxes, missiles and rocket launchers, and ammunition. Then he zips the tent flap closed behind them, shutting them off from the outside world.

'I wish you hadn't washed off all the dragon blood,' says Gethin. 'It might have helped to convince people.'

'Convince them of what?' she asks.

He sighs. 'I think you know what. About this queen business.'

'Look, it's okay,' she says. 'I'm not sure I'd be the best queen anyway. Somebody else can do it. I'm not ... I know I'm not ...'

'Dai's dead,' says Gethin.

That makes her fall silent. She looks down at the sword in her hand. Clenching her fist around the hilt. Thinking back to the lorry, dressing his wounds, trying to stop the bleeding. If she'd known what she was doing then maybe she could have saved him.

'I'm sorry,' Mariam says. 'I'm so sorry. But I don't—'

'No, listen,' says Gethin. He takes a deep breath and holds out his hand like he's trying to calm down an animal. 'If I'm being honest, I don't like this any more than you do. You seem like a very nice young woman, but I've only just met you a couple of days ago. I've no bloody idea whether you'll make a good queen or not.'

'Exactly. So why are you—'

'He wanted you to come after him. Now, there's lots of other people here who'd love to have a go at being king, but I know for a fact that they wouldn't be able to do it. Too much infighting and jealousy, like there is everywhere else. Won't be long before they're fighting over who should replace him, and the whole Kingdom of New Gwynedd will come crashing down. Unless we find somebody else.'

'But it's crazy,' she says. 'I'm not from Wales. I don't speak Welsh. I don't even like leeks!'

'But you have slain a dragon,' says Gethin. 'Look, this whole business of restoring the Welsh monarchy, it was all Dai's idea. Twenty years ago, people would have laughed, if you told them there ought to be a King of Wales. But then Dai came along, and he took himself seriously. And we believed in it because *he* believed in it. He was the one holding it all together. Through sheer bloody-mindedness and force of will. He made us want to believe in it. Because he believed in himself. And that's all that matters.'

Mariam covers her face with the hand that's not holding the sword. She doesn't want this conversation to go any further.

'Why me, though?' she asks.

'Because he's chosen you,' he says. 'You've got a good story, and that's more important than anything. Queen Mariam the Dragon Slayer. We might be able to hold this all together, if you're willing to give it a go.'

She peers through her fingers, down at the sword. The blade gleams slightly even in the dim light of the tent. She stares at it for a long time, and Gethin seems content to let her. She finds herself wishing that Kay was here, but then she scowls at herself. That's the point of heroes, like Roz says. They absolve you of responsibility. They reassure you, because there's someone else around to save the world and make the hard decisions.

She's the one who has to make the hard decisions now.

What would Hassan want her to do?

'Okay,' she says. 'Conditions.'

'Right.'

'Wales has to go green. You have to stop using fossil fuels.'

Gethin looks pained. He scratches the back of his head. 'I'm not sure how feasible that is. We can't get anywhere without trucks or boats.'

'You can use potato fuel. We'll show you.'

'Okay,' says Gethin, spreading his hands.

'And hospitals. You have to look after people properly. Even if we ... I don't know. Even if we take over London, we have to make sure that we've got nurses and doctors and the proper facilities.'

'Fine,' he says. He's looking down at the sword. Mariam realises that she's been gesturing with it, pointing it at him, using it to drive home what she's been saying. She lowers it slightly.

She tries hard to think of any other demands, but nothing comes to mind. She wishes that the rest of her sisters were there to make suggestions, but then she changes her mind. They would all have too much to say. It would start to get ridiculous. It's better, sometimes, when somebody just takes charge and does something. So maybe that's what she should do.

'How does this happen, then?' she asks.

'Well, we have to burn Dai first,' he says, staring at the ground while he says it. 'That'll be in the morning, once it's light. Then we'll get to the business of crowning you. So, uh. You might want to have a think overnight, about what you're going to say.'

He turns around and unzips the tent but stops at the last moment and looks back at her. 'You'll do a brilliant job,' he says.

She's left standing in the dark tent full of strange boxes, with the sword in her hand.

25

Kay drifts through thought and memory, blown about like a boat on the stormy sea. This mushroom is taking him to strange places. Dark forests and yawning caverns and gloaming faerie halls. He remembers weird deeds done long ago, in his first life. Dreamlike deeds that seem impossible now. He fought a giant cat on the isle of Mona which had scales and gills and fins like a fish. He slew an army of toad men, wading up to his belly in a flooded cave. He spoke to eagles and crossed the sea on the back of a giant salmon. Did any of it actually happen, or is it just the mushrooms curdling his brain? They ate enough mushrooms in the old days that you could believe it either way.

There were no giant salmon or angry giants, in the wars that came afterwards. But that didn't make them any easier to understand. He doesn't want to remember those wars now and live through all of his deaths again. Not even in this dream.

So he tries to wake up. But the mushroom won't let go of his brain. When he does wake up, he's in his father's stable, in

Londinium. He's been sleeping out with the dogs again, in the yard. Trajan's stall is empty, and it takes him a moment to remember why. His father's ridden off to war, selling his lance.

This was a long time ago. Kay couldn't have been more than five years old, when it happened. But the mushroom has dredged his memory and brought it up as clear as day. He knows what's happening. He knows which day this is.

His mother is in the house, singing while she weaves a basket. An old Mauritanian song that he doesn't know the words to. Whenever his father was away fighting, she managed the household herself. Wove baskets and sold them to pay for food. He helped sometimes. Learnt the craft. Always enjoyed twisting one strand of thin rattan over the other. Slowly but surely giving form to the final thing. Then he'd go with her to market. Hear all the different tongues being spoken, see all the colourful fabrics, smell the spices and the dyes and the different meats sizzling on different pans. Part of him wants to go and help now, but that wasn't what he did on the day, so he can't do it now. Instead of the warm and friendly sounds of the market he hears commotion out on the street. People shouting things. Hoofbeats on the broken Roman road.

He brushes some strands of straw from his crumpled tunic and toddles out of the stable yard to see where the noise is coming from. Into the road, where he could be trampled by any passing oxcart.

There are horsemen riding slowly down the street, and the people of the city are running in front of them. His father used to ride with a band of mounted spearmen who fought in the Roman style, serving a magistrate called Aurelianus, an old-fashioned cavalryman with old-fashioned ideas about duty. It lifted your heart, the sight of them, returning from war on their dusty horses. Clattering in their mail, with fresh wounds on their shields.

'A giant did that,' his father would say, and Kay would believe him. Sometimes if they'd won they'd throw treasure into the crowd, plunder from their vanquished enemies. They aren't throwing treasure on this particular day. And there are fewer of them than there were when they set out. Aurelianus himself failed to return from this battle, and Kay wondered why. He didn't understand, at the time, what had happened to the missing men.

The other Britons on their street are running wildly, eager to share the terrible news with everyone else. Uther the Dragon is dead, and his forces broken. Their hero, who might have ridden down to deliver them from peril, pushing the Saxons back into the sea. He has been slain by murderous Picts, or by treachery, or by the Saxons themselves. There are a dozen different stories, disappearing down a dozen different alleyways and side streets, where they will be picked up and changed and spread throughout the city, until word reaches the Saxons on their island fortress, downriver. And nobody knew what would happen after that.

Kay stands in the street with other Britons panicking all around him, watching his father ride towards him. He remembers this day. His father never looked more tired or sour or war-beaten than he looked on that day. Hunched beneath his red cloak, holding a bundle in his arms and riding somebody else's horse. Wounded in the leg, with a deep cut that didn't mend well on the road. Red blood adding more lustre to his black skin.

His father's name was Hector – or, that's what the Romans called him. They couldn't pronounce his Numidian name, and he reminded them of a prince called Hector from the old stories, so Hector he became. When he rides close enough, Hector sees his son standing in the road. He pulls up his new horse and almost falls from the saddle. Passing the strange bundle down into Kay's arms.

Kay remembers this part much more clearly. Finer cloth than

he'd ever touched before, at that age. Then he felt the bundle move in his arms, and realised that the bundle was a child. Beneath the folds of silk he saw a pale white baby with copper-red curls of hair. He was barely big enough to hold a baby without dropping it, but his father told him to take the baby inside, and that's what he did. Running indoors to find his mother while his father led his weary horse into the stable yard. Bringing the last of the Roman horsemen with him.

There were a lot of arguments, after that. Kay sat silently at the dinner table while his mum and dad shouted at each other and the baby cried.

'Doesn't matter what he's called or where I got him from,' his dad would say, sighing heavily. 'You were saying that we could do with a boy around the house. Fetch water for you. Sweep the yard. All of that. Well now you've got one. I thought you'd be grateful. We'll have to rear him up a bit, but they grow big, these lads from out west. Broad shoulders.'

'Never mind his fucking shoulders. If this is your son that you've had in the heath with some pasty Welsh trollop then I'll not have him in my house. I'll leave him out on the street.'

'Blood of Christ, woman, I wasn't gone long enough for that, was I?'

'Don't blaspheme!'

'And he'd hardly look like that, would he, pale as the moon, if he was my lad? Even if I'd sired him on the whitest woman in Britannia.'

'So where did you find him?'

'You don't need to know that.'

'I suppose we'll need to baptise him as well, if he's from that part of the country. All pagans over there. And if you think I'm the one who's going to bribe the priest then you've got another thing coming.'

'Does it matter, whether he's been baptised or not?'

'I'm not bringing him up a pagan!'

And so it went, for a while. His mother wasn't happy at first. She would leave the baby crying in the corner of the kitchen, tutting at him and telling him to be quiet. But then she started to go soft for him. It wasn't long before she was feeding the boy on goat's milk, from a special wineskin that she ordered from the tanners in the marketplace. Then she would bring him to the dinner table and bounce him on her knee, smiling and making baby noises.

Kay can remember feeling jealous, at first. He was only a boy. If he'd known that he had a brother coming then he might have felt differently. But to have one turn up from nowhere, without any warning, seemed unfair to him. He never said anything about it. Just silently got on with everything that his father expected him to do, polishing spearheads and cleaning out the stable yard and oiling his father's mail. But his mother didn't take him to the market as often as she did before. She took the baby instead, wrapped in a sling against her chest. So he stayed at home more often, worked with his father more often. Learnt how to lace his father's mail together and how to put a new leather rim on a round shield. How to haft a spear and shoe a horse. And eventually his father took a good long look at him and put a wooden sword in his hand. 'Hit me with that. Hard as you can. No, harder. Good. Do it again.'

So while his mother went to market with the new baby, Kay learnt how to use a sword.

By the time his baby brother was old enough to walk and talk, Kay knew how to fight. He started roaming the streets with the other Christian boys, looking for trouble. Wrestling with Saxon boys and throwing stones at soldiers. Arthur used to tag along, just wanting to play with the bigger boys. Addy, they called him then. Sometimes they'd send him on quests around the city, to find things that didn't exist. Just to be rid of him for a while.

But Kay felt protective of him, then. Feeling a keen urge to shield him from the worst cruelties of the world. Trying to bring him up tough. Teach him life's hard lessons earlier than he needed to learn them. He tripped him up, pushed him over. Held his face down in a drinking trough until he nearly drowned. Told himself he was doing it out of love. Maybe he wasn't. Maybe it was laced with anger, even then.

Eventually their father decided that if they were going to be brawling with Saxon boys then they both needed to know how to fight. It might have been because of how the realm was going. Londinium was nearly burnt, three or four times. More raiders kept coming upriver. Irish in the west. Picts in the north. No sign of Rome sending any help. Every man or boy had to hold a sword.

So their father put a sword into Arthur's hand as well. He started teaching them properly. How to fight like common horse-men. Where you should stick your Saxon if you want to lame him quickly, and where you should stick him if you have the time to keep him dead. How to break bones or bite ears if you couldn't get your swordpoint somewhere vital. When they knew all that, their father set them against each other, had them beating each other with old, blunted spears.

Kay usually won, at first. He'd started learning earlier, so Arthur had to catch up. He would knock Arthur flat on his arse with a slam from his shield, or wind him with a sudden jab from his spear. And then he'd offer Addy a hand up. Smiling down at him. Trying to give him some advice. He remembers Addy sitting on the straw and cobbles, still a beardless stripling, pale as milk. Pushing the long red hair out of his face. Looking up at him with tempered scorn in his eyes.

'Don't tell me what I'm doing wrong,' said Arthur.

'How else are you supposed to learn?' he said back. 'How else are you supposed to get better?'

'I don't need *you* to tell me,' Arthur said.

And Kay began to realise that he'd done something wrong, with all of his hard teaching. Addy didn't look up to him or worship him. Addy resented him. Addy would always, forever, do the opposite of whatever he told him to do.

That look in Arthur's eye never left him, even years later against the Saxons. Tempered scorn. He wanted to beat his brother. He wanted to beat everyone. He spent hours at night dancing in the dark stable yard, practising his footwork. Kay might have started earlier, but Arthur started younger. He learnt quickly. He got good. It got to the point where he was winning as often as he lost.

And that was when Merlin rode in on a white horse. He appeared from nowhere, back from his travels to distant lands, weighed down by the things he brought back with him. He was still young enough then that his hair and beard were raven black, but his eyes already had that mad rainbow light behind them that made men tremble, staring in two slightly different directions.

He climbed down from his horse and brushed the dirt from his robes and asked Hector, their father, what he had done with the boy. The same boy that he gave to Hector in the far north, long ago. The son of Uther the Dragon. The boy who would be king.

Kay wakes up with a jolt and bangs his elbow on something, looking around in a brief panic while he figures out where he is. A dark and cramped space which seems to be moving around him. He can hear music, fake music from a speaker, the same few notes over and over again. Barry scampers up to him in the darkness.

''Ello,' says Barry. 'Look who's awake.'

'Where are we?' asks Kay, confused.

'Erm,' says Barry. 'We're in the van, with this faerie. They've been driving us somewhere. No clue where.'

Kay sits up, unsteadily. Barry's right. This is the back of the ice cream van. He's on the floor between the cupboards and the cardboard boxes. He has to brace himself against the refrigerator, because the van is moving over bumpy ground. Barry struggles even more, bouncing around and scrabbling for purchase.

'How did I get in the van?' he asks.

Barry looks at the fay and does a tiny squirrel shrug. 'They're stronger than they look.'

Kay follows Barry's gaze to the front of the van, where the fay is hunched over the steering wheel. The chiming music is playing from somewhere above them. A child's tune, over and over again.

'You were out like a light, mate,' says Barry. 'I wouldn't buy from him again, like. Dodgy dealer.'

Barry's not wrong. Now that he's figured out where he is, the panic leaves him, and he realises how rough he feels. His brain feels wet. There's a sharp pain behind his eyes. His limbs are trembling. He's still trying to piece things together, trying to remember what he saw in his dream. He rubs his eyes. 'I saw Arthur,' he says, mostly to himself. 'I dreamt about Arthur.'

'Who?'

He's about to explain when the jingling tune from overhead slowly fades into silence. The fay brings the ice cream van to a stop and turns around with a grin on their face.

'Here we are!' they sing.

It's difficult to get out of the van. Kay has to clamber over boxes of waffle cones and bags of mushrooms and all manner of other detritus, then squeeze into the cab. Down out of the passenger-side door, which the fay holds open for him. Then he's standing

317

on damp earth, with the instant sense of being somewhere wild and remote.

In the glow from the van's headlights he can see that his sword is here, driven into the ground, with his shield lying next to it. The van has stopped at the end of a tiny winding road, with thick woodland on either side. A strange wind wails through the trees, and a solid cliff face stands in front of them. A sign with an oak leaf on it says ALDERLEY EDGE.

The fay walks forward and waves their hand in a circle. Suddenly the cliff face isn't quite so solid. A cave appears, with a pair of rusty gates hanging across the mouth.

'Is Merlin in there?' asks Kay.

'You must enter,' says the fay. 'Leave the squirrel.'

Kay sighs. He looks at Barry, sitting on the van's passenger seat. 'Best stay here. I'll go in and talk to him for you. Ask him if he can turn you back.'

'Whatever you say, mate,' says Barry. 'I'll just . . . be out here with them, then.'

Kay gives the fay a stern look. The fay grins back at him, sharp-toothed. Then he goes to retrieve his sword and shield.

When the sword is back in his scabbard and the shield is back on his arm, he walks towards the cave. The old gates are nearly off their hinges, and they collapse inwards with a single kick. A rusty chain falls to the floor.

Inside there is darkness. Hard to know what you might find, in a place like this. In the old days it could have been anything, any otherworldly thing that had slipped through the veil in search of dark refuge. A young dragonling trying to build a hoard here, or giant spider laying its eggs. An ancient giant that somehow survived the purge.

Kay tries to empty his head. You have to be careful, thinking about beasts like that when there's a lot of magic about. If you're not careful you can think them into being. Would be good if he had his staff with him. But Morgan has the staff now, and that's his own fault.

He steps inside. He doesn't have an electric torch, so he looks around to see if he could make an old-fashioned one. Any piece of timber, a dry rag, some stones with which to strike a fire. But he doesn't have to look for long because he sees a switch on the wall instead. Could be for anything. There's a wire leading upwards, somewhere. He whispers a short prayer to God and then an even quieter one to whatever old god might have chosen to slumber in this cave. Then he reaches out and flicks the switch with one green finger.

The gods deliver. A dim strip of light flickers on overhead. Why does a place like this still have electricity running to it? If there are any answers, he'll probably find them further inside. He takes a breath, then forges onwards.

The cave widens, leading deeper into shadow. There's another ice cream van sitting in here, on piles of bricks, with the wheels removed. Cardboard boxes lying around with MISTER FRUITY written on the sides. The air around him is close and dank and fuggy, with a smell that he remembers from somewhere. It's like the bodies at the camp. The ones overgrown with mushrooms. Not a pleasant memory.

He decides that it's time to draw his sword. It feels strange, gripping the hilt with his oak hand. Hand bark against hilt leather.

There's a sound carrying down the cave. It takes him a while to realise what it is. Somebody humming. He thinks that he might have heard the tune before, a long time ago. It might have been in a dream. Maybe he hasn't heard it yet, or ever before, but he remembers anyway. His mind working backwards. Magic can play tricks like that.

There are wires snaking along the floor. They lead to wherever the sound is coming from, or so it seems. He follows their course to a curtain hung across the cave, a veil made from strips of plastic or something else synthetic. The wires lead under it. The humming is coming from the other side.

He takes a deep breath. He puts his shoulder through the curtain, pushing aside two of the dangling strips. Leading with his sword hand. Going through the veil.

The other side looks the same but makes less sense. He is still in the cave, still lit by electric lights, but now there are rows of planters with something growing in them. Tubes and pipes snaking the ground in disorderly bundles. Computers whirring, banks of light blinking in the semi-darkness.

And there, among the mess, is Merlin. Sitting at a metal work-table and staring through the eyepiece of a microscope. He isn't wearing the bedraggled blue mantle that he used to wear in the old days, stained from the road. He is wearing shorts. Socks and sandals. A colourful short-sleeved shirt with a floral print. But he is still the same Merlin. With his gaunt face and his banded beard, and his white hair tied behind him.

'Late!' Merlin shouts, without looking up. 'You should have been here days ago. What on earth have you been doing?'

Kay slides his sword back into its scabbard. He finds that he's laughing, despite himself. Happy to be getting a lecture from Merlin again. It's been more than a thousand years since the last one. He wants to run over and wrap his arms around him, but Merlin wouldn't understand what he was doing, or why he was doing it. He doesn't know what to say to him now.

'What have I been doing?' asks Kay. 'What the fuck have *you* been doing?'

Merlin tuts to himself. He still doesn't lift his eyes, but he moves a hand to adjust the focus on his instrument. 'You've forgotten your lessons,' he says. 'Foul language never got anybody anywhere.'

'What have you been doing, though? All this time?'

'You say that as if I haven't been doing anything,' Merlin grumbles, 'when in fact I have been quite busy.'

'Doing what?'

Merlin finally looks up from his work with a scowl on his face. His rainbow eyes staring in two slightly different directions.

'I have been working powerful magics upon the realm,' says Merlin, 'if you must know. And setting delicate schemes in motion, which you are threatening to entirely ruin, by blundering about the land causing your usual mischief, and arriving here later than you ought to have arrived!'

'You could have made yourself a bit easier to find, in fairness.'

'Are you blind, as well as stupid? Did you not see my name written on the walls? Did you not think to ask earlier where you might find Ambrose?'

'Who?'

Merlin pinches the bridge of his nose. Kay remembers him doing that in the old days when he was particularly exasperated. 'I should have thought that it was perfectly obvious,' he says. 'Perhaps this is my error, in failing to account for your stupidity. Ambrosius was my Latin name. I couldn't very well have gone around writing "Merlin" everywhere, could I? There are people looking for me! People trying to hinder my progress. Oil men and Morris dancers and other servants of evil . . . even time travellers! I've seen them, coming back to try and stop me!'

'Stop you from doing *what*?'

'From saving the realm and banishing evil. The tree of time splits ahead of us, as always.'

'Not the bloody tree of time again,' says Kay.

Merlin's scowl grows fiercer. 'Yes, the tree of time! There are

321

two branches ahead of us. The first is a blasted bough of blackness and corruption, down which we must not travel or the realm will perish and all will be wrought to ruin. And on the other hand, the faintest shoot of green. Hope, Kay! Hope for a bright future! But we must act hastily. Come with me.'

And then Merlin is up, out of his seat with more agility than somebody ought to have at the age of sixteen hundred. He leads Kay further into the cave, sandals flapping against the stone floor. Past plants and computers and experiments and cardboard boxes full of wafer cones. Kay follows, shaking his head. He's always tried his best to understand the tree of time, and Merlin has always tried his best to explain it to him, but Merlin's brain just works differently to the brains of ordinary men. Merlin sees time all at once. That's what happens when you go mad on the battlefield and spend the rest of your life eating strange mushrooms. Licking the backs of toads. Other people remember the past and imagine the future. Merlin can see time spread out in front of him. He sees it like a giant tree. He can see all the way back to its earliest roots, and all the way forward into its highest leaves. Branches that haven't even grown yet. He can see how the tree weaves and wends, how it splits and branches off. Thousands of possible futures. Or that's what he's always said. Kay tries his best to comprehend.

'I thought we'd already gone down the wrong branch, or whatever it was,' he says. 'You said that when Arthur died.'

Merlin scoffs. 'Yes, we are on a black bough, when we might have gone down a far greener one. We missed that chance a long time ago. But even black boughs have green shoots. There are still good strong branches that might grow ahead of us, if we nurture them.'

'And how do we do that?'

'If you would stop interrupting me, then I shall explain it to you. Goodness gracious. Now, first we must determine … we must try and determine which version of things is already happening. Have you found Mariam?'

'Yeah …'

'Excellent! She's important. Must keep her safe. Where is she?'

Kay reaches up to scratch the back of his neck. 'Well, I found her once, but then I bumped into Lancelot and we ended up killing each other. So I don't actually know where she is right now. But—'

Merlin stops and spins around, glaring up at him. You forget how short Merlin is until you're standing a head taller than him. It doesn't make him any less imposing.

'What was the point of finding her once only to lose her again?' asks Merlin. 'Do you have the staff, at least? The Rod of Amaethon? Where is it?'

'I did have it. But now … Morgan's got it.'

Merlin stares at him for a long, uncomfortable moment. Kay can see Merlin's mind working behind his eyes, trying to discern which branch of the tree they have travelled down. Which branches still lie ahead of them. Once he has thought about it for long enough, he shakes his head and walks away again.

'I don't know why I bothered using resurrection stones on any of you,' Merlin says. 'Immortal warriors … quite useless. I'd have been better off training a flock of seagulls. Perhaps they'd have been more use.'

They reach another plastic curtain hung across the cave. Instead of going through it, Merlin starts moving furniture around. There is clutter everywhere, steel tables piled up and objects hidden under sheets. Merlin was always like the centre of a storm, surrounded by chaos and confusion. Eventually he finds what he is looking for: a kind of mechanical chair, with arm and leg restraints. Somebody could be strapped into it and held down, if they needed to be kept from fleeing. Merlin drags it out into the centre of the cave and takes a moment to recover from the effort. Then he turns to look at Kay.

'Well, come on,' says Merlin. 'Kit off, sit down. Let's have a look.'

'I . . . what?'

'This oak-flesh business. Isn't that why you came here? Do you want me to have a look at it, or not?'

He learnt a long time ago that Merlin already knows everything. It's no use resisting it. He sighs and starts to ungirth his sword belt. A minute later he's stripped to his waist again and sitting back in the strange chair. He doesn't need Merlin to tell him that the oak flesh is getting worse. His wrist has grown a solid crust of bark that cracks whenever he bends it. It seems to be spreading to his hand, his forearm. There are spots of bark emerging through the skin. And the great knot in the centre of his chest seems bigger, feels tighter.

Merlin is fussing around him, muttering to himself, prodding him with something that might be a doctor's implement but could equally be the stick from an iced lolly. It's oddly relaxing, giving himself over. Letting Merlin cluck and grumble around him. Trusting himself to Merlin's wisdom. The danger is that he'll forget why he came here. If he lets Merlin keep talking over him and tell him what to do, he won't get anything useful out of him.

'There's a friend of mine outside who got turned into a squirrel,' he says, 'and he wants to be turned back again.'

'Why on earth should he want that?' says Merlin. 'Much less complicated, being a squirrel. No concerns loftier than food or shelter. Much easier to live in harmony with nature, as a squirrel. Much less destructive than being a person.'

'Could you sort him out?'

'All in good time, dear boy. It's very peculiar, this oak business.

324

I didn't write anything like it into the spell. It must be caused by some sort of natural change. The magic that's been bringing you back for all these years is drawn from the earth, the rocks, the trees. I can't imagine what's causing it.'

Natural change. Like the changing weather, the rising oceans. 'Well, the world is changing,' he says. 'It's different. Warmer. The weather's broken. There must be something you can do to stop it. Didn't you know that all of this was going to happen?'

Merlin scoffs again and chuckles to himself. 'Kay, my dear boy. Of course I knew about it. I foresaw all of this *two thousand years ago*. It has been my life's work to try and stop it! To save everyone from destruction. I couldn't tell you all, at first. You would have thought I was mad.'

'Yeah, well, we all thought that anyway.'

'But I knew I had to do something. There are all sorts of world-ending cataclysms on the tree of time. There are blackened boughs that end with disease, or famine, or catastrophic warfare. Rocks hurtling through space, and so on. We have avoided most of those. Travelled down different branches. But far more numerous than any of them are the branches where we cook ourselves to death. Almost every branch, every shoot and leaf, ends with the earth getting too warm. Half the tree is burning, dying. Only very few branches tend away from that towards a long, bright future. We have already missed most of those chances. But there are still some precious shoots ahead of us. And I have been guiding us towards them for centuries – or trying to. If we'd managed to spread druidism across the world then things would have been a lot easier ...'

'So what are you doing to stop it now?'

Merlin isn't listening. He picks up a pair of metal tweezers and goes back to his work, prodding at the oak flesh, muttering to himself. 'If I made one mistake it was giving Arthur to your father. Brought him up Christian. Filled his head with nonsense. That's what set us off down the wrong bough. Next time I'll look after him myself. Take him into the woods, bring him up to love nature . . . but no, that wouldn't work either. If turning him into a fish couldn't get it into his head, then I don't know what . . . bah! Well, never mind. Enough kings. *This* plan! This will work.'

Kay sighs and feels himself relax. Merlin has a plan. That fact alone is cause for relief. It gives him a glimmer of hope, even before he knows what the plan is. If Merlin has a plan then there might be a way out of all of this. A way to actually save the realm. This is why he came here, really. Not for Barry, or even for the oak flesh. Because he wanted to know Merlin's plan. Because he wanted Merlin to tell him what to do.

'So what is the plan?' he asks.

Instead of answering, Merlin tears a sizeable chunk of bark from Kay's finger. It comes away with a crunch and a string of wet sap, stinging like hellfire and making him scream through clenched teeth. He holds his trembling hand up in front of him to stare at the wound. Removing the topmost layer has left a lighter patch of bark underneath, younger and smoother and greener. Merlin goes and puts the piece of bark in a glass jar, closing the lid.

'Really quite extraordinary,' says Merlin. 'Now, you wanted to know the plan, didn't you? Come this way and I'll show you.'

He doesn't have time to stand up and get dressed, or even to ask Merlin how the oak flesh can be cured. Merlin pushes through the next curtain, into the space beyond.

26

There isn't much wood up here in the mountains, so the Welsh can't build Dai a proper funeral pyre. They make a small mound of cargo pallets and lay his body on top of it, adorned with daffodils. Once they've spoken some words they douse him in petrol and stand back to watch the fire.

Mariam stands with everyone else, her nose full of fumes, trying not to choke. The petrol doesn't seem like a great start to Wales going green. It doesn't feel like a funeral fit for a king. But then the Welsh start singing their anthem, one voice, then three, joined quickly by all the others. It's beautiful. Mariam wishes she could join in, but she doesn't know the words. She stares into the fire, wishing that King Dai had lived long enough to give her some advice. Wishing strangely that Kay was here, next to her.

She's grateful to have Teoni and the others standing behind her. Willow gave her a piece of camping gear to clip onto her belt so that she can hang the sword through it and wear it on her hip, instead of carrying it around all the time. Bronte stayed up late last night making daffodil crowns for all of them. It would feel mean not to wear them. But neither of these things make her feel more like a queen.

While the fire's still blazing Gethin leads them all across the moor to something ancient, a low pile of jagged grey stones. There's grass growing through them and they're speckled with moss. Mariam doesn't know what they are or how long they've been here, but Gethin has told her how important this place is. The name means something like 'The Hill of the Throne'. The outermost stones look like the edges of a crown, jutting up towards the sky.

The Welsh stand around the stone circle and wait for Gethin to speak. Mariam glances carefully between them, avoiding eye contact. None of them look thrilled to be here. None of them are giving her kind looks.

'Sons of Wales,' says Gethin.

He speaks in English. There are instant shouts of protest, in Welsh. Gethin puts up his hands and waits for silence before continuing. 'We have guests with us who don't know our language,' he says, 'and they need to hear what is being said. So I ask you all to speak English, for these proceedings.'

Some of the Welsh turn and leave immediately, shaking their heads. Mariam would quite like to leave with them. She's almost glad that she can't hear what's being said. One or two of them do switch to English, just for her benefit.

'It's a bloody disgrace!'

'Now, lads,' says Gethin. 'You'll have heard by now that Dai named this woman, Mariam Alsiham, as his successor, before he died.'

'Who is she?'

'He's not even finished burning yet and you're trying to replace him with some stranger!'

'How do we know that Dai named her as queen? We're just taking her word for it!'

Gethin tries to calm them down. 'Anyone who was with Dai on the drive up here will have heard it for themselves,' he says. 'You can ask them. Rhys was there.'

Mariam recognises Rhys from the lorry, with his gaunt face and scraggly moustache. He looks uncomfortable, having been named.

'I don't know what I heard,' he says. 'Dai wasn't making much sense.'

The Welsh start shouting. She stands silently clenching her teeth. Wanting to grab the flower crown from her head and throw it on the ground. Here she is at another meeting, *another* meeting, watching people shout at each other for stupid reasons. There's smoke rising from across the moor where Dai's body is still burning. More carbon floating into the atmosphere. She stares at the smoke for long enough that her anger outweighs her nervousness. The words rise up out of her throat unbidden.

'I'm sorry that I'm not speaking to you in Welsh,' she says. 'I'm sorry that your king is dead. He seemed like a pretty good king. I know you must all be feeling lost and confused right now without him. I'm feeling pretty lost and confused myself.'

'Fuck off back to London, then,' somebody shouts, 'or wherever it is you're from.'

'Actually I'm from Manchester,' she says. 'But King Dai must have thought that it didn't matter where I was from. He thought I'd make a decent Queen of Wales. I don't know why he thought that. But I'm willing to give it a go, if you're willing to have me.'

'I'm not having some bloody feminist being Queen of Wales!'

Chaos again. Gethin shouts at the other Welsh, telling them to show some respect. Her sisters are shouting behind her, furious and indignant. Bronte looks almost thrilled. It makes it easier to disagree with people if they reveal their true nature. The tent gets smaller, and the Welsh are placed outside of it, and everybody goes on hating each other. Mariam just stares at the pile of stones on the ground. It doesn't really look like a crown, if you stare at it for long enough. It just looks like a pile of stones.

'Look, we don't have time for this!' she shouts over the noise. 'There's been enough arguing and shouting and disagreeing already. It's time to take action, now. We can't afford to waste any more time with this bullshit.'

There is uproar, but she shouts over it. 'No, I'm sorry, it is bullshit. I don't care who the King of Wales is. I don't care whether it's me or Gethin or King Arthur or whoever. But I care about the planet. And I care about stopping the people who are destroying the planet. And they're the same people who are destroying Wales. The same people you're fighting against. Every moment we waste arguing, they're using it to burn more oil, and make more money, and cut down more trees, and make the world more miserable. They like it when we argue. So I think we should stop arguing and start going after them instead. Because that's the only way we're ever going to stop them. And if I have to be Queen of Wales to make that happen, then fine. I'll be Queen of Wales.'

Teoni whoops and cheers, behind her. The Welsh seem less happy.

'Lads,' says Gethin, 'when I was in Manchester, yesterday, I saw this woman kill a dragon. Those of you who weren't with us might struggle to understand that, but I'm telling the truth. I'll swear it on the bones of Saint David, or whatever else you like. You can ask Rhys or Ieuan or any of the others – they saw it too. And more importantly, Dai saw it. And he thought that was enough for him to name Mariam as his successor. So as far as I'm concerned, we should do as he said.'

One of the other Welsh leaders is shaking his head. 'Sorry, Gethin,' he says. 'But I came here to fight for Dai. If you're asking us to fight for her instead, then me and my boys are going home.'

Welshmen from other places start to agree. They start melting away, in groups. Retreating to different parts of the camp. Until it's just Mariam, and her friends, and Gethin, left standing around the pile of stones.

'That could have gone better,' says Gethin. 'I'll go and talk some sense into them. Maybe we can try again this evening, once we've had time to calm down.'

'No,' says Mariam. 'Don't bother.'

Gethin frowns at her and leaves, walking back towards the camp. Mariam reaches up and pulls the crown of daffodils from her head, throwing it into the stones in front of her.

Willow places a hand on her arm. 'It's not your fault, Mar. I thought you did really well.'

'Not well enough.'

'Don't beat yourself up about it.'

'They were never gonna let you convince them, were they?' says Roz. 'This is all too weird. I think we just back out of it and get the fuck out of here.'

'But we've got a whole army here!' says Teoni. 'If we can get them to listen to us then we can just go and murder everyone on the Avalon rig.'

'Um,' says Bronte, 'I feel like maybe murder shouldn't be our end goal here?'

'No,' says Mariam. 'Roz is right. I can't be the Queen of Wales, can I? It's just mental.'

'Why not?' asks Teoni. 'Just fake it 'til you make it. Be like, "I'm the queen now, deal with it".'

'That's probably what King Arthur did, to be fair,' says Willow. 'Or William the Conqueror, or whoever. That's how it gets started. Some rando just decides that they're in charge. Why can't it be you?'

The mist has thickened around them, blowing down off the mountain, bringing a cold chill with it. Dampness hanging in the air. Mariam scowls against the cold. 'Because none of these people respect me. They're not going to listen to me. Maybe if King Arthur was here, they'd listen to him, but—'

'Now,' says a new voice, 'that's an interesting idea, isn't it?'

Mariam looks up. Regan is standing in the middle of the stone circle, where she wasn't standing before. Here she is, not burnt alive or eaten by a dragon but standing in front of them, leaning on a stick. Not just any stick. Kay's staff.

Nobody runs over to hug Regan this time. They stand silently, letting their confusion speak for them. Eventually Mariam swallows to clear her throat.

'How did you get here?' she asks.

'You wouldn't believe me if I told you.'

'No,' says Mariam, 'I don't think I would. This is the second time you've done this.'

'Done what, my dear?'

'Disappeared during a dragon attack. Then reappeared again, from nowhere.'

'It is starting to look pretty sketchy,' says Willow. 'Not gonna lie.'

Regan looks surprised for half an instant. Then a smile spreads across her face. 'There's no fooling you, is there?' she asks. 'You're far too smart for me to pull the wool over your eyes any longer. Not like Kay and his friend.'

'What the fuck are you talking about?' asks Roz.

'Why don't we all sit down,' says Regan, 'and I'll explain.'

So that's what they do, slowly and cautiously. The members of FETA seat themselves at intervals around the stone circle. Regan lays the oak staff across her legs and starts rolling a cigarette. Mariam holds the sword firmly in one hand.

'There are some secrets I've been keeping from you all,' says Regan. 'Secrets that I've been keeping for a very long time. I'm sorry for deceiving you, and I'll try and explain everything in due course. The important thing right now is that you have that sword, Mariam, and I have this staff. And with those two things together, there's a chance that we can bring an end to all of this. To all of this greed and corruption and cruelty. If you're willing to trust me.'

Mariam glances away, down at the ground. Aware that Regan is speaking to her in particular, more than any of the others. But it's the others who start asking questions.

'So, what, you're part of all of this?' asks Roz. 'All of this magic bullshit? King Arthur and everything?'

'Very much a part of it, I'm afraid,' says Regan. 'I turned my back on all of it, a very long time ago. Tried to live a quiet life of helping and healing. But now I fear I have to get tangled up in it again. Use my powers to try and change the world.'

'Powers?' asks Teoni. 'Like, supernatural powers?'

Regan smiles demurely. 'You could say that.'

A small pebble lifts itself from the pile of stones, guided only by Regan's gaze. It floats towards Teoni, who takes it gingerly in her hand.

'That's so cool,' says Bronte quietly.

'It's not cool,' says Roz, drawing herself back from the circle. 'It's fucking weird.'

'Why are you only telling us about this now?' asks Willow, squinting.

'I'm not sure you'd have believed me until recently,' says Regan. 'And we have so little time left, now, in which to save the world. I used to think we could do it without the use of magic. By protesting, campaigning, bringing down the oil industry ... but I'm starting to think that magic might be our only hope.'

Hope. It's almost embarrassing, how quickly it floods back. Is there some magic solution to all of this? Wave a magic wand and climate breakdown goes away? It can't be as easy as that. Mariam remembers what Roz said, that heroes absolve you of your responsibility to take action. But right now she wants to be absolved of responsibility. She doesn't want to pick up that crown of daffodils again from the stone circle.

'So,' she asks, 'can you just ... zap carbon out of the air, or ...?'

Regan laughs sadly. 'No, my dear. I'm afraid there's not enough magic left in the world for something like that. And my powers aren't as strong as they used to be. But there is something else we can do. If you're willing to give up that sword, we can give it to somebody who's held it before. We can bring back Arthur Pendragon.'

Mariam feels relief washing over her. She'd happily give the sword to anyone if they wanted to take it. It might as well be King Arthur. He'll probably know what to do with it. She imagines him like a Greek god, tall and muscular and glowing slightly. Coming alive again. Saying the right things to unite everyone behind him. Commanding their confidence with some legendary force. She imagines herself in the crowd, with nobody looking at her and asking her what to do. The relief of being able to melt into the shadows.

It feels as though Regan is reading her thoughts. 'Mariam, I think you'd make an excellent leader if you had the time to learn

334

how. But time is a luxury we don't have. If we want to save the planet then we need a strong leader *now*, to unite the country behind him. To remind people of what they should be fighting for and who they should be fighting against.'

'So how do we do it?' she asks. 'Bring him back?'

Regan smiles. 'We have everything we need. We have Excalibur. We have the staff. We have a queen who's willing to give up her throne. And it must be done on Glastonbury Tor, tomorrow morning.'

Bronte gasps. 'The vernal equinox!'

Regan nods. 'The start of spring. The proper day for waking up dead kings.'

'Hang on,' says Roz. 'So your plan for saving the planet is to bring some mouldy old king back from the dead and make him the king of England? I mean, it's not exactly very feminist, is it?'

'I know,' says Regan. 'But I have some sway over him. I believe he can be brought around to our way of thinking.'

It seems too good to be true. Mariam remembers what Kay said about Arthur. It was never anything specific. But the way he seemed to talk about him. The look on his face, when they mentioned his name. She got the sense that there might be more to Arthur than the legends, the shining golden king.

'Are you sure?' she asks. 'Kay said it would be bad, if we brought him back . . .'

Regan pulls a face. 'Kay was Arthur's brother. He's always been jealous of him, ever since they were children. And you saw in Manchester what Kay has to offer. You don't need to listen to the advice of ancient men like him. You can decide your own destiny.'

Mariam finds herself nodding. She stares at the ground for a long moment before she looks back up into Regan's face. 'Does King Arthur know about climate change?'

'I imagine not,' says Regan. 'But I shall try and explain it to him.'

They find Gethin in the Welsh command tent, sitting at a cluttered table with his head in his hands. When she walks in, he tries to make it look like he wasn't despairing.

'You all right?' he asks. 'I'm sorry about all that. The lads can get a bit worked up sometimes.'

'It's fine.'

'It was a good speech you gave,' says Gethin. 'I'm sorry it didn't work. But we can have a think now about what you're going to say at the next meeting, if you want. How you can win them over.'

'We don't have time for that,' she says. The world is already burning. The seas are already rising. 'But I think I've got a better idea.'

'Go on.'

'What if I told you that I could bring back King Arthur?'

Gethin blinks at her at least ten times before he says anything. In the silence, Regan slips into the tent. She seems taller than usual, taking up more space. Holding Kay's staff in her hand.

'Well,' says Gethin, 'the lads would like it. I suppose Arthur's the only other person they'd settle for, if they can't have Dai. But surely you can't ...'

'There's a certain way of doing it,' says Regan. 'But we need to be in Glastonbury at the stroke of dawn, tomorrow morning.'

Gethin shakes his head and stares at the table in front of him. It has a map of Wales laid out over it. When he's stared at it for long enough he sighs and shrugs his shoulders. 'Well, it's no more daft than anything else, is it? If there's dragons flying about then

I suppose Arthur's the man for the job, isn't he? We can tell the lads tonight.'

Mariam feels the weight lift from her shoulders as Gethin gets up to leave. She thanks him on the way out, and he claps a hand uncertainly on her shoulder. He doesn't look her in the eye as he goes past.

27

Lancelot is lying back on a tanning bed, with a towel draped over his lap and slices of cucumber resting on his eyelids. Feeling the absence of Galehaut's ring.

The spa on the Avalon is, admittedly, quite nice. Sun beating down on him through the glass ceiling. The air is agreeably warm and humid against his skin. Marlowe has given him a new music box, a more modern contraption than the old cassette player, and he has soothing panpipe music playing in his years. They have an arrangement with the masseurs and the serving staff to ensure there's always a cold glass of gin within arm's reach.

So he tries to relax. Swallowing his qualms with his gin. The alternative doesn't seem worth the effort. Climb up onto his high horse, draw his righteous sword, start passing judgement. Like rescuing Gwenhwyfar all over again. It didn't turn out very well back then. There's no reason it would turn out any better this time around. And he is very tired of all that. Playing the hero. Making sacrifices. He's lost enough recently without making things worse for himself, just to prove some notion of chivalry. Galehaut's gone. There's nobody left to fool – except for Marlowe, who cannot be fooled.

The spa is mostly empty today, besides him and Marlowe. Down in one corner of the swimming pool there's a handful of old men who might be CEOs or media barons or corporate warlords. He recognises some of them from the old days. Good Protestant men, like Marlowe, from the time of Elizabeth. Strange to see them in swimming trunks.

'How much do they know about your little scheme?' Lancelot asks. Tugging one of the headphones from his ear.

Marlowe groans on the couch beside him. 'Can't we just relax for a while?'

'Do they know more than I do?'

'They know all about it,' says Marlowe. 'Everybody here is completely au fait with what we're doing.'

Lancelot frowns. 'Au fait with bringing Arthur back?'

'Absolutely,' says Marlowe. 'He's the man they need to get the job done. The once and future king. There's a lot of power tied up in that prophecy.'

Lancelot removes a cucumber from one eye. 'Power of the temporal kind, or ... ?'

Marlowe is lying back impassively, calm and serene. Hands folded over his stomach. 'The power to save their skins,' he says. 'They know how it works, all of this magic rubbish. They know that Merlin sealed the barrier between the worlds, and so on. They know that it all rests on Arthur coming back. So they bring him back, stick him in some ermine, put a crown on his head, and hey presto. Magic returns to the realm. That opens up some options.'

'What kind of options?'

Marlowe sighs. 'Look,' he says. 'These people know that the

world is dying. They know that they need a way out. So they tried to find solutions. They looked into underground bunkers and luxury colonies on Mars and all of that rot. But it was all too impractical. And there was still the problem of food. Once the world gets hot enough and the surface dies, you can't grow anything. That's what it comes down to. They wanted to find something that would magically solve all of their problems.'

'And you helped them?'

Marlowe shrugs. 'They were willing to look anywhere. Entertain any possibility, however fanciful. And that brought them to the Department. That's why GX5 wanted to buy us out, really. So they could get their hands on my files.'

Lancelot feels the spark of outrage rising up through him, but it fizzles out like a damp squib. When you've lived through fifty kings and seen the world change beyond comprehension it's hard to maintain outrage about anything for very long. Otherwise, you'd be permanently outraged. But this still feels like a violation. He remembers how fiercely Marlowe used to guard his shadow bureau, his library of secret things. Ancient manuscripts and parchments and stone tablets, all neatly catalogued and locked away. The safest library in the world. Until now. Now Marlowe's friends have got their grubby hands all over it. The likes of Colonel Nashorn thumbing through it, suddenly knowing all the unknowable secrets of the land. Hidden places and sacred groves. Swords in damp caves. Sleeping giants. Portals to forgotten realms. All the places where old warriors are sleeping under trees.

He swallows his anger. 'I thought you and your friends were supposed to stop this sort of thing. I thought you were meant to look after all of the old secrets.'

'I'm sorry to disillusion you,' says Marlowe. 'But my superiors have always been principally concerned with looking after their own interests. Sometimes those interests have aligned with the interests of the Crown, or the interests of the realm. But not in this instance.'

'You used to say that if the bureau fell into the wrong hands it could mean the end of civilisation.'

'Well, yes,' says Marlowe, 'perhaps I did used to say that. But we're already looking at the end of civilisation, old boy. Staring right down the barrel of it. Now I'm just finding ways to push the barrel away.'

Away from himself and towards somebody else. Lancelot takes a slug of gin to stop himself from saying that out loud, but the gin tastes wrong. There's a bitter, chemical note to it now. Something wrong with the ice. Spoiling the drink, as it melts.

'Whose fault is it, exactly, that the world is dying?'

Marlowe finally clears the cucumbers from his own eyes, putting them on the table beside him for somebody else to clean up. 'There's no sense pointing fingers now,' he says. 'The game's up. It's sink or swim, at this point. And personally I'd rather swim.'

Lancelot shakes his head. 'It's like that restaurant on Mayfair that you took me to. In 1922, I think it was. You and your friends have trashed the place, and you're happy for somebody else to pick up the bill.'

'Precisely. Just scale that up to a planetary level. I'm glad you understand.'

'I'm not sure I do. You still haven't told me what this magical solution actually is.'

'All in good time, old boy,' says Marlowe.

Lancelot curls his hands into fists. The number of times he's heard those words from Marlowe, in a coach-and-four, or a railway carriage, or the back of a C47. It still feels like nails on a chalkboard. But he knows that getting answers out of Marlowe is like getting the sword out of the stone. There's no sense straining away at it all day.

'Whatever it is you're planning, it can't be worth bringing Arthur back,' he says. 'You weren't there, you don't know what he was like.'

'Ohh,' says Marlowe, dismissively, 'I'm sure he can't be all that bad.'

Lancelot doesn't know how to explain. He once saw Arthur kill a man by punching through his abdomen and tearing out his bowels like rope, but that's not the worst of it. He wasn't just Arthur the great bear warrior. He was also Arthur the dragon, the serpent. His gift was cowing men into following him, convincing them that he would lead them to glory. Making promises that sounded good but never seemed to come to fruition. Starting wars just to get people feeling spiteful, so they wouldn't notice the problems at home. Drumming up hatred. Unmoved by bloodshed, by loss of life. Incapable of feeling shame or understanding mercy. Gathering cruel men around him and stoking their worst instincts until their hate boiled over. It won't take him five minutes to adapt to this new world, even with its strange technology. The fighting, the division, the hatred. He'll find new followers, new people to turn his followers against. If not Saxons then somebody else. Foreigners. Immigrants. Riding the tide of hate like he always did.

'Christ,' he says. 'I think I need another gin.'

'Only one more,' says Marlowe. 'We have to be up at the crack of dawn tomorrow morning.'

'Dare I ask why?'

Marlowe smiles. 'Early bird gets the worm. We wouldn't want to be late for the return of the king.'

28

Merlin's cave stretches into distant darkness. Endless rows of metal racks with strange growths sprouting from them, spilling out onto the ground. Mushrooms. Thousands of them. Growing up the walls until they meet at the ceiling overhead.

Kay stands, uncomprehending. 'What is this place?' he asks.

Merlin chuckles. 'This is the nerve centre of my little mushroom empire. We're shipping to America, to Eastern Europe, to Africa, to Amsterdam – well, to the parts of Amsterdam that are still above water, anyway.'

There are boxes at Kay's feet, full of little plastic bags. Kay has seen them before. The paupers in the Preston camp, pinching the contents and placing them on their tongues.

'So it is you, selling this stuff?' he asks.

'Yes! We need to get it out to as many people as possible.'

He stands, thinking, shaking his head. 'I don't get it. The whole planet's dying, and you've known about it for centuries, and you're ... what? Selling mushrooms? So that people can get wasted and forget about it? How's that going to help?'

Merlin sighs heavily. 'Perhaps I should break it down for you. Are you at all familiar with the *Cordyceps* fungus? Zombie ants? No. I don't suppose you can watch many David Attenborough documentaries when you're under a hill. Come and look at this.'

There are glass tanks along one side of the cave. Merlin leads Kay over to them and hands him a magnifying glass. Kay does what he always used to do when Merlin had something to explain. He swallows his questions, he sighs to himself, and he does as he's told. Through the magnifying glass he can see insects inside the tank. They look like ants. But they are moving strangely, writhing in awkward patterns.

'A very nasty fungus,' says Merlin. 'It takes over muscle control and drives the ant to somewhere nice and high up, where it will get a lot of sunlight. Then it grows, piercing through the ant's exoskeleton. Eating the body from the inside out. Very nasty. But very ingenious.'

Kay looks higher up in the tank, where ants are hanging from leaves. Their bodies are furred over, with tiny mushrooms growing from them. Exactly like the paupers that he saw in the camp. The memory turns his stomach, and he has to put down the magnifying glass.

'Right,' he says. 'What does this have to do with—'

'Now,' says Merlin, 'here are my mushrooms. The common panther cap, crossbred with the *Cordyceps* fungus, and grown from the bark of one of your resurrection trees. I took a little bark from your tree, a little from Lancelot's, and so on ...'

Kay's mind struggles to make sense of all this. There's nothing to grab onto. He cannot fathom any of it. 'You did what?'

Merlin is leaning over one of his racks of mushrooms, cupping the mushrooms in one hand, sniffing them, peering under their caps. He carries on speaking.

'It's taken me two hundred years of *very* careful selection to bring out the right traits, to isolate the right enzymes. At first I was confined to spellwork and incantations. But it's much easier with modern technology. A bit of high-tech genome splicing, a bit of old-fashioned hockety-pockety, and I made my own special fungal cocktail! What do you think of that, eh? I'm rather proud of it.'

Kay stands silently, with his eyes narrowed. Still uncomprehending but feeling a kind of anger building in his breast and shoulders. Eventually the enthusiasm falls from Merlin's face.

'Oh, for heaven's sake, Kay. Do I have to spell it out to you? I've made a mind-control mushroom!'

'Why would you want to do that?'

Merlin shakes his head. 'You have a singular lack of vision, my boy.'

'Is this really what you've been doing, for two hundred years? Growing mushrooms? Why haven't you been doing anything useful? What are you doing to stop the waters rising? Can't you do a spell to take all of the corruption out of the air?'

Merlin laughs. 'What, wave my hand and reduce the amount of carbon dioxide in the atmosphere by two hundred parts per million? If I could do that, don't you think I'd have tried?'

'But you're a wizard. You're Merlin. You can do anything.'

'I'm a druid, Kay. My primary medium is plants. Living things, green things. No – there's always been a magic solution to the whole mess. Right under our very noses. Able to clean the air, to produce oxygen, to replicate itself. It's so brilliantly simple.'

'What is it?'

'Trees, Kay!' Merlin nearly explodes with excitement. 'Ordinary trees. We must give the great old forests time to recover. And then the forests will clean the air for us. But people keep cutting them down and burning them and making things worse.'

'Right,' says Kay. 'Okay, then. We just need to get the right people into power. Like in the old days. Find people who want to save the realm and plant some trees.'

Merlin is scowling now. 'No, no, no. Tried that. People are the problem, Kay. I'm tired of people. Tired of getting them to see sense and look past their own greed. It's quite impossible. I've been trying to convince *people* for two thousand years! And I've tried everything else, as well. All manner of contrivances. I've tried sorcery. I've tried muddling around behind the scenes. I've tried standing on the rooftops and shouting. I tried to find a half-decent king who'd do something about it, and we both know how that turned out. It's all become quite impossible. No. I've found a much more elegant solution.'

Merlin hands him something that he recognises instantly. Cold and smooth and bean-shaped, like something you'd dig out of the ground. Heavier than it ought to be, for something natural. Full of a strange weight. Kay swallowed one, a long time ago. It was the beginning of all this.

'You're using the resurrection stones?' he asks. 'The same ones you used with us?'

'Of course!' Merlin smiles. 'This is why I wanted to experiment with the stones in the first place. I needed to know if they could be enchanted to cause resurrection *conditionally*, you see. If such-and-such a thing is true, then alakazam! Resurrect this person. In your case, the condition was, "If Britain is in peril", but it really could have been anything.'

Merlin keeps pottering about, sniffing his mushrooms, never looking up while he speaks. Kay feels a chill creep up from his feet, all the way up to his stomach, then up his spine. It bleeds

346

slowly into his shoulders. He swallows a few times to clear the sudden lump from his throat.

'We were an experiment?' he asks.

'Hmm?' asks Merlin. 'Oh! Yes, one of my more successful ones, if I do say so myself. The results were mixed. I think the concept of "peril" needed a little refinement, which taught me that I needed to be more precise in future. Useful data. But, crucially, it showed me that the principle was sound. And once I knew that, I knew there was a chance of survival. You proved my theory.'

'Right,' says Kay, slowly. The coldness has reached the centre of his chest, where it is building into something solid. He can hear his heart beating in his ears.

'And now I can put that theory into practice!' says Merlin. 'I've enchanted these mushrooms with a different condition: they will resurrect their hosts *when the sky is clean again*. When carbon is down to an acceptable level of parts per million. Don't you see? Half the world's population, sent into a peaceful slumber! If they're asleep, they can't burn any more fuel or cut down any more trees. They'll stay safely underground until the forests have regrown, and the earth has cooled, and the sky is clean again. It will only take a few hundred years or so. And then they'll be reborn! They'll blink the sleep from their eyes and wake up in a new green world. What they do after that is their own business. But I can always spread the fungus about again, if need be. And, more importantly, it will give me time to keep working! To find a lasting solution!'

Kay realises that the cold feeling in his chest is naked rage. It has made its way into his arms. He grabs Merlin, taking fistfuls of his flowery shirt and lifting him out of his sandals. Slamming him against a tank of ants and pressing him there. Standing so close that there's not an inch between them. Merlin barely weighs anything, and he also stinks; he probably hasn't washed himself

347

for fifty years. One of Merlin's eyes is mostly blue, and the other is mostly yellow. But they are marbled and ringed, with strands of amber, golden halos, orbiting flecks of green. They can see in four dimensions. They contain galaxies. At this moment, they are both full of terror.

'All of this,' says Kay. His jaw is trembling. 'Two thousand years. Of sleeping under a fucking tree. Of crawling back up from the dead. Never getting to see my wife, in heaven. I had to fight at the fucking Somme. I had to fight in Malaya. I can't remember how many times I've died. Or how many people I've killed. And it was all just because you needed to test a *theory*? Because of these mushrooms?'

Merlin looks baffled. 'Well . . . there's no need to be angry, my boy. It was a very important theory! It . . . it might prove to be the salvation of everyone on the planet!'

Kay shakes him against the glass. 'That's not good enough. You told us that it was about protecting people. Saving Britain from peril. That's what you said. That's why we all agreed to it.'

'Well, yes!' says Merlin. 'I needed you to agree to it. I needed Arthur to agree to it! If I'd said that it was just about trees and carbon dioxide, you wouldn't have volunteered!'

'You're fucking right I wouldn't have volunteered.'

'Precisely!' says Merlin. He is blinking in confusion. He genuinely doesn't realise what the problem is. That was always the thing with Merlin. Smartest man in Britain – Merlin the sage, Merlin the sorcerer. He could see into the future. He could see the world ending from two thousand years away. But he couldn't see into people's hearts or minds. Not really. Kay stares at him, breathing raggedly through his nose. Then he begins to nod.

'You knew that Arthur would like the idea,' he says. 'Immortal warriors. Protecting Britain. Protecting his legacy.'

Merlin hazards a smile. 'Yes,' he says. 'It was ... the only way to sell it to him, you see.'

Kay looks away, at the rows of mushrooms, receding into the distance. He nods his head at them. 'That's why I'm here? That's why me and Lance and Galehaut come back from the dead. Not for any higher purpose. Not because you needed us to win wars or do anything halfway noble. We were ... a trial run. For these mushrooms.'

'Yes!' says Merlin. 'That's it exactly. I'm glad you're beginning to understand.'

Kay remembers the fires in Malaya. He remembers what it felt like to choke on mustard gas. He remembers digging through the pile of corpses at Malplaquet. All the wars that he could have been long dead for. He looks back at the mushrooms. Then he drops Merlin and runs his oak hand over his head.

'Do you have anything to drink?' he asks.

Merlin has an ancient bottle of rancid mead stowed away, for reasons beyond Kay's capacity to care. He sits in a collapsible chair and necks it from the bottle. Merlin is moving about uncertainly, pacing and muttering and scratching his beard.

'I don't see why you're angry,' says Merlin. 'You *have* been saving the realm, in your own way! You were a vital part of my experiments.'

'Just shut up, for a minute,' says Kay.

'Well!' says Merlin. 'Really. I've never heard such ... I don't see why I deserve ... Surely you understand that ...'

'Wise old Merlin, smartest wizard who ever lived, and the best plan that you can come up with is to turn everyone into a mushroom, for a hundred years or so, so that they can't burn any more coal.'

'That's right, yes.'

'I think it's a fucking terrible plan.'

Merlin draws himself up and scowls again. 'Well! Have you got any better ideas, Kay the Cupbearer? Kay the Fool? Hmm? Because I don't. I've tried everything else. Fresh out of ideas. It's mushrooms or Armageddon at this point.'

'Why not people? There are good people, in the realm.'

'Because people can't be trusted to make sensible decisions! So we must make the decisions for them. Put them to sleep. It's the only thing to do.'

'What about Mariam? You said she was important.'

'Yes,' says Merlin. 'Yes. There are quite a few branches of the tree where she ends up being very important indeed. She could be the start of something new. There will need to be some people still alive, to guide things in the right direction. Dismantle the old world. Build a new one. Restore the balance of nature.'

'All right,' Kay says. He drinks more mead. 'How many branches are there where Mariam succeeds? What do we need to do to make that happen?'

'Well, I ... hmm,' says Merlin. 'Just a moment.' He reaches for a rack of glass phials on the nearest table, nearly knocking it over. The phials are full of a brownish liquid, some kind of mushroom extract. Merlin lets several drops fall onto his extended tongue. He places the phial carefully back in its rack. Then he sits down on the chair opposite Kay and plants his hands on his knees, waiting for the effects to kick in. Kay drinks silently. It's not long before Merlin is somewhere else, seeing different things. The tree of time. His gold eye has travelled round to stare inside his head, only the yellowy white visible. He is murmuring and muttering in old languages beneath his breath. Then he sits up very straight.

'We should go back and stop Constantine from becoming emperor! Why didn't I think of that before?'

'No, no, come on,' says Kay. 'Get closer. Look ahead.'

'Oh, yes, of course,' says Merlin. He brings up a hand to cover his blue eye, helping him focus on what he can see with the other one. 'Closer. Yes. Let's see ... sack of Rome ... no, later than that ... Genghis Khan ... Spanish Armada ... David Bowie ... almost there. Oh, this part always upsets me ...'

'Stay focused.'

'There were so many warnings,' he says. 'So many green shoots branching off towards better futures. All of this ... could have been avoided. All of this suffering and ruin.'

'Keep going.'

Tears begin streaming down Merlin's face. He shakes his head. 'We're on a black bough,' he says. 'A very black bough. Hurtling towards a bleak future. Death and misery for everyone. I can see it, Kay. I can see the earth rendered barren ... a lifeless husk with burning skies. It looms ahead of us. Almost inevitable, now. So few shoots of green. We've ignored so many of them. So many chances wasted. Now we have so few left.'

'Merl,' he says. 'What about Mariam?'

'... Mariam,' says Merlin. 'Yes, Mariam. I was looking for her, wasn't I? She ... she can change things. There are still green shoots. Tender shoots that might become mighty branches. I can see them. Stretched out ahead of us. She stands at a podium. She is speaking. People are ... listening. They're actually listening.'

Kay feels pride blooming in his chest. He can't stop himself from smiling. 'Great,' he says. 'How do we make that happen?'

Merlin falls silent and begins to twitch. He is coming down from his trance. Kay puts the bottle on the ground. He walks over and shakes Merlin's shoulders. Slapping him gently on one cheek until his eye rolls around again and he returns fully to this branch of time. He looks up crossly and brushes him off.

'There's no need to manhandle me, my boy, I'm quite in control of my faculties.'

'Did you see what we have to do?'

'I did,' says Merlin. He stands up and brushes off his shirt. 'There's five or ten branches where Mariam does quite well for herself and makes the world a better place, but only if we stop her from being killed at the Tor.'

'When does that happen?'

'In about five minutes. So perhaps we ought to get a move on.'

A pit of dread opens in Kay's stomach. 'What?'

Merlin starts heading down the cave, back towards the entrance. Looking through his mess for something in particular. 'We're on the branch where Morgan has the staff and tries to bring Arthur back. We should try and stop that, if we can. That is a very black limb that we don't want to travel down.'

Kay wants to pick Merlin up and shake him again, but he restrains himself. 'Forget about that, we need to help Mariam. We need to go and save her.'

'One and the same thing, my boy. There's not a moment to lose.'

Merlin finds what he's looking for, bundled up in a corner. It's his old blue mantle, his druid's cloak, the same one that he used to wear centuries ago. He shakes it out and pulls it over his head, draping it about himself, over his shirt and shorts. Then he heads out of the cave as quickly as his old legs will carry him. Kay follows, willing him to move faster.

The van is still parked where it was, headlights blazing. The fay is standing outside, cheerfully licking an ice cream.

'You!' Merlin shouts, levelling his finger. 'Fly home and tell your faerie king that the veil is opening. Tell him that under no circumstances is he to let Arthur back into the world.'

The fay frowns. 'Can we finish our 99 first?'

'Certainly not! You must hurry!'

The fay looks crestfallen. They explode into dust with a sound like a whipcrack. A bright spark of light weaves away into the night sky. The ice cream falls to the ground and nearly lands on top of Barry.

'Oh, er,' says Kay, 'Merlin, this is Barry. I mentioned him earlier. He was hoping you could turn him back into a man.'

'No time!' says Merlin. He dodders his way past Barry and opens the far door of the ice cream van, climbing up into the driver's seat.

Kay knows Merlin well enough to know that he's liable to drive away without them if they don't hurry. He picks up Barry and climbs into the passenger seat, closing the door behind him. Merlin is scratching his beard, looking at the steering wheel and pedals as if they are a manuscript written in a language that he can't remember.

'Do you want me to drive?' Kay asks.

'No, no,' says Merlin. 'No time for that. Strap yourself in.'

There are times to disobey Merlin, but he can tell this isn't one of them. He scrabbles for the seatbelt and clicks it into place, Barry scrambling up onto his shoulder. Merlin is waving his fingers in front of the steering wheel, mumbling in some ancient and terrible language.

Kay feels a change of weight and tension in the ice cream van. The whole structure creaks and groans around him. There's an uncomfortable tension building in his stomach. And when he looks out of the windows, he can see why. The cave and the trees are slowly sinking around them. The ice cream van is rising gently into the air.

'Aw, no, Merlin . . .' he says.

'Much better!' says Merlin. He laughs, turning the steering

wheel. The van slowly turns around, mid-air, to face in another direction. Once they've cleared the treeline, and they're out in the open air, Merlin reaches down and puts the van into a different gear. 'Hold on, my boy!'

Kay does as he's told. The van is shaking and groaning, vibrating with a whining sound that gradually gets louder and more concerning over time. He barely has time to brace himself against the dashboard before Merlin's sandal comes down against the accelerator.

The heavens begin to twist and whirl, like water draining down a hole. And then the van shoots forwards, punching through the dawn firmament like a bullet through a piece of muslin. Kay is pressed back against his seat so hard that he can feel each rib trying to get through his skin. Barry flies backwards, screaming, and Kay hears him smack against the back window of the van. The view outside makes no sense whatsoever, every colour at once, colours he can't comprehend, a glimpse of the Otherworld that he doesn't want to see. He squeezes his eyes closed against it, trying to stop his brain from leaking out of his ears.

'Merlin!' he shouts.

But Merlin is staring ahead of them, into the churning rainbow, with a wild and terrible purpose in his eyes.

29

They take the boats across the Bristol Channel, leaving Swansea at midnight. Twelve silhouettes packed into each boat. Mariam tries not to be sick, bouncing over the waves, battered by salt spray in the darkness. She has the sword between her knees, clutching the hilt with both hands, resting the point between her shoes. Slightly worried that she'll burst the skin of the boat with it if she's not careful. She doesn't feel any great power coursing through it. It just feels slightly heavier than she thought swords would feel. It will be a relief not to have to bear the weight of it anymore.

They stay as far as they can from the Avalon platform. They can still see it in the distance, lit up with spotlights. Huge and ugly. Red lights blazing on the crane towers like evil eyes in the darkness. She can't help staring back at them. Gethin sits beside her, cradling a rifle. Keeping his new queen safe, until the moment she isn't queen anymore. She's noticed that he talks too much when he's nervous.

'They've built it right there on the floodplain,' he says. 'Used to be Somerset, but most of Somerset's underwater now. Big bloody marsh. Easier for them to build these things when there's nobody left to complain, isn't it? We've no hope of taking Cardiff back as long as they've got that thing sitting there. Like an aircraft carrier, sending drones out at us and what have you. But we'd lose half our numbers if we tried to take it by force. Which is why you and your girls might come in handy.'

The word 'girls' annoys her, but she doesn't say anything. They have an average age of about twenty-five. It might be higher, if Regan's as old as she says she is. Mariam looks over at the dark shape which is Regan, sitting in the prow of the boat. Holding Kay's staff in one hand. Giving off waves of scary determination. How did they never realise that she was a witch? It seems so obvious, now. Not weird or hard to understand.

There are moments, during the crossing, when she remembers just how mad this is. It seems even stranger than Kay or the dragon, even wronger, even harder to take seriously. There's a part of her that would rather keep King Arthur firmly in the realm of myth. Not bring him into reality, a living breathing person.

But there's a bigger part of her that feels relieved. As soon as they do this, she won't be queen anymore. That's enough of a reason to go and do it.

It's hard to know where the channel ends and Somerset begins. Twenty years ago the difference between sea and land might have been more obvious, but now the waters have risen, and there's a shallow sea over most of the county. They have to cut the engines and move over it slowly, breaking through reeds, trying their best in the darkness to avoid sunken hedgerows or half-drowned trees that might slow their progress. The Welshmen bring out poles and use them to drive the boats forward, probing the water for solid earth to push against. She can't tell which way they're facing in the darkness, but she trusts that the Welsh are better at navigating these waters than she is – that is, until one of them turns around and whispers in the darkness.

'Which bloody way are we going, Gethin?'

'How should I know?' Gethin hisses back at him.

'Straight ahead,' says Regan, not bothering to whisper.

Her voice is clear and calm, and it doesn't invite disagreement. The Welsh fall silent and push their boat through the reeds. Putting their faith in sorcery or old gods or whatever it is that makes Regan so confident.

They drift pass dark shapes, angular and strange. Avalon is far enough behind them that one of the Welshmen risks switching on an electric torch. The light passes quickly over brickwork and roof tiles. The shapes are houses, flooded past the height of their ground-floor windows. In one of the upstairs windows Mariam sees a child's drawing sellotaped against the glass. Crayon people in a green field, with a rainbow overhead.

The Welshman turns his torch back off, and Mariam looks down at her feet.

By the time they reach where they're going the sky has turned from pitch blackness to the deep blue colour of a bruise. There's a hill in front of them, a giant purple mound rising from the wetlands. Regan steps ashore as soon as the boats bump against the hillside and starts climbing up the hill, moving more quickly than she should be able to, using Kay's staff as a walking stick. Mariam stays behind to help the others, dragging the boats ashore, getting her legs wet in the cold floodwater. It's only after-wards that she wonders whether queens are supposed to help with that sort of thing.

She picks up the sword and takes a deep breath. Standing at the foot of the hill and staring upwards after Regan, with her sisters gathering behind her.

'There's still time to not do this, you know,' says Roz.

'I know,' says Mariam. 'But we're here now. Might as well get it over with.'

'You don't have to go through with it,' says Willow, 'if you're not sure.'

'I am sure.'

'Well, I hope you're right.'

She can't find the words to explain it to them. She doesn't know how to wave this sword and make the sea level go down. She doesn't know how to make men do as she tells them to do. Maybe Arthur will. That's all the reason she needs. The sword feels almost hot, in her hand. She wants to pass it on as quickly as she can.

They climb upwards, in the blue twilight. The hill is long and narrow, with a dirt track leading up its spine, and some sort of tower standing at the top. Not a new metal tower but something much older, its rough outline slightly darker than the sky behind it. Regan is already doing something in the darkness, scratching marks on the ground with the end of Kay's staff. Marking a circle around the tower.

When Mariam reaches the top her mind goes blank for a moment, emptied by the view: a sea of mist stretching out in all directions over the marsh, with black tree shadows poking through in places where the land is high enough. The sun is still hidden, away to the east somewhere, but there is already a narrow band of orange on the horizon. The sky above is dark indigo blue, like the deep ocean or the edge of space.

It might be the most beautiful thing she's ever seen.

When she turns around to look back the way they came, she can still see the red lights of the Avalon, closer than she would have thought possible. Ugly even in the dark. Whatever she was feeling a moment ago is replaced by something worse: the urge to destroy. She grips the sword more tightly in her hand.

But then Regan is at her shoulder, reaching out to take the sword away from her. Mariam finds herself hesitating. Regan waits, with the ghost of a smile on her face.

'Are you sure this is a good idea?' Mariam asks.

Regan sighs. 'I think the last king did a very cruel thing, taking someone so young, with their whole life ahead of them, and making them into a queen. Putting all of that responsibility on your shoulders. This was never your destiny. You never wanted it, or sought it for yourself. You're a healer. A very good healer. And you fight for what you believe in.'

Mariam opens her mouth to speak, but she doesn't know what to say. She wishes, briefly, that Kay was here.

'You can let somebody else be the leader,' says Regan. 'Why not let Arthur do it? It's what he was made for.'

She stares down at the sword, still stained with flecks of dragon blood. She doesn't even know how to clean a sword. Arthur probably would.

So she holds it out to Regan, offering it clumsily. Regan manages to take it without injuring herself. She rests it sideways across both hands, reverently, like she's done this kind of thing before. Then she carries it slowly towards the tower.

Mariam stands where she is, clenching her empty hand into a fist. Her right arm feels lighter, as if it's going to float upwards and leave the rest of her behind. When does she stop being queen? Is it now, or when Arthur has actually returned?

The Welsh are staying down near the boats, not wanting to come uphill and give too much credence to this spectacle. Willow and Teoni and Roz and Bronte have moved to the eastern side of the hill, sitting in the grass and waiting for the sun to come up. She sits and joins them, savouring the feel of the wet grass beneath her hands. Feeling like she can already breathe more easily.

'I still think you'd have made a great queen, for the record,' says Willow.

'Thanks,' she says. She manages to smile.

Roz is sitting with her arms folded, staring at the ground. 'I can't believe we're just . . . giving up this much power.'

'I don't want power,' says Mariam. 'I wouldn't know what to do with power.'

Roz stares at her unflinchingly for a long moment, with her pale blue eyes. 'You really don't see how amazing you are, do you?'

Mariam can't stop herself from scowling. 'What?'

'You're the kindest and bravest and most determined person I know,' says Roz. 'You always think about others before you think about yourself. You're way too hard on yourself, but only because you want to make the world better. I think Willow's right. You'd make a great queen.'

'No,' says Mariam, flustered. 'You'd be way better. You're much tougher than me.'

'I couldn't have killed that dragon,' says Roz. 'I couldn't have blown up that fracking site, or talked to the Welsh like you tried to talk to them.'

Mariam presses her hands to her eyes. 'I . . . I shouldn't have to be queen. Okay? I'm too young. I don't know what I'm doing. I'd just get it wrong. There should be somebody else, somebody older, who knows what they're doing. Regan's right. It might as well be Arthur. Just anyone, as long as it's not me.'

When she looks up from her hands again she sees that the others have fallen silent.

Regan is standing over them.

'It's time,' says Regan. 'Mariam, could you come with me?'

She stands up, nodding, brushing the mud from her trousers. Her sisters stare up at her. She feels that she'd rather stay with them, on the grass.

'I love you guys,' she says. 'I won't be long.'

The tower is old and made of stone. It has two archways built into it; one facing vaguely east, the other vaguely west. Mariam tries to think about why it might be here and when it was built. It's easier to think about that than it is to think about anything else. She looks upwards and sees a perfect square of dark blue sky. The tower is roofless.

Regan has drawn something on the ground. A symbol that Mariam doesn't recognise, etched in chalk on the rough flagstones. A wheel of three spirals, twisting in different directions. Regan leads her to the centre of the tower, so the chalk spirals are beneath her feet.

'What do I have to do?' she asks.

'It's quite simple,' says Regan. 'Don't be alarmed.'

The sword is propped in the corner of the tower. Regan takes it up again and holds it in one hand, as if she intends to wield it.

Mariam frowns and shrinks back slightly. 'Erm,' she says, 'you're not going to stab me, are you?'

Regan smiles at her as if that was a funny thing for her to say. 'The blood of a king is a powerful thing. We don't need much of it. Hold out your hand, and close your eyes.'

Mariam feels a moment of plunging doubt. But this is still Regan, standing in front of her. Wise and kind and smiling harmlessly. So she holds out her right hand, turning the palm slowly to face the sky. She allows her eyelids to shut.

She feels Regan's hand on her shoulder, holding her firmly in place. Then she feels the sword plunge into her stomach, driven up to the hilt. The coldness of the blade and then the terrible cramping pain.

She's not sure what she was expecting. Perhaps she thought that Regan would draw the sword gently across her palm, making a line of blood. Something that would be over quickly and would heal easily. A few drops of blood on the ground. That must have been why Regan said it. To put her at ease. To make her expect one thing, so she'd be less prepared for something else.

The first noise she makes is a whimper that dies in her throat. Her eyes open to find Regan staring into them, any kindness in her gaze replaced by steel.

Her feet fail underneath her and she has to lean against Regan to stop herself from falling. Regan holds her briefly in a kind of hug, but only long enough to draw the sword back out again. Then everything hurts even more.

She starts to lose moments of time. She is kneeling on the ground but can't remember how she got there. Warm blood soaking her clothes and pooling on the chalk spirals beneath her. The eastern archway of the tower is in front of her, and she can see the sun's edge peering over the horizon. The sky turning red.

Then Willow and Teoni and the others are running up the hill with terror on their faces, trying to get inside the tower. Roz looks more distraught than any of the others, which surprises her. But something is stopping them from getting through. They are hammering their fists on a wall of glass. Mariam can't understand what it is until she remembers Regan drawing a ring around the base of the tower. A spell to keep them out. They can't get in and help her. They can't stop the sun from rising. She can't hear them shouting – but then, she can't hear anything else, either. She can't even hear herself screaming. It sounds like she's deep underwater, like when Teoni fired the rocket launcher at the dragon.

When enough of her blood has been spilled on the floor, Regan props her up carefully in the corner of the tower and smiles at her, cupping her face. It's a proud smile, as if Regan is happy for her.

Instead of panicking, Mariam sits back against the wall and presses both hands hard against her stomach, trying to prevent blood loss. But she's lost so much already. It's soaking into the stones, filling the gaps between them. The drawings on the ground have started smoking. Now Regan moves to stand in the middle of the spiral, holding the sword in one hand and Kay's staff in the other. Her lips move, and she stares into the west with wide, unblinking eyes. When the sun has risen high enough behind her she drives Kay's staff down hard against the stones.

The universe seems to blink. Mariam sees the air change. Dust falls from the old brickwork. Something like electricity jolts through her bones, driving her back against the wall. And then rays of sunlight stream through the tower, in one archway and out the other. Regan's eyes are wide and her face is pale, looking at whatever it is that she's done. She begins to change, her hair darkening, her face growing younger.

The next thing Mariam sees is a kingdom of light floating in the sky. An island in the clouds, higher and brighter than any island ought to be. She can still see the red lights of the Avalon in the distance, but the ghostly island looms in front of them. Occupying the same space. There and not there at the same time. It takes her a moment to notice that there's something moving between the island and the Tor. Something gliding across the sea of mist. A white sail from some kind of ship. Growing slowly closer.

But now the blood is draining from her brain. The darkness wells up again and she lets herself fall into it, seeing nothing ordinary or extraordinary anymore.

30

Kay's fairly sure that this ice cream van wasn't designed to travel faster than the speed of light. When it returns to the normal bounds of space and time it is in broadly the right place, but it is falling from a great height, and parts of it are falling off. Kay braces himself against the ceiling, for all the good that will do. Below them there is a glistening sea of silver wetlands, with a purple mound rising from it, and a strange kingdom of mist on the horizon. It would be beautiful if it wasn't rising up to meet them quite so quickly.

There are other things happening in the sky, but Kay is falling too quickly to make sense of anything before the windscreen fills with green hillside.

He was in an aeroplane that came down somewhere over Burgundy, in the last big war. This is much worse. The plane didn't bounce, or flip nose-over-tail and land on its roof. He didn't hit his forehead against the dashboard of the aeroplane. It didn't shatter and crunch. It didn't roll slowly down a hill afterwards and end up in a flooded marsh, gradually filling with water. There wasn't a frightened squirrel bouncing around inside it.

When the van finally settles, he feels the chill of water rising past his chest. He knows that he has to move, get himself and Merlin and Barry onto dry land before the van floods entirely. But his head is spinning. There are black spots in his eyes. When his hand goes to his brow it comes away slick with yellow sap.

He slumps forward against his seatbelt, feeling the water rise past his chest. Until firm hands grab him, under his shoulders. Pulling him out of the water and onto dry land.

The next thing he's conscious of seeing is a yellow sky full of flying machines, making the air hum. Circling the Tor like vultures. That's another reason to get up, to find Mariam, to move his bones and bark as quickly as they will move. But he finds that he can't. Somebody has bound his ankles. Tied his hands together, behind his back.

If he can't free himself then he can't find Mariam. He strains against his bonds, squirming on the ground like a worm, trying to make sense of where he is. Down at the bottom of the Tor somewhere, in the fields that aren't quite flooded. He can see Saxons moving on foot, securing the area; trying to look busy, like soldiers have been doing for thousands of years. More of them stand around him, guarding him, in thick ranks. But his eyes are drawn past them, away to the distance, where far worse things are happening.

There are two fortresses on the horizon. One of them is dark and worldly, an ugly machine spawning Saxon whirligigs like a nest of hornets. But the second frightens him more. A glass fortress glittering in the sky.

He closes his eyes. That's the Otherworld. It presents itself as a castle, to make itself easier to understand. But truly it's a realm of dreams and nightmares, a dark reflection of the waking world which overlaps uneasily with God's creation. Things used to slip through in the old days, ogres and dragons and worse.

When Arthur died they shipped him off to fairyland and sealed the way behind him, trapping him beyond the veil. Now the veil's been torn back open, long enough for Arthur to come back through.

Tempting to give up, at this point. The damage is done. The veil is open. Arthur will come back through with all the cumulated fury of a thousand years. Ancient grievances avenged upon the realm and the people living in it. Precious little Kay can do to stop that, now. And even if he could, there's still everything that Merlin said. There's no grand purpose to any of this. No great evil to overcome. No end times for which his sword and strength are required.

But he can still try to find Mariam. He can still try to save her. Get her clear from all of this. This mess that she wouldn't be in if not for him. He can still do that much, at least. So he strains against his bonds, again. Trying to stand, in the slippery earth. He just needs to find Mariam. Find Merlin. Get them both out of here, to somewhere safe. If he can do that, then there'll be some hope left in the world.

He's still struggling when somebody walks up beside him in a pair of leather brogues. They throw down the end of a cigarette and grind it into the mud beneath their heel.

'Hullo, old boy,' says Marlowe. 'That wasn't much of a rescue, was it?'

Contempt forms like a fist in his stomach. It starts to dawn on him that this has all been planned. When he manages to twist his neck around, he can see Marlowe and Morgan standing over him. Marlowe looks insufferably pleased with himself. Morgan looks young again, and regal, like the queen of ravens. Wielding the staff in one hand and Caliburn in the other. The blade is stained with blood.

Hope dies in Kay's heart. 'What did you do?'

'Only what was necessary,' says Morgan.

'Where's Mariam?'

She looks for a moment as if she's about to answer him. But then she turns and walks away towards the water's edge, leaving him where he is.

'Just for the record,' says Marlowe, 'this is what's liable to happen when you pick the wrong side.'

Kay would very much like to stand up and strangle Marlowe with his own intestines. But Marlowe is walking away, and he can't do anything but watch. Trying to stand and failing. Face falling back against the mud.

Where's Merlin? Where's Barry? Did they get dragged from the wreckage too? Did they drown in a flooded ice cream van? That's not a death befitting of Merlin Ambrosius. That's not how the last of the druids should offer up his ghost. He must still be alive. But if he's alive, then he should be here. He should be doing something.

The Saxons are changing ranks. More of them descend from the Tor, dragging prisoners with them. Lining them up to be processed. Most of the prisoners look like the Welshmen from Manchester, but he sees Mariam's friends as well. Fighting tooth-and-nail. Struggling against their captors.

And suddenly he sees Mariam, sprawled on the cold earth with her eyes closed. Willow is kneeling over her, trying to help her, but the Saxons tear her away. There are flying machines on the grass, waiting to carry the prisoners away to somewhere else. The Saxons don't bother moving Mariam. They leave her lying where she is, undignified, unattended. Pale and drained of life.

He can't save her, bound up like this. He can't save her friends. He can't get close to her and see if she's all right. He shouts her name until his throat is ragged, but she doesn't

367

shout anything back. He drags himself towards her, over the grass, until the Saxons stop him. Kicking him in the chest and stomach. Stamping on his hands. Driving their rifle butts down into his face.

He lets them beat the sap out of him. Not much point resisting anymore. Nothing left to achieve. Might as well die like this, before he has to face Arthur again. Slip away into oblivion. Let these Saxons take him there, with their boots and fists and blunt instruments.

They don't kill him. After a while they haul him up by his armpits, dragging his knees through the mud. Throwing him down again, by the water's edge. There's another pair of nice shoes, standing next to him.

'Body of Christ,' says Lancelot. 'I'm sorry, Kay.'

Kay rolls over and leers up at him. Hard to tell, from down here, whether he's sincere or not. Standing there in his leather shoes and his cream suit. Sword at his hip.

'Did you know about this?' he asks.

'No. Not until about five minutes ago. There ... wasn't much I could do.'

'If you knew about this, I'll kill you,' he says. Seething, now. 'I'll flay you alive. I'll peel your skin off.'

'We've been stitched-up, Kay,' says Lancelot. 'Both of us. Pawns in a much bigger game. I didn't know any more than you did.'

'Help me stop this,' he says. He can hear the desperation in his voice, but he doesn't care.

Lancelot sighs. 'Bit late for that, isn't it? He's on his way, now. Let's hope he's in a forgiving mood ...'

The nightmare fortress fades back into nothingness, on the horizon. Like mist burnt away by the sun. You could almost convince yourself that it was just an illusion. But the white ship is still material, and it's drifting closer. Gliding through the water now as if it were an ordinary ship. The Saxons have formed a guard of honour by the water's edge, ready for Arthur's arrival. Marlowe and Morgan are nearest the shore, talking like old friends.

'I've kept my end of the bargain,' Morgan says. 'I trust you'll keep yours.'

'One miracle at a time,' says Marlowe. 'We'll move him to the Avalon, as soon as we're finished here. Then you work your charms on him. Get him on side. Once he's been crowned king, we'll worry about saving the planet.'

Kay spits soil out of his mouth. No way to stop this. None that he can think of, anyway. He tries, again, to strain against his bindings. Hopeless. Even if he could break free, what would he do then? Get shot and fall back through the earth again. Would he be saved from the darkness a second time? Would he come back with even more of him turned to oak? This might be the last time he walks the earth, breathes the air, before he's plunged into darkness forever. If he did have any chances left, he'd give them to Mariam. He turns his eyes to heaven, wondering if there's anything that Wyn can do. He might have used up all of his favours from her as well.

The ship draws close. Kay waits, feeling his heart tighten. And then he sees his brother standing in the bows.

He has twelve dozen feelings for Arthur, all wrestling in his belly like a mass of eels. He hated the baby Arthur that his dad brought home from the war. He grew fond of the younger brother that he never asked for. He loved the stripling ginger lad, made king.

The Arthur he can see drifting closer now isn't the baby Arthur, or the boy Arthur, or the young king Arthur. It's Arthur the lord of war, as he was in his final years. Arthur who broke the realm in two because he thought his wife was lying with other men. Here he is now, dressed as he was when he died. Bearskin cloak hanging from his shoulders. Coat of scale mail gleaming like dragon skin. Gold circlet on his head, holding back the waves of his copper hair. Beard braided in front of him. Scowl on his face. Empty scabbard at his hip.

The ship comes near to the water's edge and strikes ground with its prow. Arthur vaults over the side, plunging up to his thighs in the floodwater. Wading hungrily ashore. The first thing he does is fall to his knees and grab a wet fistful of English dirt, smearing his face with it. Then he spreads his arms and offers up a silent prayer to God.

Kay waits to be noticed. Lancelot kneels down beside him, and the Saxons kneel as well. Marlowe joins them, careful not to muddy his trousers. Only Morgan remains standing. She drives the oak staff into the earth so that it stands freely of its own accord. Then she goes forward, holding Caliburn in both hands. Balancing the blade across her open palms.

Arthur crosses himself before he stands. He grasps the hilt of Caliburn and takes it up again. Testing its weight in his hand. Staring down the length of it to check the keenness of its edge. Making some experimental strokes, as if he's cutting long grass in front of him. When he's satisfied, he returns it to its old scabbard. Then he comes forward.

Kay glares up at him, and Arthur glares back down. Sixteen hundred years of unspoken conversations, silently communicated over the space of a few seconds. Old tenderness turned bitter and scored over with resentment. Contempt. Mutual disappointment. When Arthur gets bored of the conversation, his gaze flickers towards Lancelot. Then he snorts, shifting ancient phlegm inside his nostrils.

'All right, lads,' he says. That deep gravel in his voice. 'How's tricks?'

'Sire,' says Lancelot.

'Addy,' says Kay. 'Long time no see.'

The gift of tongues, again. They're talking proper old Brythonic to each other, coarse as a hermit's undershirt, but their words carry strangely on the breeze. Warped and wefted into something else by all the old magics. Christ knows how it sounds to the surrounding company. But then Arthur never cared much for purple words, Roman oratory, even in the old days. He's sniffing the air of his kingdom now, like a farmer savouring the smell of pigshit. Looking over at the Avalon, and then back down at them. Less than thrilled.

'Can't say I like what you've done with the place,' he says.

'That's not the half of it,' says Kay.

Arthur scowls at him. 'Why are you trussed up like a sow?'

'Well, I—'

'Your Majesty,' says Marlowe, interrupting, 'might I be the first to welcome you back, to—'

Kay and Lancelot both wince, on Marlowe's behalf. He doesn't know the rules. Arthur used to hate it when people spoke out of turn. He used to like it when people knelt in front of him, because it made it easier to kick the shit out of them. He does this now, sharply and suddenly, reducing Marlowe to a wheezing pile of limbs.

'I'm sorry, did I ask you?' says Arthur. 'No, I fucking didn't. One more word, I'll tear your tongue out of your head and turn it into a belt. Now who the fuck are half of these people? Where are my best knights? Where's Gawain? Where's Bedwyr?'

Morgan moves to Arthur's side. Getting inside his bear cloak;

one hand resting on his back, the other pressed flat against his chest. Kay had almost forgotten how good she was at this kind of thing. She might be able to cool his temper before anyone loses an arm.

'My love,' she says, 'much time has passed. The realm is not as it was. Have patience, and I'll explain.'

Arthur sneers down at her, but he does wrap an arm around her waist. 'Don't tell me to have patience,' he says. 'Been patient long enough. Was your bright idea to ship me off to fairyland in the first place. I haven't forgotten.'

'Marlowe serves us well, darling,' says Morgan. 'You should heed his counsel.'

'Your Majesty,' says Marlowe, slightly breathless, 'Britain is in dire peril. You could not have returned at a better time. We need you to restore order to the realm.'

Arthur nods, as if this is what he was expecting. He doesn't care what the problem is. He already knows that he's the solution. He lifts his hand, palm upwards. Marlowe rises from his knees. The Saxons follow his example. Only Kay and Lancelot stay kneeling in front of him. Lancelot out of ancient habit. Kay because his ankles are still tied together.

'I need men I can trust,' says Arthur, looking down at them. 'You've both betrayed me in the past. Slighted me. Done things I shouldn't forgive you for. But I know your faces. I know your hearts. Not like this bunch of melts. So I would have you both by my side, if you'll swear your loyalty. Would you both fight with me again? Help me tame this land?'

Kay thinks about serving Arthur again. Living through another reign of horror. Making war across Britain, and then carrying it to foreign shores. Planting Arthur's banner over burning battlefields. More chaos and destruction, to pile on top of all the chaos and destruction he's already seen. All while the world burns and the oceans rise, and the forests die. Wyn would be looking down on him with contempt if he agreed to that. But perhaps it would be better than the alternative: plunging through oblivion until the end of time.

'Well?' asks Arthur. 'Do I have your loyalty?'

There's that word again. Loyalty. Arthur always expected it, but never earnt it, never rewarded it. It raises Kay's hackles. Sets his teeth on edge. It's enough to make him say something rash.

'I'll follow you,' says Kay, 'if you listen to what I say. If you heed my counsel.'

Arthur looks away and shakes his head. He takes a deep breath and then allows it out again. Containing his anger. 'I don't need your advice,' he says. 'I never have. I need men who'll do as I tell them.'

'Everything's different, Addy,' he says. 'The realm's dying. If you're going to be king, then you need to do something about it.'

'If the realm's dying, it's because I was absent from it!' says Arthur. 'With my return it will thrive again. Lancelot, do I have your loyalty?'

'Of course, sire,' says Lancelot.

Kay bridles against his bonds. Lancelot's loyalty is worth less than pitch. He used to change his gods more often than he changed his undertunic. Arthur must remember that. But the words are enough. Arthur nods. He looks back to Kay.

'Swear loyalty,' says Arthur. 'If you don't, then you're my enemy, and I won't suffer to let you live. I've made that mistake before.'

Kay swallows. He keeps his eyes on Arthur's boots, with their crescent buckles. He can't bring himself to say a word, never mind swearing loyalty.

It was a good thing when Arthur died. That's a foul thing to think about your brother, but it's true. It stopped the chaos – for a little while, at least. It brought an end to the endless war. And that's how things should have remained. Arthur should have stayed in the Otherworld, locked away behind the veil, until the end of time. Kay ought to be kneeling in front of Mariam, who might have changed things. Not Arthur. Not again.

'There's a young woman,' he says, 'Mariam, who died to bring you back. She'd have done a better job than you. She had my loyalty. But now she's dead.'

Arthur can't comprehend that. 'A girl? Britain would never bear the shame of being ruled by a woman.'

Kay snorts. He shakes his head. Laughing at Arthur was always the quickest way to put him in a foul mood. That much hasn't changed, it seems.

'If that's your answer,' says Arthur, 'Lancelot: you'll prove your loyalty to me by striking my brother's head from his shoulders.'

Lancelot stands up. Kay doesn't give Arthur the satisfaction of looking up at him. He looks down at the earth, giving Lancelot a cleaner stretch of neck to slice through. There's something about this that makes perfect sense. If some soothsayer had told him a thousand years ago that it would be Lancelot who'd finally destroy him, he wouldn't have been the slightest bit surprised.

He hears Lancelot's sword scrape out of its scabbard. Lancelot's boots move in the wet earth, getting better purchase. You need the right stance for a blow like this one, coming down with enough force to cut clean through the spine. He wonders for half a moment what might be going through Lancelot's head, but he's killed enough people himself to know that you rarely think about anything at times like this, other than the practicalities of it. Your conscience doesn't trouble you until afterwards. Lancelot's might not trouble him at all.

Better to spend the last few moments thinking about something else. Might be a good time to ask God for forgiveness.

Might be a better time to swear some oath to the old gods – Herne or Brigid or somebody else – but you can't do both. That was always the problem, in the old days. Hedging your bets.

He thinks about Hildwyn, instead. The first time he saw her, with her golden hair. The strained wedding. Everything that came after. She said she'd rather have been a nun than marry a pagan. Then she said it was her Christian duty to stay with her husband and care for his soul. She started turning her eyes to heaven and smiling at his jokes, despite herself. He remembers the first time she ever laughed in his presence. Covering her mouth with one pale hand. Nice thing to think about while Lancelot's blade comes singing down.

But then a voice rings out, crying Arthur's name. Merlin. Standing over Mariam's body in his wet mantle, with a squirrel on his shoulder.

Some of the Saxons take aim, but Arthur puts out his hand to stay them. He hasn't been back for an hour yet and already these men are following his every whim. That was always the way. But he looks uncertain. He has soldiers ready to follow his orders. He has his brother bound in front of him. He has Morgan whispering in his ear.

'Arthur!' says Merlin, again. 'If you're to be king again then you must keep your brother alive, and heed his counsel. You must heed my counsel. You must follow the example of young Mariam, here. The realm has changed. It is being killed by greed and complacency and wilful ignorance. You must take up your sword against these things, if you wish to save it from destruction.'

Arthur is already shaking his head. 'I don't need advice from some crusty old piss-drinking tree worshipper. I didn't need it in the old days, and I don't need it now. Fuck off back to whatever rock you've been hiding under.'

Merlin draws himself up and scowls. 'If you won't lift a finger to save the realm from peril, then you should stand aside – and make room for someone who will!'

Just for a moment, Mariam seems to move. Kay's heart soars. He calls her name. She only twitched, moving her head slightly on the ground. But it was enough. It was life.

Arthur squints. Then he looks at the nearest Saxon soldier, and the rifle in his hand. 'Is that a weapon?'

'Yes, sir,' says the Saxon.

Arthur nods. He points at Merlin. 'Show me how it works.'

The Saxon takes aim and fires three bullets.

But something else soars through the air. The old oak staff, wrenched from the ground. It flies into Merlin's outstretched hand. And then magic happens. The progress of the bullets slows to a crawl. Kay can see individual cartridges being ejected from the Saxon's rifle, falling to the ground at a snail's pace. He can see the slow realisation dawning on Arthur's face. His countenance changing from cold indifference to an even colder rage.

Merlin's beard crackles with a cosmic charge, and he drives the staff into the ground. Time forks around him, like a rainbow cleaved in two, or a river parting around a rock. The rest of them are caught in his wake.

Whatever happens next gives Kay a kind of temporal vertigo. Time is churning visibly, nauseatingly, somehow green and orange and purple at the same time. He can see the tree of time, as he has never seen it before. It's not something he enjoys seeing. He can feel the past stretching out behind him, through a hundred battles and half as many resurrections, past his death and through his mortal life, all the way back to Caer Moelydd and Londinium and the moment of his birth. And he can see the future stretching out in front of him, through his next death and beyond. He can feel Lancelot's sword swinging down to carve his head from his shoulders. But that is just one death, one branch ending itself. And there are thousands of other branches. Millions. In most of them he can see the world burning, the air unbreathable, the ground a barren desert. Bones burning away to dust, leaving no trace that people ever walked and lived and loved. But down some branches there is still hope. There are still green trees. There are still people living their lives, in peace.

In this strand of time, Merlin is being cut down by a hail of gunfire. But Merlin is taking them down a different branch, away from death. Towards something else.

31

And then they're back in the dim light of Merlin's cave, where the air tastes of mushrooms. No need for an enchanted ice cream van on the return journey. Not while Merlin has the staff in his hand, his eyes still bright with power, beard still crackling with energy. Dust whorling in the air around him.

'Aw, fucking hell,' says Barry. The squirrel is still clinging to Merlin's shoulder, looking ill. 'I've had enough with all this magic bollocks.'

Kay's bindings turn into tiny snakes, slithering away into the dark corners of the cave. He is free. He picks himself up, grasping for his sword. But he sees no enemies here. Merlin didn't bring any Saxons with them. He didn't bring Arthur, or Morgan, or Lancelot. Just Mariam: she is here on the floor of the cave, still pale as death. Still breathing, with her eyes closed. There's a bandage on her stomach, sodden red with blood.

Kay kneels down to pick Mariam up, laying her down on the cushions of a mouldy old sofa that sits among all the rest of

Merlin's rubbish. Then he stands over her, scratching the back of his neck, not knowing what else to do. He was never a healer. Not like his wife.

'Will she be all right?' he asks.

'Hardly matters anymore, does it?' says Merlin.

Merlin is moving busily around the cave, rifling through his heaps of clutter. Casting some things aside and keeping others, packing them into a cardboard box. Kay can't stop himself from scowling. It's a wonder that he can still be surprised by Merlin's lack of pity, after all this time. But Merlin was always full of surprises.

'Why not?' he asks. 'Why doesn't it matter?'

'Because this branch of time is beyond saving now!' says Merlin. 'Rotten and corrupted. Beyond any hope of salvation.'

'That can't be true,' says Kay. 'There has to be something we can do.'

'I'm afraid not,' says Merlin. 'Now that Arthur's returned, there won't be any convincing him. You ought to know that better than anyone. All will come to ruin and destruction.'

'So we defeat Arthur, then,' says Kay. 'We ... we can kill him again, if we need to. Send him back to Avalon.'

Merlin shakes his head. 'That would be a waste of my energies,' he says. 'I must abandon my efforts here. Travel to a different branch. See what good I can do elsewhere. Perhaps I *will* go back and stop Constantine ...'

'But what about your mushrooms? What about your plan?'

'Won't make a blind bit of difference now, I'm afraid,' says Merlin. 'Not here, anyway. I'll take some samples with me. Try it out on a different branch of the tree, where there's still some hope remaining.'

Kay feels the white heat of anger building up within him again, the same anger he felt the last time he was here. 'So you're just leaving? You're just giving up on the world?'

'Only on this particular *version* of the world. I know the concept of parallel quantum realities might be a little beyond you, but do try to keep up.'

'What about us? What about all of the people who live here?'

Merlin scoffs, as if this was a foolish question. 'Try to take the broad view of things, my boy! Perhaps in this branch of the tree you're doomed, but in some of the other branches you're probably very happy. Doesn't that bring you some comfort?'

'Not really, no.'

'Well, suit yourself, then.'

Merlin picks up a small bronze mechanism, ancient and intricate. He holds it up to his ear and shakes it to check that it's still working before dropping it into the box. Then he wades further into his hoard, sorting through clutter and muttering to himself. Deciding what he'll need in whatever branch of time he's going to. Kay glances at Mariam on the sofa before he follows after Merlin. Not sure whether he wants to reason with him or strangle the life out of him.

'You said that there were still green shoots,' he says. 'That Mariam could change things. If we kept her alive.'

'That was then,' says Merlin. 'There were still green shoots ahead of us, but we went a different way. Down a different path. Towards doom!'

'There has to be a chance, still,' he says. 'If we keep Mariam alive maybe we can still turn things around.'

'No!' says Merlin. 'Hopeless. Utterly hopeless.'

Kay can't stand it anymore, following Merlin around, watching him pack to leave. He grabs his arm, rough oak hand grasping Merlin's frail old bones. Forcing Merlin to turn and look at him.

'Heal her,' he says, 'before you go wherever it is that you're going. The least you can do is make her better first. Then you can leave.'

Merlin sighs. He looks exasperated. Keen to be gone. 'Well,' he says, 'if you insist. If you'd be so good as to unhand me . . .'

Kay lets go of him, against his better judgement. The box of things is temporarily put down. Merlin makes his way back through the hoard, closer to Mariam.

There's a kind of cistern at the side of the cave, a barrel hewn from plastic, not wood or iron or stone. Merlin must have put it there to collect water, which trickles down the cave wall from somewhere up above. Faint light shines down through a gap in the bricks, catching the dust in its beam. The water in the cistern seems strangely limpid, clearer and brighter than it has any right to be.

Merlin opens an old suitcase and pulls out a cloth sack. When he strips the sack away, he's holding something that Kay recognises from the old days. A cup of tarnished bronze. Ordinary and extraordinary at the same time. Lots of men went searching for that cup, for a number of misguided reasons. Most of them didn't come back. Good to know that Merlin's been keeping it in an old suitcase on the floor of his cave.

'Here we are,' says Merlin. He dips the cup into the cistern and brings it back up, half-full and dripping. 'Should do the trick.'

Kay takes it carefully in both hands, as if it was an unexploded bomb. He carries it carefully to the sofa where Mariam lies, not wanting to hold it for any longer than he has to. Feeling droplets of water on his fingers and trying not to think too hard about them.

Does he pour it over the wound, or try and make her drink it? He opts for the latter, kneeling before the sofa and putting the cup's edge to her lips. Slowly emptying the contents. He doesn't hear a choir of angels singing or see the glow of divine intercession happening before his eyes, but he does feel his hackles rise. A strange energy moves through him. Faint wisps of smoke rise from the dressing on Mariam's abdomen. She seems to stir slightly in her sleep. Her face showing confusion, then calm.

Kay gazes at the cup, in his hand. Thoughts going to places that aren't helpful. If he'd had that cup in the old days, when his hall burnt down, then perhaps things could have been different. Could it have undone fire?

The wonder of the moment is ended when Merlin drops and shatters something heavy, across the cave. Combing through his hoard again. Kay sighs and crosses back to the cistern, placing the cup upon a sideboard beside the water barrel. Willing himself to leave it there. He feels strange, just turning his back upon it. But he does. Going after Merlin.

Deeper into the cave there's another rack of plants growing beneath a strip of purple light. Small trees growing in bags of soil. Merlin is kneeling beside them, making cuttings. Scions that he can plant elsewhere if he needs to. Kay goes to stand over him, waiting for him to finish. But it doesn't take him long to notice something strange. Strange and horrible. There are twelve trees. Each of them is labelled in Merlin's untidy hand and stuck to the frame in front of them. Gawain. Bedwyr. Tristan. Bors. Percival. Safir and Palamedes. Agravain and Caradoc. Lancelot. Galehaut.

And Kay. His own name.

'What is this?' he asks quietly. Afraid of the answer.

'Hm?' asks Merlin. 'I told you, didn't I, that I took cuttings from all of your trees? Well, I planted them here. Think of them as backup copies, I suppose. A good wizard always has a redundancy plan.'

Backup copies. Kay swallows, slowly. 'If I went and planted that somewhere, would I ... would there be another ...'

'Well, I've never tested it,' says Merlin. 'But yes, that's the theory! Clever, isn't it?'

'And you thought it was all right to just make backup copies of all of us? Without asking us first?'

'I didn't see why you'd object. You yourself are a sort of clone, after all.'

Kay has to close his eyes. There can't be anything more, surely. There can't be anything else today to break him down further, to make him feel worse. But the question is already on his lips. Not that he wants to know the answer.

'I'm a what?' he asks.

Merlin laughs. 'You're not the *original* Kay. You're a facsimile! A crude copy. Every time the spell detects sufficient quantities of peril in the realm it churns out a new version of you. Muddles you together from whatever materials it can find. A new copy, each time. I should have thought that was perfectly obvious.'

'But,' he says, 'I remember. I remember the last war. And the one before that. And all the other wars. I remember the old days. Caer Moelydd.'

Merlin stands up, brushing the soil from his shorts. 'Yes, yes, all part of the spell. You wouldn't be much use otherwise, would you?'

'We're . . .' he says. 'We're just replaceable, to you. Aren't we? We always were. And now you're just going to fuck off and save your own skin. You're going to leave me here, in this doomed version of the world. Me and Lance. After everything we've done. Everything we've been through.'

'This is no time to start getting emotional.'

Kay can't stop himself. 'You just . . . you didn't even think, did you? All that time ago. About what it would be like, for us. For me and Lance and all the others. You didn't think for a moment what it would actually be like. To keep coming back and fighting. To keep dying, over and over again. And we all kept going because we thought you had a plan for us. We thought we were protecting the realm. Helping people. Making the world a better place.'

Merlin stares at him for a long, uncomprehending moment. Then he reaches out with one frail hand and pats him carefully upon his shoulder.

'You *were* helping people, my boy. Just, perhaps, not quite in the way that you imagined. It's a shame you had to go through all of that unpleasantness, but ... well ... it was all worth it, in the end. I got important data out of it! Try to remember that.'

Kay stares at the floor of the cave, suddenly unable to meet Merlin's gaze. Then he remembers that this might be the last time that he'll ever see him. Merlin, who took him from his father's home and taught him something of the world, all those years ago. So he forces himself to look back up again into those strange eyes. There isn't much tenderness there. Only hesitance. Confusion. Eagerness to get away.

'You can rest easy, now,' says Merlin. 'You've done your part. Nothing more you can do here. I'll pass on your regards to which-ever version of you I run into next!'

'What happens to me, then?' asks Kay. 'And all of us, here in this world? How does it end for us?'

Merlin has already turned around. He doesn't look back. 'I honestly don't know,' he says. 'Goodbye, Kay.'

Time bends, again. It forks either side of Merlin. Strange colours churn in the air. And then Merlin is gone. The dust is left to settle in peculiar spiral patterns. Only the oak staff is left behind, clattering to the floor.

Kay stands in the dark cave. He looks over at Mariam, sleeping on the sofa. Then he sinks to his knees.

32

Morgan feels a migraine developing.

It's not just Arthur, it's being here on this monstrosity. This profane clunking thing, poisoning the sky and the water and the earth. Her soul is crying out for trees and rivers, not silicone floor tiles and polyester sheets and electric light. It's like the place is sapping her magic.

Now she stares at the ceiling, absent-mindedly tracing her fingers along Arthur's back. He lies half on top of her, panting like a bear. The bedsheets are soaked with his sweat. He smells of copper and something fungal. Something mordant.

She wants to bathe in asses' milk, or the blood of a basilisk, or something else extravagant. A deep cleanse. Sleeping with Arthur again is awaking some very old impulses. It would have to be almond milk, nowadays. But even almonds are bad for the planet. She read that in the *New Yorker*.

In the absence of asses' milk, she would settle for a cold shower. But Arthur gets up and lumbers to the bathroom, scratching his arse. He coughs something up in the sink, something black and foul that's been in his throat for a thousand years. Then he starts to piss with the door open.

She gets up and pulls on a dressing gown, which crackles with static. Some synthetic fabric that she doesn't want next to her skin. She starts rolling a joint on the bedside table.

'Have you thought about what I said?' she calls into the bathroom.

'Christ's weeping sores, woman,' Arthur grumbles. 'Let me piss in peace.'

Morgan closes her eyes and licks the rolling paper. She could get up and slink into the bathroom, wrapping her arms around him and kissing his shoulder blades. He has shoulders like an ox. It would probably put him in a more receptive vein. But she's done enough for him already since they came aboard the Avalon rig. She doesn't have the energy left to slink.

'You dislike my new counsellors?' he asks, still in the bathroom.

'I do,' she says. 'Marlowe and his friends don't have your best interests at heart. You're surrounding yourself with enemies and fools.'

'They're the richest men in the realm,' he says. 'They command great armies. They have powerful friends in foreign lands, across the sea.'

'Those are not the qualities that I would seek in a good counsellor,' she says.

'No?' he scoffs. 'And what qualities would you seek?'

'Loyalty,' she says. She turns over, to face the bathroom. 'And bravery. Send for Kay again. Listen to his counsel. He's brave enough to tell you the truth.'

Arthur laughs. It's a bitter, unkind laugh. He looks around for a jug or basin, to pour water on his hands, but he cannot find one. He doesn't know how to turn on the taps and use the sink. He wipes his hands on a towel instead, standing naked in the doorway.

'Loyalty?' he asks. 'I gave him the chance to prove his fucking loyalty. He threw it back in my face. And I haven't forgotten his old treachery, either. He didn't come when I needed him. He's the real enemy of the realm. Not these new men.'

Morgan asks the old gods for the strength not to roll her eyes. She smiles instead, leaning on her elbow, trying to look even more beguiling. The things she does for Britain. In the old days she used to think about the good of the realm. All the ordinary women of the realm who she could save from the perils of war and famine, if she put the king in the right mood. Said the right thing on the right pillow. Now she thinks about the wild grass and the rivers and the trees. All of which will be gone soon, if she can't convince Arthur to save them.

'Merlin, then,' she says. 'Send for him. Call him to you.'

Arthur shakes his head. 'Old fool. He tried to trap me. Banished me to the Otherworld. Thought he could protect Britain without me. Now look at the state of it. Whole bloody realm's gone to the dogs. If I'd come back sooner, I wouldn't have let it get out of hand. This is all his fault. So much for the wisdom of druids.'

She can tell how embarrassed he is by the state of things. How much it angers him, undermines his sense of himself. It always did have a profound effect. The idea of mighty Albion always put him in a good mood. Britain, conqueror of Ireland, enemy of the Saxons, feared in Gaul and Rome. All fiction, but sweet fiction. He used to talk about sacking Byzantium. Calling him Arthur Rex or Arthur Augustus used to be the quickest way of putting him in a good mood. But the idea of a diminished Britain has the opposite effect. A small, shrivelled country. Laughed at, in other lands. The serpent eating its own tail. It makes him seethe.

'They say that Britain is much reduced,' says Arthur. He is pouring himself some more wine. 'For a time, we had an empire that spread the breadth of the world. As far as India! That's what these men are telling me. But it has fallen into ruin. They want me to rebuild it. Restore these isles to glory. I like that notion.'

'You don't know them,' she says. 'You haven't been here. They only seek to enrich themselves. They want to use you to win the hearts of the people. They will flatter you and beguile you and give you an empire, but you'll be giving them the world. And they'll destroy it.'

Arthur drinks his wine and shakes his head, standing by the foot of the bed. 'I asked them about that. About what you told me. They say it's all nonsense. There's still snow, in the winter. And we need to burn these fuels to keep our war machines rolling. That's what they say. Why would God have put this stuff in the ground if he didn't want us to use it?'

She blinks twice, formulating an answer. 'To test us, perhaps?' she says. 'Leading us into temptation. And if we succumb, we fail his test. By destroying creation.'

Arthur's face becomes grave and dour. The fact that he's staring at her breasts is unimportant. She's lodged that thought in his brain. The canker of doubt. Arthur's fear of the Christian God was always a good way of getting into his head and checking his wilder passions.

She crosses the bed on her knees and wraps her arms behind his neck. Kissing his foul-smelling beard, staring up into his dark green eyes. The green of a forest, deep and inviting, full of deer to hunt and beasts to slay.

'Your realm is flooded, and dying,' she says. 'And these men are the cause. Serpents and dissemblers, poisoning the air. You should cast them into the sea. Like Saint Patrick, clearing the snakes from Ireland.'

He is not meeting her gaze, but staring away at the floor. Thoughtful. Receptive. 'And what would I do then?' he asks.

She gently bites his ear and whispers into it. 'Rule with me by your side. Be the saviour of Britain. The saviour of all creation. Earn God's favour for all time. I'll show you how.'

His eyes harden. She can feel his shoulders tense. She's said something that displeases him.

'The only serpent here is you,' he says. He grabs her wrist and pushes her away, back onto the bed. Then he stares down at her, balefully. 'A snake at my ear, whispering poison. As ever. And I allow you into my bedchamber. At my bosom. You have bewitched me, temptress! I shan't hear another word from you.'

He knocks back his wine and fights his way into his discarded tunic from the night before. Then he bellows at the computer system in the ceiling, the way he's been taught to do. 'Oberon! Summon my counsellors!'

'Okay,' says Oberon, through the ceiling speakers. 'I'm summoning your counsellors.'

Morgan lies where she fell, grasping the bedsheets with white knuckles. She could harness all of this rage and use it for something deeply profane, turning Arthur's bowels into eels or summoning flies to lay their eggs in his eyes. Instead she pulls on her dressing gown and gathers up her smoking paraphernalia. She doesn't want to be here, half-naked, to be patronised by Marlowe's friends again.

He hasn't told her to leave, but she leaves anyway. There are eight stories of luxury apartments on this monstrosity. Arthur's new staterooms take up the entire eighth floor, and he has a private balcony. The whole western wall is sliding windows. When Morgan pushes them open, she lets in the wind and the smell of petroleum. She scowls and closes the window behind her. Then she is alone, outside in the baking heat, staring out over the flooded fens.

There is no peace out here. She can hear the sounds of the earth being drilled and defiled. The sounds of fuel being burnt and generators spinning. It's everything that she wants to see destroyed in the world. And they have the temerity to call it Avalon.

She walks over to the railing, cradling her lighter, struggling to get her joint lit in the cold wind until she remembers that the veil is open: she can waste magic on little indulgences, like she would have done in the old days. She throws the lighter over the side. Then she snaps her fingers, and a curl of flame is dancing painlessly on the pad of her thumb. She lights the joint with it and draws the smoke deep into her lungs, shaking her hand until the flame is gone.

A spark in the right place could blow this whole monstrosity to ruins. It would be nice to destroy it, to send it up in flames. She could flee to Anwyn and claim sanctuary. Her uncle Gwyn is still the king of the Fair Folk, as far as she knows. She could abandon the world of men to the fire and the slaughter.

But that wouldn't help her cause. That wouldn't save the trees, or the fields, or the women of the realm.

Once she's taken a couple of drags, she throws the joint over the balcony. Then she unties her dressing gown and shrugs it off. She lets it blow away in the wind, not particularly caring if Arthur or his counsellors can see her through the windows.

She waits for the wind to blow from the east, against her back. Then she slips over the railing and falls like a stone towards the marsh below.

There are already feathers growing on her back. Before the marsh rushes up to meet her, she has sprouted wings. Her eyes become keener, and her nose becomes a sharp beak in front of her. And then she is a red kite, riding on the wind, soaring above the water.

She could just circle for a while until her mood improves. She could slip through the veil and fly to Anwyn. Then she wouldn't have to worry about her form or appearance. She could just be a fay spirit, formless, five dimensional, incomprehensible to the human mind. But that would require speaking to other fay, explaining her absence to them, and she doesn't want to do that. Not just yet.

She turns her tail and arcs away, swooping towards land. Earth. Britain. Circling over the marsh. Gliding and coasting, gradually closer to the water. There might be something to eat there, a fish that she could swoop down and catch in her talons. She could carry it ashore and rend its innards with her beak. That would be therapeutic.

But the marsh seems strangely empty, even when she swoops down close to it. No fish or eels or anything else. No herons nesting in the reeds. The water becomes inviting. Perhaps she wants to swim, to cleanse herself of Arthur and oil rigs and the taint of corruption. Maybe once she's in the water it will be easier to find prey. Her feathers become a thick hide, glistening and sleek. Her beak becomes a whiskered muzzle. She drops into the water as something otterish, not quite fay or human or animal but some combination of the three.

The water feels wrong, instantly. Harsh and sour against her hide. Unctuous. Acidic. Burning her eyes and her sensitive nose. She doesn't want to swim through this oily murk for any longer than she has to. She powers towards shore, thrashing her whole body from nose to tail. Fighting through the reeds and a bobbing cluster of plastic bottles until she feels mud beneath her claws. She scrambles ashore and shakes herself dry to try and rid herself of the corruption. But it stays, stuck to her coat.

She wills herself human again and sloughs off her lutrine skin as if it was a fur coat that she'd grown tired of. Standing with human feet on a soggy stretch of land in the middle of the marsh. Sun baking down on her wet skin.

The monstrosity still looms in the distance, poisoning the earth. There was nobody out here to see her, crawling out of the water like a half-drowned cat, but she still feels embarrassed, foolish. She imagines a dress into existence and lets it unfurl around her skin, tying it at the waist.

There is a blighted tree stump on this stretch of land, and she sits on it, trying to get the oily water out of her hair. While she is sitting and thinking and wringing her hair she sees a shape rising from the water. A familiar face. Sharp teeth. Yellow eyes. Silver skin.

A few minutes later they're sitting together and smoking. Nimue is half in the water and half out of it, soaking her tail, not bothering to disguise her fins. Morgan can't help but notice that she doesn't look well. There's a whitish plaque building up on her scales.

'You shacked up with him again, didn't you?' asks Nimue.

Morgan shrugs. 'I'm not ashamed of it.'

'You told me you were finished with him. "I'll never go near him again", that's what you said.'

Morgan frowns. 'Well, perhaps I did say that. In 521 AD. But that was then, and this is now.'

'I don't care how long it's been, love. You're better than he deserves. Mortals have a saying for this kind of thing.'

'I'm sure they do,' says Morgan. 'But it's easy for mortals. If they vow never to sleep with somebody ever again then they only have to keep it up for eighty years or so. Then they're dead. It's much harder to stay away from somebody if you both live forever.'

'That's a shit excuse,' says Nimue. 'And he's still your cousin. I know I've said it a billion times, but it's proper sketchy.'

'It's necessary,' she says, raising her chin. 'For the good of the realm.'

'Yeah, keep telling yourself that, love. I thought you said you had a plan. Was your plan just to keep shagging Arthur until the end of the world?'

Morgan lets out her frustrations with a ragged sigh. With the hand that's not holding her cigarette, she pinches the bridge of her nose. Her plan was to get him back on the throne and then use him to save the planet. If she can find a way of persuading him, he might do something useful. Plant some trees. Throw some oil barons into the sea. That sort of thing. But the barons have him in their thrall. There's no clear path to salvation. No hopeful light shining through the thorns. 'I do feel bad about the young woman,' she says. 'Poor Mariam. It would have been worth the bloodshed, if Arthur had actually listened to me, but now ...'

Nimue smokes silently for a minute, blowing smoke out of her rheumy gills. She shakes her head. 'I expected better from you, you know.'

Morgan frowns at her. 'Why?'

'I don't mean shagging him. That's very on brand if you don't mind my saying so. But I mean ... you're trying to save the planet, and your big idea was to try and get *some bloke* to fix everything?'

'He's Arthur Pendragon, he's not just "some bloke".'

'Now you listen to me,' says Nimue. 'Arthur Pendragon is the definition of Just Some Bloke. He thinks he's all that, but he's not. He's a nasty piece of work. You can wrap him round your little finger all you want, but you can't change who he is.'

Morgan doesn't try to hide her confusion. 'But you gave him the sword,' she says. 'You looked into his soul and you gave him Caliburn. If you hadn't done that then he could never have been king.'

'I gave him the sword because Merlin told me to,' says Nimue. 'He said it was the only way to save the realm from peril. And I trusted Merlin, back then. But it turns out Merlin was Just Some Bloke as well.'

A wind blows in across the marsh from somewhere in the west. It brings foul dust with it, blown up off the surface of the water. Morgan closes her eyes against the grains of corruption, wondering just how she allowed this to happen, this complete ravaging of the world. She had visions of it long ago. She tried everything to stop it. You might have thought that a sorcerer of her ability could have done something more tangible to save the world. Born of magic. Granddaughter of the faerie queen. It's not that she didn't try. Inveigling and enchanting and working magic under different guises. But it never seemed to make much difference. There is no evidence of her labours, here, in this foul place. Fifteen hundred years of wasted effort. She might as well have cast off her immortality long ago. Ended the charade. Allowed her bones to crumble into dust. It wouldn't have made a difference, in the long run.

'I'm tired,' she says. She takes another long drag on her cigarette.

'I'm bloody knackered,' says Nimue. 'Suppose we have to see it through, now, though. After all, we've hung around this long. Be a shame to miss the end.'

Morgan draws her knees close to her chest. 'How do you think it will end?'

Nimue scoffs. 'Humans being humans. Being greedy. They'll burn everything, and they'll run out of food, and then they'll blame each other for it. And that'll be the end. Nowt we can do about it.'

Morgan imagines what it would be like, living through that. Surviving it. Wandering through the ruins of the world. What would be the point? Nothing left to save. Even if she ruled over the ashes, she would be queen of nothing.

'I thought this would work,' she says. 'With Arthur. I'm not so certain, now.'

'You could have asked me. I'd have told you that it wouldn't.'

Nimue starts coughing and then she can't stop. Wet sounds, horrible and grating. Gills flaring. Morgan watches, apprehensively. Can gods die from ailments like this? Nimue's only a minor god, in the grand scheme of things. The god of British rivers, lakes, freshwater confluences, tidal wetlands. If the water is poisoned, perhaps Nimue is poisoned too.

Morgan stares at the monstrosity across the water and finds new reserves of loathing for it. A foul mass of cranes and towers and chimneys, shimmering in the heat of its exhaust fumes. Not just a font of corruption but a black fortress for all the guiltiest men in the world, the most culpable, the men whose greed is fuelling this mess. She thought that Arthur would sweep them away when he came back. Perhaps that was foolish of her. She ought to have known that Marlowe would be in their pocket. Not quite the steadfast public servant that he pretended to be. Not so concerned with the good of the realm as he led her to believe. He should suffer, for that.

There might be ways of ensuring that he suffers. There is one advantage to this situation which she'd overlooked before. All of the guilty men are in one place.

'Perhaps,' she says, 'between the two of us, if we combined our magic . . .'

Nimue makes a sceptical sound. 'We could what?'

'We could turn things in a different direction.'

'Ohh, no,' says Nimue. 'I already had this from Kay. I'm not getting involved.'

Morgan frowns. 'What did he want you to do?'

'Wreck that thing, somehow,' says Nimue, gesturing across the water. 'I told him that it wouldn't make a blind bit of difference, even if I did.'

'But could you do it?' says Morgan.

Nimue looks away and shrugs. Staring at the water. At the sky. And at the monstrosity, in the distance. 'Maybe,' she says. 'Why? What d'you have in mind?'

Morgan allows herself a smile. She will have to return, for a little while, if this plan has any chance of succeeding. A few more days of nursing Arthur's ego and walking among the serpents. But if it succeeds, it will be worth the cost.

'I have a few ideas ...'

33

Mariam wakes up on a mouldy sofa, somewhere that feels cold and smells bad. When she cracks her eyelids open she can see the ceiling arching overhead, lit weirdly and covered in slime.

She groans faintly to herself. Just once she'd like to wake up in a nice hotel room or something. Somewhere clean.

The sofa is damp with sweat or condensation. Her mouth feels as dry as leather. If she gets up to see where she is then she might find something to drink. But the moment she tries to move, she feels a sharp stab of pain in her stomach. She screws her eyes shut against it and lets her head fall back against the sofa, trying not to faint. Riding the waves of pain with her teeth clenched together, until her ears stop ringing and her heart stops pounding.

She reaches down slowly and feels under her shirt, expecting to find a dressing. But there's nothing there, no bandages or open wound. Just raised scar tissue, as if it's been healing for months.

Maybe it has been. Maybe she's been in a coma or something,

and the last few days of weird shit didn't actually happen. That would make a lot of sense. She got shot by a Saxon goon outside the Preston fracking plant, and Regan dug the bullet out of her stomach. Now she's in a FETA hideout somewhere, getting better. Everything else was just a fever dream. Otherwise she has to believe that Regan stabbed her to bring back King Arthur. She has to believe that Dando was killed by a dragon. Those do seem like the kinds of things you'd hallucinate. She lets her hand droop off the side of the sofa in case Dando wants to pad over and lick her fingers. But he doesn't, because he isn't here.

When she moves again she does it more carefully, trying not to strain her abdomen any further. It still hurts, but she manages to get upright. Sitting on the sofa with an old blanket wrapped around her. She sniffs at it and pulls a face.

Somebody snores, in the gloom. She reaches to her hip for a gun that isn't there. But then she sees that it's Kay. Sleeping in an overstuffed armchair with his head against his shoulder and a squirrel dozing in his lap. He's wearing just his tunic and his old cloak draped over him like a blanket. The same cloak that he left in the clothing bins in the Preston camp. Did he go and get it back?

She feels relieved, for half a moment, seeing Kay. But then the familiar dread returns. If Kay is here then it all happened. The dragon and everything else. Regan stabbed her. Kay didn't do anything to stop it. The relief turns to anger. Why didn't he do anything?

Maybe he did. She can barely remember what happened. She was lying on the stone floor of the tower, in Glastonbury. Staring up at the square of sky overhead. She remembers an old man, standing over her. The sky looked strange behind him. He was the kind of old man who you sometimes used to see at climate protest camps, selling drugs and raving about spiritual energy.

Wrinkly and bearded and harmless, but totally batshit. She can remember his eyes. They were hypnotising, bright and weird and multicoloured.

She needs to drink something, so she stands up on shaky legs. Closing her eyes while she overcomes a wave of dizziness. She leaves the musty blanket on the sofa and goes searching for water.

Exploring this place doesn't help her to understand its purpose. It's like a mix between a science lab and an antique furniture shop – the kind that always seemed like they must have been a front for something. There are glass tanks full of strange plants that she doesn't want to look too closely at. Water running through pipes and under shelves, like something from a space colony, but no taps anywhere for her to drink from. Eventually she finds a rain barrel, full to the brim, collecting water from somewhere up above. There's a manky old cup sitting on the table next to it, so she grabs that and rinses it out a couple of times. Then she fills it and drinks from it. The water tastes better than she expected, cool and clear and metallic. It makes her think of moonlight.

She fills it again and walks back over to Kay, planning to offer him some. But he is still asleep and snoring. Her boots clink against something on the ground beside his chair: an empty bottle of booze. That makes her wrinkle her nose. She decides to pour the water over Kay's head, instead.

The squirrel chitters and bolts for a distant corner of the cave. Kay jolts awake, with panic in his eyes, grabbing for a sword that isn't there. The cloak falls away from him, and Mariam hears herself gasp.

'Oh my God,' she says. 'What happened to your hand?'

Kay blinks the sleep from his eyes. He stares at her, then stares down at his right hand. It looks wrong, crusted over with something hard. Green and tufted, in places. Green shoots growing from it, like a young tree. He flexes his fingers and pulls a face, then hides the hand back under the folds of his cloak.

'Where are we?' she asks. 'Where are my friends?'

Kay groans to himself. Probably the empty bottle catching up with him. Bowing his head and rubbing his eyes. His left hand looks fairly normal. Nothing growing on it that shouldn't be.

'We're in Merlin's cave,' he says. 'He brought us here.'

Mariam presses her lips together and breathes in deeply through her nose. She's just about reached her capacity for legendary people.

'Right,' she says. 'Great. Is Robin Hood going to turn up next, or ...?'

Kay looks pained, as if that was a silly question. 'No, he's been dead for hundreds of years.'

'Oh, right, *sorry*,' she says. 'How stupid of me. Is Merlin going to help us save the planet?'

'No, he's ... gone,' says Kay. 'He left us here.'

'Brilliant. Where are my friends?'

Kay grunts. 'Saxons took them.'

That's almost more painful than getting stabbed. Almost, but not quite. She has to stand silently for a moment before she speaks again. She needs her sisters to still be alive. None of this would be even slightly bearable without them.

'So what's the plan? How do we get them back? What are we going to do?'

Kay heaves himself up out of the armchair and pushes past her, trying to wave away the questions with his weird hand. She stands where she is, uncomprehending. Watching him stumble groggily across the cave. When he reaches the rain barrel he plants his hands on its rim and plunges his head underwater, to wake himself up. Staying down so long that she almost worries about him drowning. It's only when she takes half a step towards him that he comes up gasping, shaking his head, spraying water everywhere. Then he stands panting for a while, water streaming down his dreadlocks and back into the barrel.

'The plan right now,' he says, 'is to stay here. And wait until you've healed properly. You need rest. Time to recover.'

'All right,' she says. 'And then what? What do we do once I've healed? How do we save my friends?'

'Urgh,' says Kay. As if he's disgusted by her. Annoyed by her. She walks closer to him, feeling hesitant. Confused.

'You have to have a plan,' she says. 'We have to stop Arthur and Regan, right?'

'It doesn't matter anymore,' says Kay. 'None of it matters.'

He stands where he is, rubbing his eyes. She can't believe that he's saying these things. He's hungover, but it must be more than that. Now that she looks closely she can see other signs that something is wrong. Leaves in his hair. Strange hard spots on his face.

'It still matters to me,' she says.

'There's nothing we can do. Merlin said that there's no green shoots. Nothing we can do to make the world better. It's too late.'

'I don't believe this,' she says. 'You're just giving up? Because of some fortune cookie bullshit that your friend told you?'

'He's Merlin. All-seeing, all-knowing, all of that bollocks. If he says that it's hopeless, then it's hopeless.'

He is rummaging through an old cupboard, looking for something. Eventually he pulls out a glass bottle that looks like it's been there for a million years, gathering dust. Once he's brushed the cobwebs away and bitten the cork out of it, he takes a sniff and pulls a face. But he drinks from it anyway, grimacing at the taste. Walking back over to his mouldy armchair and sitting back down again. The squirrel comes out of hiding, clawing its way up the back of the chair. Kay offers him a swig.

'But you're you,' she says. 'You're Kay. Your whole thing is that you come back when England needs you, right? You come back and save the world, whenever it needs saving. If you're not going to save the world then who is?'

'Christ knows,' says Kay. 'Not me. I've spent the last thousand years saving England from peril. Reckon I probably deserve a holiday.'

Mariam realises that she's trembling, with shock or rage or something halfway between the two. Her abdomen hurts, but she's too angry to care about that at the moment. She badly wants to grab the bottle from his hand and beat him over the head with it.

'You know who doesn't get a holiday?' she asks him. 'My friends, who've been locked up by Saxon and are probably being tortured right now. Or the people up in Manchester laying down their lives for a cause that they believe in. Or any of the kids in refugee camps, all over the country, who don't know where their next meal is coming from. They don't get to have a holiday. They're all waiting for the world to change. They're waiting for somebody to stand up and bring this government crashing down so that something else can come after it. They're waiting for a new world. They're dying, waiting for it. And you're not going to help them? You're just going to sit here on your arse drinking beer?'

Kay has closed his eyes. He looks broken, sitting like he is, with his shoulder slumped. Holding the bottle loosely in his weird wooden hand. He slowly starts to shake his head.

'I'm sorry, Mariam,' he says. 'I really am. I don't know what you were expecting from me, when you first met me, but whatever it was . . . I'm not going to magically save the planet. I'm just some mouldy old geezer who doesn't know what he's doing. Should have been dead long ago. I'm out of ideas. No use to anyone.

Might as well just sit here and let this happen, whatever it is. Turn into a tree.'

'Do you know how pathetic that is?' she asks. 'Do you know how pathetic you sound right now? There's nothing noble about giving up.'

Kay puts his head in his hand, covering his eyes. 'I'm tired,' he says. 'I'm done. Nothing left in me. If you still want to go and save your friends, then be my guest. Best of luck to you. But there's nothing I can do to help.'

Mariam stands and stares at him, with her fists clenched at her sides. Blood boiling in her cheeks. Part of her wants to scream at him, rain down her fists on him, find something to bludgeon him with. Instead of doing that she turns and walks away, through this cave, to wherever it leads. Wanting to get away from all the clutter. Leave it all behind her. Find fresh air, somewhere.

At the entrance to the cave there's an old ice cream van and then a set of metal gates that somebody has kicked in. And then she's out in the open, in the middle of a forest, on an evening that's warmer than it should be for the time of year. The fresh air doesn't make her feel better because it isn't fresh. It tastes of ash and corruption. She has to pull her scarf up over her nose.

She could just walk away into the forest. Put all of this craziness behind her, for good. Try and make a life for herself somewhere. She knows about other camps that need help, other communes that she could join, if they haven't been burnt and raided and destroyed. Tilling the earth somewhere and trying not to think about the wider world. Trying to forget Kay. Trying to forget that she picked up that sword and killed that dragon and was almost Queen of Wales.

But then she thinks of her friends, locked up somewhere. Saxon don't follow any code. They don't have to. They torture prisoners. They execute terrorists. They enjoy it. She can't let that happen to Willow and Teoni and the others. She couldn't live with herself if she just turned her back on them, knowing that she didn't even try to save them.

So she stays, for now. She walks up one side of the valley, into the trees, looking for somewhere to sit. Near the top there's a fallen tree, mouldering on its side, which tore a big hole out of the hillside when it fell over. She goes and sits in the hollow, with her back against the cold earth. Staring downhill and thinking.

Storming the Avalon rig by herself probably wouldn't achieve a great deal. She's not even sure how she would go about it. Those huge unscalable legs. With the Preston plant, she did reconnaissance for weeks before. She knew the layout, knew the guard rotations, knew the right place to put the explosives. And she still managed to fuck it up. With the Avalon rig, she'd know nothing. She'd be going in blind. That seems like a great way to get herself shot. And her friends might not even be there. They might have been shipped off to some Saxon black site somewhere. They might have been taken back to Saxon HQ in America, extradited for execution. They might have been killed already and dumped in the sea . . .

This is all her fault. They could have just stayed in Wales, with the sword. She should have stepped up and tried to be a leader. But Regan offered her a way out, and it seemed too good to turn down. If she'd just tried harder – if she'd risen to the challenge and suffered through it – then maybe her friends would still be safe. Maybe they'd still be alive.

There's a sound somewhere behind her, like somebody breathing out through their nose. Her first thought is that the Saxons must have tracked her down. She turns so that she's crouching inside the hollow, trying to ignore the stab of pain in her stomach from moving too quickly. Peering over the edge, uphill, towards the sound.

A huge deer with giant antlers is standing among the trees. It must have already seen her, because it's frozen still and staring down at her, looking her right in the eyes. It really is massive, taller than she would be if she stood at her full height. Taller than Kay, even without the antlers. It has shaggy brown fur around its neck, which must make it too warm in all of this hot weather.

'Hi,' Mariam says.

The deer doesn't move. It only blinks.

'Are you . . . going to talk to me?' she asks.

It would make sense. After dragons and King Arthur and everything else. Talking deer. Maybe it's some kind of deer god – which is probably haram to even think about, but she's way past the point of worrying about that. What would her foster mother think if she knew? Her daughter who talks to deer gods in the forest.

'Look,' she says, 'if you're here to tell me what to do or give me the wisdom of the forest or whatever, then let's just get it over with.'

The deer doesn't say anything. It stands and stares down at her as if it doesn't like her. As if it was hoping to find somebody else. Or maybe she's just imagining that.

She sighs. Then she stands up. Straightening her back and balling her hands into fists. She takes a deep breath and tries to look serious, staring the deer dead in the eyes.

'I am Queen Mariam,' she says, in a deep voice. 'Queen of Wales. Queen of the Forest! And I demand that you speak to me and tell me how I should save the world!'

The deer's eyes widen in panic. It doesn't bow its head or start speaking in words that she can understand. It takes a few steps back, away from her.

'No, I'm sorry,' she says. 'It's okay. Don't go. Just tell me how I can save my friends!'

But the deer turns and moves away through the forest, stepping over roots in no particular hurry. Neither frightened of her nor interested in staying.

Mariam sinks back down into the hollow and buries her head in her hands. Maybe if she waits long enough another animal will come, a talking fox or a talking bear or something else. But she knows how stupid that is, even as she thinks it. Why is she expecting help from animals? Why is she asking a random deer to solve her problems? Why is she waiting for Kay or Merlin or any other old tosser to wave their magic wand and fix everything? Roz was right about heroes. About relying on other people. It would be nice if she could just sit back and let a talking deer tell her what to do. It would be so much easier than figuring it out for herself. But that isn't going to happen.

It's just like slaying the dragon. If she wants to save the world, she'll have to do it herself.

34

Lancelot can't decide what to wear. There will be two nights of coronation feasting on the Avalon platform. Arthur will be crowned on Glastonbury Tor the day after tomorrow. If it's anything like feasts used to be in the old days, the time between then and now will be spent gorging and fucking and vomiting.

It doesn't really matter what you wear for an occasion like that. He doesn't want to wear his mail shirt and his thick fighting tunic. Not to a feast. He remembers a bliaut that he used to own a thousand years ago: bright red, gored sleeves, trimmed with thick bands of embroidered interlace. He'd have worn it with gartered stockings and a mantle of marten's fur fastened at the shoulder. But he doesn't have that bliaut anymore. He doesn't even have his officer's dress jackets from the last few wars. Can't pop back to Chingford just for those.

He settles for a modern look. White tuxedo. Red cummerbund. Shirt open at the collar. Sword hanging from his belt. If anyone accuses him of breaking their dress code then at least he can stab them.

Marlowe has gone for classic black tie, leaning into the spy aesthetic. Lancelot can't pretend that it doesn't look good on him. They admire each other briefly in Marlowe's suite before they head out to the feast. Marlowe straightens his lapels for him.

'I'm not sure I have the stamina for coronation feasts, anymore,' Lancelot admits.

Marlowe places a hand on his shoulder. Squeezes it gently. 'We can leave early if you want. Come back here for a nightcap . . .'

'I like the sound of that,' he lies.

'I'm glad you're with us,' says Marlowe. 'I was worried for a while that you might be developing a conscience.'

Lancelot makes himself smile. 'Not much danger there.'

They leave together. Out into the air-conditioned corridors, where people are already moving, wearing a strange hotchpotch of clothes. Nobody knows how to dress for the return of King Arthur. The Saxons have bizarre dress uniforms, azure jackets with gold lapels and too much braid. For everyone else there's black tie and long gowns and sequined cocktail dresses, but musty old things as well. All manner of doublets and bliauts and veiled hennin steeple hats like costumes from a play. They must think that this is what people used to wear. Groups of them block the corridor, hanging from each other's shoulders, taking photos of themselves.

They're all going to the same place, a huge conference space that has been transformed into a banqueting hall. Lit by flaming braziers and draped with the Pendragon banner. The sight of it makes Lancelot's stomach quail. The last time he saw that banner it was at the head of an army marching against him. The crude dragon's head, in profile, staring out at you with its single hungry eye. Jaws open, teeth bared, ready to snap you in half.

They've brought in the Round Table from wherever it was being kept. It can be quartered and broken up, then reassembled. In the old days they carried it from one mead hall to the next, while Arthur progressed around his kingdoms. Trailing it on oxcarts through Gwynedd and Powys and Dumnonia. Now it is here. There are other tables, long and covered in green cloth, for people beneath the king's attention. The Round Table is reserved for honoured guests.

Arthur sits in his old place with his legs splayed and his elbow on the back of his seat. Still crownless, for now. Curls of red hair spilling down onto his shoulders. Somebody's convinced him to trade his mail for a military jacket, with a sash across the chest, but he still has Caliburn girthed to his waist. He looks uncomfortable and bored. The other seats are taken up by Marlowe's friends, the oil men and the media men and mercenary men. The good old Protestant men. The CEO of Saxon is one of them, with armed thugs standing behind him and more of them in every corner of the room. No question of Arthur's legitimacy, when the mercenaries are on his side. Now there's a sort of scramble to earn his good favour. Supplicating and entreating. The government of the nation now consists of King Arthur and whoever can hold his attention for longer than half a minute. Just like the good old days.

Lancelot finds it all faintly nauseating, and he hasn't even started drinking yet.

Arthur seems pleased to see him, waving him over with one massive arm. 'Lancelot! I want you at my right hand, not these chinless Saesnegs. Get up, you fat sow. Make way for a real sword-Briton.'

Arthur cuffs the man sitting next to him until the seat is emptied, and Lancelot takes his place. There is a general reshuffling. Marlowe somehow smoothly ends up in the next seat down.

Morgan is on Arthur's left, looking forlorn in a beautiful dress. She smiles thinly at him.

Lancelot is still deciding whether to smile back or not when Arthur slams a pint glass down in front of him, then fills it to the brim with wine. He claps a hand on Lancelot's shoulder, staring into his face. Breath smelling heavily of drink already. Lancelot had forgotten the sheer size of him, the broadness of his shoulders, the thickness of his neck. Beard like an autumn forest. Arms like iron rope.

'They say Britain forged an empire while I was sleeping,' Arthur says, 'greater than Rome. We ruled India. We ruled lands on the other side of the world. Is that true?'

'For a while, yes,' says Lancelot. 'But we ... gave them back again.'

Arthur scoffs. 'Well that was fucking stupid of us, wasn't it? When these rebels are broken we'll send ships to build our empire back. I'll make you King of India.'

Lancelot swallows. 'I'm sure I don't deserve the honour, sire.'

'Bollocks,' says Arthur. 'Don't be such a nancy. I've forgiven you. You'll take an army to India. You'll become king. You'll grow rich. Then you'll send me tribute. First, these rebels. Then India.'

Some of the oil men rap their hands against the Round Table. Lancelot stares down at it. The ancient wood, set with cheap paper napkins. He has been to India before, during the Raj. He remembers how beautiful it was. Drinking gin in cool palaces. He knows that it has changed, now. He read about it in one of Marlowe's newspapers. Hit worse than anywhere else by rising temperatures. He will be King of India, where the rivers have dried up and the cities are roasting, and people are fighting over clean water.

'Do you intend ...' he begins. 'Do you intend to do anything for the environment, my liege?'

He has surprised himself. Morgan looks surprised as well, but pleasantly so. Marlowe delicately clears his throat. Arthur squints at him like a huntsman squinting at a distant elk.

'For the *what*?' asks Arthur.

'He means the planet, my love,' says Morgan. 'Like I've been saying to you.'

Arthur groans from deep in his throat. 'Christ preserve me. I thought a red-blooded Briton like you would take all of that for the cack that it is. Archbishop, tell him.'

There's a priest sitting at the table in a mixture of diving gear and liturgical vestments. Stole and surplice, snorkel and goggles. It's not the strangest thing that Lancelot has seen since he came back up, but it ranks pretty highly.

'This second great flood is as the first,' says the archbishop, through his snorkel. 'God has sent it to remake the earth, as punishment for our sins. Only through prayer and Christian virtue can we deliver our salvation.'

'See?' says Arthur. He extends his hand towards the archbishop and looks at Lancelot as if the matter is settled.

'Couldn't agree more, Your Grace,' says the CEO of Saxon, wiping his mouth on a serviette. He sounds American. 'All this eco-terrorist hogwash is just socialism by the back door.'

Lancelot feels very old instincts taking over. Don't stick your neck out. Don't go out on a limb for anyone or anything. Look after yourself. Look after your prospects. Those are the instincts that he used to live by, in the old days. Courting Arthur's favour. Fearing Arthur's displeasure. But then he sees Morgan sitting across the table from him, with hope in her eyes. And he hears more words coming out of his mouth.

'That being said, my liege,' he begins, 'India won't be much of a kingdom if the world gets any warmer. There must be something we can do to—'

Arthur slams his fist down against the table, rattling the cutlery. The world shakes slightly. Old fears leap up in Lancelot's chest, and he tries to drive them down again.

'Not much of a kingdom?' asks Arthur, seething. 'Fucking ingratitude. Whole of India not good enough for you? I let you back into my trust. I offer you *half the world* to rule over. And you turn your nose up at me?'

Morgan is trying to calm him down. 'Lancelot means well, my liege.'

Arthur sneers at her. 'Keep your teeth together, woman. I won't hear any more about the world being too warm. It's as warm as God wants it to be. Why should I defy his will? Now, have the hog brought out. I'm fucking starving.'

When the food arrives it tastes of chemicals. Arthur sneers at his plate. Instead of a boar's leg that he could seize by the bone and gnaw upon, he has pork steaks drowned in a greasy white wine sauce. Lancelot worries that he won't know how to eat it, but it seems that Morgan has taught him to use a knife and fork since his resurrection. Nobody else would have had the forethought. Arthur looks uncomfortable, using womanly eating utensils. Hacking inexpertly at the meat. Like somebody using chopsticks for the second time. But he manages to get a hunk of meat into his mouth. He frowns halfway through chewing it and spits it on the ground, washing away the taste with a swig of wine. 'Who killed this boar? Tastes like stewed shit. Bring me something else.'

'Nothing wrong with this meat, Your Majesty,' says the Saxon CEO. 'Finest American rump steak, so you know it's good. Flown in all the way from Tennessee.'

Arthur screws up his face. 'What, so pigs fly now, do they?' he asks. 'It's rancid. Bring me another. Or I'll ride out and kill one myself. Be good to hunt some boar again.'

Lancelot clears his throat. 'There are no boars left in Britain, my lord.'

'Bollocks,' says Arthur. 'The forests are teeming with boar.'

'Most of the old forests are gone,' says Morgan. 'If you were to go and ride through your realm, you would find it barren. You could see the destruction for yourself.'

Marlowe speaks up. 'The king cannot possibly ride anywhere until the realm has been purged of undesirable elements. He would be placing his royal person in too much danger.'

'I'd like to place my royal person at the head of an army,' says Arthur. 'Ride one of these new war machines into battle.'

'All of Britain's hopes rest upon your shoulders, Your Majesty,' says Marlowe. 'It would be a tragedy for you to be killed again in battle, so soon after your return from your exile. Why not send Lancelot to hunt them down?'

Lancelot turns and glares. Marlowe smiles back at him, smooth and serpentine.

Arthur grunts. 'Well, I don't trust any of these fucking melts to lead my army. I trust you to do it. Find the hole that these rebels are hiding in and burn them out of it. I'll join you on the field, after I'm crowned king.'

'As you say, my liege,' says Lancelot. He stares into his wine.

More food comes. It isn't any better. Arthur eats it anyway, which means they all have to eat it too. Disdaining it would be an insult to the royal tastebuds, and insulting the king's tastebuds is a good way to get your tongue ripped out. So Lancelot eats, washing it down with bad wine. It's depressingly easy, falling back into old habits.

Between courses they can leave their seats and wander freely around the hall, dipping their cups into huge tubs of strong wine. Half the guests are drunk already. Colonel Nashorn is here, all the way down from Manchester, wearing medals on his breast. Regaling people with tales of his dragon slaying.

413

Lancelot resolves to get as drunk as possible, as quickly as possible. He's plunging his cup back into the vat of wine when he feels a familiar chill by his shoulder. Morgan is standing by the buffet table, where she wasn't standing half a second ago.

'Christ,' he says. 'Do you have to be relentlessly terrifying all the time?'

'Only when I choose to be,' she says.

He drinks from his cup and scowls at her over its brim, thinking of what to say. This is the same Morgan who once trapped him in the cellar of her castle for three months, back in the old days. The first rumours about him and Gwenhwyfar probably passed as whispers from her lips into Arthur's ears, to sow discord at Caer Moelydd. He has a glut of reasons to dislike her. But there was always something about her that he faintly admired. She rejected the Christian notions of how a woman ought to comport herself. What a woman ought to want and how she ought to go about acquiring it. He finds himself pleased, now, to find her here. Somebody else from the old days. Even Morgan is better than these awful modern people.

'I wanted to return this,' she says. 'I have no further use for it.'

On her pale and outstretched palm is Galehaut's ring. He stares down at it in mute surprise before he snatches it up in his spare hand. Turning it over to see whether it is damaged. The ancient stone is still where it should be, burnished with orange warmth. The twisted silver bands are untarnished. He puts his cup of wine down long enough to twist it onto his left forefinger, running his thumb over the stone. Part of him has felt empty since he lost the ring. Now it feels whole again. He lets out a long breath. Strange to feel grateful when Morgan was the one who took it in the first place. But he feels a surge of goodwill towards her.

'Thank you,' he says.

Morgan smiles. Her face seems to lay bare his secrets. 'I was

414

sorry to have to take it from you. But it was necessary, to achieve all of this.'

'Hmm,' he says. Looking around the room. 'I didn't realise we were on the same side. How long have you been working with Marlowe?'

'Long enough,' says Morgan. 'He made a deal with me some time ago. If I brought about Arthur's return, he'd banish these vultures and end the devastation of the earth.'

Lancelot scoffs. 'And you thought he'd keep his word? I wouldn't have expected you to be that naïve.'

'I warned him that if he betrayed me I would wreak my unholy vengeance upon him. But it seems that the unholy vengeance of a sorceress inspires less fear than it used to.'

Lancelot presses a hand to his chest. 'I'd still be afraid, if you threatened to wreak vengeance upon me.'

She smiles, gratefully. 'Thank you. What a kind thing to say.'

'Still, it's a shame I didn't know sooner,' he says. 'We could have worked together in Manchester if Marlowe had mentioned it to me.'

'That may not be the only thing that Marlowe hasn't mentioned to you,' says Morgan, sipping her wine.

Lancelot pulls a face. Here she goes. Morgan the deceiver, dark lady of ruinous whispers, dripping poison, sowing doubt. He knows better by now than to be drawn in by it.

'You may not choose to listen to me,' she says, 'but there's something amiss here. Why did Marlowe want Arthur back? How do these people benefit from his return? It's still unclear to me.'

'He hasn't fully explained himself to me, either,' says Lancelot. 'But that's just Marlowe. Keeping everything close to his chest.'

'You're far closer to his chest than I am,' says Morgan. 'I'd hoped that he might have told you. But perhaps he doesn't trust you either. Do you trust him?'

She's very good at this. Part of him wants to tell her that she's being ridiculous. But the truth is that she isn't. He doesn't feel like he can trust Marlowe any more. It's like the carpet's being pulled out from under him.

'I trust him to look after the realm's best interests,' he says. But he doesn't believe himself, as he says it.

Morgan looks at him as if that was a pitiful thing to say. 'I trust him to look after his own best interests,' she says. 'And perhaps the best interests of those close to him. Not the best interests of the realm.'

'Well, I'm close to him,' says Lancelot. 'So I have nothing to worry about.'

'Hm,' says Morgan. 'I wonder if Galehaut felt the same way.'

Lancelot's fist tightens, and he feels the ring pressing against his finger. He doesn't want to hear Galehaut's name in her mouth. Not used like this, like something rotten, dragged out of the bushes to sow discord.

'What are you trying to say?' he asks.

'Don't you think it's strange that none of the others are here? Galehaut, and Gawain, and the rest? I don't know exactly what happened to them. But I suspect that Marlowe does. Why don't you ask him about it?'

'He wouldn't give me a straight answer.'

'Hm. Perhaps I can help with that.'

She draws something from her dress, or conjures it from the Otherworld, or summons it by some other means. A phial of glass, ancient and opaque, stoppered by a small bone or tooth. He can't see what manner of substance is contained within, even when she hands it out to him.

'What's this?' he asks.

'My unholy vengeance.' She smiles. 'It will loosen his lips. Make the truth spill from them. Surely you're curious? To find out what secrets he's been keeping from you . . .'

Lancelot swallows. He can't deny the temptation. But then temptation was always Morgan's bread and butter, in the old days. She would dangle something tempting in front of you, and all you had to do to get it was betray your principles. All you had to do to uphold the realm was resist temptation – that's what Arthur used to tell them. If even one of them forsook their virtue, the whole kingdom would come crashing down.

He looks up at Arthur on the dais now, sitting behind the Round Table. He looks at Marlowe standing behind him, whispering in his ear. Then he takes the phial from Morgan's hand and puts it in the inside breast pocket of his jacket.

They stay for another hour or two. After three drinks they're doing lines in the toilets. After five drinks they're going back to Marlowe's suite.

Marlowe throws his jacket on the couch and goes to the bathroom. Lancelot opens the drinks cabinet in the corner of the room and sees a dusty bottle of Terrantez with the year 1704 chalked on the side. They laid down a few dozen bottles just before the Peace of Utrecht; this must be the last one.

Lancelot opens the wax with his thumbnail, pulls out the cork and pours two glasses, without letting it air first. He's greeted with the familiar deep auburn colour; the smell of dried peaches, banana leaf, varnished wood. But he doesn't have time to enjoy the bouquet. He takes Morgan's vengeance out of his pocket, pulls the stopper out of it and tips the contents into Marlowe's glass. A black ichor that turns clear as it meets the Madeira. Hopefully flavourless.

'I hope you're not too upset about being sent after Kay again,' says Marlowe, reappearing. Running a finger under his nose. 'I was going to tell you. You're more likely than anyone else to know where he's gone to ground.'

'Hm,' says Lancelot. 'I have a few ideas.'

'There's another pistol for you there, on the cabinet. Nineteen millimetre. I know you prefer revolvers, but we all have to move with the times.'

He picks it up, disgruntled by it. A boxy thing that says MADE IN CHINA on the side. Not cool gunmetal under his hand but some sort of rough synthetic polymer. He drives a new magazine into the grip and draws the slide back, but the mechanism sticks and he has to try again. Not a weapon that he feels any sense of kinship with, nor one he'd like to depend upon in the middle of a battle. But he puts it down with the Terrantez, on a silver cocktail tray. Carrying them over, easing them down onto the table, sitting down on the couch across from Marlowe with as much nonchalance as he can muster.

'Ah,' says Marlowe, seeing the Madeira. Not looking entirely pleased. 'Well, I suppose I did promise. What shall we drink to?'

Lancelot shrugs. 'New beginnings?'

Marlowe nods, with a thin smile. 'Quite so.'

They sniff their wine, rolling it in the glass, savouring the smell. Trying to delay the inevitable as long as possible. Then the first sip: august, sophisticated, incredible complexities of sweetness. Everything good about the old world distilled into a single glass. The burnishing warmth of the alcohol, the dry aftertaste. An edge of bitterness. They both sit for a long moment, unable to do anything but make small appreciative noises. But Marlowe's face turns into a frown, wrinkles deepening on his face. 'Do you know, I think that might be slightly past its best.'

'Hm,' says Lancelot. 'Not everything improves with age.'

Marlowe chuckles, staring at the amber liquid in his glass. 'Francis Bacon said that age is best in four things; old wood to burn, old wine to drink, old friends to trust . . . and I've forgotten the fourth.'

'Your memory's not what it used to be,' says Lancelot. He puts his drink down on the table, next to the gun.

Marlowe takes another long sip of his Madeira, washing it round his mouth with a deeper look of contemplation on his face. Then he swallows and looks Lancelot in the eye.

'I remember seeing you and Morgan having your tête-à-tête by the wine table, earlier,' says Marlowe. 'What were you talking about?'

'That's our little secret.'

Marlowe arches an eyebrow. 'You don't keep secrets from me, do you?'

'You keep thousands of secrets from me.'

'Occupational hazard.'

'Perhaps if you tell me a secret, I'll tell you what Morgan and I were talking about.'

'Dangerous territory.'

'Just one secret.'

'What kind of secret? I can tell you all about the aliens if you want.'

'I don't want to know about the aliens.'

Marlowe is looking drowsy, all of a sudden. Stifling a yawn behind his fist. Blinking to stay awake. 'I'd honestly quite enjoy telling someone about the aliens,' he says. 'I've been keeping schtum about them for decades, now. There used to be a whole office for dealing with aliens. And then on the floor beneath them were the boys looking after your crowd. Magic knights and faerie kings and all of that rot. Neither of them knew that the other existed. It was a nightmare keeping them from finding out about each other – at Christmas parties, and so on.'

Marlowe keeps talking, and Lancelot keeps staring at him. He doesn't know how quickly this stuff works, whatever potion he's slipped into Marlowe's wine. He doesn't know how long it lasts. There are questions he ought to ask about Arthur, about this place. Everything that Morgan wants to know. But that's not the question he wants to ask. He worries Galehaut's ring under his thumb.

'Did you kill Galehaut?' he asks, bluntly. 'Did you cut down his tree?'

'Hm?' says Marlowe. 'Oh ... well, not me personally. I'm not a lumberjack.'

'But you let it happen,' he asks. 'You made it happen.'

'Yes,' says Marlowe, blearily. As if it's the least important thing in the world. 'They told me to do it, so I did. And the others.'

Lancelot feels the powerful urge to draw his sword. His arms want to do it. Go over and plunge the blade into Marlowe's throat. But he doesn't do it yet. He has more questions to ask first. So he sits still, tension building in his stomach.

'What others?' he asks.

'Oh, Gawain, Tristan, Bors. Whole bloody lot of them.'

Something pinches in Lancelot's chest, like an iron band around his heart. His jaw feels numb all of a sudden. Quivering. He has to wrestle back control of his voice before he can speak.

'Why not Kay?'

Marlowe frowns at the floor. Almost as if he's in a trance. He doesn't look entirely sure of why he's saying what he's saying. But he says it anyway. 'The staff,' he says. 'We needed the staff. Morgan told us that Kay could get it.'

'And why not me?'

Marlowe actually laughs at that. 'We knew you'd be on side. You don't let your conscience get in the way of doing what's necessary. You never have.'

'I don't understand,' says Lancelot. He can hear a thin note in his own voice that he doesn't like. A mix of things. Rage and sorrow and contempt. 'You kept us around for ... thousands of years. And then you just decide that we've outlived our usefulness? You cut down our trees? Why would you do it now?'

'Because you're the last remnants,' says Marlowe. 'You and your chums. You're all that's left of ... whatever it is. The thing we're trying to get rid of. All the old laws and protections and traditions. The red tape. The people I work for have been trying to scrub it out for centuries.'

'Why?'

'Urgh,' says Marlowe. As if this is elementary stuff. 'Because it stands in the way of progress. It stops them from achieving what they want to achieve. They want it all broken down and done away with, to make everything easier for themselves. And when they want something done, I'm the one who ends up doing it.'

'You cut down their trees,' he says again. Just to make sure. 'You snuffed them out of existence.'

But Marlowe is rambling now, unguarded and uncaring. 'We didn't know how it was going to end, when we started all of this. Business and slavery and empire. We didn't know it would end like this, with turning the world barren. But we're hardly going to stop now, are we? We'd have to give up the game. Undo the whole progress of the last five hundred years. Muck in with everybody else, farming radishes or goodness knows what. Not my cup of tea, really. I'd much rather be sitting here in some sort of comfort. Everyone on this facility feels the same way. We can't back down now. So it all has to just keep going. The march of progress. Preserving itself. Destroying anything that gets in its way. That's why we built this place.'

Lancelot can hear his heart pounding in his ears. 'And what is this place?' he asks. 'What's it for?'

But Marlowe looks tired. Lying back again and frowning, with his eyes closed. 'It's all on my computer pad,' he says. 'Over there.'

Lancelot tenses every muscle in his body, trying to stay calm for a moment longer. Using his last reserves of patience to ask another question. 'Does it have a passcode?'

'1592,' says Marlowe. 'The year we met.'

'Ah,' says Lancelot. 'Faustus.'

He spares a thought for Marlowe the playwright, the rake-hell, the dashing rogue. How things were in the old days, before Marlowe sold his soul. Then he picks up the pistol from the table and shoots Marlowe three times through the chest. It jams on the fourth round. He throws it down, with no intention of picking it up again.

Marlowe looks puzzled, staring down at the holes in his chest. Realising the extent of his miscalculation. He blinks back up at Lancelot as if he can still change his strategy, still somehow worm his way out of this. But he can't. The bloodstains on his shirt are already smouldering, beginning to blacken. Immortality and invulnerability are two very different things.

'Ought to have read your own play, old boy,' says Lancelot. He drains his glass of Madeira, flavour exploding on his tongue, feeling slightly sacrilegious for drinking it off so quickly. Then he gets up and goes to the side counter, where the computer tablet is sitting.

He hears Marlowe croak behind him, but he doesn't look back. Focused on the mission now. His own mission. The one he's given himself.

It takes him a while to figure out how the bloody tablet works. The passcode is accepted. Eventually he finds a folder called AVALON, stored in some sort of secure file system. Ancient secrets digitised, uploaded. There's something called PROPOSAL PRESENTATION. He opens it. Flicks through it with vague contempt.

He doesn't have the faintest idea what half of this stuff is.

Graphs and charts, mostly. Maps of Britain with parts of the country shaded bright orange. Some of them have words along the bottom, or up the side. Food system collapse. Death spiral. Total human extinction by 2100. None of it sounds particularly encouraging.

There's the sound of something going up in flames behind him. He glances over long enough to see tongues of hellfire licking at Marlowe's dinner jacket. The room already smells of brimstone. Marlowe and his friends must have known what they were getting themselves into, surely. Sensible men of business, signing their souls on the dotted line. They must have known that the dividends would be pretty steep. They must have tried to delay the inevitable for as long as possible. Maybe that's the way to understand this whole plan of theirs. Rich old men, scared of death, trying to stave it off for a little longer. Willing to do the unthinkable.

The next few pictures in this presentation are drawings of Avalon from old manuscripts. The court of the fay, where guests are treated like kings and fed the sweetest ambrosia. Kept young and beautiful forever until the end of time. But that was all sealed beyond the veil when Merlin did his spell over Arthur's corpse. There's a drawing of Merlin, an oil painting of Arthur's death. Ships coming to bear him away.

'. . . So that's your game, is it?' Lancelot says quietly. He can feel heat on the back of his neck. See flames reflected in the pad and the picture frames on the walls.

It's not a bad idea, really. Move this whole facility through the veil for a long holiday in the faerie realm, where they don't have to live with the consequences of their actions. That's why they need Arthur back. Crown on his head. Magic returned to the realm.

Even then, they'd need a massive quantity of magic to pull it off. Punching a hole through the veil and breaking the barrier between worlds. But it seems like they know that. The next few slides are maps of Britain, overlaid with strange patterns and colourations. Surveys for resource exploitation. Offshore oil deposits and underground gas pockets. Ley lines. Magnetic anomalies. Geothermic energy. Lancelot almost swipes through them all, but then he frowns and swipes back to that last one again.

Not geothermic. Geothaumic. He mouths the word to himself, wrinkling his nose. What on earth is geothaumic energy? How do you measure it? Yet here it is, mapped across Britain in its various concentrations. Some of the brightest deposits are labelled. LANCASHIRE SUMP. 500 megathaums. There's a 900 megathaum concentration somewhere in the middle of Wales. But the biggest by far is in Somerset. A huge bright spot, in the flooded wetlands. Three gigathaums. He doesn't know what a thaum is, but that sounds like a lot of thaums.

He can guess what the next slide will be. Plans and concept art for the Avalon platform. They've built this thing right in the middle of the bright spot. There are three gigathaums of magical energy stored in the ground somewhere beneath his feet. And Marlowe's people are drawing it up, harvesting it. Draining all of the magic from the realm. Storing it for their own purposes.

The presentation ends. There's a picture of hell, full of demons, torturing the damned. Then there's a picture of men sunbathing on a beach. These people know what will happen if they punch a hole through the veil, breaking the barrier, releasing untold horrors into the world. And apparently they don't care. They'll be in Avalon, safe from harm. Drinking the nectar of the gods.

'Rats fleeing a sinking ship,' he says.

When he looks back at Marlowe, he grimaces at what he sees. The fire is spreading to the sofa and the carpet underneath. It's probably time to leave, before any alarms go off. Lancelot takes the pad with him, with the vague idea of giving it to somebody.

Somebody who knows how to blow up oil rigs. One of Kay's friends, if he can find them. That seems like a good plan. Galehaut would like that plan.

He changes back into his tunic and his mail, as quickly as he can. When he looks at himself in the mirror now, he finds that he can maintain eye contact. Appropriately dressed, for once.

Smoke has filled the room by the time he's finished. Sprinklers activate. Marlowe is already toast, clothes turned to ash, flesh and sinew burnt away. It's hard to feel sentimental about an immolated skeleton. He walks out of the door, taking the bottle of Terrantez. Leaving Marlowe behind.

The feast has spilled out onto the rest of the platform, now. The whole of Avalon is strewn with debris. Lancelot walks back towards the feasting hall, passing a discarded bowtie and a castoff item of lingerie. Nearly stepping in a puddle of sick. Wary of distant laughter echoing down the corridors. He feels slightly ridiculous, in mail, holding a computer pad and a three-hundred-year-old bottle of Madeira. But at least he knows that his cause is just. He hasn't had the luxury of knowing that for a very long time.

If Arthur's taken Morgan to bed already then his escape plan's out the window. But as he nears the epicentre of the celebrations he sees a band of revellers carousing down the corridor. Arthur is at the centre of them, lumbering like a drunk bear, with three or four women in short dresses leading him by the hand. The rest of the group are Marlowe's people, media men and private security men, Saxons and GX5 men, laughing and smoking cigars. Arthur is roaring drunk. Shouting about capturing Jerusalem and building a new temple there. But he seems quite willing to go where he is led, until he sees Lancelot coming the other way. Then his face lights up.

'Lancelot!' he says. 'Come here you fucking stallion.'

Arthur grabs him by the shoulders and pins him against the wall, growling, grinning, laughing. Breath like corpse rot, eyes wide like saucers. They've given him something. Arthur on coke is a terrifying thought.

'I'm glad you're back with me, Lance!' he says. 'Not like Kay and the others. No share of glory for them. We'll rule the world between us. You and me!'

He pounds his fist against Lancelot's heart, like he's trying to batter down a castle gate. It's only when he hurts his knuckles that he notices the mail. He looks down at it, then back up again. Suddenly suspicious. 'You're dressed for battle,' he says. 'You weren't, earlier.'

'Sire,' says Lancelot, 'I thought I'd ride out early. Leave tonight and begin my search for Kay.'

The suspicion on Arthur's face is replaced by joy. He turns to his entourage. 'You see,' he says. 'You fucking see! He puts you to shame. All of you craven milksops. You call yourselves men. You're like field mice. You've all got slits between your legs. Not like Lancelot!'

Lancelot feels his testicles squeezed in Arthur's iron grip. Arthur punches him in the chest again for good measure, then seizes the bottle of Madeira, wresting it from his grasp. Lancelot has watched Arthur do many horrible things, and now he watches him swig a bottle of 1704 Terrantez straight from the neck, drinking it down in great thirsty glugs, some of it spilling down his beard and clothes. Stopping once he's drunk half of it to frown and spit and hand the bottle back.

'Foreign swill,' he says. 'Now go with my blessing, Lance.

Bring Kay back to me in irons. Or bring me his head. I don't care which.'

And then Arthur goes, dragged off by the men in their suits and the women in their short dresses. Lancelot leans back against the wall until his balls stop hurting and his heart stops beating in his ears. Then he makes himself continue on his quest. Towards the feasting hall.

The place is abandoned by the time he gets there, tables turned over and food scattered on the floor. The music has stopped. He sets the bottle down on a damp tablecloth and casts his eyes around the place, not sure exactly what he's looking for until he feels a cold breeze on the back of his neck. It blows through the place, filling the dragon banners like sails and then letting them settle flat again. One of the windows is open, looking out onto the balcony and the open sea.

When he steps through into the darkness he finds Morgan standing there, surely freezing, with her shoulders bare. But she doesn't seem to feel the cold. She is smoking a roll-up and staring out over the ocean. Her hair looks darker than the night.

'Was he talkative?' she asks.

'Very,' says Lancelot. 'We had a flaming row.'

She turns her head, slightly. 'I hope you found out what you needed to know.'

'I did,' he says. 'I know what they're trying to do.'

'And are you going to try and stop them?' she asks.

He swallows, thinking for a moment. His left hand is clenched into a fist. Galehaut's ring is pressing into his skin.

'Yes,' he says.

Morgan throws her roll-up over the side. 'Good. Come with me.'

She moves her hand through the air in a slow arc, fingers straightened, palm outwards towards the sea. Lancelot feels the air bristle. He can tell somehow that the space in front of her

427

has changed. It has a new sheen. It has become a membrane, pervious, leading somewhere. She has created a doorway to another place. Now she takes his hand and leads him through it, to wherever it is that they're going.

35

Kay sleeps in his chair and turns slowly into bark, dreaming of strange things.

There must be a time when strange becomes normal, though, mustn't there? His normal has been strange for so long. Now other people's normal would be strange to him. Living between four walls somewhere and having normal worries, normal fears. How will we eat this month? That would be stranger, almost. Stranger than turning into a tree.

His dreams take him through the centuries. Slewn under-hoof. Clubbed to death. Burnt alive. Boiled alive. Standing in a boggy trench, feeling just as terrified as the boy standing next to him, before somebody blew a tin whistle and they all climbed over the top. Except now he knows that those things didn't actually happen to him; they happened to different versions of him, different copies. Ogres made from mud in his image. They died and he was reborn. Hardly seems fair, then, that he has to keep their memories in his mud-brain. That his dreams are troubled by the things they saw, the things they had to do.

These dreams always end up in Malaya, watching British soldiers burn down a village. Gangly young lads who'd never seen action before. They seemed to be enjoying it, sweating in the heat with wide grins and their sleeves rolled up while the flames leapt from bamboo roofs to the rotten leaves of overhanging trees. People fleeing. Ordinary, frightened people. Somebody empties a Bren gun into the jungle, spraying bullets after them. In the dream he muscles up to them, tries to stop them. Tries to tear the gun out of their arms and talk some sense into them. Then he realises that it's him. A different version of him. One of his clones, but still him. Staring back at him without a trace of mercy in his eyes.

Kay wakes up soaked in jungle sweat. Smelling of mushrooms. Still in the old chair, in the dark cave.

It was a loud crash that woke him up. Mariam's still here, sorting through Merlin's collection, moving great heaps of it aside. Not trying to be particularly quiet or gentle with whatever she's doing.

He runs his hands down his face and feels the bark scratch against his skin. Feels the strange nodules on his cheeks. Dear Christ, he feels like death. Whatever he was drinking last night was poisonous stuff. He should have known better than to touch it. Now his body is punishing him for his foolishness. Wyn would have taken the bottle from him, in the old days. Stopped him from corrupting himself. But it's a bit late for that now.

His dream stays with him. It was easier to deal with the memories when he knew that he served a purpose. He used to tell himself that he was coming back for a reason. It made everything an ounce more tolerable. He used to tell himself that he was part of Merlin's plan. Well, he was – just not in the way that he thought. None of what he did was part of the plan, was it? None

430

of the wars. None of the killing and the suffering and the death. It didn't make a blind bit of difference either way. He could have just stayed under his tree.

Might be better to go back there now; he's been putting it off, after all. An old voice pipes up in his head to tell him that he has a duty to Mariam. A duty to stop Arthur. But he pours scorn all over that voice. He doesn't have a duty to do anything, does he? Merlin told him that. He's done his bit. He could take up his sword and open his veins. Then oblivion, in the dark place between worlds. Or heaven, with Wyn. Or rebirth again, but worse. Maybe the realm will spit him back out as a tree golem. Or maybe it will let him rest for a little while. Sleeping in the earth's cool bosom, until it isn't cool anymore.

He's thinking these dark thoughts when Barry climbs up onto the arm of his chair. He clears his throat, in a squirrelly kind of way.

'What?' asks Kay in a dry, croaking voice.

'Just . . . wondering if we could have a word, is all.'

Kay grunts. 'Don't see why not.'

'Well, it's a couple of things, I suppose. First off, I noticed you've got your big stick back. And I know this Merlin bloke went off walkabouts, but I was wondering if you could see your way to turning me back?'

'I might,' he says. The staff is still propped up against his chair, and he's content to leave it there for the time being. Unless it can magically cure his hangover.

'And the other thing is . . . ' Barry wrings his squirrel hands together. 'I heard that little bargy you were having with your lady friend yesterday. And it sounded to me like she was talking sense.'

He screws up his face. 'About what?'

'About giving up on everything. Or not giving up on everything. Might want to listen to her.'

'I'm not taking life advice from a squirrel who used to be racist.'

'Harsh but fair. Look, all I'm saying is, maybe it seems like it's all doom and gloom, but I think you're underselling yourself, mate. I don't think you realise how much of a difference you could make, if you wanted to.'

'How's that?'

'Well, you've brought me round, haven't you? I'm a reformed squirrel. Maybe you could bring other people round as well, if you put your mind to it. It's just a thought.'

Something happens in Kay's stomach which feels unrelated to last night's drinking. It feels like a small door opening, and cool water pouring through it. He's too tired and mouldy brained to know what it means. He feels itchy, festerous, scabbed over. Like he wants to shed his skin. But he feels tenderness for Barry, as well. He finds himself nodding.

'All right,' he says. 'I'll keep it in mind. Now let's see about this spell, shall we?'

He has to peel himself away from the armchair. Parts of him have grown through the fabric. His whole body is stiff from sleeping in his mail coat and from whatever else is happening to him. The bark on his arms is starting to grow around the mail, now, swelling through the iron links and crusting over them, so that the mail is part of his new oak skin, and he couldn't take it off if he tried. Worrying. How long until his feet put down roots and anchor him to the ground?

That's the kind of thought he can push to the back of his mind until this good deed is done. So he takes up the staff and turns back to Barry, who is waiting patiently on the arm of the chair.

'Now, I'm not sure if this'll work,' he says.

'Just give it yer best shot,' says Barry. He closes his squirrel eyes and tenses every muscle in his squirrel body, as if that will help.

Kay runs his hands over the staff. Bark against wood. Maybe that'll help. Better point of contact. He takes a good grip of it, like you'd hold a spear for fishing. Raising the knobbled cudgel-end of it above his shoulder. Pointing the narrow walking-stick end of it towards the chair and Barry.

And then he tries to bend the universe. Only a small miracle, in the grand scheme of things. Only undoing what he already did. But it was easier then. A moment of tension, trying to save Mariam and her friends. A few half-connected thoughts. There was urgency then, to make the magic happen. Now there isn't. He'll have to find a different kind of fuel.

Mercy might do the trick. Common kindness. Though Christ knows he hasn't got much mercy left in him. It feels as though his store has run dry. The hard oak parts of him aren't brimming with benevolence for men like Barry. But he finds an ounce of sympathy for this man-squirrel. Maybe he was kind and good when he was a child. Maybe the world made him cruel. People do cruel things, trying to save themselves from cruelty, and it's all downhill from there. Fall in with the wrong company. Learn the wrong habits. Easy to start hating people when that's what everyone else is doing. Hate is the path of least resistance. Maybe Barry really is a reformed squirrel. Maybe he wants to find a different path, now. A harder, better path. That's a good enough reason to change him back.

So Kay takes the ounce of mercy and uses it as fuel. Sending it down his arms. Through his hands. Coursing down the old grains and whorls of the staff until it leaps from the end and hops across to Barry like a meagre bolt of lightning.

There's a great screaming and tearing of fur as Barry outgrows his squirrel skin, bursting through it suddenly as a pale and naked human. Perched on the arm of the chair for an awkward moment and then falling back into it. He runs his hands over his body to confirm that various bits of himself are all where they're supposed to be. Then he grins and punches the air with both fists.

'WAHEY!' says Barry. 'You fucking beauty!'

Kay smiles, for a brief moment. He doesn't have time to lower the staff before Barry scrambles out of the armchair and crosses the distance between them. Grabbing him by both cheeks. Kissing him square on the mouth.

He pulls away and clears his throat. They enjoyed a kind of closeness, while Barry was still a squirrel. Climbing up his mail, perching on his shoulder. Sleeping in his lap. That closeness seems strange now that they're both men again. Easier to feel goodwill towards a talking squirrel than towards a pale and gangly naked man.

'Aw, mate,' says Barry. He has tears in his eyes. Suddenly penitent for his past life. He kneels down, clasping his hands awkwardly together. 'How can I pay you back? I'll do anything! You name it, I'll do it.'

Kay stands over him, looking down. Briefly holding this man's fate in his hands. He looks up and sees that Mariam has stopped her rummaging. She's standing and watching, with a face that's hard to read.

There were times in the old days when Hildwyn would do some small kindness for him and he'd be overcome with gratitude. Putting honey in his porridge when he hadn't asked her to. Praying for him when she made her prayers up to God. And he'd ask her then what he could do to pay her back. But she would always shake her head. That's not the point of kindness, she'd say. Kindness ought to be like a river, flowing downhill.

'Pass it down to someone else,' he says, now, to Barry. 'Do a kindness for them. Like I just did for you. That's how you pay me back.'

Barry starts nodding. Grinning with relief. Like he just got off lightly. Three days a squirrel, and a good deed passed down to someone else. Is that sufficient penance for half a lifetime's hatefulness? Barry seems to think so. Kay isn't so sure, all of a sudden. He feels contempt creeping into his chest, breaking through the fragile mercy that was there a few moments ago. Maybe Barry's been having him on.

'Now go,' he says, using the staff to gesture outside.

'What?' asks Barry. Grin falling from his face.

'Get out of here. Go on. Go and find your mates.'

'Oh,' says Barry. 'Right. Yeah, I'll uh ... I'll do that. Go and find some clothes as well, I suppose.'

'Might be a good plan.'

'Right. Yeah. Well, thanks again. I mean it. For this, and for uh ... well, for the rest as well. Real life-changer.'

'You're welcome.'

'I'll be off then. Be seeing you. And, uh, good luck saving the world and all that!'

Barry backs out of the cave, waving clumsily. Cupping his manhood with his other hand. Letting the plastic curtains fall down behind him.

Then there is silence, apart from the hum of the earth and the dank trickle of cave noises. Kay looks back to Mariam and feels as if he's seeking her approval. She doesn't seem inclined to grant it.

'What are you doing, over there?' he asks.

'Did Merlin have a TV?' she asks. 'Or a phone? Laptop?'

'What?'

'Somewhere in all this trash. Does he have a TV?'

'Why?'

She gives him a withering look. 'Because I'm tired of sitting here being useless? It's boring. I want to see what's happening, out in the world.'

435

He sniffs. It makes a certain amount of sense. 'All right,' he says. 'I'll help you look.'

Mariam is already deep in the pile of clutter, and he goes to help her. Bones creaking like young branches. He doesn't want to think what his skeleton would look like, right now, if you sloughed all the flesh away from it. But he tries not to let his thoughts linger on such things. Better to give himself a little quest to keep his mind from all of that. Find the lost Box of Moving Pictures; for, without it, we cannot see what is happening in distant corners of the realm. Kay ventures into part of the cave that Mariam hasn't searched yet and starts poring over things, trying not to stare at his hands. They are covered in thick plates of bark that crack and shift when he moves his fingers to grasp anything.

Merlin has a harpsichord under a tarpaulin. He has a giant brass model of the planets, with painted spheres on revolving arms. He has ancient clay jars that might contain anything – wine or demons or petrified yoghurt. Why does one wizard need so much? How did he get it all here? Why did he abandon it so readily if it was so important to him? There are no answers to any of these questions, now that Merlin has gone. He stays away from the rack of little trees in the corner. His backup copy. He doesn't want to venture close to it. He doesn't like to think of what might be germinating in the soil beneath it.

Eventually he finds what he's looking for, hidden under an old carpet. A big wooden box with a glass screen set into it. He remembers how amazed he was, the first time he saw one of these things. A box full of moving pictures. More impressive than any of Merlin's magic, because people invented it, figured out how to get it working. It makes him smile, even now. But when he carries it over to Mariam she pulls a face.

'Urgh,' she says.

'What? I found one.'

'It looks, like, a million years old.'

He can't fathom that. This marvel of technology. He shakes his head. 'What does that make me, then?'

'Never mind,' she says. 'It'll do. Put it over here.'

They put it on a stool in front of the sofa. Kay brushes the worst of the dust off it. Mariam tries to find somewhere to plug it in, but he hazards a guess that Merlin didn't bother with that sort of thing. He presses a button on the front panel and it switches on anyway. Mariam looks at the television as if it must be haunted. Then she seems to remember where she is. She shrugs and drops the cable on the ground.

Once they've found the news channel they sit down together on the sofa. People are talking around a table, somewhere clean. They are rendered grey and silent by the television. The box doesn't make any noise until Mariam kneels in front of it and turns a dial.

'... unusual, but there is a vacancy, since the abdication of King Charles.'

'Do you have any concerns about whether this is unconstitutional?'

'No, Julia, I think that's rubbish. I think the British people are tired of soft constitutional politics. They want a proper old-fashioned king who'll lead the country out of this crisis and back to greatness. And that's exactly what Arthur's going to do.'

'I think you might be right about that. We go live to Glastonbury now, where King Arthur's coronation will be taking place tomorrow morning. It looks like preparations are already well underway ...'

'Don't listen to any of this,' says Mariam. 'It's just bollocks. Propaganda.'

Kay grunts. Of course it is. Heralds of news say things that powerful people pay them to say. That's been the way of things since before Rome fell. He'd like to think that ordinary people are clever enough to remember that. Maybe he's wrong.

The television shows a moving image of the damp plain around the Tor. There's a stage being built, a place for Arthur to stand and be beheld while his crown is placed back upon his head.

It wasn't supposed to happen like this, Arthur's return. But then, they never really agreed how it was supposed to happen. They decided it on the field at Camlann, standing over Arthur's corpse. Good to have a king in reserve in case things got really hairy. In case the realm was ever overrun. But maybe that's just what they told themselves. It made them feel better about shipping his body off to Avalon. Because they never did bring him back, not when the Danes came, or the Normans after them. Kay always had it in his head that Arthur would return as the world itself was ending. When the realm was cast into fire and shadow, blighted by fiends from hell or foul things from the Otherworld. The end of the days. That's when Arthur would finally return. Then, and not before.

But perhaps this *is* the end of the days. He didn't imagine it looking like this. No horde of demons slavering through the hills for Arthur to bear his sword against. No band of warriors riding behind their king. Just corruption in the air and a stage being hammered together by men in bright waistcoats.

'Why aren't they doing it on the oil rig?' asks Mariam. 'Or in, like, Westminster Abbey, or whatever?'

Kay doesn't see much point in asking questions like that now. He shrugs. It makes his shoulders creak in a way that he doesn't like. The people in the box keep talking.

'... I'm sure security's going to be very tight, Ian.'

'Well, obviously we heard yesterday that the left-wing extremists in Manchester have finally been defeated. But the terrorists responsible for the Lancashire fracking explosion have been arrested as well, and they're being held on the Avalon platform itself, which just shows how versatile the facility is.'

'Absolutely. A really clever investment by the government ...'

Mariam stands up too quickly, then has to sit down again, her hand going to the place where she was stabbed. But her eyes are wide.

'They're on the Avalon rig,' she says. 'We know where they are.'

'Doesn't change anything,' says Kay.

'Why not? If we know where they are then we can go and find them. We can go and save them!'

'And then what?' he finds himself saying. 'What good will that do? Even if we save your friends, the realm's still dying. Arthur will still be king.'

He looks up into Mariam's eyes and sees the way she's looking back at him. It brings cold shame burbling up through his chest.

'I don't care what good it will do,' she says. 'They're my friends. If I can find a way of saving them, then I will. Are you going to help me with that, or are you going to sit here being a miserable tosser?'

He grunts at her, because he can't think of what to say. Why should he try and save people? He's spent long enough trying to save people. It didn't make the world a better place, in the end. He looks back at the television, which is showing the Avalon platform, the great monstrosity looming over the shallow marsh.

'I wouldn't even know how to get inside that thing,' he says. He starts to think about it, though. How it might be done. He did a few missions in little boats in the last big war. Sneaking around in the water. Climbing up the side of a German warship, a great iron monster. But that was different. This thing's bigger, higher above the water, harder to scale.

'I don't know what happened to the Welsh,' says Mariam. 'I think they took Gethin, at Glastonbury. But maybe they'd help us? If they still have their boats ...'

The television changes, suddenly. The screen shows a flag, the one with the overlapping crosses. He remembers thinking that it looked daft the first time he ever saw it. When was that? Marlborough's war, maybe. The union flag. Flag of a united country. Doesn't seem very fitting at the moment.

'*There now follows an address from His Majesty, King Arthur,*' says the television.

'Oh, shit,' says Mariam.

And then Arthur himself appears, sitting behind a desk. Wearing his mail and his bearskin cloak and his gold coronet. They've cleaned him up a bit. Got the blood off. Have they explained to him how televisions work? He seems uncertain, sitting there in front of the camera. Kay feels a pang of sympathy. It must be strange for him. Like a fish out of water.

But then Arthur stares into the camera. He clears his throat and starts to speak.

'Britons,' he says. '*Long have I slumbered. And as I slept, Britain grew weak. Now I rise and find this land a shadow of its former greatness. Riven by violence and beset by outlanders. But no longer. Now that I have returned, I will take up my sword and make Britain great again.*'

They sit and watch the speech for a little while. Arthur talks about putting down rebellions. Slaying dragons. Driving

440

foreigners into the sea. Britain for the British. Purify the land with blood. Kay wonders if he wrote this himself or whether they've compelled him to read it. It hardly matters, either way. This is how Arthur always was.

'Fucking hell,' says Mariam.

'What?' asks Kay.

'I mean, listen to him. He's King Arthur. He's supposed to be the best king ever. Right? But he isn't. He's just as shit as everyone else.'

'So what?'

'So none of it fucking matters, does it? All that history and privilege and ancient bollocks. If King Arthur's just as shit as everyone else, then none of it matters. Anyone can run the country and do a better job. You could do it. Bronte could do it. I could do it.'

He turns to look at her for a long moment. Looking at her while she looks at Arthur. Holding her head up and frowning at the television. There's conviction on her face, not cynicism or despair. She hasn't given up, like him.

'Yeah,' he says. 'Yeah, I think you could do it if you wanted to. I think you'd do a fantastic job. So maybe you should go and do that. Go and lead. Go and make the world a better place. I think you could do it, if you put your mind to it.'

She turns to look at him. Surprised, at first. Then thoughtful.

'Will you help me, then?' she asks.

He thinks about it. He could draw his sword and kneel in front of the sofa and pledge himself to her cause, like he did with Empress Maud. The start of a long fight. Killing people for a good cause. It didn't do Maud much good. He's not sure how much good it would do now either.

'Look, Mariam,' he says. 'I've done ... bad things. Over the years. Things I still have nightmares about. And I thought I was

441

doing it for a good reason. I always thought I was doing it to make the world a better place. But it turns out that I wasn't. I don't think it made much of a difference, in the end. And I don't want to do any more of it, if I can help it.'

Mariam is quiet. Arthur speaks of fire and blood in the background, and they both ignore him. Eventually she shakes her head. 'I trusted you,' she says. 'When you came back. I trusted you to fix everything. I thought you were going to come along and save the world, and everything would be all right.'

'Mariam—'

'No, just listen. I trusted you because it was easy. And I trusted Regan because it was easy. I gave her the sword because it was easy. It meant I didn't have to do anything. I could just trust somebody else to fix the problem. But I think I've figured out now that I can't keep doing that. I can't keep hoping that somebody else will come along and magically make everything better. It has to be me.'

'So what do you need me for?' he says.

'Because you can't do it either. You can't sit here hoping that *I'll* magically save the world. It's the same for everybody. We all have to get up and do it together.'

Kay hears something from the mouth of the cave. Only a faint sound, but there it is again, louder. The scrape of a footstep. Somebody approaching.

He stands and draws his sword from its scabbard, casting the empty sword belt down against the sofa. Wincing at a stiff, wooden pain in his shoulder.

'What are you doing?' asks Mariam.

'Quiet,' he whispers. 'Get behind something.'

There's still the plastic curtain hanging across the cave. The intruders are on the other side of it, whoever they are. If he gets close to the curtain he can wait for them, surprise them as they come through. But it's too late for that. The curtain is pushed aside.

Two people step through who tried to kill him the last time he saw them. Morgan and Lancelot. Lancelot sees him and smiles thinly.

'I thought we might find you here,' says Lancelot.

Kay holds back his contempt long enough to be cautious. He tries to look past Lancelot, past the curtains, to see if there's a platoon of Saxon thugs in the cave behind him. But he can't see anything.

'We haven't come here to kill you,' says Morgan, stepping forward. 'We've come to help.'

'Help with what?' he asks.

'With vanquishing evil and removing peril from the realm.'

'Sorry if I struggle to believe that.'

'Perhaps if you allow us to explain,' says Lancelot. He shrugs off a satchel that he's wearing over his mail and drops it carefully against the wall. Then he takes a few steps further into the cave. Towards Mariam.

Kay goes straight for him, bringing his sword singing down from overhead. He's not going to let Lance get him on the backfoot this time. Lancelot draws his own sword just in time to block. Panic crosses his face for an instant before it's replaced with disdain. And then they're fighting again, hacking away at each other in the strange purple light. Mariam and Morgan are shouting at them both, but Kay doesn't listen. He is trying to keep up with Lance. His creaking bones can't seem to move as fast as usual, and he still feels wretched from drinking Merlin's noxious brew the night before. He can hear his heart beating in his ears. At least he knows that he still has a heart and not a lump of wood.

After they've traded a few blows Lancelot catches him off

balance, throwing his weight behind the blade, pushing him back into the pile of furniture and old flotsam. Kay knocks over some kind of ancient obelisk on his way down and lands beside it on the floor, with Lancelot standing over him.

Mariam gets between them and holds out her hands.

'Stop it,' she says. 'Both of you. If you're just going to kill each other again you can go and do it somewhere else. It's not helping anyone. If you want to help with saving the realm or whatever, then put your swords away. Actually, give them to me.'

Kay screws up his face. 'What?'

'New rule,' says Mariam. 'No swords in the cave. If I can't trust you not to wave them around everywhere then I'm going to have to take them off you.'

'Don't be absurd,' says Lancelot.

Kay picks himself up, climbing to his feet. 'Sorry, Mariam,' he says. 'I'm not giving you my sword while he's here.'

'We're sword-Britons,' says Lancelot. 'Warriors of the Round Table. You can't just ask us to surrender our swords.'

'Yeah, I can,' says Mariam. 'I just did. So stop whining and hand them over. Both of you.'

Mariam holds out her hands. Kay looks at Lancelot, and Lancelot looks back at him. Both of them are still tense. Swords held ready for another bout. Neither willing to be the first to disarm themselves.

And then Kay surprises himself. He reaches out slowly with his sword arm, offering his sword to Mariam. But he keeps staring straight into Lancelot's eyes. Daring him to do the same.

He sees Lancelot hesitate. Thinking obvious thoughts. Should he strike now? Cut down the foe while he's unarmed? He'd think the same thing if their places were reversed, and not even out of malice. Just out of instinct.

But no. Lancelot hands over his sword as well. Mariam stands clutching them both like toys taken from children who were playing too roughly.

'Right,' she says. 'Now whatever beef the two of you have with each other, go outside and talk about it. Use your words. Come back in here when you've settled whatever this is and you're ready to act like adults.'

'You can't be serious,' says Lancelot.

'You sure you want to be alone with . . . ?' says Kay, gesturing to Morgan.

Mariam points both of the swords towards their former owners. It doesn't look like she knows how to hold two swords at once, let alone shed blood with them. But it doesn't look like she cares. She'd give it a fair go.

So, grumbling and scoffing, Lancelot and Kay both walk down along the cave. Through the curtain. Clearing their throats and scratching the backs of their necks. Emerging into daylight and the forest. Staring everywhere apart from at each other.

Kay balls his fists. He's tempted to cut across and punch Lancelot in the jaw. But what would that solve, wrestling out here, in the mud? They've both spent enough time in the mud.

'Look,' says Lancelot, 'do you fancy a pint?'

Kay can't hide his confusion. 'What?'

'There's a decent pub, not far from here. We could get a swift one in, then come back and tell her we've buried the hatchet.'

Kay considers this. 'All right,' he says. 'That sounds good, actually.'

They walk away together into the woods.

36

Mariam holds a sword in each hand, still surprised that Kay and his friend did what she told them to do. She's hoping that they come back, eventually. She wouldn't know what to do next if they just abandoned her.

Now she turns her anger on Regan, who still looks like she did at Glastonbury. A younger version of herself, with pale skin and jet-black hair, wearing a velvety green dress that clings to her curves. It's weird, finding Regan fit. Regan, who's been like a grandmother to her for the past few years. Regan, who drove a sword into her.

'You stabbed me,' she says.

'Yes.'

'You said that you wouldn't stab me, and then you did.'

'Sometimes it's necessary to make sacrifices, Mariam.'

'Yeah, but not *literal human sacrifices*, Regan. Or whatever your name is.'

'My true name is Morganna, though many people call me Morgan. Now, I'm sure you have many questions, but—'

'Yeah, I do. And I'm going to ask them all now, if that's all right with you. Because I deserve to know the answers.'

This person – Regan, Morgan – looks like she's about to protest. Then she seems to think better of it. She nods. 'Very well. Proceed.'

Mariam stands momentarily at a loss. Now that she's allowed to ask questions, she doesn't know what to ask first. Finally her curiosity pushes everything else aside. 'Do you really look like that?'

Regan smiles weakly. 'No. But I don't really look like this, either.'

She ages as she speaks. Hair turning silver. Face wrinkling. The green dress becomes cargo trousers and a woolly gilet. Sensible walking shoes appear on her feet. Mariam feels a strange swell of relief, seeing the old Regan come back again. But it doesn't make sense to be relieved.

'You wouldn't be able to comprehend what I really look like,' says Morgan.

'There's a lot of things I can't comprehend,' says Mariam. 'Why did you join FETA? Did you just need to find some young women and get us to trust you so you could use our blood for a weird ritual? Because that's pretty fucking creepy, honestly.'

Regan closes her eyes and sighs, taking a moment to think things through before she speaks. Then she looks up again. 'Do you mind if I smoke?'

They end up sitting by the TV. Regan is smoking a roll-up in Kay's chair. Mariam sits on the sofa, holding the swords. The people on the news are still talking nonsense when Regan starts speaking.

'It may be difficult to believe,' she says. 'But my motives were sincere. After the whole affair with Arthur was over, I spent a very long time ... trying to keep my nose out of other people's business. I had a little house in the woods. But men are always doing their best to make the world a miserable place, so I started trying to stop them. Not with sorcery or enchantment or anything like that. I just ... tried to be an ordinary woman. I may have threatened people with the occasional curse here and there, but mostly I did what other women were doing. There were food riots and revolts. Desperate people trying to make the world a better place. I helped, where I could. I marched for Women's Suffrage. Nuclear disarmament. Women for Life on Earth. Everything I could to save the planet. But I started to realise that it wasn't making much of a difference. Peaceful protest. Non-violent action. That's why I joined FETA. Not because I wanted to bewitch or sacrifice anybody. Because I was angry, and I thought FETA might make a difference.'

Mariam sits staring at her, unblinking. Not wanting to put the swords down. Trying to process everything. Part of her thinks it's very cool that Regan was a suffragette. But she's not going to ask about that. She's going to ask sensible, serious questions.

'And then what?' she asks.

'I got frustrated. With FETA. You know why. The same reasons you got frustrated with them. Inaction, arguing, focusing on the wrong things. Hiding in tents. Feeling powerless. In the old days, I used to have influence. I used to have the ear of King Arthur. So I thought, well, why not bring him back? And I think you know the rest.'

'No, I don't. Tell me. Walk me through it.'

Regan sighs again. 'I sought out ... the right people. Marlowe, that horrible man. I've had one or two dealings with him before, over the years. He keeps tabs on people like me. And I made a bargain with him. That we'd work together to bring Arthur back. I thought it was a good bargain. I didn't realise what he was planning.'

448

Mariam feels her face tightening with anger. She has to swallow before she can speak. 'So it's all your fault,' she says. 'It's your fault that the others are all locked up on that thing. You sold us out. You grassed on us.'

Regan frowns, as if she objects to that particular expression. 'He already knew about FETA. Of course he did. We weren't exactly secretive. He was using us as a sort of bogeyman. Eco-terrorists in the woodwork. It gave his people an excuse to keep making things worse. Emergency powers, that sort of thing. He could have swept into Preston and arrested us all whenever he wanted. But he didn't want to.'

'And you knew that, the whole time. Is that why you wanted me to blow up the fracking site? Did . . . did he want us to do that?'

'Yes, I'm afraid he did.'

Mariam finds herself standing up, limbs moved by anger rather than thought or reason. She steps closer to Regan, with the swords still in her hands.

Regan looks down at the swords. Then she takes another drag on her roll-up. 'You can stab me, if it makes you feel better. I suppose that would make us even.'

'They've taken them prisoner,' says Mariam, 'everyone else. Willow and Teoni and Roz and Bronte. They're probably torturing them right now because you sold us out. That's your fault.'

'I know,' says Morgan. 'And I feel sorrow for them. But I felt that their sacrifice was worth the cost of saving the planet from destruction.'

'You don't get to make that decision!'

Regan looks intrigued by that. 'Don't I? Who does, then? Perhaps you would like to start making difficult decisions? Deciding who needs to be sacrificed and who deserves to live. Are their lives really more important than the lives of everyone else? More important than the protection of the whole planet?'

'They are to me,' says Mariam. She hears a sob in her voice and tries to swallow it down. There was a time when she could go to Regan for comfort whenever she felt tears in her eyes, but now she can't. She wishes the old Regan was still here.

'Ah,' says Regan. 'Well, that is a shame. More sacrifices might be necessary if we are to triumph against evil.'

A tear breaks free and streaks down Mariam's face. She resists the urge to raise a hand and wipe it away. That would be a good way to stab herself. She moves the swordpoints closer to Regan's throat instead. Regan looks worried for half an instant.

'I'm not sacrificing them,' Mariam says. 'They're my friends. I'm going to save them. And you're going to help me.'

She makes that decision right then, as the words are leaving her mouth. She will save them. She just needs to figure out how.

Regan is smiling, faintly, now. Recovering from her moment of uncertainty. 'Very well,' she says. 'Why don't you put those down? I have something to show you.'

Mariam doesn't exactly put them down; she just lowers them, stepping out of the way long enough for Regan to stand up. Kay's blonde friend brought a satchel with him and left it against the side of the cave. Now Regan goes to find it, retrieving a computer tablet from inside.

They end up sitting next to each other on the sofa. Regan takes painfully long to type the password in, then painfully long to find what she's looking for. It must be hard to use an iPad when you're eighty million years old.

'Here,' says Regan eventually. 'Plans for the Avalon platform.'

'Oh my God,' says Mariam. She snatches the pad as Regan offers it to her. These are detailed blueprints – the sort of thing that they always dreamt of having when they were planning direct actions. She's studied plans before, learnt how an oil rig works, how a fracking site is built, how to put them out of action without damaging the environment. They went through all of that in Manchester, years ago, in the cold cellars where they held their student meetings. Long before she went to the Preston camp. But the plans they had then were never as good as this. These are deck-by-deck schematics. Nothing blacked out or hidden. She scrolls through it all, unblinking, leaning over the pad.

'Where did you get these?' she asks.

'Lancelot acquired them for us.'

She has a momentary lapse of concentration. 'Wait, that guy's *Lancelot*?'

'Yes.'

'The guy who … didn't he … hook up with Arthur's wife? In the stories?'

Regan takes a deep breath, as if she's about to explain it all. But then she thinks better of it and just says, 'Not exactly.'

'Is that why Kay has beef with him?'

'Something like that. I fear that might be a story for another time.'

'Okay, well, whatever,' Mariam says, turning her attention back to the screen.

She looks for the wellhead first – the place where the oil is pumped up into the rig itself. Avalon is huge, but the wellhead is right where it's supposed to be: in the middle of the lowest deck. There's a manual blowout preventer – the thing you can clamp shut to stop any oil from getting up through the wellbore. She would need to close that first, if she wanted to destroy the rest of the rig without causing an oil spill.

But that's not what she wants to do. She wants to find her friends. She hunts through the upper levels, floors and floors of stuff that shouldn't be on an oil rig. Everything is neatly labelled. Luxury suites. Day spa. Retail outlet. Indoor golf course.

And components that she doesn't understand. A huge tube runs up through every level of the rig, labelled GEOTHAUMIC SUPERCAPACITOR. That looks important.

'What is all of this stuff?'

'As far as we can tell,' says Morgan, 'the Avalon platform isn't just an oil rig. It's some sort of magical harvesting device. Drawing up the latent magic from the under the earth and hoarding it in one place.'

'What for?'

'To break through the veil between worlds. To leave this earthly realm behind and transport themselves elsewhere.'

Mariam blinks at Regan. 'So all of the worst people in the world are going to ... leave?'

'Yes.'

'Is that a *bad* thing? We could just ... let them go. If we save the others first.'

Regan shakes her head. 'Punching through the veil in such a manner will release a huge amount of latent magic into the realm. Dark spirits from the Otherworld will use that magic to come through and manifest in our world. Dragons, giants, trolls. Interminable horrors. All manner of foul things that were banished to the realm of nightmares a long time ago. Our waking realm will be overrun with monsters.'

'Oh,' says Mariam. 'Fuck.'

'Fuck indeed,' says Regan.

Mariam stares at the television. Arthur's speech has finished, but the news people are still talking and nodding. Agreeing with each other on how regal he is. Safe in their studio, on the platform. Are they being taken advantage of? Held hostage, even? Or do they know about all of this? Maybe they know what the plan is and they're okay with it too, as long as they know that they're safe. They're on the inside. No matter how bad things get,

452

it won't get bad for them.

'How do we stop that?' Mariam says.

'The simplest way would be to destroy the Avalon platform before they can complete their ritual,' says Regan.

That can't be the simple option, surely. Sneaking onto a maximum-security oil rig and blowing it up.

'I'd have to save the others first,' says Mariam. 'I can't blow it up while they're still locked up there.'

'Hm,' says Regan. 'As I said, more sacrifices may be necessary.'

'No.'

Regan sighs through her nose. 'Mariam, I understand that they're very dear to you. But you have to think about the greater good.'

Mariam laughs because that's such a stupid thing to say. The greater good. 'The greater good for who?'

'For everybody,' says Regan. 'For everybody on the planet. If you care about saving the world then that has to be your first priority. Above everything else. Even above saving your friends.'

'Why?'

'It will be hard enough to break into that facility and destroy it. If you try to save your friends as well, you're far more likely to be captured. And then these people will win. Arthur will be made king, they'll complete their ritual, and the world will be cast into ruin. Even another oil fire would be preferable to what these people are planning.'

'Would it? Really?'

Regan holds her ground, staring her down. 'What do you think? On the one hand, a slow descent into chaos as the ecosystem continues to collapse upon itself. On the other hand, fiends and dragons and pandemonium.'

'Those can't be the only two choices.'

'I'm afraid that's the situation in which we find ourselves.'

'Well, why don't you stop them? You're magic, aren't you? Why don't you save the world? And while you're doing that, I can save the others.'

Regan stands up, and suddenly she looks terrifying, like an evil queen. Drawing the warmth out of the room, with white fire burning in her eyes. Hair writhing like a mass of snakes. Skin glowing with dark light. Mariam gets the faintest glimpse of what she really looks like, and she can't deal with it. She closes her eyes against it, clenching her teeth.

'I can do that, if you wish,' says Regan. She seems to have three or four voices. 'But I will bring down such fire and destruction upon that oil rig that they'll still be talking about it a thousand years from now. And your friends will surely be destroyed.'

Mariam feels the need to edge away, backed up against the armrest of the sofa. Staring up at this thing in front of her, this thing which tricked her for so long, pretending to be her friend. This thing that stabbed her. Is this what she really looks like?

And then she finds herself laughing. Pressed up against the armrest and laughing up at Regan's face changes. Even like this, this horrible evil version of herself, she looks confused.

'Bullshit,' says Mariam. 'If you could do that, why didn't you do it years ago? Why don't you go and do it now? Why are you here talking to me?'

Regan tries, again, to make her afraid. She tries to make herself look twice as awful. But it doesn't work. The light returns to the room, in flashes, like something electrical. The strange glow leaves Regan's skin. She looks human again, but older. Withered and white-haired. Frail and weary. She sits heavily down on the sofa, hiding her face.

'I'm old, Mariam,' she says. 'I'm old and I'm weak. And I don't have the strength left for this sort of thing. That's why I need you. That's why I needed all of you, you and your sisters. I knew I couldn't do it by myself. I was just getting so tired of it all. Centuries of fighting hard and getting nowhere. And I felt so helpless to do anything about it.'

Mariam keeps staring at her, this old woman on the sofa next to her, covering her face with one hand. She knows that she ought to feel pity or compassion, but this is the same woman – the same creature – that stabbed her a couple of days ago. She's probably faking this as well.

Mariam swallows. 'That's why you went to Marlowe,' she says. 'You were tired. You were ready to give up. You were ready to bring Arthur back and let him deal with it.'

Regan starts to nod. 'Yes. Yes, I suppose that's right.'

'Well, I'm tired too,' says Mariam. 'I wake up every day feeling tired. Because I should be living a normal life right now. There should be people older than me, people like you and Kay, keeping the world safe. But you and Kay and everyone else, you just keep throwing your hands up and stepping back like it isn't your prob-lem. And that's why I have to keep waking up in tents, and caves, and wherever else. That's why I have to go and blow up oil rigs. That's not what I *want* to be doing. But I have to do it – because none of you are doing it. So don't talk to me about being tired. I'm fucking exhausted.'

'I—' says Regan.

Mariam shakes her head and interrupts her. 'I'm not betray-ing my friends, just because I'm exhausted. I'm not giving up on them. Maybe you felt like you had to do that, but I don't. I'm going to figure out a way to save them. And I don't want to hear anything about sacrifices, anymore. Not from you or anyone else.'

'Then you're a fool,' says Regan, quietly.

It sounds petty. Childish. Mariam feels like she doesn't have any patience left.

'You know what?' she asks. 'If you're not going to help me,

maybe you should just go. You go and have a nice rest, some-where. I'll figure it out by myself.'

Now she's the one who stands up. No swords, this time. She just stands and waits, staring down at Regan on the sofa. Saying nothing.

And eventually Regan gathers herself up. It seems to take a hundred years for her to get up off the sofa. Mariam stands where she is, with her arms folded, and watches this old woman hobble towards the entrance of the cave. It's only when Regan gets near the plastic curtain that she turns around.

'I don't suppose . . .' she says. 'If I could take Kay's staff with me? Only to use as a walking stick?'

'Just go.'

Regan lingers, with her face in shadow. Then she nods. It's hard to tell what she looks like, now. Like the old and the young version of herself at the same time.

'I'm proud of you, Mariam,' she says. 'I want you to know that.'

And then she leaves. Pushing the curtain aside and stepping through it. Leaving Mariam alone.

37

Kay doesn't understand why this pub is here, but he tries not to think too hard about it. If he thinks too hard about it then the whole pub might vanish back into the faerie realm, and then he wouldn't get to drink his pint.

There's a car park outside the pub with a horse tied up in it. The same horse Lancelot was riding in Manchester. It must have somehow known to find its way here. Lancelot takes a moment to stroke its nose and scratch behind its ears. Around the back of the pub there's a motorcycle sitting under a tarpaulin. Somebody has put two or three jerrycans of petrol next to it. Lancelot seems happy about that.

'I stopped here on the way up to find you,' Lancelot explains. 'Spoke to the landlord. He's a decent sort.'

When they go around the front of the pub they find the door unlocked. But the pub is empty, and deadly silent. Some of the tables are turned over. It doesn't take Kay long to notice the bullet holes in the furniture. The buckshot embedded in the walls. There aren't any bodies, but there are red stains on the tiles. Streaks of blood where people have been dragged outside.

Lancelot sighs. He looks weary, all of a sudden. He goes behind the bar and gets down two pint glasses from a shelf. Then he starts filling them with beer.

'What happened here?' asks Kay.

Lance shrugs. 'I don't know. Might have been some friends of yours. Might have been Saxons. Hardly matters, does it? Just the sort of thing that happens when the realm's in chaos.'

Kay tries not to bristle at that. They take their beer and find a table where they can sit and drink it. The one they settle for is small and round, with three soft stools under it. Lancelot looks at the empty stool and then back at the bar.

'Should have poured one for Galehaut,' he says.

'Or Galahad,' says Kay. 'He might have turned up if we waited long enough.'

Lancelot sniffs with mild amusement. It doesn't seem to break through whatever else he's feeling, looking down at the blood-stains on the floor.

They sit in silence. Uneasy truce. Kay finds that Lancelot is studying him, running his eyes over him. Looking at the oak hand and the mossy hair, and the stuff growing through his mail. Kay tries to ignore it. He takes his first sip of the fizzy stuff sitting on the table between them. Then he screws up his face.

'Tastes like piss,' says Kay.

'You look dreadful,' says Lance. 'I hope that's not catching.'

Kay shrugs. 'Merlin said that the realm's dying. And magic's dying with it. So, might happen to you, as well.'

'Christ,' says Lance. 'Did he say anything else?'

'Yeah. Yeah, he said a few things, actually.'

So he tells him. He tells Lancelot everything he can remember. He tells him about the dying realm. About the tree of time and the black boughs and the green shoots. He tells him about Herne, and Nimue, and Merlin, and Mariam. And finally he gets onto the important stuff, telling Lancelot all about the mushrooms and the resurrection stones and the vast pointlessness of everything they've been doing for the past thousand years. By the time he's finished they've both drunk their pints down to the bottom of the glass.

'We were all just part of this . . . experiment,' Kay says. 'There wasn't any reason for us to keep coming back and saving the realm from peril and all of that bollocks. No higher purpose. No sacred duty. He just needed to see if it worked. The magic. So he could do it on his mushrooms.'

Lancelot stares at the floor, for a while. He looks about as horrified as Kay felt when Merlin told him for the first time. Kay drains the dregs of his beer and gives Lance however much time he needs to wrap his head around everything. And eventually Lance starts nodding.

'Sorry,' Kay says. 'But you did ask.'

'Right,' says Lancelot. 'I think I'm going to need another pint.'

'Good idea.'

They get another round in. Something about it reminds Kay of the last big war, drinking in London pubs between air raids whenever they had leave. Pretending to be normal people. Except the ale was better then, and the pubs were full of friendly faces. Things didn't seem quite so bad. Maybe that's just because of where they were sitting. But things didn't seem hopeless. Even with bombs raining down. Not like they do now.

'Christ,' says Lance, again. 'Why did we bother? Bosworth and Naseby and . . . all of that. Could have just stayed under our trees.'

'Seems that way,' says Kay.

'Makes one wonder why we're bothering now.'

Kay frowns at Lancelot over the rim of his pint. Swallowing

down another mouthful of dreadful beer and wiping off his foam moustache. 'Yeah, why are you bothering?' he asks. 'Why are you here? Arthur finally get sick of you again?'

Lancelot narrows his eyes. 'I don't suppose you'd believe that I'm here out of adherence to my principles?'

'Not for a moment,' says Kay. 'I don't think you've done a selfless thing since the day you were born.'

'Are we really going to go over all of this, again?'

'Apparently.'

Lancelot sighs. He squeezes his eyes shut. Thinking back, to the old days. Looking more tired than Kay has ever seen him.

'Look,' says Lancelot, 'I saved Gwen from the fire because she was a terrified young girl and Arthur was going to burn her alive. It wasn't because I wanted to start a war. I just couldn't stand by and watch it happen.'

'Well, what about all the people who burned afterwards, in your war on Arthur? You could stand by and watch them burn, could you?'

Lancelot scoffs. 'This is getting off to a tremendous start, isn't it?'

'You killed my *wife*, Lance.'

He says it too loud. He can almost feel people staring at them from other tables, their conversations falling quiet. But there's nobody there, of course. The tables are empty. Perhaps he's disturbed their ghosts. Maybe they're eavesdropping from the afterlife.

They sit for a long while in silence, nursing their pints and their ancient grudges. Then Lancelot closes his eyes and begins to speak.

'I am truly sorry, about Hildwyn. I only met her once, but she seemed like a charming young woman. And when I went to the Saxons for help, I never dreamt, not for a moment, that they would take things as far as they did. It was never my intention for them to burn down your hall or do harm to anyone that you loved. I'm sorry that they did. I'm sorry that I haven't apologised for that until now.'

Kay tries to stay angry. He remembers Wyn. Remembers her alive and laughing. Then remembers her dead, under the fallen rafters. Subjects himself to the memories again, and then feels bad for doing it. She wouldn't want him to do that, call up the memory of her death and use it as fuel for his anger.

The worst thing is that part of him understands. It's not something he readily wants to admit about himself, but he can imagine how it might have happened. War is chaos. Like the death here, at this pub. You give orders, and things get set in motion, and people die. Even when you didn't mean them to. He knows that. He knew it at the time. But he was angry that Wyn had died before they could grow old together. He tracked down the Saxons who did it and slaughtered them, and that didn't make him feel any less angry. So he let himself be angry with Lancelot instead. It wasn't difficult, in times past, when Lancelot refused to apologise. But now he has apologised, hasn't he? The fuel is burnt away. The fire starts to simmer down and burn cooler.

'All right,' he says.

'But while we're on the subject . . . ' says Lancelot.

Kay groans. 'Lance.'

'If you'd only stood with me, then it wouldn't have happened. If you'd declared for me we could have ridden against him together. Brought an end to the madness.'

'I vowed not to raise my sword against him. I kept that vow. And he was my brother, Lance. He still is.'

'Which means you know better than anyone how awful he is.'

'He's just . . . sick,' says Kay, 'I think. He's not right in the head. Never was. Makes it easy for people to manipulate him.'

Lancelot nearly knocks his pint off the table. 'So let's go and kill all of the people who are manipulating him! You could have done that back then, helped me to kill Mordred and Agryfan and all the others. You can still do it now. And if you're going to do it now then I want to do it with you. Because it seems to me like the people running the country all deserve what's coming to them.'

'Including Marlowe?'

Lancelot looks taken off guard. He swallows before he speaks. 'He's already had what was coming to him. I killed him.'

Kay feels suddenly, worryingly, sober. 'What?'

'He killed Galehaut,' says Lancelot. 'Had his tree cut down. So I killed him. Seemed the right thing to do.'

Kay feels shock, then anger. His oak fist tightens of its own accord. They did whatever Marlowe told them to do, for so long. No matter how nasty it was. They trusted him to keep their secrets for them. Seems like that was a mistake.

'Right,' he says. 'Well. I'm ... I'm sorry about Galehaut, Lance. I know you were, um ... I know you were very ... I know that you ...'

Lancelot tries to help him out. 'That we were gay and had lots of sex?'

'Yeah,' says Kay, clearing his throat. 'Yeah. I'm sorry.'

'That's not the half of it, either,' says Lancelot. 'Let me get another round, and I'll tell you the rest.'

More dreadful beer. Lancelot tells him about what they're planning, these false counsellors. Draining the magic from the land and using it for evil purposes. Tearing the veil open and disappearing off to the faerie realm. Now the stuff in Lancashire makes sense. The dragon coming up from the earth. The weird magic around the fracking facility. It makes him sneer. If they've read all of Marlowe's files, they must know that it's a bad idea. They must know what will happen to the world, when there's no barrier anymore between the waking realm and the realm of nightmares. But maybe they don't care. Just trying to get away from the mess they've made. Bugger everyone else.

Near the bottom of his fourth pint, Kay has a brief moment of caring, of thinking they ought to do something – lift a finger, take up their swords. But it doesn't last long.

'I left the plans with Morgan and your friend,' says Lancelot. 'If she can make any sense out of them then maybe we can do something. I don't know. Blow it up. Sabotage it, somehow. Wouldn't be much harder than the Paderborn raid in forty-five, I shouldn't have thought.'

Thoughts of Nazis and worse things threaten to rumble up through his mind, so he drowns them in beer and shakes his head. 'Even if we can blow it up, it won't make a blind bit of difference,' he says. 'I told you. Merlin says there's no hope. No way this turns out well.'

Lancelot blinks at him. 'Not with that attitude, it won't. Come on, I haven't come all the way up here just for us to sit around being a pair of miserable cunts.'

'Look, Merlin can see the future. He can see all possible futures. And he said that on this branch of the ... of the tree of time ... there's no hope for anything good happening. We've missed our chance. Everything's shit, from here on out. No green shoots. So what's the point in trying?'

'Oh, fuck the tree of time,' says Lancelot. 'I don't believe that everything's all mapped out, and that things are hopeless just because Merlin says that they're hopeless. I think we get to decide the future ourselves. Maybe the fact that you've given up is what stopped him from seeing those green shoots. Did you think of that?'

'That's not how it works.'

'Has your friend Mariam given up as well?'

'No,' he says. 'No, she still wants to do something. She still has hope.'

'Well, there you are, then!' says Lancelot. 'If she still has hope, then I still have hope. That's good enough for me.'

Kay stares at a spot on the table where Lancelot has spilled some beer, watching it spread slowly over the surface towards the table's edge. Just sort of waiting for it to run over the side and drip onto the floor. But then it doesn't. Something stops it from spreading any further.

'How long does it go on for, then?' asks Kay. 'Say we manage this, somehow. Save the world, again. Remove peril from the realm and go back to sleep. How long do we keep it up, knowing that it's not achieving anything? Knowing that it's all going to happen again, sooner or later. There'll be another war, or something else, fifty years down the line. And we're the ones who'll have to get up and do something about it.'

Lancelot shrugs. 'I don't know. Until Judgement Day, I suppose. Until the earth gets eaten by the sun. I can't say I'm overly enthused about it either, but that's just the way it is.'

Kay wipes a hand down his face. 'I suppose I thought that Merlin had a plan for us. I suppose that made it easier. But if that's not true, then ... I'm not sure I want to keep doing it.'

Lancelot looks sympathetic. 'It's different for you, I suppose,' he says. 'You might get to see Hildwyn again, once all of this is over. I'm not sure I'll ever get to see Galehaut again.'

Kay thinks about the weird trees, back in Merlin's cave. Then he stands up from the table and suddenly realises how much he's had to drink. The blood – or perhaps the sap, in his case – rushes to his feet.

'Come on,' he says. 'I've got something to show you.'

'Hold on,' says Lancelot, raising one hand. 'Let's get another round in first.'

38

Mariam sits and studies the plans.

It's not just blueprints on this tablet but climate data, heatmaps, casualty projections. Evidence of crimes against the planet. She imagines a courtroom somewhere, in the world after this one, a safe world where the war is over and the ecosystem has been saved. That all seems pretty unlikely, now. It never seemed very likely at all, but she always had the sense before that there were other people, other FETA cells, other climate warriors, who would do what needed to be done. Winning the war. Holding people to account. Setting up climate trials, in the better world that came afterwards. Now she knows that there isn't anybody else. Just her, in this cave, with this tablet.

That's not what she should be thinking about right now. She needs to focus on what's right in front of her. How to destroy this thing without causing more damage to the environment. How to save her friends without getting killed herself.

She finds an area on the blueprints labelled DETENTION

CENTRE. That sounds promising. The platform has twelve levels, as far as she can tell. The detention centre is up on Deck Two, near the very top of the platform. The wellhead is right down at the bottom, on Deck Twelve.

Regan's absence is very loud. She can hear Regan's voice in her head, telling her to do the smart thing. Far safer to get in and out again as quickly as possible. Sabotage the rig. Blow it up. Not get distracted. Not go out of her way to save her friends. But she doesn't listen to that voice.

There's another voice, a more insistent voice, telling her that this whole plan is crazy. She's just one woman. She can't possibly think that this will work. It will all go wrong, like it did in Preston. Kay will have to rescue her again.

Maybe she should wait until he and Lancelot get back before she makes any plans. Kay has probably done this kind of thing before. In the meantime, she does everything else that she can to prepare. She packs and repacks her bag. She'll take the tablet with the plans. She still has all the Semtex and the climbing gear. Those are two things you need to blow up an oil rig, but they don't feel like enough for the Avalon platform. The ropes probably aren't long enough. The explosives are probably too weak.

Mariam repacks everything for the third time and feels like she can't justify a fourth. Kay and Lancelot haven't come back. Did they kill each other? Did they just fuck off and leave her here to do this by herself?

She sits and watches the TV until she can't stand it anymore. Then she switches it off. The cave feels twice as silent now. Twice as empty. The despair creeps up and settles coldly in her stomach, closing its fist around her heart.

She jigs her right foot absent-mindedly against the floor, twisting her prayer beads until the skin on her wrist grows sore. Can you save the world with good intentions? Can you save it with a backpack full of climbing gear and plastic explosives? You can't rely on peaceful protests and voting for the right people. You can't rely on the Welsh and the communists, people with more optimism than ammunition. You can't even rely on all of the weird old stuff, on people like Kay and Regan and King Arthur coming out from under the earth and magically making things better.

So maybe she'll have to do it. Get back down to Glastonbury, climb onto a giant oil rig, blow it up and save the world. It doesn't look like anyone else is going to do it.

Mariam finds a paper and pen among Merlin's stuff and scribbles a note for Kay to read when he gets back. And then she can't think of any more ways to waste time. The only thing left to do is to walk out into the trees. She needs to somehow get to Glastonbury by noon to stop all of this. That's what Regan said.

But she finds herself standing and doing nothing. Feet glued to the floor. Holding the straps of her rucksack against her shoulders and feeling numb. She doesn't even know what part of the country she's in. She doesn't have a car. She doesn't have a map. It might be too late, even if she sets off now. Even if she wants to save the world, there might be no way of doing it. No magic way of getting down there overnight.

Well, there might be one.

Kay's staff is still propped up against his chair. Mariam looks at it for half a second and then tells herself that she's being stupid. You probably need to be an ancient tosser like Kay or Regan to use a magic staff. Don't you? It wouldn't make sense if everyone could use it. What would be the point of wizards or witches or heroes if everybody had the power to wield it? If any ordinary person could pick it up and use it to change the world?

She stares at the staff for a long, silent moment. Then she crosses over to it and picks it up. It feels warmer than it should, like a phone that's been left charging in the sun. The wood feels

467

somehow rough and smooth at the same time. She tries different ways of holding it. In both hands it feels like a rounders bat, like she could brain somebody with it. When she touches the end to the floor and holds it near the top, it comes up to just above her waist, like a walking stick. That feels a bit more natural. But she still has no idea what to do.

She starts to experiment. Pointing the staff at the wall, as if something useful might shoot out of it. Bringing the end down against the floor of the cave. Softly at first, then harder. Swinging it in wild arcs through the air. It doesn't seem to do anything except disturb the dust.

Oh well. She didn't really believe it would work.

But maybe that was the problem. Maybe she needs to actually believe it. She holds the staff in front of her, in both hands, touching the end of it against the ground. She shuts her eyes. She controls her breathing, as if she's doing one of Bronte's meditation sessions. It feels ridiculous, but she makes herself do it anyway. And then she starts speaking quietly to herself.

'I can do this,' she says. 'I can do this. I can make it work.'

Mariam thinks about magic. Old things. Forests and knights and castles. Wizards. She thinks about the deer that she met in the trees yesterday. That's the kind of world that magic comes from. Not from her world. Maybe she needs to draw it up from somewhere. Maybe she needs to convince somebody, or something. Prove herself worthy.

'I want to save the world,' she whispers. 'I want to save the forests, and the animals, and everybody living in the world.'

Nothing happens. So she thinks about her friends instead. She thinks about where she wants to go. She imagines seeing them, saving them. Maybe if she screws up her eyes and wishes hard enough, the staff will take her to them. She wants to save them. She focuses on the thought. Clenching every muscle in her face and arms, until she feels like she's going to pass out.

Maybe there isn't a magical solution to all of this. She can't just wave a magic stick and zap herself across the country. She can't save her friends, or stop the world from ending. Why did she think for a moment that she could? She's just an ordinary person. That's not the kind of thing that ordinary people can do.

But then Mariam remembers what Kay told her, on the dark walk over the moor towards Manchester. Ordinary people can do miracles, if they put their mind to it. If they choose to believe in themselves.

That becomes her mantra. She closes her eyes again.

Ordinary people can work miracles if they believe in themselves. Ordinary people can work miracles if they believe in themselves. *Ordinary people can work miracles if they believe in themselves.*

The staff gets warmer in her hands. She hears a keening sound, getting louder. She feels a change in the air around her, like the pressure before a lightning storm. Her hair stands on end. And then she opens her eyes, and everything looks different, as if her eyes can see new colours that they couldn't see before. There's a rainbow churning around her, moving the dust in spirals. It picks her up and takes her somewhere else.

39

Kay and Lancelot stagger out of the pub, six pints worse. The road is dark. The sky is black. Kay stares up at the moon to check what time it is. He didn't think they'd been in there for that long. Arthur's coronation is tomorrow. The veil will be torn and all manner of horrors will be released into the world. And here they are getting rat-arsed in the whatever corner of the country this is. Fine protectors of the realm, they are.

They stumble back through the woods towards the cave, singing an old song about trying to sleep with a giant's daughter. Lancelot stops to piss against a tree, with his mail and tunic hitched up around his waist. Kay waits, kicking at leaves with one foot. But he hears Lancelot chuckling behind him.

'What?' he asks.

'So this girl,' says Lancelot. 'Mariam. Are you and her, uh . . . intimately acquainted?'

'No.'

'Not even a little bit?'

'It's not like that.'

'Why not?'

'Because it isn't.'

'There's nothing wrong with having a bit of fun every now and again, you know.'

'Hm.'

Lancelot clears his throat. 'Kay, you have had carnal relations since the sixth century, haven't you? Please tell me you have.'

Kay turns his eyes briefly to heaven.

'Oh no,' says Lancelot. 'That's tragic. You poor man.'

'Some of us take our vows seriously.'

'It's "till death do us part", isn't it? You're dead, she's dead. You're both dead. I'm sure she wouldn't want you to— And don't start talking to me about vows, again.'

'Just 'cause she got up there first doesn't mean I can do whatever I like down here.'

'Urgh, God,' says Lancelot. 'That's the most— You do know that everybody was at it like rabbits, in the old days? Under Arthur's nose? It can't have escaped your attention. All that chivalry was . . . well, you don't have to keep it up. Especially not a thousand years later.'

'Not sure I agree.'

'Well then,' says Lancelot, dropping his mail around his waist again, 'you're a better man than me.'

'Already knew that.'

'There's no need to be rude.'

It's pitch black by the time they get back to the clearing. They help each other down the slope, careful not to slip. Trying to walk quietly through the caves in case they wake Mariam and Morgan. They might have gone to bed, if they haven't killed each other by now. Instead of going straight through to the main chamber,

Kay leads Lancelot down to the damp cave where Merlin grows his mushrooms.

'Look,' he says. 'In here. Something you should see.'

Past the rows of mushrooms are the feeble saplings growing from their bags of soil, with their labels sellotaped to the planter. Kay. Lancelot. Bors. Agravain. Galehaut. It's still not an easy thing to behold or think about. Lancelot looks just about as horrified as he felt himself when he saw them for the first time.

'What in the name of Christ,' says Lancelot.

'He went around and cut bits off from our trees,' says Kay. 'And ... well, I'm not exactly sure what he did to them. But they're here now. Maybe he saw that our trees would get torn down. I think he was growing these in reserve.'

'Do you think ...' says Lancelot. He reaches out slowly, with uncertain fingers. Touching Galehaut's sapling with his left hand. Rubbing the leaves gently between his thumb and forefinger.

'I don't know,' says Kay. 'Maybe. If you planted it out in the wild somewhere. Waited long enough.'

Lancelot lets out a mournful groan. 'Long enough for it to grow into an adult oak tree. How long is that? Eighty years? A hundred?'

'Well, yeah, but ... what's that to us?'

'I suppose you're right. I've waited this long.'

They stand in silence, regarding the young trees in front of them. Then Lancelot rests his right hand on Kay's shoulder.

'Thank you for this,' he says.

'Don't mention it.'

'What are we going to do with the others?'

'Oh, I'm gonna burn mine,' says Kay. 'No question. Don't want two of me walking around.'

'Good idea,' says Lancelot. 'One of you's bad enough.'

They leave the saplings in their soil for the time being, hoping

472

that Merlin's magic will sustain them, bolstered by the tubes of water and the purple lights.

When they go back through to the main chamber they find it empty. No sign of Morgan or Mariam, nor any sign of where they've gone. The television has been switched off. Then Kay finds a piece of paper left on top of it and neatly folded.

Kay,
Gone to save the world.
Mariam

'Lance,' he says. 'She's gone.'

'Gone where?'

He palms the note to Lancelot and goes to find his things, his sword and shield. He worries that Mariam may have taken the sword with her, but no, it's there lain across the armchair. What's missing is the staff, which gives him pause. Did Mariam take it, or Morgan? He's not sure which would be worse.

'Ah,' says Lancelot. 'Down to the Tor, do you think?'

'Come on,' he says. 'If we hurry we can still get down there.'

'And do what?' asks Lancelot. 'You said yourself that we're obsolete. Long past our best. Even if we do charge to the rescue, I don't see how we're going to achieve anything. Swim up the bloody thing in our mail and try to shimmy up it?'

'No,' says Kay. He tries to sober himself up. Marshal his thoughts. 'But we . . . we can cause a distraction. Draw attention away from her, so she can do whatever she's trying to do.'

'And how are we going to do that?'

'I'll challenge Arthur,' says Kay, picking up his sword. 'Which, you're right, I should have done a very long time ago. But I'll do it now. I'll call him out. We just have to get to him first.'

'Hang on, though,' says Lancelot, squinting through his own

drunkenness. 'We'll probably only get one shot at this. I'm all for fighting Arthur, but ... is this the smartest way to go about doing it?'

Kay straps his shield to his arm, remembering something that Mariam said a few days ago. 'It might not be the smart thing to do,' he says, 'but it's the right thing to do. If we can't save the world then the least we can do is make it easier for people like Mariam to save it.'

Lancelot seems to think about that, for a moment. Then he starts nodding. 'All right,' he says. 'But I'm taking the bike.'

40

Mariam flies through a rainbow kaleidoscope, clutching the staff tightly in both hands. She sees things in the swirl of colour, filtered through the prism of time. She sees a sky full of dragons over a burning city. There are things stalking through the ruins, creatures that her brain can't even process. She sees a world without people, without water, with air too thick to breathe. Dust blowing over the ruins.

And then she sees herself, in a better world. She stands and speaks to a crowd of listeners, looking older and more comfortable in her own skin, with long grey hair and gold bangles on her wrists. The air seems to taste cleaner. There are low grass-covered homes, greenhouses full of fruit and vegetables, fields of young and newly planted trees. Solar panels glittering in the distance, and windmills turning. And people are sitting in the middle of all this, listening to her speak. Why would they do that? Why would they come and listen to what she has to say? She's not worth listening to, not worth following. She already proved that, on the hills in Wales. But here they are anyway. These people, in this better world.

She is standing on the grass and watching her older self in this green future when she feels the presence of somebody else beside her, as if she's been noticed by some watchful force. She looks down slowly, wary of what she might see.

Standing beside her is a small child, no more than twelve years old. Thin arms and messy hair and skin that makes Mariam think of acorns. Naked, apart from some kind of animal loincloth. Weird stubs sprouting from their temples, like baby antlers poking through their hair. But the most unnerving thing about them is their smile. And the fact that they've taken her by the hand.

The green future slips away. Now she sees a dark green past. Thick forests of moss and tangled roots. People sheltering in the wilderness, wearing fur, hoping that the thorns and branches will keep them safe from whatever is chasing after them. Wolves and beasts and men on horseback – and worse things, nightmare things.

It all passes so quickly that she barely has time to make sense of it. But the child is holding her hand, and she finds that she can't let go. This is what the strange child wants her to see.

She sees a family hiding beneath a tree, in the cavity beneath the twisted roots. A woman and her two daughters, taking refuge from a monster. Something that has slithered out of a bog, now clambering over roots, sniffing with its nostril slits. Drawing close to its prey. Laying three long talons on the tree above them.

But then something else comes bounding out of the undergrowth. A giant bear, bigger than a bear has any right to be, knocking aside the swamp creature with one shoulder. Rearing up on its hind legs to rend the monster with both claws. Tearing off a gangly green arm between its teeth.

476

The monster runs back into the darkness, trailing blood behind it. The bear stays, sniffing at the woman and her daughters like it might try and steal the monster's prey. But then it turns and lumbers away, leaving them in peace.

Mariam sees other things, a quick flash of images. Women wearing tiny bear totems, carved from wood or bone, on strings around their necks. People building shrines and praying to bear statues. Men wearing bearskins, bear heads, and dancing around a fire. A warrior being painted in blood, given a sword in one hand and a shield in the other.

Then the images stop. And she finds herself in a green clearing with blue sky overhead. Skin cooled by a soft breeze. It sounds peaceful here, and it takes her a moment to realise why.

Birdsong. She hasn't heard birdsong for a long time.

In the centre of the clearing is a hollow tree, with room inside the trunk for somebody to build their home. The child is sitting inside on the soft earth. There's a fire in front of them with a cauldron boiling on it.

Mariam finds herself walking closer. She stops at the threshold of the tree, where she puts a hand against the bark, waiting for the child to invite her inside.

'Who guards the gate?' asks the child, stirring their cauldron.

'Um,' she says. 'Hi. Who are you?'

'Call me what you want,' says the child. They sound Welsh and Irish at the same time. 'Some people call me Herne. They're no more wrong than most.'

'Look,' says Mariam. 'I'm trying to get somewhere, and I think I must have done something wrong, so . . . '

'No, no,' says the child, 'you're on the right path. I just brought you here for a moment. I'm good with the in-between bits. Dreams, mushroom trips, planar travel, that sort of thing.'

'Right,' she says, unconvinced.

'Won't keep you long. Will you sit? Have some broth?'

So she does, sitting cross-legged in front of the fire. The cauldron contains a deer skull floating in a thin bubbling liquid. The child scoops up some of the broth in a cup made from an animal horn and hands it to her. It's warm in her hands. She doesn't drink from it yet.

'What were those things you showed me?'

'That's how this all started,' says the child. 'With Arthur. He has a job he's supposed to be doing. Guarding the gate. And he's been making a pig's ear of it recently, I don't mind telling you.'

Mariam blinks at him. 'Guarding the gate?'

'Protecting the forest,' says the child. 'Protecting the earth. Keeping nightmares from leaking into the world. Guardian of the greenwood and the vale. That's been his job for a very long time. Longer than even he can remember, I'd wager. That's why we created him in the first place. But he seems to have lost his way. An abdication of responsibility is what you'd call it, I think.'

'What does this have to do with me?'

'Well,' says the child, 'if he's not guarding the gate, then I wondered if you might fancy the job. Doesn't seem like any bugger else is going to do it.'

Mariam shakes her head. 'I don't want to be the fucking guardian of the greenwood, or whatever it was. I'm just trying to rescue my friends. And maybe save the planet.'

The child smiles again, more widely. 'That's the beauty of it. You're already doing a grand job.'

'I'm not a hero. I'm not like Kay.'

'I reckon that might be where we went wrong the first time,' says the child, 'creating heroes. Reckon we should have trusted normal people to guard the gate in the first place. Reckon that's what we should do now.'

Mariam drinks from her cup of broth, almost absent-mindedly, and feels the warmth of it bleed through her. Feels things happening behind her eyes. When she lowers the cup it knocks against something. A kind of talisman has appeared around her neck. A bear totem, carved from white bone.

'Will you help me?' she asks. 'If I agree to ... whatever this is. Will you help me save my friends?'

'Oh, you don't need my help,' says the child. 'Like I said, you're doing a grand job already. Just wanted to tell you that you're on the right path.'

'But I ... I don't know what I'm doing,' she says. 'I don't even know how to use the staff properly. Can't you tell me?'

'It ought to work beautifully where you're going,' says the child. 'Plenty of magic for it to draw from. You'll figure it out, I'm sure.'

She can't help from scowling at them. This god-child-faerie thing, who could probably turn her into a newt if they wanted to. But she's too angry with them to care about that.

'What's the point of you, then?' she asks. 'If you're not going to help. What's the point of me being here?'

The child just laughs. It's somehow innocent and terrifying at the same time. 'The point of me?' they ask. 'I'm every leaf on every tree. I'm every worm in the ground. Every root and acorn. That's the point of me. I keep the world turning. I keep the air clean.'

As they speak, they start to decay in front of her. Their antlers grow. There are flies on their cheek and moths in their hair. Mariam tries to shrink away from them, but they grow inside the tree trunk until they're looming over her.

'What's the point of you?' asks the child. 'That's more the question. What's the point of people? Nought but a nuisance to me. You'll make the place unliveable for yourselves if you carry on the way you're doing. And I've half a mind to let you. So that's the choice you face. Guard the gate well and make the world green again. Or make it barren and destroy yourselves. I offer you nothing, except that choice.'

Mariam scrambles backwards, out of the trunk. Tripping on a root. Falling against the ground. And then reality rushes up to meet her. She falls down hard against something flat and warm, feeling granules of dirt beneath her hands.

She only had a vague idea of where she was trying to get to when she set off from Merlin's cave. The Avalon platform. Somewhere outside, on the superstructure. She didn't know whether the staff would do what she wanted or not. It could have taken her to anywhere in the world. But it has dropped her on one of the landing pads. There were eight of them on the plans. This one has a big yellow '9' written on it. That's not great.

She stands with the sun baking down on her and dust blowing against her skin. The sky is orange and cloudless overhead. The floodplain is glittering below. No way down from here except a long fall into shallow water. But there's a metal walkway with a door at the end of it, leading into the Avalon. She takes a deep breath before she heads down it, holding the staff in both hands.

There's nobody guarding the door. No security system to stop her from getting in. They must have thought that nobody could get up here, past all the defences. No need to bother keeping the door locked. It glides open as she draws near, and then she's inside.

Beige corridors. Light fixtures. Potted plants and dull paintings. The place seems weirdly quiet. Air conditioning cycles through empty corridors. Mariam had imagined more people, more oil men, more Saxon guards. There are probably cameras watching her, somebody sitting in a room with a bank of TV screens, sending Saxons to find her. But she can't hear any alarms or announcements.

She knows from the blueprints that this place has twelve levels, and the landing pads are on Deck Four. The security centre is up on Deck One. The wellhead is right at the bottom – Deck Twelve. But if there are nine landing pads instead of eight then the plans might be out of date. Everything might have changed while this place was being built. She tries not to think about that. Before she does anything else, she has to find a lift or a stairwell.

It turns out that looking at the blueprint of an oil rig and trying to move around an oil rig by foot are two very different things. Mariam has to stop, swearing under her breath, in a little nook in the corridor where people are meant to sit and enjoy the bad art hanging on the walls. She puts the staff down for a moment. Crouching behind a massive plant pot. Getting the tablet out of her bag. Scrolling through plans.

There's a lift not far from where she is, if the plans are accurate. Left, right, and right again. She's halfway to standing up when she hears heavy footfalls against the carpet.

'Down this way,' somebody says. They sound American.

Mariam crouches down again behind the plant pot and presses a hand over her mouth. Back against the wall, holding the staff across her chest. The Saxons lumber past her in their khaki trousers and their combat boots, heading down the corridor, the way she came.

She waits at least a minute before she dares to breathe again. Then she gets up and heads for the lift. It's only once she stands up that she realises how quickly her heart is beating.

Left, and right, and right again. The lift is wood panelled and mirrored on the inside. She finds herself confronted by her reflection, for the first time in days. Confronted by the row of buttons for different floors.

The smart thing to do would be to go straight down to the wellhead and close the blowout preventer, so she can safely destroy the whole facility. She should do that quickly, before she gets caught by Saxons. She can hear Regan's voice in her head telling her to do the smart thing. Telling her to make sacrifices. But she doesn't listen to that voice. She presses the button for Deck One. Up to where her friends are.

Her reflection looks like somebody with their shit together. Somebody who might actually be able to save her friends and disable an oil rig at the same time. That's not how she feels inside, but maybe she should try harder. Stand taller. She allows herself a moment of hope that she can manage to do this.

But then the lift stops on Deck Two, earlier than she expected. They must have locked down the elevators. The doors slide open to reveal a crowd of Saxons, eight or nine of them waiting with their weapons levelled. As soon as they see her, they start screaming. Get on the floor. Put down the weapon. Hands on the wall.

Mariam's first instinct is to do as they say – because they're shouting so loud, because they have guns, because they're dressed how they are. Stupid to think that she could have come here all by herself and that this wouldn't happen, that she could somehow fight these people and win. Now they're probably going to zip-tie her hands and drag her to a cell and waterboard her, or worse. The same things they've been doing to Willow and Teoni and Roz and Bronte. The same things they'll keep doing, if she doesn't stop them.

Why didn't she wait for Kay and Lancelot to come back? Why didn't she bring one of their swords with her? All she has is this staff. This length of wood. But the Saxons keep shouting, 'Put down the weapon!' Is it a weapon? She did see Kay use it to turn that guy into a squirrel. She remembers, again, what he said. Ordinary people can work miracles if they choose to believe in themselves. So she grips the staff more tightly. Then she points it at the Saxons, lunging forward with it. Thinking about what she wants to do to them.

The air becomes thicker. The walls of the lift creak and groan. Rifles clatter. War gear and khaki trousers slump to the floor in heaps. She can see feathers and beaks and tails. Not just squirrels but pigeons, aardvarks, pelicans. Fighting their way free from sleeves and waistbands and bulletproof vests. Mariam stares for a moment at the thing she's done. Then she runs through the menagerie, past the fluttering of feathers and the twitch of tails. The pelican tries to chase after her, tries to get his beak around her leg, but he doesn't follow her very far. Metamorphosis probably wasn't covered in his danger pay.

It's only now that alarms start blaring. Emerging onto the second floor, she sees some sort of shopping mall for rich people, like the kind you have to walk through at airports. Handbags and whisky and diamond necklaces. When she steps out into it there are more Saxons charging towards her, filling the corridors. A whole line of them kneel down and start firing, their guns thundering. Terror cracking through the air. She brings up the staff in one hand and holds out the other towards the Saxons, with her palm towards them. Reflexively, protectively. Flinching behind the staff and turning her eyes away.

She doesn't die. When she looks back at the Saxons, the air is shimmering in front of her. The bullets have stopped, tiny deadly lumps of metal suspended motionless. Held there only by her desperate force of will. But the Saxons keep firing. More and more bullets crashing against the hard air, gathering like flies on a windscreen. So many of them that she feels her heart shrink, starts to ask herself what the fuck she thinks she's doing. These are men who've been paid to kill people like her, men who probably disdain everything she stands for, men who are now scared of her because of what she's done to their mates. Men who have lots of spare bullets to burn through. How long can she keep doing this, holding them back?

Doubt takes hold of her. The barrier grows thinner. One or two bullets break through, cracking the window of a perfume shop behind her. Makes her realise that doubt is the problem. The more she doubts herself, the more her fears become true.

So she chooses to believe that she can win. She thrusts the staff forward in both hands, and the bullets fly back to where they came from, tearing through their former masters. The Saxons fall down dead.

Did she always have the power to do this? When she saw Kay and Regan doing this kind of stuff, she thought it was because they were special. Now she's starting to wonder why she thought that. Maybe everyone can do it. Maybe you don't need to be part of a special club if you want to wield this kind of power. You don't need to be ancient and powerful and clever. You just need the willingness to try.

More Saxons, coming from everywhere. Mariam starts to get creative, testing the limits of what the staff can do. Using it to levitate Saxons from a distance and throw them through shop windows, hurling mannequins at them, pelting them with sharp diamonds, tearing their guns away from them. It becomes a running battle of bullets versus whatever she can come up with on the hoof. Turning them into hamsters, flamingos, giant snails. They chase her past some kind of spa wellness centre, so she draws the water up out of the swimming pool and sends it roaring at them like a tidal wave. Knocking them down with tanning beds and gym equipment. Right at the end of the mall there's a big metal statue of a man holding the world on his shoulders, but she tears it down, sending the iron globe rolling down the concourse. Bowling over any Saxons who are still standing. She leaves the place ransacked and flooding, covered in broken glass and dead Saxons and scattered tiaras. The giant snail moves slowly through the wreckage, looking for plants to eat.

She feels a twinge of guilt. It doesn't bring her any pleasure, doling out justice like this. They're all just humans, behind the war gear. But they're humans who didn't see a problem with becoming mercenaries and shooting at her. Overgrown boys playing with their lethal toys. It's probably easy to feel inhuman when you can hide your humanity behind masks and helmets. Makes it easier to do inhuman things. If she does end up being queen of anywhere, when all of this is over, she'll get rid of uniforms before she does anything else.

Right now she'll settle for saving her friends. She heads for the stairs, thinking about the future. About green trees rustling in the wind.

41

There's a checkpoint just north of Shepton Mallet manned by a few bored Saxons watching a monsoon roll south towards them. They have sunglasses and concrete roadblocks and a heavy machine gun that doesn't work in hot weather, but they're being paid to guard this stretch of road, so that's what they're doing. They stand sweating in the damp heat with their rifles slung low across their chests, weighed down with gear that they don't need, wishing they had a crate of cold beer to slake their thirst. Waiting for the rain to come.

They probably feel prepared for any Welsh insurgents who come down the road towards them. They're not prepared for Arthurian knights. But that's what they see, drawing closer. Two men in chainmail, one of them riding a Brough Superior, the other riding a white horse and keeping pace. It's such a strange thing to see that the Saxons don't raise their weapons until the knights are almost upon them. Then they start blazing from the hip, rifles chattering. But the bullets seem to fly in strange directions, steered awry by some magnetic force. The machine gun jams, as usual. And the knights sweep through them, with the thunder of hooves and the growl of the engine. Their swords flash in the sunlight. Three dead Saxons are left in their wake.

Kay likes this horse. She seems to know where he wants her to take him. She can somehow keep pace with Lancelot's two-wheeled contraption without tiring, though they must have galloped a hundred miles without pause since The Wizard Inn. He doesn't question what magic allows her to run so fast or for so long. All he has to do is hold on.

This used to be their old stomping ground: the heartland of Britain, the frontiers of Arthur's kingdom. But the frontiers of men often become the frontiers between other worlds as well, where the map is unsure of itself and territory is always shifting. It's places like this where one could easily slip through into the fay realm, if one wasn't careful. Where magic flows a bit more freely, up from the earth. And so it hastens their journey, quickening their way. Roads of the realm bending to their aid, as they used to do in the old days.

'How much further?' he shouts.

But Lancelot can't hear him. He's listening to something called 'The Final Countdown' on his little music box. Galehaut's tree is lashed very carefully to the back of his bike, still in its bag of soil.

They can only find one road leading to the Tor. Glastonbury made into an island once again; a narrow land bridge connecting it with the rest of Britain, as in the old days. They ride down it, water on either side of them, trampling and exsanguinating a few more Saxons on the way. A helpful force lends weight to their blades, and Kay is grateful for it, wherever it comes from. God working through them, or old Herne granting them the last of his power, if he has any left to give.

Then the Tor stands tall in front of them, with the sun behind it. Even from a distance they can see the host of people gathered in the fields beneath, packed together. Thousands of them. Making noise and chanting something. Chanting Arthur's name.

Kay feels fear gripping coldly at his heart. He's fought dragons and worse. Faced the Viking horde. Weathered the French and German armies in their multitudes. Fear was a constant companion through all of that, but he can't remember feeling this frightened before. Not for a long while, at least. Not since he was a boy.

He knows that he might not come back again this time. That might be why. Harder to be a hero when you know you're just as mortal as any bugger else. Nothing brave about dying when it doesn't mean anything; plenty brave about dying when you might not come back. First time he's had to be brave in a thousand years or so.

Well, time to be brave, then.

They stop a safe distance from the crowd, in an empty field that's mostly dry, leaving their mounts under a row of trees. Kay stops to stroke his horse's neck once he's down from the saddle, feeling grateful.

'Can make yourself scarce, if you want,' he says to the horse. 'We might not be coming back.'

The horse seems to know what he's saying, but it stands its ground. Waiting to see if he survives and comes back. He's even more grateful for that.

Lancelot has taken Galehaut's tree from the back of his bike. Now he stands and holds it awkwardly, looking for somewhere good to plant it. It seemed like a better plan when they were still in the cave. Now they're here in a nice green field, with no spades or picks to break the earth.

So they kneel and use their swords, driving them down into the earth two-handed. Then scrabbling with their hands to clear the broken earth away. There probably isn't time for this, not really. But if they get killed, which they probably will, then Galehaut's tree will just wither and die in its plastic bag. And Kay wouldn't want that to happen.

They put the tree in place and pack the earth around the roots. Then they stand to admire their handiwork.

'Thank you for that,' says Lancelot.

'S'all right,' says Kay. He sniffs. 'Nice spot.'

'Hm. I think he'd like it here.'

It feels like they ought to say something else. Like they ought to kneel and pray, perhaps. But Galehaut was never the most Christian man, even in the old days. And Kay can scarcely hear himself think over the chanting, let alone pray. There's still a field or two between themselves and the crowd, but that doesn't seem to deaden the noise.

'He wouldn't have liked all of that racket, though,' he says.

'No,' says Lancelot.

'Shall we go see if we can shut them up?'

'Capital idea.'

They stroll towards the crowd on foot, across the damp field. Hiding behind a hedge, as they draw near. Kay peers through the leaves and finds himself looking at an army. Several armies, in fact. The Welsh and the Cornish and the Army of Saint George, getting into vague and muddled ranks. The racists are standing around getting sunburnt in cheap crusader costumes, clapping their hands, chanting. *We love you Arthur, we do. We love you Arthur, we do.* Drinking beer out of plastic cups.

Nobody is keeping watch. If Kay had a decent body of men with him, even just archers, he could take the whole lot of them by surprise. Attack them from behind the hedge and drop a fair quarter of them before they knew what was happening. But he doesn't have any archers. He just has himself, and Lancelot, and their swords. That will have to do.

489

In the centre of the crowd, near the foot of the Tor, is the stage that he saw on the television. Built for Arthur's coronation. It's empty now, but it may not be empty for much longer.

'What's the plan?' asks Lancelot.

'I reckon we just walk through.'

'Ah,' says Lancelot. 'The "get shot as quickly as possible" approach. Yes, very cunning. Very astute.'

'Come on,' says Kay, moving forward.

Lancelot grabs him by the sword belt and tries to hold him back. 'Are you mad? There's thousands of them.'

'Exactly,' says Kay. 'Nobody'll notice two more, will they?'

Lancelot seems to consider this, for a moment. Then he nods and lets go.

So they scramble through the hedge together and start moving through the crowd. Swords at their hips and shields strapped to their arms.

It's like a festival, this place. There are huge television screens showing better views of the stage and whirligigs buzzing over-head, which must be filming everything. The crowd is packed in tight, Welshmen and Cornishmen rubbing shoulders with Cumbrians and Soldiers of Saint George. Hard to press through. Some of the Saint George men see Kay and start making monkey noises. He ignores them, walking past.

'Even if we do kill Arthur,' says Lancelot, close behind him, 'they're not going to let us get away with it.'

'I know,' says Kay.

'So what's the plan for getting out?'

'There isn't one.'

Lancelot sighs. 'I was afraid you were going to say that.'

That was how they did things in the last war. He tries to treat it like that. Just another mission. Walking into danger, surrounded by Nazis. Nothing he hasn't done twelve times before. The only difference this time is that he might not come back again, if he dies again here now in this place.

Something about that starts to feel right. If he has to go then maybe it should be like this. Him and Arthur and Lancelot, in the shadow of some damp hill somewhere. That's how it all started. Maybe that's how it all ends.

They wind their way slowly through the mass of bodies, closer to the stage. Further up the Tor there are men in suits and sunglasses behind a line of Saxons. He can see them on the big telly screens, drinking champagne, like this is some kind of garden party. Those are probably the people that Mariam doesn't like, if he had to guess. The real enemies in this war. They have their backs to the water, to the Avalon platform, looming hideous in a haze of heat behind them. Big whirligig sitting on the Tor beside them, in case they need a quick exit. Could press uphill and start doing slaughter to them before the whirligig gets away, but that wouldn't achieve much. He knows why he's here.

There's a bodyguard of short-sleeved Nazi bruisers standing with their backs to the stage, arms folded, cross of Saint George painted on their faces. Holding back the crowd with glowering stares. Behind them a wooden throne sits on the empty stage. Arthur has yet to show himself.

'What do we do when he turns up?' asks Lancelot, shouting in his ear to be heard above the crowd. 'Take him together?'

Kay shakes his head. 'I'll go up first and tire him out. Then, once I'm down, you step in and finish the job.'

Lancelot doesn't look happy about that notion. But he nods.

They work their way down the line of Saint George men, looking for an opening. Pressed in by bodies behind them. Deafened by the crowd. Until Kay sees a bodyguard who looks shorter than the others. Thinner and reedier, with slightly squirrelly teeth.

'All right, then, Barry?' he asks. 'Fancy seeing you here.'

Barry swallows, looking him up and down. Glancing at the bruisers on either side of him. They don't look impressed.

'You know this fella, Baz?' asks the bruiser to his right, with gravel in his throat.

'Uh . . . yeah,' says Barry. 'Yeah, he's sound. He's a mate of mine.'

The bruiser sneers. 'Doesn't look like a mate of yours.'

Lancelot appears at his shoulder with a broad white grin. Always was good at this sort of thing. 'We're part of the ceremony,' he says. 'We go on halfway through.'

'Isn't that right, Barry?' says Kay.

Barry looks uncertain. He licks his lips. Weighs up his options. And then he starts nodding to himself. 'Yeah,' he says. 'Yeah! That's right. We have to let them on, halfway through. That's what the Saxons said, anyway.'

The other bruiser scowls at them like he doesn't believe it. But then he looks again at what they're wearing. Swords and chainmail. Old stuff. Coronation stuff, maybe. He shrugs. He goes back to watching the crowd. He lets them stand there. Kay winks at Barry, and Barry grins back at him.

So they wait, facing the bodyguard. Deafened by chanting behind them. And eventually figures appear, walking down from the Tor. Their image is projected onto the television screens for anyone too far away to make them out. A great cheer goes up.

Arthur leads, slowly and determinedly, wearing a robe of ermine and the kind of scowl that he used to reserve for state occasions. There's a train of priests behind him – the priests of Noah that Kay saw in Manchester, garbed now in golden vestments, with their snorkels and flippers and diving masks. One of them is carrying a crown.

Kay remembers the first time he saw a golden band placed upon Arthur's head. Surrounded by gruff chieftains in the hoary wilds of Gwynedd, with tall trees around them. Back in the time when anyone could call themselves king. He spent that whole morning wondering if it ought to have been him instead. Not because he wanted to be king – because he wanted to spare Arthur the weight of that crown on his head. Still a stripling youth. The young king with fear in his eyes.

No such fear today. Arthur probably thinks this is his right, now. No less than he's due. When he reaches the stage he kneels on a red cushion in front of the throne, holding Caliburn in front of him like the cross. Whispering a prayer into the hilt, with his eyes closed. One of the priests approaches from behind, slow and stately, and begins to speak. Warbling into his snorkel. Raising the crown to place atop Arthur's head.

Kay nods at Barry, who moves aside to make a gap.

He didn't stop the first coronation, all those years ago. But he can still stop this one. He steps up onto the stage and draws his sword.

'I challenge you!' he says. His own voice echoes back from speakers, all around the Tor. There are whirligigs buzzing. Cameras filming. This might be going out to everyone in the country. He feels a thousand eyes on him from the crowd. But mostly he's concerned with Arthur's eyes. Sharp and green and staring at him with a tangle of hard feelings. There's a strain of contempt woven in there, but there's other things as well.

'You what?' asks Arthur.

'I don't think you're worthy of being king,' says Kay, 'so I'm challenging you. Like in the old days. Single combat. You can prove yourself worthy by defeating me.'

Arthur kneels where he is. Kay knows the worn tracks of Arthur's mind well enough to guess what he must be thinking. He could just order the Saxons to shoot him, but would he do that in front of this crowd? In front of the nation? Not now that his worth has been called into question. There's only one thing he can do to preserve his sense of honour. He gets slowly to his feet, holding Caliburn down at his side.

'All right,' says Arthur. 'Come on, then. I accept your challenge!'

He bellows the last part, and the crowd roars back at him with cheers and thunder. They think this is part of the festivities. Like a wrestling match. When was the last time they had a king who actually fought people?

Arthur lets his robe fall to the ground. Scalemail gleaming underneath. Forearms bulging as he hefts Caliburn in both hands. No shield, which might put him at a disadvantage if he was anybody else. But Arthur is Arthur. He never needed a shield to beat anyone. Two hands on the sword will make for a stronger parry. It will give him more power on any thrusts or downward strokes.

Kay tightens his oak hand around the hilt of his own sword. He brings up his shield to cover himself, feeling oddly calm about all of this. If this is how he's ordained to die, then so be it. Long overdue.

They circle each other on the stage. Sizing each other up. Been a while since they did this. Normally Arthur might wait for him to make the first move, but the crowd is already chanting his name. Cheering him on. He won't want to look weak in front of them.

So Arthur calls up a primal bear cry from somewhere deep in his soul and comes forward, swinging Caliburn down mightily from overhead.

Not much room to give ground, here. The stage is a small arena boxed in by Saxons, who are trying to hold back the baying crowd. So he has to keep circling, sidestepping. Not much point trying to attack, trying to outmatch Arthur's strength. Better to try and outlast his fury. Let him burn through his anger, use it up, tire himself out. Kay is happy to defend, favouring his shield. Circling around the stage as much as he can. All about the footwork. Letting Arthur hack away at him, taking chunks from his shield.

He knocks Arthur off balance with a timely shield bash and sees a fleeting chance to plunge his sword into Arthur's belly. But he doesn't take it. Arthur recovers his form and goes back on the offensive. Kay has to fall back and circle again.

Stupid to have passed up an opening like that. He's dragging this out to try and make Arthur tired, but that's not the only reason. Might as well admit it to himself. Even now, after all of this, he doesn't really want to kill Arthur. It was the same in the old days, when Arthur started burning pagans, seeing enemies everywhere, going slowly mad. Paranoid and wild-eyed. Even then, he couldn't quite bring himself to raise his sword against his own brother. The same brother he'd grown up with, sparred with in the stable yard, seen kneeling in the wilds of Gwynedd with fear in his eyes.

Maybe it's different now. If Arthur puts that crown on his head then the world will be filled with nightmares. But that was true in the old days as well, wasn't it? Nightmares of a different sort. Maybe he should have killed him centuries ago. Ended the madness, before any of this could come to pass. Maybe it's his fault if the world gets plunged into fire and chaos. His fault for not doing this earlier.

So he starts to take more chances. Lashing out more often. Looking for more openings. He waits for another downward swing, then he lunges for the stomach.

But Arthur is Arthur. He's not going to run onto your sword-point and make things easy for you. The great downward swing was just a feint to make his chest look open. Now Caliburn comes crashing down hilt first, with the weight of both of Arthur's fists. Batting Kay's swordpoint low. Nearly knocking it from his hand.

And the next thing he knows is Arthur's right fist cutting across to catch him in the jaw.

It goes on like this for a while, Arthur constantly changing style. Going from a street-brawler's low and hungry stance to a sudden kingly posture between sword strokes. Coming on with Roman poise and grace, then going in for a knee to the groin. That's how he used to win in the old days. Besting anyone who dared to spar with him. Changing from brawn to elegance and back again, faster than anyone could keep up with.

But that was a thousand years ago, or more. Kay's been up and about a bit, since then. He learnt things from the Saxons, from the Normans, and everyone after. Learnt things that Arthur doesn't know. How to kill with a bayonet and a trench club. How to kill with just his bare hands. He learnt ungentlemanly warfare in the last big war. Throats, shins, eyes and ears. He tries to use some of that now. Sticking out one foot to try and trip Arthur.

It doesn't work.

Arthur goes for his outstretched leg, plunging Caliburn down through the back of his thigh. Blade scraping against bark and bone. His leg goes limp beneath him, and he shifts his weight to his other side, struggling not to fall. Hopping backwards. Dragging his left foot.

The crowd roars. Arthur lets him retreat a few paces. Busy scowling at Caliburn, eyes moving up and down the blade, which is coated with yellow sap instead of blood. Arthur looks at him with disgust. No brotherly love beneath that sneer. It's probably easier to kill your brother when he starts bleeding tree sap. Easier to think of him as a monstrosity, something from the Otherworld. Not your human brother after all.

Arthur comes forward again, and Kay raises his shield.

42

Mariam stands in Avalon's security centre, a dark room full of bright TV monitors. The floor is covered in rabbits who used to be people, hopping between piles of their clothes and war gear.

She looks over the bank of screens in front of her, scanning from room to room. Looking for signs of her friends. There are so many levels, so many corners of this thing. She can see prison cells, but the cells are empty. There are Saxons running down the corridors, but they're not coming up here to try and kill her. They're going to the landing pads, getting into big drone gunships, flying away. Where could they be going that's more important than here? One of the feeds is showing Arthur's coronation, and it's only now that she sees Kay on the screen. Fighting with Arthur, on the stage.

She reaches out towards the screen, then snatches her hand back. There's people who need help, but Kay isn't helping them. He's decided that stabbing somebody is the best solution to the problem. Like the fight in Manchester, all over again. Wrestling in the mud when he could be slaying dragons. At least now he's fighting the right person. Drawing the Saxons away. She lets herself feel grateful for that. Forcing down any other feelings that she doesn't have time to deal with right now.

There's something else, on one of the other screens. Down on the lowest levels of the Avalon she can see a procession of people in weird robes. More Saxons following behind them. And with them are four figures with their hands tied behind their backs. Hoods over their heads. She can't see their faces, but she knows who they must be.

Five minutes later she kicks open a door and finds herself outside, exposed to the wind. It's not spas and tennis courts down here, on the lowest levels of the Avalon. This must be where the ecocide happens. She can see pipes bundled together, running next to dirty metal staircases. Machinery whirring. Oil being pumped up from the ground. Catwalks hanging over nothing, with floodwater far below them.

She's never been keen on heights. But this is the only way to get where she's going, as far as she can tell. The pipes and the walkways all lead to a donut-shaped structure hanging beneath the oil rig. The wellhead. That's where the controls are, to cut off the oil flow. That's where she'll find her friends.

Can she just zap herself there, with the staff? She has the sense that you shouldn't use power like this just to make things easier for yourself. You should only use it when you have to. So she doesn't zap herself across. She puts one foot down on the thin mesh catwalk, with her teeth clenched together. It feels fragile underfoot, but it doesn't break or bend. It holds her weight. She puts the other foot down and starts running.

There are more Saxons behind her, charging down staircases, shouting orders. Boots ringing against the catwalks. How many of them are there on this thing? She jabs the staff at them, almost lazily at this point. Turning them into lemurs, armadillos, porcupines. One of them becomes an octopus, wrapping his tentacles around the walkway, trying not to ooze through the holes in the grating.

There's nothing between her and the wellhead, now. She dares to hope that she might actually be able to do this. But then she hears death buzzing in the air. A big drone gunship flies down from somewhere and drops below the oil rig, coming level with her. Already spooling up its guns.

No time to lift the staff or think of magic. Mariam dives down behind a hub of pipes and valves, some kind of substation, bashing her knees against the catwalk. Just quickly enough. The drone starts firing, guns roaring to life with a horrible solid noise, burring and electronic. Filling the air with bullets, peppering the catwalk, throwing up sparks. She makes herself as small as possible, hugging her knees, feeling soft and fragile and easily killable. One of the bullets punches through a pipe above her, and she hears hissing. Smells petrol. Looks up to see a jet of gas discolouring the air.

The old despair comes back. How long will this go on for? How can it be stopped? This is what happens when you just keep building, hoping that technology will solve everything, without caring about the planet. Without pausing to think about how the technology will interact with the world. The whole process becomes automated. It reproduces itself without any need for human input. Reaping the world for fuel. Destroying the world that it's supposed to protect. Spiralling out of control, like a dance of death.

Well, she can't stop the whole dance of death, but she can try to kill this one expression of it, this one avatar of what's wrong with the world.

She looks at the staff. She can't pop out of cover and turn the drone into a whale, or whatever; there's too much death in the air. She'd be cut down before she could stand up. But there might be something else she can do. She has about eight pounds of plastic explosives in her backpack. If she uses them now then she won't have any left to blow up the Avalon. But if she doesn't do it then she's never going to get past this thing. Her friends will die. This weird ritual will happen. Everything will be fucked.

It might not be the smart thing to do, but it's the right thing to do.

She rifles through her bag and pulls out the C4, taped together. Shoving the detonator pin down into it and setting the timer. This is the part of the plan that she knows how to do, the part that she's been trained for. They learnt years ago, in secret workshops, how to use explosives properly. They practised it in the camp. It doesn't take much C4 to blow something up, even something big like this machine. It's all about planting it in the right place.

The gunship fires again. More bullets, more dents and sparks and ricochets. More chance of death. She's less sure about the other part of the plan, the magic part, but she can't think of any other way. So she grits her teeth and arms the detonator. The timer starts counting down. Ten seconds. She closes her eyes, holding the staff so tightly that she can feel it shaking in her fist. Thinking about where she wants to be.

It feels like being sucked through a keyhole, or folded up and fed through the eye of a needle. Then she's in the air, buffeted by the wind. She has zapped herself to five feet above the drone, and now she falls towards it, terrified that she'll be minced by the rotor blades. But she lands between them, on its broad back, in the space between the engines. The buzzing in her ears is far too loud. The surface is smooth polymer, not providing many footholds. She scrambles to stay where she is, pinning herself with her knees and elbows. There's five seconds left on the timer, so she sticks the charges down and holds the staff up high again, zapping away. She feels time bending around her. She feels the urge to be sick. Then she's back on the walkway, falling against it, banging her knees again. Rolling back into her hiding place and covering her ears.

The charges detonate. Mariam hears the sudden bang, the note of distress in the drone's engines, the crunch of polymer and the tinkle of glass as the drone is shattered, broken like an expensive toy. And then she feels safe standing up, watching it fall. Burning and spinning, trailing smoke, plunging alongside fragments of itself, until it ploughs into the water far below.

She has no explosives left, but she doesn't care. The only thing she regrets is that her friends weren't here to see how cool that was. She should probably go and rescue them, so she can tell them about it.

Tiredness washes over her. Limbs numb and ears ringing. Adrenaline wearing thin. She'd like to lie here and close her eyes for five minutes. But she can't do that. She's the guardian of the gate, now, isn't she? Whatever that means. She has to stop bad things happening. Has to stop nightmares from leaking into the world. She has to save the planet. And she has to save her friends. If she doesn't do it, nobody will.

There's nobody on her heels as she reaches the hatch. Nobody to follow her through.

The wellhead is dark and round, like an old Roman theatre plunged into shadow. Mariam is expecting the pipes and tubes and machinery running round the edges, the giant Christmas tree of valves and ducts that crawl up from the well itself. She knows all of that from diagrams and plans. She's not expecting twelve men in black robes, standing around a hole in the floor. She's not expecting the column of pale light burning upwards from somewhere far below. She's not expecting the big grey stone hanging weightlessly in the air, in just the way that big stones shouldn't.

Her friends are here. Willow and Teoni and Roz and Bronte. Kneeling around the hole with their hands bound behind them and the hoods still drawn over their heads. She can hear Bronte crying, faintly. Somebody else, one of the nameless men, is chanting in Latin.

She doesn't know exactly what they're doing, but she knows that she's not going to let them finish. The staff is so hot against her hand that it's almost painful. She holds it out towards the black-robed men and thinks about destroying them. Turning them all to dust.

But nothing happens. Sparks fly upwards from the staff's end and rise towards the giant stone. She sees the air shimmering. The carvings on the stone glow brightly for an instant.

It's enough for the robed men to notice her. One of them wears red robes, different from the others. He has Bronte kneeling in front of him. Now he grabs her by the arm and pulls her up. Pulling off her hood. One of his hands moves to cover her mouth. The other holds an ornate knife to her throat. Bronte's eyes are wide and brimming with tears.

The man with the red robes reveals a gaunt, liver-spotted face under his hood, like a man who's lived too long and somehow cheated death. Now he grins at her with yellow teeth.

'Hello, Mariam,' he says. 'That is your name, isn't it?'

She doesn't know the names of these people, but she knows exactly who they are. They're what's wrong with the world. They're the old men who try to make things worse instead of better. She wants to turn them into snails and stamp on their shells so there wouldn't be anything left of them but slime and fragments. But Bronte wouldn't want her to do that. Bronte would want her to try compassion first.

'I'm afraid that stick of yours won't do much good in here,' says the old man. 'The lodestone is far more powerful. It absorbs any latent geothaumic energy in the room. We're collecting it for our little ritual. So you might as well put the staff down.'

She can hear muffled sounds from Bronte and the others. Shouting her name through their hoods. Fighting against their handcuffs. The four strongest women she's ever met, reduced to this. It makes her so angry that her mouth starts quivering.

'Let my friends go,' she says. 'You can keep me if you want to. But let them go.'

'That's very courageous of you,' says the old man. 'But I'm afraid that wouldn't suit our purposes. We need quite a lot of blood, you see, to do what we're trying to do. All of this old magic needs blood. It's frightfully barbarous, but that's ancient druids for you.'

'If you let her go then I'll let you leave,' she says. 'You can run away somewhere. Somewhere far from here.'

'Well,' says the old man. 'Clearly, you're a reasonable young woman, Mariam. And that's a very generous offer. But I'm afraid there isn't anywhere to go. Oceans dying and crops failing, and so on. I don't need to tell you that, do I? And there's not a great deal that can be done about it, I'm afraid. It's far too late to try and save the world.'

'That's not true,' says Mariam. 'Maybe you've given up, but I haven't.'

The old man just laughs at her. 'It's not a question of giving up,' he says. 'My friends and I made a deal with the devil, a very long time ago. We're going to live forever. And now that we know what forever looks like, we'd rather spend it in the faerie realm. Not here, in the real world, on a dead planet.'

'But you're the people who killed it,' says Mariam. 'This is all your fault. You can't just run away from that.'

The old man shrugs. 'That's immaterial now. Why don't you put the staff down, and perhaps we can continue this conversation like reasonable adults?'

She stares at him long enough to realise something. There's fear, real fear, in his old, dead eyes. Hidden behind the brash smug attitude and the condescending smile. He's afraid. Afraid of a young woman with power. Afraid of what she might do.

'Just wondering,' she asks, 'if the staff won't do any good in here, then why do you want me to put it down?'

The old man loses his composure. Then he cries out in pain because Bronte – gentle, non-violent Bronte – has bitten down hard on his fingers. Mariam sees blood. She sees Bronte duck away and fall against the floor, leaving the old man standing, stunned, with two fingers missing from his hand.

Mariam has half a second in which to do something.

She only has one idea. The great floating stone above them is like a big magic battery. And Kay told her out on the moor that the staff is a kind of lightning rod. So maybe this will work.

She points the staff up at the lodestone, thinking hard about what she wants to do. Letting herself get angry now. These men, standing in this room, are the men who stole her future. They've been putting the stone of despair on her chest every morning and pushing down with it, to crush the hope out of her. They've burnt through any compassion that she had left for them. All she has left is anger. And it's anger that draws the magic down. Not any noble or kind-hearted feeling, like her desire to save the world. She just tells the lodestone that these men are evil. And she feels as if the lodestone agrees with her. Like it wants to help.

She feels her face tingling. Her hair standing on end. She feels a shift in the magnetism of the room. Something changing, deep in her marrow. The old man must have felt it as well. He looks up at the lodestone for an uneasy moment.

And then a bolt of lightning arcs down towards her, striking the tip of the staff. Burning itself into her eyeballs. Thundering through her bones.

When you get hit by lightning, you should die, shouldn't you? All the wet meat parts of you should fry and sizzle. You shouldn't survive. You definitely shouldn't start floating into the air and seeing in five dimensions. But that's what happens. When Mariam can see again she looks down and finds that her shoes have left the floor. She is floating, slowly, up towards the ceiling. Lightning crackling around her. The staff is red hot, smoking against her hands, but she can't unclench her grasp. Not now. She can feel times in the past when her hand wasn't burning. Times in the future when the wound will have healed. She focuses on those moments. Not the painful present.

She can see other things as well. Not just the inside of the room, and the deep shaft yawning underneath her, and her friends kneeling around it. Not just the past and future. The lightning has done something to her eyes. It's like she can see physics. Waves arcing off in all directions. Field lines and particles and other things that she doesn't understand. She can see the heat in the old man's skin. She can see his fragile skeleton. The electrical signals firing in his brain. The fear in his heart.

She points the staff down towards him and sends all of her anger surging through it.

The old man's eyes flash with terrible knowledge. Then

505

lightning strikes him squarely in the chest. He doesn't turn into a rabbit or a squirrel or anything else harmless. This is worse. His skin wizens and shrivels, turning to leather on the spot. Fire erupts from his heart and starts burning outwards, turning his flesh to ashes. And when there's barely any of him left, he falls forwards, into the great pit. Plunging downwards.

The lightning tears through the other twelve men, leaping from one to the next. Burning through them, until there's nothing left but a bad smell. But Mariam is barely aware of that, anymore. She is everywhere and nowhere. Then and now and forever. Mind growing quickly, to fill the world.

43

Kay falls to his hands and knees. Arthur stands over him with a sneer on his face, fist curled around the hilt of Caliburn.

'Stand,' says Arthur. 'Or I'll kill you on your knees.'

Kay tries to wipe the sap from his mouth. He's been killed on his knees before, but now seems like a bad time to mention that. It appears that Arthur doesn't share his qualms about fratricide.

The crowd are still cheering, baying for blood. They want to see their new king kill this unknown challenger. Arthur seems happy to oblige them. The admiration of his people is more important to him than the love of his brother. That was always the way.

There isn't enough strength left in his oak limbs to stand and fight another bout. Caliburn has bitten his shield into a state of uselessness. He tries to take up his sword from where it lies, but Arthur stamps on the blade, bringing his foot down hard so that it snaps in two. He's left holding the hilt, with a jagged stub of blade protruding from it. First time that's ever happened in a thousand years.

Kay drops it, lets it fall to the stage with a clang. It hasn't been doing him much good recently, that crude killing tool. It wouldn't have saved him here. Wouldn't have saved anybody else either. Only thing that will save him now is the tongue between his teeth, if he remembers how to use it before Arthur cuts it out of his head.

'Listen,' he says. 'Addy.'

'No,' says Arthur. 'The only thing I want to hear from you right now is prayer. Prayer for your immortal soul.'

That might not be a bad idea. Offering a silent prayer up to heaven. Wyn, if you're up there. Bake some more honey cakes. He turns his head far enough to see the Avalon tower, still standing hazy in the distance. There is lightning in the sky above it. Part of him was hoping to hear a great boom, like he did at Preston, while he was still fighting Arthur. See the whole thing burning, black smoke rising from the ruins. That would have been good enough. He'd have known then that Mariam had achieved something. It wouldn't have been a bad thing to see, in his last moments. But Avalon still stands.

Arthur changes his stance. Plants his feet for better purchase. Brings Caliburn up, so that he can bring it crashing down again.

And then he stops, because somebody else has joined them on the stage.

'Oh, Christ,' says Arthur. 'Not you as well.'

Kay looks up in time to see Lancelot shrug. 'I'm nothing if not consistent.'

'I should never have placed my faith in you again,' says Arthur.

'Yes,' says Lancelot. 'Even for you, that was particularly stupid.'

Kay smiles down at the stage. This is Lance trying to goad Arthur, and it's working. No quicker way to inflame his wrath than to insult his intelligence.

'That's how it is, then,' says Arthur. 'No castle walls to save you now.'

Arthur steps away to clash with Lance. Kay doesn't watch. He hears the chanting go up again, hears their footwork on the stage and the sound of Caliburn eating into Lance's shield. But he focuses on himself. On finding the strength to stand up. Getting his bad leg under him and trying to put weight on it. Clenching his teeth against the pain. There are still bald men shouting foul things from the crowd. They're starting to get impatient. One of them throws a can full of beer that sails past him, inches from his face. He ignores it. Ignores the laughter. Ignores the other missiles bouncing off the stage around him. He manages to stand, shaking uncertainly. Barely hearing anything, as the sap rushes to his feet. Like the crowd are shouting through an ocean of water.

Arthur has Lancelot on the ropes, but there's a new wound on Arthur's cheek which wasn't there before. It looks like Lance is about to push back when somebody from the crowd reaches up and grabs his ankle. Pulling him off-balance for half a moment. Long enough for Arthur to strike. Kay can't quite tell whether Caliburn cleaves straight through Lancelot's shoulder or whether it just strikes him flat-edged with enough force to beat him down. Either way, Lancelot falls from the stage, dragged down into the crowd by clawing hands.

He shouts Lance's name, but he can't hear himself.

Arthur's attention turns back to him. He's earnt some measure of respect by standing back up again. Arthur always respected steadfastness, bloody-minded doggedness, more than he respected compassion or reason. A good soldier stands back up again when he gets knocked down. And he keeps standing back up again while there's breath left in him. That's what their father taught them both, a very long time ago. It feels like they're back

509

in the stable yard, not here on this stage at the end of the world. Maybe that's why he feels like he can speak his mind.

'Addy,' he says, again. 'Just listen. For a moment. Let me speak.'

'You always thought you knew better than me,' says Arthur. 'Always trying to tell me why I was wrong.'

'And you never used to listen.'

'So what makes you imagine that I'll listen now?'

'Because they're using you, Addy! They think they can take you for a mug.'

'The fuck are you talking about?'

'Those men on the Tor,' he says. 'They're only feigning fealty. They're laughing at you, behind your back. They've got you doing tricks for them like a dancing bear.'

Arthur never liked being laughed at. He always feared that friends and allies were scheming against him, behind his back. Now he lowers his sword, eyes burning with fury. Fury tempered with curiosity. He wants to hear the rest.

'They brought me back to save the realm from peril,' says Arthur.

'They brought you back to weaken the veil! That's all they need you for. That fortress of theirs, it's a ship. They're going to ride it off to the other side and let all the horrors through. They'll leave you ruling over the end of days.'

'You're just like Lance and Morgan,' says Arthur. 'Lies and treachery.'

'Lance didn't betray you – he left because he figured out what they were doing! There's still time to stop them. Still time to make things right.'

Red lightning flashes in the distance, and Arthur looks away towards Avalon, over the crowd and the flooded plain. Kay knows that look in his eyes, the slow turning of thoughts. The slow tilting of the golden scales in the royal mind.

'Let me tell you how people remember you, Addy,' he says. 'You've never heard the stories, have you? You've been asleep the whole time. You've got no idea, the stories that people have been telling about you, for the past thousand years.'

Arthur feigns disinterest, but he feigns it poorly. He always used to worry what people would think of him after he was gone. Now he needs to know.

'What stories?'

'King Arthur was virtuous, and kind-hearted. That's how you are in all the stories. That's what they're expecting, from you. Kindness. Chivalry.'

Arthur looks around at the crowd baying for blood. He looks sceptical. 'Doesn't seem to me like they want kindness.'

'But there's more people than just them in the country,' says Kay. 'These people are here, and they're loud, and you might think that they speak for everyone. But it's not just them watching. The whole of Britain's watching.'

There are still whirligigs buzzing, cameras rolling, filming everything. Their words might be lost beneath the noise, but the picture's still going out. Beamed around the country into people's homes. Does Arthur understand that? He looks up at the giant screens with his eyes narrowed. Comprehension dawning.

Kay finds himself grinning, through the sap on his teeth. 'What do you want them to think, Addy? All the people in their homes, in the camps, wherever they are. All over the world. Do you want them to think you're some hard-edged bastard who'd kill his own brother? Or do you want them to think you're the king from all the stories? Do you want to look like a hero? It's up to you. How do you want to be remembered?'

Arthur stares out over the crowd, looking into their faces. Kay can read him like a book. There was always an idea in Arthur's head of how a king ought to be, but the idea was everchanging.

Kings are remembered for their strength. Kings are remembered for their virtue. Kings are remembered for their just laws and the happiness of their people. It was always the best way of checking his worst habits, making him compare himself to that model king in his head. Weighing himself on the scales of history. There will be more history, after this. There's always more history. He's wondering what that history will look like, and how it will be written.

'Why would they flee?' asks Arthur, eventually. 'Why would they leave this world and cross the veil?'

'They've been poisoning the world! Making the air foul. And they've been doing it for so long that the whole world's getting warmer. Ice melting and plants dying. All the old forests have been cut down. There's no boars in Britain anymore, no bears, no lynx.'

Arthur licks his lips. 'They told me about that. They said it was bollocks.'

'Well, they would say that, wouldn't they?'

Arthur looks over at the oil men in the distance. His eyes narrow. 'Yeah,' he says. 'I suppose they would.'

'And they know that they're doing it, but they don't care, because they're making a lot of money out of it. Spoiling the realm for everyone.'

'Like Vortigern,' says Arthur, eyes blazing suddenly. 'Growing fat while the realm starved. Letting the Saxons onto our shores.'

'Exactly,' says Kay, grinning. 'And if you took up your sword against them, then you'd be the hero, wouldn't you? You'd be just like Uther, killing Vortigern. You'd be the one who saved the realm from peril.'

The crowd are getting quiet now. They're getting bored of whatever this is. They want less talking and more fighting. Arthur looks over them, this band of Britons massed around him. He looks at the Saxons on the hill. He raises Caliburn above his head.

'People of Britain!' he bellows. 'You have been lied to. You have been misled. Do not fight amongst yourselves. The true enemy stands there, gorging themselves on the realm like fat leeches as they've done for a thousand years. Fleecing the coffers to line their own purses. Turning one Briton against another. While you fight your neighbour, the men on that hill are despoiling the land and plundering its riches. But no longer! Lay down your petty hatreds for one another. Take up your swords against your common foe. Come forth with me, and we'll rid their foul scourge from the realm forevermore! Forward with me! Forward with me!'

A great cry goes up. All of these people finally given a target for their rage, a target that isn't foreigners or people who look different. Arthur points Caliburn towards the Tor, then leaps down from the stage to lead the charge.

Kay feels proud of him, for the first time in sixteen hundred years. He doesn't have time to move before the stage is swarmed, people charging after Arthur, people slamming into him from all sides. He can't stand up again on his bleeding leg. Somebody kicks him in passing. Somebody else treads on his hand. On his calf. Feet stamping madly around him. Christ, he can't die like this. To get through everything and then to be killed like this and not find out what happens? He's been trampled to death before, and it's not an experience he'd care to repeat. Especially not now.

But then there's somebody helping him up, hauling him up by the arm, getting their head under his shoulder. When he looks to his saviour he finds that it's Lancelot, bloodied but still standing, dragging him up through gritted teeth.

'Come on, old thing,' says Lancelot. 'Can't have you falling behind.'

They stagger down the steps from the stage and find themselves being carried along by the crowd. It's one of the least orderly charges he's ever been part of. A few thousand men with bats and bars and chains and pipes, swarming uphill against a line of Saxons with assault rifles. Not good odds, all told. They only have the element of surprise for a few seconds before the Saxons start firing. Guns chattering. Whirligigs firing down from the sky. Shells arcing over the crowd and bursting into clouds of smoke. Kay sees the first glimpse of blood, the first few bodies falling. Arthur is right out in the vanguard, wearing only scalemail. Not enough to stop bullets. But you'd need an elephant gun to bring down Arthur mid-charge when he's wild with battle fury. There he is at the front, felling Saxons by the half-dozen. Caliburn gorging itself on Saxon blood. Like Badon Hill all over again.

Kay tries to catch up, hobbling along with Lancelot as the horde rushes past them. Armed with nothing. Most of the people around him aren't armed with anything either. Just their own vague ideas of what they're fighting for. Welshmen and Cornishmen and Cumbrians, and the Army of Saint George, charging after their new king. All charging together. That's got to count for something.

Some of the Saxons have batons and plastic shields. They form a shield-wall and stand their ground while their fellows fire down from further up the hill. Bodies start piling up. The smoke is thickening, burning his eyes and throat. Kay tries to push forward, tries to break a hole through the Saxon lines, but he can't get through the mob in front of him. Too thickly packed. It's all elbows and shoulders and firm backs. People can barely move. Like sardines, crammed in together. Bullets still pattering down into them, sending up spurts of blood, punching through two or three men apiece. He sees hesitation on people's faces. One or two people regretting their courage. Thinking of turning back, pushing back against the men behind them. There'll be a stampede if this turns into a rout. People scrambling over each other, trampling each other, to try and retreat. He's seen it happen before.

But then the Saxons start firing upwards, at something in the sky. He turns his gaze to trace their bullets, squinting through the smoke.

Morgan, riding a new dragon. Not a huge white queen like the one up north but a smaller bull, horned and bearded, with scales of burnished green. Where did she get that from? She must have conjured it up from somewhere, found it coiled and sleeping in some deep hollow beneath the earth or drawn it through the veil with sorcery. But here it is, snaking through the sky with death in its eyes. Swooping low, above the battle. Taking a deep breath.

Kay throws himself down and covers his head, pulling Lancelot down with him. Tasting soil. He hears the gout of flame before he feels it. Feels the searing heat on the tops of his fingers, the back of his neck.

It's a scene of devastation when he looks up. Grass blackened and Saxons chargrilled in their war gear. Shields melted and smouldering on the ground. Morgan is wheeling her dragon up again to wrestle with the buzzing whirligigs above, but she's burnt a path clean through the Saxon lines. And Arthur is already charging through it, with the crowd following at his heels. Wading through the fire and death towards the huddle of oil men terrified behind.

Kay picks himself up and limps after Arthur, struggling uphill, with Lancelot somewhere behind him. Looking for Saxons to kill. But he can't seem to find any. The crowd is spreading now in all directions, getting behind the Saxons, breaking up their lines. Breaking their helmets with pipes and bars. Some of the Saxons are trying to fall back, but there's nowhere to go, except the water. Or the top of the Tor, surrounded on all sides. The whirligigs are burning, spinning, falling from the sky. Morgan's dragon swooping down to grab a clutch of Saxons in its talons. Dropping them back to earth from a great height.

He feels a shift. It's the part of the battle that always sneaks up on you if you don't get killed before you see it. You never truly know whether you're winning or losing until it happens. And then it happens one of two ways. Either the enemy's behind you, and your own side's broken, and you feel your smallest hopes getting trampled. Or you realise suddenly that the day's won, and the fight's already over. The enemy's broken, and they'll flee to the hills or kneel and surrender, if they don't get butchered first. Arthur always leaned towards butchering in the old days. Doesn't seem like anything has changed there.

The charge reaches the oil people and it doesn't stop. It keeps going through them. Bats and chains and pipes swinging. People shouting. People fleeing. People begging. People getting beaten to the ground.

Kay stops. He's not eager to join the bloodbath. It wouldn't give him any satisfaction, stabbing these people through their suits. Staining their shirts red. He doesn't relish the sight of other people doing it either, but there's nothing he can do to stop it now. He set Arthur on this path, and Arthur ran down it, taking everyone else with him. All of these people with the scales fallen from their eyes.

Arthur will be somewhere far uphill by now. Near the top of the Tor, probably. No sense trying to find him until all the chaos is over. But this is how battles end – how they've always ended. A wild, murderous confusion that can't be stopped until it burns itself out. So Kay hobbles away towards the outskirts of the slaughter, through the smoke and blood. Not looking for anything except a moment's peace. A clear space of ground where he can fall down and bleed for a while.

He reaches the land's edge, where the smoke thins out over

the water. Some of the Saxons have been pushed back into the salt marsh before being slaughtered. Now the water is red. He slumps to his knees as he reaches it, bowing his head to whisper a quick prayer.

When he looks up to heaven he sees something dire through the smoke. A great column of pale light guttering upwards from the Avalon sea fort. A waxen light, ghostly and unwholesome. Piercing the heavens like an ashen spear. Clouds gyre around it, darkening as they gather. Lightning crackles in the heart of the storm.

Maybe Merlin was right. All their efforts for nought, and no green shoots remaining. Only doom.

44

Mariam feels as if a door has opened in the back of her skull and her mind has leaked out through it.

Is she still Mariam, or is she the world? Or is the world Mariam? There used to be a clear boundary between those two things. Now it's difficult to tell. She feels *old*. Older than Kay, older than Regan. Older than Arthur or the deer child in the woods.

She can feel water bubbling up from springs a hundred miles away and streaming down into rivers to join the sea. Blades of grass striving up towards sunlight. Ants digging in the soil. Trees stretching their limbs slowly and patiently. Leaves brushing against the sides of deer in the wilderness. Birds soaring on updraughts of warm air above the mountains. Whales moving slowly through the deep, black parts of the ocean. The whole world spinning slowly around the sun. Half of it warm and half of it cold.

It's beautiful for a brief moment before it becomes terrible. There are people starving in camps across the world, and she can feel the hunger in their bellies. The thirst in their throats. The sun baking down on them. She can smell tarmac bubbling on the streets of empty cities. She knows the confusion of a mother elephant who leads her calf children to a watering hole and finds only a dry lakebed. There are bodies withering in the sun, without any birds or flies circling to pick the flesh from the bones. Because the birds and flies are dead as well.

She tries to focus on the room around her, where smaller things are happening. Gethin helping the others out of their handcuffs. When did Gethin get here? He must have freed himself from the cells. Willow and Teoni are shouting up at her, trying to reach her shoes and pull her down. But they feel like very small things. She's aware of her little human body in the same way that she used to be aware of her little toenail. Hard to focus on just one room when she can hear the screaming of the earth's magnetic field. Taste the colour of the universe. Feel the weight of the moon tugging against her heart, as if her heart was the sea.

It's all too big. Her brain wasn't built to know all of this, to see all of these things at once. She wants to curl up somewhere and ignore it, make herself small, make herself unnoticeable to the world. But the staff is like a live wire, and the muscles in her arm are clenched around it, holding on too tightly to let go.

She's made herself part of this, this ritual. Part of the circuitry of the great, bad thing that's happening. The magic flows up from its source, through her, into the lodestone. Into the framework of the Avalon platform. She can feel the whole structure straining against itself. Tension building. Pipes rattling. And the sky chang-ing outside. Clouds broiling. Pressure building. Air warming as it moves inland, becoming more and more humid until the magic can leap freely through the moisture. And then it does, up from the ground, through the staff, through her, through the metal frame of the Avalon platform. Sending its bright fingers up into the sky.

She gets the feeling that they haven't stopped the world from ending by killing the old geezer and his mates. Bronte spilled some of his blood when she bit his fingers off. And there's far more blood outside, on the old hill. The ground is soaked with it. The water has turned red. The sacrifice has been accepted.

The veil is beginning to thin. It seems strange to Mariam now that she didn't already know about the veil between worlds. Now it seems so obvious. It was always there. Such a thin barrier, with so many horrors trapped on the other side of it. She can feel them, rather than see them. Things that should only be seen in nightmares, or on very bad acid trips. Things that have to take the form of dragons when they wriggle through into the waking world.

The world is already bad enough without it getting any worse. There are enough man-made horrors without these things getting through. She can't curl up and shy away from them. She's the guardian of the gate, isn't she? That's what Herne said. If she doesn't stop them, then nobody will. Not Kay or Regan. She can't rely on anyone else to do it for her.

If she's made herself part of the circuitry then maybe she can change what the circuitry is trying to do. This whole facility was built to help such a small number of people. Casting the rest of the world into darkness. Harnessing the surge in magic to do bad things. But maybe she can use the magic for something else if she wants to. Maybe she can use it to do good instead.

So she tries, gently at first, to change things. Trying to draw up magic from the earth. Into the staff. Into herself. Willing the veil to knit itself closed again with every ounce of courage she can dredge up.

As soon as she tries to change things, she attracts the attention of the monsters. They don't want her to impede their progress. Who is she, to try and stop them? They start probing for her, grasping and reaching. She can sense their anger – feel their dark, searching thoughts – until one of them blazes through her mind. Like a dragon, roaring, blazing electrically in her brain. Moving this tiny obstacle out of its way.

She falls, thrown down against the hard deck of the wellhead. Just Mariam again, and not the whole world anymore. Feeling like a huge part of her brain has been torn out. The staff clatters down next to her, smoking.

The light in the room has turned red, for danger. She can hear alarms blaring. The whole platform is shaking and groaning. She stares up at the ceiling, the image of the dragon still burnt into her eyeballs. Forgetting to breathe. But then there are faces looming over her. Willow and Teoni, kneeling at her side.

'You all right, pet?' asks Willow. 'You were fucking flying!'

'Yeah,' says Mariam. 'Yeah, I know.'

'Come on,' says Teoni. 'We've gotta get out of here. We've gotta go.'

'Aye,' says Gethin. 'Might be able to steal one of their drones, if we're quick about it.'

'No,' says Mariam. Shaking her head. Trying to sit up. 'No, I've got to stay here. I've got to stop them from breaking through.'

Willow scrunches up her face. 'Stop who? What are you talking about?'

'The bad things. I've got to keep them away. You guys go. I've got to stay here.'

She reaches for the staff and tries to pick it up again, but her hand is raw and painful from the first attempt. The top layer of skin has burnt away from her palm.

'Are you fucking mad?' asks Teoni.

'I don't have time to explain,' she says. 'I just have to stay here. I have to do this.'

Willow and Teoni share a glance over her. Roz and Bronte

521

come back from clamping the oil pipe, sealing the blowout projector. They look confused. Bronte still has blood on her face.

'Can she walk?' asks Roz.

'Yeah,' says Teoni. 'But she wants to stay here.'

Roz looks baffled. 'I don't know what you did with that stick, but this place is coming down. If you stay here you're gonna die.'

Mariam rolls over and grabs the staff with her left hand. Not quite as hot as it was, but still warm with potential. She uses it to help herself up, leaning on it like a walking stick.

'You guys go,' she says again. 'I've got to stay here. I've got to stop them. Nobody else is going to do it.'

Nothing happens for a long moment. There's silence, apart from the blaring klaxon. Mariam struggles to stand. They could pick her up and carry her if they wanted to. She'd be too weak to stop them.

But Roz starts nodding. 'Okay,' she says. 'Well, if you have to stay here, we'll stay here with you.'

Mariam shakes her head. 'No,' she says. 'I have to do this alone.'

'Bollocks,' says Willow. 'We can do it together. Whatever it is.'

'Fuck yeah!' says Teoni.

'Maybe we can help?' says Bronte.

'Aye,' says Gethin. 'What do you need?'

Mariam closes her eyes, feeling tired and grateful and overwhelmed. Knowing that there isn't much time to feel anything else. She has friends, standing around her, who are willing to help. Waiting for her to tell them what to do. It would be such a relief, to fall back on them. To let them help. But if there's one thing she's learnt in the past few days it's that she can't rely on anybody else. She has to do this herself.

'I'm sorry,' she says.

When you've done something painful once already it becomes that slight bit easier to do it again. She turns to face the lodestone and raises the staff. Lightning comes down and judders through her bones again.

And then she is everywhere again. In fields and deserts and cities and deep ocean trenches. In the clouds and the mountains and the stones on the beach. Floating here in this room, but everywhere else as well.

Before all of this she never really believed in any of Bronte's bollocks about energy and spirituality. About the Earth Mother. About the world having its own life force. But now she feels it so strongly that she can't deny it any longer. Because the life force is being torn from the earth, through the stone. Through her. She can feel the earth resisting, but the pull is too strong. The dark things are circling, from beyond the veil. Drawing closer.

Nothing stands in their way, except her. And she feels far too weak to stop them. Like she's guarding the threshold between worlds, with just the staff to wield against them. And they are so much larger than her. So much more devious. So much more willing to inflict pain. She can feel their tendrils reaching towards her. Ready to burn her up and cast her aside.

But then she feels a hand on her shoulder.

She's vaguely aware, in the real world, that her sisters have started meditating. It must have been Bronte's idea. They are sitting in a circle on the floor beneath her, cross-legged, with their eyes closed. Holding hands. Roz is sceptical. Teoni is scared. But they are all trying to help her. Lending her their strength, however they can. She can feel their thoughts, their hopes. They want to help.

Maybe she doesn't have to do this alone.

At the moment, they're all thinking different things. They all hold slightly different hopes in their hearts. So she tries to guide them, shepherding their thoughts, moulding their hopes, twining them all together into one single hope. All of their minds thinking the same thing, working towards the same goal, in harmony. Telling the magic what to do. Telling it to close the veil again, and shut out the darkness.

And the earth seems to listen. As if it understands. As if it agrees with them and wants to help.

There are other minds, out in the world. Other thoughts. She feels Regan, riding a dragon, circling the platform. Feeling shock, and then pride, and then warm mischievous hope. Closing her eyes and coming to their aid, bringing all of her ancient knowledge, her ancient power. Becoming part of whatever this is.

She feels Lancelot, limping away from the battle. Trying to reach a tiny sapling that means so much to him. Throwing his sword away as he draws close. He slumps down in front of it and hopes, with all of his heart, that the tree will grow tall and strong. That it will bear some kind of fruit. And Mariam feels something else beneath it, a faint intelligence stirring in the ground. Something in the soil that's half-aware of its surroundings. Half-aware of being loved.

She feels Kay, kneeling in prayer at the water's edge. He is startled by her sudden presence inside his head. He opens his eyes and looks out towards the Avalon in the distance. Then he bows his head again. Creasing his brow. Offering all his might to help her. Willing his strength down into the earth.

She feels Nimue, the woman from the water. Not in any one place, but in every stream and tributary in the realm, every lake and reservoir, every place where water stands. Drawing the power from those places. Lending it to their cause.

And she feels Arthur, wounded but victorious. Planting a dragon banner at the top of the Tor. He frowns and remembers his purpose, raising Excalibur into the air.

They have strength, together. She tried to explain it to Kay in Merlin's cave, but it's only now that she really understands.

Nobody has to do this alone, fight all of the evils in the world alone, save the world alone. The weight that would be crushing becomes bearable when it's spread over ten or twenty shoulders. When it's spread over a hundred shoulders it becomes feather-light. It becomes easy to overturn.

They have the power to change things. They don't have to let this magic explode out into the world and tear a hole through the veil, letting these creatures through. But they have to do something else with it, instead. They have to find a kinder, better purpose for it.

Can they draw all of the carbon out of the air? No, she feels Regan telling her. Where would it go? They aren't trees. They can't turn carbon into oxygen. They can't cast their minds wide to all of the blighted forests in the world and grow them back up again from seed to sapling, filling the planet with tall, healthy trees again. That will take time and work, in the real world. Work they must do later.

But what they can do is destroy this place. Bring a great wave to wipe it clean from the earth. It won't solve everything at once and make the whole world right again, but it's a good place to start.

She feels agreement, from everyone. From her sisters. From Kay and Regan and Nimue. From the earth itself. She feels the horror of the dark nightmares, and the veil draws shut in front of them. And she feels a growing force, in the deepest parts of the realm. Something begins to build. It flows up from rocks and streams, spreading into rivers. Nimue moves with it, guiding it, building it up, bringing it rushing downstream. Into the channel. Into the sea. Building into a great wave.

Then she feels the shock of water, and a pair of arms wrapped around her, holding tight.

45

Kay lends his mind to this great struggle like he'd lend his weight and muscle to a shield-wall, digging his heels into the mud. He feels, for a moment, the soft touch of Wyn's hand upon his shoulder.

Then he feels the tide coming, and he looks up from his prayers.

Waves shouldn't come from inland, from rivers. They should come from the sea. He's never known it to be otherwise, in all his years. But now he sees a great torrent surging from the north, from the Severn, like a dam has burst that was built by giants. A wave larger than any he's ever seen. It crests above the Avalon platform, still standing tall and hazy in the distance. And then it crashes down against it.

The wall of water breaks against the metal tower and carries it sideways, reeling from the blow. It looks as if it might weather the brunt, but then he hears metal groaning. The mighty iron legs begin to bend and twist, echoing across the flooded plain like the cries of some great beast surprised by its own downfall. And he gets to watch, grinning, kneeling in the mud, while the whole thing falls sideways. Parts of it shearing away and crumpling and twisting. Landing with a boom that shakes the earth.

It's not what he expected. He imagined slaying Arthur and seeing the great sea fort burning on the horizon. But perhaps this is better. He feels a small swell of hope in his heart, and he lets it grow for once without pouring pitch all over it. Maybe Merlin was right, and there are no green shoots left ahead of them. But they have still done a good thing. They have vanquished a great evil. Merlin didn't foresee that. They've done something unforeseeable, hitherto undreamt of. He likes the thought of that. He finds himself laughing quietly, looking up towards Wyn in heaven. Knowing that Mariam succeeded.

The ruins of Avalon start to sink beneath the brackish water, and it's only then that his smile falls. Grief hits him like a club to the stomach. Mariam and her friends must have perished as the thing came down. They must be caught in the ruins. Drowning, perhaps. He stands quickly, drawing himself up, stumbling on his injured leg. But what can he do? Swim out there, across the marsh, and find them? Bring them all ashore? No. So he stands in the mud instead, red waves lapping at his feet.

He's trying to think of a short prayer that he could offer up, asking Wyn for the safe deliverance of their souls, when he sees a freak wave surging towards him across the marsh. Moving strangely, like a whale or dolphin, like something with a mind of its own. He's too tired to stand and flee, so he kneels and waits for it instead. Letting the wall of water slam into him, nearly knocking him backwards.

When he's wiped the salt from his eyes he sees Mariam and her friends lying on the sand around him, coughing, swearing, looking around in confusion. Standing in the water is Nimue, hands on her hips.

'Saved your mates,' she says.

He doesn't thank her yet.

He hurries to Mariam, nearly slipping, kneeling beside her and grabbing her by the shoulders. The others crowd around as soon as they've picked themselves up. The Welshman, Gethin, is right beside her.

Mariam opens her eyes. She blinks at him, once or twice. Then she throws her arms around him.

'Told you I didn't need you,' she says.

He can't actually remember the last time he was hugged by anyone. He's stunned, for a moment. Then he hugs her back, laughing.

There's a strange truce over Glastonbury. This throng of people who don't agree with each other, who want wildly different things for Britain, sizing each other up. Staying in their camps. There might still be more blood spilled, today or tomorrow.

But then Lancelot climbs up onto the stage and connects his little music box to the speakers near the stage. He starts dancing, slow movements at first, getting slowly wilder. Willow and Teoni run to join him, holding hands. It doesn't take long for everyone else to join in: for the camps to mix, and the lines to blur. They have just fought together. Defeated a common foe. They're willing to cele-brate together – for one evening, at least. Maybe longer. Hard to tell.

The shadows lengthen and the sun begins to set, but the music keeps blaring. Kay limps up the Tor, towards the stone tower. Morgan's new dragon is coiled near the top, resting its head upon its own tail. Looking down at the festivities with curious eyes, as if it might quite like to join in.

Arthur is lying in the tower, bleeding. Resting his head on Morgan's lap. Pressing his hand to the wound in his side. Slain again, by one Saxon or another, during the charge. Nothing so dramatic as last time. It's hard to feel anything but a kind of grim humour, really. What did he think he was playing at, charging at them like that? His own stupid fault that he got himself shot, that he ended up like this.

'My people rejoice,' says Arthur. Pale and quiet, but gratified. 'We've vanquished peril from the realm.'

Kay nods. 'For the time being.'

Arthur grimaces. Not because of his wound, but because of what he's trying to say. 'You gave me good counsel,' he says, after some effort. 'I was ... wise, to listen.'

'Very wise,' says Morgan.

Kay leans against the wall of the tower, with his arms folded. 'I hope you'll heed my counsel more often in future,' he says, 'if you're planning on sticking around. We've still got a war to win.'

Arthur narrows his eyes. He stares up at the square of sky through the empty roof of the tower. 'Been having a think, about that,' he says. 'Seems to me ... that I might not be the right man for the job, anymore. Horses for courses, innit. I was the right man, back in the old days. Not so sure about now. Might be that the crown should go to someone younger. Someone who knows their stuff, if you get what I'm saying.'

Kay smiles, feeling proud of him again. Thinking again of the young red-haired lad kneeling in the wilds of Gwynedd, all those years ago.

'And what'll you do?' he asks. 'Take up knitting?'

'I'll go back to Avalon,' says Arthur. Announcing it as grandly as he can while lying on his back. 'The real Avalon. Heal up a bit. Semi-retirement is what I'm thinking. But I'll be back like a shot if this all goes south. Mark my words.'

'I'll ensure his safe passage,' says Morgan. She winks at him, over Arthur's head.

They both know what this is. An excuse for Arthur to slink back to Avalon and heal his wounds again, with some of his dignity intact. It was always important to make him feel like he was doing things on his own terms. But it shows some wisdom, as well.

They get him up, between the two of them, joking about his weight. They carry him out to Morgan's dragon, struggling to get him up onto its back. Once they've managed it, Morgan climbs up behind him, wrapping her arms around his stomach to hold him up.

Arthur squints over the crowd once more, looking east over England. Then he draws Caliburn from its sheath and hands it down to Kay on the hilltop.

'Keep the sword,' says Arthur. 'Mind the shop.'

Kay nods. 'All right, Addy. You get some sleep.'

Morgan gives him a final smile, then guides the dragon up into the air with a great thrust of her hips. Kay stands on the Tor, with Caliburn down by his side, and watches the dragon fly away into the sunset. Bearing Arthur back to a warm slumber.

There are fires being lit, now, and people dancing around them. Kay sits on the side of the Tor and plunges Caliburn into the ground, watching the celebration from a distance for a while. Smiling down at Lancelot among the others. He scratches at his oak-hand, itching under his mail, in all of the places where his flesh has become tree-stuff. And a piece of bark breaks off in his fingers, leaving a patch of soft brown skin beneath. He stares down at it in mute wonder. Then he scrambles to ungirth his sword belt and to shrug off his mail.

Some of the bark comes away with his mail. The rest can be torn in great pieces from his hands and chest and shoulders, from the small of his back and the top of his scalp. He's never known anything more crudely satisfying than the crunch of it sloughing away. Like tearing the crust from a scab. Finding his old self remade beneath.

He runs his hands over his smooth forearms. There's only one explanation that he can think of: magic restored to the realm, returned to the ground. Not hoarded in one place anymore but spread out evenly underfoot, throughout the country. Enough of it left in the earth now to hold his ancient bones together for a little while longer. That's a comforting thought. He smiles up at Hildwyn in the clouds and mumbles an apology. Might be a little longer yet, before he goes up to join her.

When he's pulled his tunic back on again he draws Caliburn from the ground and walks down to the outskirts of the festival.

There's a white tent with boxes of equipment in it, left by the Saxon broadcasting people. Full of lights and cameras and wires and other things. Now Mariam has taken it as her headquarters. It warms his heart to see her taking charge. Newly confident. Speaking closely with Gethin the Welshman, and with any other leaders who aren't out dancing. Barry's here as well, with some of his friends, nodding at what Mariam tells them to do. That might be a good sign of things to come.

Kay lingers by the entrance, peering in. Knowing better than to get involved at this stage of the proceedings. This is roundabout when he'd usually make himself scarce, disappear from history, walk off into the shadows. End up back under his tree one way or another. But he feels he ought to hang around this time. Not just because of Caliburn in his hand.

Mariam sends her people off with instructions to enjoy them-selves. They'll march in the morning. He waits for her to be alone before he steps inside, clearing his throat.

She smiles at him. Stifling a yawn behind her hand. 'Well,' she says. 'You lived to see the victory parade, for once.'

'Suppose I did,' he says.

'How long are you planning on sticking around?'

'Long enough to give you this, at least.'

He goes down on one knee, in front of her. Balancing the blade of Caliburn across his palms. Offering her the hilt. She looks down at him for a thoughtful moment. But then she wrinkles her nose.

'Nah,' she says. 'You keep it. I've got the staff – it's better.'

She jerks a thumb over her shoulder. The staff is leaning up against a stack of metal boxes in the corner of the tent. He prob-ably shouldn't let her keep it. He should probably make sure it stays in the right hands. But that's Marlowe talking, or Merlin. Whose hands are the right hands? What gives him the right to decide? Maybe it's time to let other people make those decisions. If Arthur can give up his crown, he can give up the staff. He can trust Mariam to do what's right with it.

'Arthur's gone,' he says, rising to his feet, 'which makes you Queen of the Britons, I think.'

'I don't want to be queen of anywhere,' she says.

'What are you, then?' he asks.

She looks out over the crowd, shrugging her shoulders. He can see the thoughts moving behind her eyes. 'Something new.'

'Suit yourself,' he says, following her gaze towards the noise and the dancing. Shirtless men getting pissed with Saint George flags hanging from their shoulders. Welshmen dancing with painted faces. Lance and Willow and Teoni, dancing in the firelight.

'You were right, back in Manchester,' he says. 'I've never really changed anything. Same people in charge, more or less. Same country. Same bollocks. But this might be different. All it takes is choosing to make it different, I suppose. Throwing out all the old bollocks. Building a new country from the ground up.'

'Are you going to stay and help, with all of that?' she asks. 'There might be another dragon, or something, that needs killing.'

'Nah, you don't need me,' he says, grinning. 'Never have done. You told me that yourself. You'll do fine without me. More than fine.'

She looks sad. 'What will you do, then?'

He's not sure. It's the first time in a thousand years that he's felt free to make up his own mind about what he should do next. He spares a glance up into the clouds, in case Wyn's looking down at him. Then he snorts to himself.

'Do you fancy dancing?' he asks.

In the cold, crisp light of morning Kay walks to the land's edge and hurls Caliburn into the placid water. Nimue's hand shoots up to grab it by the hilt. He'd love to learn how she does that without losing her fingers.

She comes up grinning, streaming water, holding the sword. It might be his imagination, but she looks a bit more silvery than she did in Manchester. Like her scales have regained their sheen.

'So,' she says, 'did you get your leg over, or what?'

He laughs at the cheek of that, shaking his head. 'Still don't see how it's any of your business.'

Nimue tuts at him. 'Christ, you're a boring old sod, aren't you?

What's the point of saving the realm if you don't even get a decent shag out of it?'

'Not sure I have saved the realm,' he says. 'Not entirely. But it's a step in the right direction.'

'Well, good,' she says. 'You've made a bit of difference. That's all you can ever hope to do. Whether you're mortal or immortal or anything else. You told me that.'

'Hm,' he says. 'I suppose I did.'

'Go on, go and enjoy yourself for a while,' she says. 'Live a little.'

'Make sure you look after that sword.'

'Nah, I thought I'd whack it on eBay, actually,' she says. ''Course I'm gonna sodding look after it. You take care of yourself.'

She sinks back down, and the water settles over her, looking clearer than it did yesterday. He stands and watches the ripples for a while and then heads back through the camp, past groaning Welshmen nursing their hangovers. All the way inland to the field with the sparse trees where they planted Galehaut's sapling in the earth.

Lancelot is sitting next to it, with his mail shrugged off and his sword cast down. Like he might sit there quite happily for eighty years and wait for it to grow. Kay sits down to join him, on the grass. He can hear gentle birdsong from somewhere overhead.

Acknowledgements

I had the idea for this book in the summer of 2016 and made a few attempts at writing it, but they were terrible enough to put me off the idea of being a writer altogether. Fortunately, I then met Beth Underdown at her book launch in the Deansgate branch of Waterstones, and she convinced me to apply for an MA in creative writing. Since then, she has done immeasurably more, reading my bad first drafts, connecting me with my agent, fighting in my corner, responding to messages at 1:00 a.m. and reassuring me that I should finish this book rather than throwing my laptop in the canal. Beth, I cannot thank you enough. It's been a long road, and you've been the perfect guide.

I'm lucky enough to have incredibly supportive parents who have always had more faith in my writing genius than I ever did. I couldn't have done this without their help and encouragement. I'm very grateful to my sister Steph (for innumerable reasons) and my brother Joe (for his polite interest in all of this Arthurian rubbish). I love them both.

I would also like to extend my profound thanks to:

Harry Illingworth, my brilliant agent. Thanks for taking a chance on me!

Jenni Hill and Julian Pavia, who are stuck with me for at least one more book.

Sam Morgan, who sold my book in America – best of luck in all of your new endeavours.

Everyone at Orbit and Ballantine who helped to turn this book into the best version of itself.

Kaye Mitchell, John McAuliffe, and everyone else at Manchester's Centre for New Writing.

Nathaniel Gage, for our long friendship and his sage advice.

Paddy Dobson, for his wit and insight, his notes on this book, and for being a good friend.

Rina Haenze, for being the finest First Officer in Starfleet.

The brave pilots of X-Flight, who always come through when the chips are down.

My fellow gadabouts and denizens of the night on Manchester's MA programme, who convinced me that 'Brexit Knights' was an idea worth running with.

My friends in Manchester's medieval re-enactment community, who gave me a unique insight into what it might be like to be repeatedly killed and brought back from the dead.

Raina Parker, my high school English teacher – to whom this book is dedicated – for encouraging my creativity at a time when I really needed the encouragement. She says I give her too much credit, but she is wrong.

And finally the dogs, Bob and poor old Duke, who slept on my feet and took me out for walks at different stages of this book's development. I hope for Duke's sake that greyhound heaven and rabbit hell are the same place.

About the Author

Thomas D. Lee is an author of fantastical and historical fiction. In 2019, he completed an MA in creative writing at the University of Manchester's Centre for New Writing. He has now embarked upon a PhD at the same institution, specialising in queer interpretations of the Arthurian mythos. He frequently considers emulating Merlin and becoming a hermit in the woods who speaks only in riddles.

Find out more about Thomas D. Lee and other Orbit authors by registering for the free monthly newsletter at orbitbooks.net.